Orphans
An Adventure Filled with Intrigue and Courage

by

Nancy Jasin Ensley

DORRANCE PUBLISHING CO., INC.
PITTSBURGH, PENNSYLVANIA 15222

The contents of this work including, but not limited to, the accuracy of events, people, and places depicted; opinions expressed; permission to use previously published materials included; and any advice given or actions advocated are solely the responsibility of the author, who assumes all liability for said work and indemnifies the publisher against any claims stemming from publication of the work.

Dorrance Publishing Co., Inc.
701 Smithfield Street
Pittsburgh, PA 15222
Visit our website at *www.dorrancebookstore.com*

ISBN: 978-1-4349-1830-7
eISBN: 978-1-4349-1750-8

*Dedicated to my grandchildren and
to Tyler Wylie, an amazing young man.*

Acknowledgments

A mystery novel is a far cry from an autobiography, poetry, and short stories. My work with young adults as a teacher and counselor, my being a mother to teenagers of my own, and my own rocky childhood had led to this theme that I tossed around in my mind—about a modern Huckleberry Finn tale. I loved adventure stories that demonstrated the resourcefulness and resilience of kids who had to fend for themselves. Personal encounters with children and young adults who had to survive abuse, abandonment, and illness have touched my heart and gave me a backdrop for this story. The most difficult part of writing for a different audience than the one reading *The Tire Swing*, my first published book, was to limit detailed descriptions of scenes, avoid deep philosophical discussions, and insert action into every chapter. Young readers aged thirteen to twenty five care little whether the light filtering through the trees in the thick woods paints dancing fairy like shadows across the damp ground. What a challenge!

Writing fiction opens up one's mind and characters fly in and out of one's imagination. Such characters don't really have to make sense all the time. You can have them performing amazing feats and acting in a most unusual manner. Once your mind is free to invent and is released from the constraints of reality and authenticity, it becomes difficult to end the story. Near impossible encounters and scenes with heart stopping action requires little explanation and weave the author into the center of the story to manipulate each character without having to explain it to anyone.

My family and friends have been so supportive of my virgin attempts to write entire novels that I am unable to stop my brain from thinking of many other books that I hope to write. I even intend to also write a text book. I fall asleep at this keyboard and dream of titles and characters, situations and messages that my fingers are too tired to transmit onto the computer. I write notes and phrases on grocery lists, scraps of paper, envelopes, and tablets I keep in my car and at my desk.

I pray each night that I will have enough time and the brain cells to get it all down. I surely will try.

Orphans

Nancy Jasin Ensley

Preface

William West and Charlie Peterson have very little in common. Will lives in Ohio, Charlie in Florida. They both have good parents and brothers and are pretty much enjoying friends, playing sports, going to school, and doing the things that boys do. Will is twelve going on thirteen, and Charlie is fourteen going on fifteen. Suddenly, separate tragedies have occurred that lead the boys on a journey filled with intrigue and twists and turns. Both boys' families are missing and the "orphans" along with Casey—Charlie's droopy eared, loyal dog—have set out to find them. Will has a race car that has a mysterious disc imbedded in its chassis. His father was helping him build the race car in the garage the day before Will's world was turned upside down. Will was so thrilled that his dad could be home for his birthday as Robert West would often be gone away from home, sometimes for weeks. Will always wondered why his mother stayed close to home and that he knew very little about what his father did for a living.

The journey of the two boys and their fateful meeting at a Greyhound bus station turns into an adventure that is filled with danger, brushes with death, terrorists, and new friendships. The people that enter their lives and the need to survive change them and expose them to decisions most adults don't even face. The plot thickens as the world is threatened with a disaster that could affect millions of lives—greed, ambition, insanity plague people with power, and respect for humanity. Each chapter brings persons into the mystery who the reader will find difficult to identify as the good guy or the villain.

Some people entangled in the web of locating the Hatham terrorists and the mysterious black box wind up with powers that surprise them and the enemy as well. Join these two young men on an adventure that will keep you guessing.

Introduction

Will's heart raced as he clutched the damaged race car to his chest and ran from the ditch to the woods, between his yard and Ted's farm. He couldn't look back as he did not want to believe what had just happened. If he didn't see it again, maybe he was just having a nightmare and he would wake up soon in his own bed, in his own room. There was a small stream that ran along the edge of the woods and his feet became numb as he moved as fast as he could through the icy water. He thought if there were dogs tracking him, they would lose his scent if he made his way through the stream. Careful not to slip on the rocks lining the stream's bed, he winced as his ankle turned when he encountered a large rock. He had to get somewhere to think—to try to plan what to do next. His stomach churned and his chest ached as real fear replaced the shock.

Charlie and his family listened to the radio that gave directions for all residents of the area to evacuate immediately. The National Guard had been called in to monitor the exodus of thousands of families along the coast as the storm swirled above the ocean gaining momentum and power as it headed toward its victims. These people had weathered many tropical storms and hurricanes in the past, but none like Helen. She was dressed in a gown of damaging winds up to one hundred and fifty miles per hour. Jake, Charlie's brother, listened with a totally different attentiveness than the rest of his family. He and Elmo, his sleek colorful surfboard, loved the waves—the higher and more ferocious, the better. He was sixteen and fearless, muscular, and tan. The girls drooled over him and it pumped up his ego, overshadowing his ability to make good decisions. Pepper was the Peterson's pedigree Golden Retriever. She had spurned many suitors anxious to impregnate her aloof self. She had chosen a vagrant, garbage scrounging mutt in a moment of heated passion to father her lone pup, Casey. Casey was born prematurely and only survived because of the tender loving care of Charlie's mother, Carolyn Peterson, RN. Because of the unusual mix of hound and thoroughbred, Casey had interesting features. He had shorter legs than a Retriever, was more muscular like his absent father, and his ears drooped along with floppy joules, making him look pensive and sad. Casey's joules would often fold under his huge set of teeth, which made him look like he was smiling. Pepper and Casey had assumed the roles of protection agents for their human owners. Pepper hated the water monster that had once grabbed her off the beach during a family outing, so she was content to sit quite a distance from the ocean, still watchful and protective, but at a safe footage.

Robert and Emily West had secrets. They thought they had locked them away when their lives changed with the birth of their two sons, Will and Toby. They had been assured the family would be protected at all times. Emily still was anxious, not for her safety, but for her boys' safety. She kept most activities close to home and rarely invited guests. They had moved several times during Will's twelve years and he had found it difficult to develop friendships. Ted lived on a farm on a road at the other side of the woods adjacent to the Wests' home. Both boys developed a bond as they seemed much older and wiser than their years due to circumstances affecting both of them. The tree house built by Ted's grandfather was located deep in the woods and was surrounded by large pine trees which made it difficult to be seen unless you knew it was there. The "Bombardiers" were a small group of guys who held meetings in the tree house and played war games in the woods. You had to be invited, and the membership had rules, such as not letting any silly girl break up the group. Ted was the chief of the fearless "Bs" and Will soon was allowed to partake of that status.

Charlie and Will had a loving mother and father and one brother. Beyond that, they had nothing in common. The story of how their lives change and the adventures they find themselves encountering intertwine from a chance meeting at a bus station to a tangled web of intrigue and disasters. Casey travels with Charlie and becomes a hero several times over. Both boys have no idea about the part that they will play in a plot by terrorists to potentially destroy most of the Western World. These three orphans will have the ride of their lives searching for their loved ones.

Chapter One

Will

The sun was buried behind a cloud that looked mysteriously like the mask Will had worn last Halloween. It lasted for just a moment, as clouds often do, and so did the twelve-year-old's attention, as boys often do. The grass was freshly mowed and tiny sprigs of pesky crabgrass where already pushing aside the more delicate greenery in a jealous reach for the few rays of sun that made their way through the haze. Will—William Edward West—the name sake for his grandfather, who, it was told, was a highly decorated General during World War II, was really too busy to notice that crabgrass or some silly clouds or even the car that pulled slowly into the driveway of his two story upper middle class home. He was too busy putting the finishing touches on his very own super duper, red and blue, unbeatable race car. He had torn open the box containing the best birthday gift ever as soon as he saw the picture on the box of the one thing he loved the most, that is, besides his mom and dad—yes, including that pesky little brother, Toby. He loved to put things together, to watch pieces of plastic or wood or paper take shape and become something awesome and usable. The first recollection he had of the excitement a creator feels was when he was about three years old. His father had taken a piece of rough pine, placed it on a machine that made a noise that hurt your teeth and moved it in such a way it evolved into a railroad car. It was magic. He didn't understand the mechanics or skill behind the creation. He just knew that his hero—his father—had made that shapeless piece of wood take on the personality of the big trains he loved to watch passing by when their car would stop behind the white and black gates.

The pieces had fallen out of the box onto the kitchen table. Will had little regard for the packaging as his hands tore the cardboard picture of the race car right across the hood of the car.

"Dad, will you help me put it together right now—right away! Please, Dad!" he shouted trying to imagine all those pieces becoming a whole red race car.

Will's father was settling into his Lazy-Boy busily flicking through the channels on their new big screen TV. Cincinnati was facing the Patriots in the playoffs and he was sure his two dollar bet in the pool would multiply when Cinci massacred those haughty Easterners. Robert West treasured his sparse moments with his family. His job took him away, often for days and sometimes weeks and he missed his wife, Emily, and his two precious sons. What he disliked most was the parts of his life he couldn't reveal—the parts that—

"Dad! C'mon, I have to put this together right now! C'mon!" Will stood between the new TV and his father and the Lazy-Boy.

Bob West refocused on his son and away from his concerns and the channel selector. He refocused on the pleading, excited brown eyes of his oldest son, jumped out of the Lazy-Boy, dropped the channel changer in the chair, left the new TV on a cooking show, grabbed his son, and threw him over his shoulder as they headed to the workroom in the garage. Will's laughter as he was carried off to the "man cave" by his hero, was music to Emily's ears.

Emily was mixing together the ingredients for her famous meat loaf. She smiled as she listened to the bonding moment and the giggles fading into the garage. Toby was sleeping inside the playpen in the corner of the dining room. His blond curls and tiny features resembled a girl's even more when he was sleeping. His lips made sucking sounds as though he was still enjoying the sweet warm milk from Emily's breast. These moments were precious to her as they never occurred often enough and never lasted long enough. "Together times" she called them. Times when the anxious feeling pushing on her chest would melt away. Times when she didn't have to scan the horizon for a danger she could not see. Times when a trip to the grocery store wasn't preceded by preparing for an ever present black cloud of intrigue.

She had practically pulverized the glop of chopped sirloin, onions, celery, bread, eggs, and seasonings (with just a teaspoon of poultry seasoning—the secret ingredient) in her mother's beige mixing bowl as she was lost in her musings. She peaked around the corner at her youngest and a tear dropped into the mixture. She wiped away the remaining tear on the sleeve of her sweatshirt and proceeded to pour their main dish for Will's birthday dinner into the baking pan.

Will got a little dizzy as the airplane glue his father had opened spread its fumes across the garage. He sat on a stool next to his father and could feel the warmth of his body as he leaned in close to focus on the pieces of the yet to be assembled race car. Their eyes were intently perusing the directions that were always typed in a print too small for the human eye. Bob had pushed his glasses down on the bridge of his nose the way that Grandpa Will used to do when he was serious about some issue or working on a project. Will Jr. missed his grandfather. Though he was stern and not subject to much smiling and levity, he loved his family and friends with his strength of conviction and a sense that "nothing could harm you" if he was standing by. The General was a mean old cuss some would say, but beneath the metal there was a heart that melted when his wife's name was mentioned, and when Will put his hand into the General's big rough one.

"Well, let's take a look at the parts list first, Will. We want to make sure we have all the pieces before we start. That's a good practice for almost any project, son—make sure you have everything you need before you start. Nothing worse than being in the middle of something and finding out an important piece is missing." A thought passed through Bob's mind as he considered the advice he had just given his son. *Maybe I should take my own advice.* He shook it off and looked down at the fuzzy crew cut and innocent eyes of his son and smiled. *I am such a lucky man...I should...*

Will interrupted his father's thoughts "I counted all the parts, Dad. There are seventeen and there are seventeen pictures of parts on the paper. I'm not sure what some of the words mean."

"Let's see, buddy. Hmmmmm...here's the frame. That's number one."

Will examined every line and curve of the frame as though he was an engineer building a landmark...

"The frame of the car, for that matter, any car is like the foundation of a house. We just have to look at the schematic and match the part numbers with the ones marked on the frame."

"What's a skeeematic?" Will tried to frown a little like his father did when he was thinking or sitting at the computer in his office. He didn't have eyeglasses to put on the bridge of his nose, but he lowered his head and peered over the top of imaginary ones.

"Just a drawing with lots of directions and numbers, symbols and...Hey, let's get down to business or your mother will wonder if we slithered out for some ice cream before dinner!" The phone rang and Emily motioned to Robert to take the call. She looked concerned turning away briskly as her husband took the phone.

Will had placed himself on one of the steps leading to the porch that covered the front of his house. They had put all seventeen parts together, laughing, grunting (even a few farts in between); male bonding until the race car was ready for its first coat of paint. Bob had handed that job to Will to complete for himself. No matter how the paint job came out, it was Will's super duper race car. Bob was just the assistant.

Will looked up from his project as two men exited the black shiny car that had pulled into the driveway while he was lost in clouds, crabgrass, and the excitement of knowing he could win the race at his Boy Scout rally with his very own race car. The men wore suits like his father did when he went to work or on one of those trips he was always taking. Will didn't like it when his dad would have to go away. He missed him. Sometimes he could hear his mother raise her voice or he would hear her crying, and he would go to find her sitting in a chair with her head in her hands or lying on her bed. He always gave her one of his biggest and best hugs even though he was way too close to manhood to be doing that sappy girl stuff. He was the man of the house when Bob was gone. His father told him so. Bob had left the day before, leaving Will in charge.

The two men looked anything but congenial as they scanned the yard, peered at the garage, and looked up to the second story. Will stood up moving the box with his precious car and the red paint can and brushes to the side of the porch. He stretched his five foot frame as tall as he could make it and said, "May I help you?" He had heard the lady at the checkout counter of the grocery store say that many times and it sounded pretty awesome.

One of the men looked at him in a way Will had never been looked at before and a little shiver went up his arms to the back of his neck.

"Is your father home?" The eyes seemed to look through Will. "Well, is he?" he repeated a little louder.

"I'm not deaf!" Will wanted to say, but remembered his manners and held his breath for a few seconds.

"He just went to the store a few minutes ago." Will crossed his fingers behind his back. Something made him tell a fib. Something about the man's eyes didn't make Will want to tell the man that he and his brother were alone with their mother.

"Who's watchin' you, kid?" The second man hid behind dark glasses and had the beginnings of a beard. "Is Em...I mean, your mom here?" The chill ran up Will's arms and down his back again.

"N...no, she went with him and I'm watching my little brother till they both get back." Will's voice was shaking the tiniest bit. *"I told too much. Mom says I shouldn't talk to strangers, but she didn't tell me what to do if they were at my house."*

"Guess we'll have to wait. What you got there, a model car?" the first man with the empty eyes started to reach into the box to pick up the race car.

Will let out a screech "Don't touch it! I just put the first coat of paint on it! Please."

"Sorry, fella."

They didn't see Emily head toward the window just to the right of the front door when she heard Will screech. She caught a glimpse of the two figures standing in front of Will and backed hastily against the front door. Her heart began to pound against her breast and some milk leaked through her bra leaving a wet spot on her dress. She laid on the floor and crawled to the desk in the dining room. The drawer slid open softly but sounded like a drum roll to her ears as adrenalin rushed through her bloodstream heightening her senses. The metal was cold as she grasped it from under the false bottom of the drawer. Her boys. She had to get her boys away from there. Her mouth was so dry she could barely swallow. Toby was upstairs in his crib. She could get to him. But, Will. How could she get to Will? She knew the front door was locked. She always kept it locked, especially when Bob was gone. *"Bob, oh Bob please don't come home right now!"* she screamed inside. *"Got to think. Get the baby. What is Will telling them? I can't believe they haven't tried to get in!"*

Emily knew there would be a time when they couldn't hide anymore. She knew they would find them no matter how many times they moved. She was trained to know what to do in any volatile situation. She was trained to shoot, to fight, to withstand pain, to sacrifice herself if she had too. That was before the kids came. That was before her taste of motherhood and being a real wife, lover, and neighbor had made her want to through down the gauntlet and be all those things and nothing else.

She laid against each step. Toby began to cry.

"Oh, baby please don't cry——please don't…"

One of the two men with the suits pulled out a gun and shot several shots at the door handle.

Will grabbed the box with his race car and ran like a hunted deer toward the bushes near his neighbor's house. He heard his mother scream "Will…run…run…r…" The red paint spilled down the porch step like blood oozing from a wound.

For a few moments Will could only hear the echo of the gunshots and his mother calling from in the house. He ran to the tall bushes separating his house from the empty lot next door. He knelt down on the cool ground and searched the porch, the injured front door and all the windows with eyes full of fear. He saw no one—not his mother, his brother, nor the two men.

The sound was like the bowels of a volcano rupturing. It came from the back of the house and erupted through the windows as the glass exploded into the newly mowed yard. The roof collapsed as fire spewed like a rocket into the air. Neighbors ran from their houses——ghost-like faces—open mouths—screams, and then silence. Black caustic smelling smoke reached its fingers into the blue sky and cast a cloud of dust over the block where Will had played.

Will couldn't feel anything. He couldn't move his feet or speak. Nothing came out when he tried to scream. He lay on the ground under the bushes and barely breathed. His mother. His brother. Those men. He could not look at his house. Maybe if he waited he would look and everything would be the way it was. Maybe he was dreaming. But those men were real. His eyes were empty—that man's eyes were totally empty.

A black car drove slowly down Maple Avenue. It turned the corner and disappeared.

Will could hear the neighbors yelling. "Call 911! For god sakes, call 911, somebody!"

Their voices merged into a muddled noise echoing in a tunnel. Will looked at the blackened porch that had collapsed onto the steps where he had sat just a few short minutes ago. He looked at a part of his house strewn across the lawn and driveway and pieces of glass thrown like tinsel into the street and into the neighbor's yard. Fire engines were screeching at top speed slowing only for people running into the street. Sirens died as they rounded the corner. Horns blared to warn the frantic neighbors that the troupes had arrived. Ambulances, police cars, a s.w.a.t. team, other fire engines poured into the usually quiet, upper middle class neighborhood. Will crouched lower into the bushes. Where were those men? Did they blow up with the house? Where was his mother and Toby? Did they run too? He could hear his mother's screams echoing in his ears——"Run, Will...Run!" She had to be okay. She was his mother. She always protected him and his brother. She would live forever. He had to believe that. His little brother...she would have rescued him. She had to. She was their mom. Dad. Where did he say he was going? Will wished he had listened to things that never seemed to be his business. He didn't know what other kids knew. He didn't know what his dad did for a living. He knew he traveled, that he went to an office downtown, but he never was told what he did there. When he asked one time because dads and moms were invited to his class to talk to the kids about their jobs, his mom had said, "He works with computers." He can't really tell the kids in class what he does because it's too complicated and they wouldn't understand. Will was a little disappointed at the time. He wanted the other kids to see what a great dad he had. It was hard making friends over and over again. They had to move lots of times and Will never got to stay long enough to get a best friend. His dad was his best friend. He was working on a best friendship with Ted, a fourteen year old guy he had met in scouts. Will seemed to get along better with older kids and adults.

"I can't let anyone see me. Those men might be out there waiting for me. I have to find my mom and dad and Toby. I have to stay away from people because they will want to take me in their house and I need to go and find my mom and dad and Toby!" Will looked through the bushes. Some men in uniforms were putting yellow ribbons around the yard and other men were chopping through the remains of the house attempting to get inside. People were moving back toward their houses, some crying, some holding on to one another. A policeman and a man in a suit were talking to the Blanchards across the street and writing things on a pad.

It was about six o'clock and lights from the houses began to cast shadows across the lawns and Maple Street. No lights shown from the West's house other than the flashlights and searchlights from the firemen and policemen. What once was an elegant upper middle class home was a pile of dark and eerie debris. Smoke still surrounded the disaster and made it look like a scene in a spooky movie. Will strained his ears and eyes to see if his mother and Toby would appear from the woods in back of the house. He prayed for someone to say they found them and they were okay. He only knew a few prayers because they rarely went to church or out anywhere except the grocery store and maybe to town. The "Angel of God" prayer came to him, at least a few of the words. He looked up at the sky that was starting to open the doors of night and prayed.

Some of the branches with fresh green foliage lay on the ground under the bushes. Will recalled helping his dad trim them before he had left for his business trip. Will had tried to negotiate his way out of helping with the yard work. He would have preferred riding his bike over to Ted Swanson's to catch some fish in the pond behind Ted's house or sitting up in Ted's tree house his grandfather had built for him. The tree house was high up in a massive oak tree several yards in the woods behind the Swanson's four acres. The pine boards nailed every six inches to the tree were formerly used by Ted's dad when he was a boy to climb to the small porch of the tree house, but they had deteriorated so the boys had fashioned a rope ladder that they pulled down from the back of the tree house with a tether rope hidden in the pine trees that encircled the old tree.

There were only a few very special guys that were asked to enter the tree house and join the "Swanson's Bombardiers". The members had to swear they would keep it a secret about the group, not let girls take over their lives, contribute a quarter a week to the club treasury for snacks and an emergency fund and no adults in the tree house—ever. It took Will almost a year after his family had moved to Ohio to convince Ted he was smart enough, brave enough, and could keep secrets well enough to become one of the bombardiers. Ted and Will were a little more mature than the other boys at school. Ted's family had lived with his grandmother and grandfather on their farm as long as he could remember. Chores were a given for everyone. Ted had muscles most of other gangly fourteen year olds hadn't developed yet from lifting, pushing, and pulling things and animals twice his size since he was three years old.

When Ted was six, his grandfather was thrown from his tractor breaking his hip. He was rushed to the hospital for surgery and was doing well until about the third day post-op. His wife and daughter had just left to go home for the night looking forward to bringing their man back home the next day. He never came home. During the night, he grabbed his chest, gasping for air. He fumbled for his call light and collapsed on the floor next to the bed. The nurses found him without a pulse, cyanotic, and not breathing. They told Muriel Swanson and her son Al, Ted's father, that it might have been a pulmonary embolus—a blood clot in the lung. Al lost himself in keeping up the large produce farm. Ted spent many hours working on the farm next to his father. It was the only way he could communicate with him anymore. His father spoke less, worked harder, and seemed to hide inside himself. No one really questioned Al's gradual loss of weight and sallow color to his skin. They thought it was because he worked so much and was outside most of the time. "It's pancreatic cancer," the doctor said. Not an easy cancer to treat by the time it is found. His was a large lesion eating its way from the pancreas to the liver. "Not too much they can do," the doctor said. "Just give him medicine for pain, special feedings through a tube when he can't eat anymore," if they wanted that. Heather—Al's wife and Ted's mother—wanted the doctor to stop talking, stop telling a horror story she didn't want to hear. She just wanted to take her strong, quiet, love of her life home, and hold him in their bed, make love to him, cook and clean for him, work side by side with him, watch their son grow with him for whatever time there was left.

Ted watched his father shrink into a skeleton covered with wrinkled, dry, yellow flesh. He watched his swollen belly be tapped over and over again to relieve the pressure of the fluid in his gut—the saliva of the cancer monster that ate away at him every day. His father was so weak that he could hardly speak during the last days of his life. One day he motioned Ted to come close to him. Ted could hardly bear to look at the person he did not recognize as his father anymore. His eyes were hollow and dark circles surrounded them. Ted cautiously moved toward the hospital bed that sat in the dining room near the window that looked out over the farm.

"Dad, can I get you something?" Ted whispered as the nausea began to creep into his chest.

"Come closer, Teddy——please." The skeleton pleaded.

His father hadn't called him Teddy since he was a toddler. Ted wondered if his father knew that he was almost grown up already. Ted leaned over his father putting his head close to his father's mouth.

His shallow breaths smelled like stale bread and somewhat sweet.

"You will be the head of the family soon, son. I want you to promise me you will take care of your mother and grandma, that you always will be honest and kind, but not weak—stay strong in what you believe in, and be a good and trusted friend." Al grimaced and let out a groan that tore at Ted's heart.

"I will, Dad...I love you, Daddy...please don't be sad...please don't l..." Ted couldn't stay there anymore. He ran out through the kitchen across the grass to the woods. He grabbed the tether rope buried in the pine tree and pulled the rope ladder from the porch. A rabbit leaped out of its cover of ash grass when it heard the whooshing sound of the rope ladder falling to just above the ground. Several birds chirped a scolding when being disturbed by the boy racing toward the tree house. The sun filtered through the tall trees and reflected off the stays of the rope ladder as it swayed with the movements of the boy as he climbed hastily toward his hiding place. He couldn't hide from the sick feeling in his stomach and chest. He couldn't hide from the vision of his father dying, melting away. He wanted so to hide from the empty space left at the dining table, from the burden of becoming a man way before he ever should have, the coat on the coat rack near the back door that would no longer cover the shoulders of the man who used to show him how to plant seeds and care for them so they would grow, the man who held him in his lap on the big combine to get him used to the power of it.

Will rode his bike over to Ted's that day after he grudgingly finished with the yard work. Ted and he had become good friends. They seemed somehow older than the other kids. Maybe it was because they had experienced more and had big responsibilities. They never tried to control what the other kids did nor criticized how they acted; they just felt a little different and looked at things a little differently. Ted's mother came to the door when Will rang the bell. She was pale and she looked as though she had been crying. Her hair was straggly and she kept twisting the dishcloth she held in her hands around her wrists.

"Teddy is out in the back forty or in the woods where he goes when he is...come on in, Will. Would you like some cookies and milk?" she smiled a little and turned toward the kitchen.

What boy would turn down cookies and milk?! Will walked softly past the living room. The dining room was dark except for a small table lamp next to a bed. Will couldn't help glancing toward the figure outlined by the small lamp. It did not move and it was covered with a white sheet. Lady, the family border collie didn't even get up from his watch beside the bed to greet Will. He just laid there on the small rug woven from children's clothes by Ted's grandmother. He looked at Will with sad eyes as if to say "I can't play right now, I have to stay by my master."

Will thanked Mrs. Swanson for the cookies and milk that he drank in a few gulps. He ran toward the woods past the barns and the horses and cows grazing lazily in the late afternoon sun. He knew Ted was probably in the tree house. He went there a lot lately. As he approached the big oak tree he saw the rope ladder was still hanging from the house. One bombardier rule was always pull the rope ladder up on the porch when you are in the tree house and fling the tether over the pine tree. "Ted must be upset about his dad, he forgot to pull up the ladder" Will said to himself.

"Hey, Ted that you up there?" Will shout-whispered.

"Go away, Will."

"C'mon, Ted. I got a cookie left that your ma gave me."

"I said go away!" Ted stepped out on to the porch of the tree house and started to pull up the rope ladder.

Will grabbed hold of the ladder just as Ted gave it a yank. "I guess you just want to sit up there and feel bad instead of letting me tell you some bad jokes and losing out on one of your mom's great cookies!"

"I…I don't know what I want. I just……"

Ted dropped the rope ladder and went into the tree house. The door slammed shut and Will proceeded to make his way up the ladder. The tree house was made from heavy three inch barn siding.

Grandpa Swanson had sealed the boards with filler and had even put dry wall boards on the inside for insulation. The club members had painted their own artistic graffiti on the drywall. A small battery operated heater, an old cooler with the handles missing, some plastic covered overstuffed pillows, maps of places they envisioned conquering someday, a couple of shelves with treasures boys collect (Bill Tracoti's pellet gun, a sling shot, a couple of someone's dad's *Playboy* magazines in a paper bag, some plastic toys extracted from someone's McDonald's kids meal), and two oil lamps completed the decor.

The front door didn't lock so one of the bombardier's had rigged up a wedge that could be jammed under the bottom of the door to give time for an escape out the one window at the opposite side of the house should they be attacked by Indians or eerie little people from outer space. Grandpa had even put shutters on the window that could be locked from the inside and also kept out the elements during the chilly Falls and harrowing Ohio Winters. There was a box with a baseball, two worse for wear left handed baseball gloves, a football, and a football helmet. Ted's mom had supplied three old blankets (none of which were pink) for the nights the guys had a sleep over.

Ted hadn't put the wedge in the door so Will took it that he wasn't shutting him out completely.

The tree house smelled like a stale cigarette mixed with the old wood smell from the planks that was always there. Will opened the door just enough to inch his arm in with his hand holding the chocolate chip cookie peace offering. Ted grunted a "C'mon, you schmuck," and Will took it as a gracious invitation and stepped into their castle.

"You been smokin'? Smells like old cigars in here." Will held his nose as he blinked his eyes trying to adjust to the darkness. "Why don't you open the window or something?"

"Don't want to. If you're gonna bug me, get outa here." Ted sat cross legged on one of the overstuffed pillows. Will could see a little of his face as he puffed on a cigar. His eyes were puffy.

"Care if I light up one of the lamps? It's gettin' kind of dark. You got one of those stogies for me?" Before Ted could object, Will lifted the glass chimney from the oil lamp, lit a match and pressed against the wick. The graffiti on the walls of obtuse shapes, signatures, drawings of animals, soldiers, and a few attempts at shapely girls came alive.

"I guess." Ted stood up and reached for a can on one of the taller shelves. He pulled out a half used cigar and began to light it from the one he was smoking. He handed it to Will who really didn't like them at all, but figured he had seen lots of guys smoking making it a kind of male bonding ritual.

Will took a big puff of the cigar and proceeded to choke as the bitter smoke hit his throat.

"What a wimp!! Ha, Ha! Your face is all red, buddy!"

"Where did you get these things, in a garbage dump?" Will dropped the cigar on the floor and stomped it out, "Now that you ask…" Will pounced on Ted and gave him a few sissy punches. Ted was about thirty pounds heavier and quite a bit more muscular than Will. He pinned Will in less than twenty seconds for a full count of ten. They laughed and grabbed a coke from the cooler. The drinks were warm but they didn't care. They both felt better.

Will had fallen asleep in the bushes. He heard the birds chirping in the trees a few yards away. The cut branches had left marks on his face as he had laid there for at least an hour. He couldn't recall why he was on the ground in some bushes then he saw it. The still smoldering blackened remnants of his home. His room, his computer, his clothes, his mother, his brother…everything was gone. Everything was black. He was thirsty and terrified, confused, and nauseated. He heard voices and peered out through his cover. People were driving by in cars and some others were walking down the street past the disaster. There is a part of human beings that harbors primitive vulture like hovering to view macabre scenes. His heart skipped a beat and he blinked his sleep crusted eyes to make sure what he saw was real. Standing in the driveway still covered with debris from the explosion was the man with the dark glasses that had shot the handle off the front door. Will was sure it was him. He wasn't wearing a suit just some dark pants and a jacket that had some sort of emblem on it. He was talking with a group of men and women with the same jackets on and there were several police cars in the driveway and the street. Will looked around for the black sedan and the man with the empty eyes but saw neither.

"I've got to get out of here! If he sees me…why is he here? Who is he? Are those other people bad guys? Got to hide somewhere until I can figure out a plan."

The vacant lot on the other side of the bushes dipped down into a little valley that became even deeper as it reached the woods that bordered Ted's farm. Will looked back toward the end of Maple Street which turned on to Kendall. There seemed to be only a few cars headed toward the end of the block. If he could slide into the little valley and crawl toward the woods he could get to the tree house and work out a plan. Surely Ted and his family had heard the explosion. It had to be all over the news by now.

"That man. I need to tell someone he was bad. I need to find out what happened to mom and Toby. Where is Dad? I know they will be trying to reach him. Please, Dad, come and help me."

Will began to sob trying so hard not to make any noise that would give away his hiding place. He bit the sleeve of his shirt to gag his mouth and choked back his tears. His dad's words: "Your in charge when I'm away, my man," swirled in his mind. He took a big breath and leaped from childhood to manhood in a few seconds. Wiping his tears and his nose on his sleeve, he laid on his belly and crawled soldier-style out from the bushes sliding in the grass into the valley. He had crawled just a few feet when he saw something lying in the grass. As he approached it he recognized his sports car or what was left of it. Two of the wheels were gone but the frame was intact. There were gouges in the roof and sides of the thick plastic body but it still looked like a race car and even had a little red paint left on the roof. Will clutched the wreck as though it was the Holy Grail. He knew it was a sign that he would find his family or they would find him. Right now he had to stay hidden. He couldn't let the man with the dark glasses find him. The ground was cool and damp as the small valley widened and grew deeper as Will pulled himself toward the woods. The smell of grass and dirt brought memories of stories his grandfather, the General, used to tell him of hiding in the foxholes during the war with dead and injured around him praying that he wouldn't be among them. He would fall to the ground when the enemy overtook them and lay still holding his breath until they passed. When he would breathe again, the smell of dead flesh and dirt, smoke and blood would stay in his nostrils. Sometimes he would have to lay there for hours and urinate on himself daring not to move. Will was mesmerized by his raw tales of war, his loyalty to his fellow soldiers, and his gruff way of letting you know you could get through anything life threw at you.

He heard the sirens in the distance growing fainter as the valley dipped into a rock bed where a spring fed a tiny creek at the edge of the woods. "Are those ambulances? Did they find mom and Toby under the debris?" Will wanted to turn back. Not knowing whether he was an orphan or just a lost child made this nightmare even more frightening. The General would say, "Don't look back, just look ahead and climb the hills you have to. Get a plan and stick to it."

Will rolled down the grassy hill and lay next to the creek. The water tinkled over the rocks as it wound through the valley surrounding the forest. Tall cottonwood and thick sassafras and oak trees shut out the sunlight that tried to sneak its way through the branches. Will laid on his back calculating it was almost ten or eleven o'clock and it had to be Sunday. Saturday, his world had exploded. He would have been going to church with his mother, Toby, and maybe his father if he came home from his trip. Where did his mother say he was going? He needed to remember but his mind and body were aching and he was so very thirsty. He turned and laid his throbbing head in the icy water. It took his breath away for a few seconds. He pursed his lips and allowed the water to flow into his parched mouth. He drank until his belly began to ache. When he rolled back onto the grass, he heard them. Dogs! In the distance coming toward him from the same direction he had taken through the valley to the woods.

"He's coming after me. Those dogs will pick up my scent." Will scrambled to his feet looking frantically through the trees toward the valley and the open lot next to his used to be home.

"Walk in the water. Run around in the forest at the other side of the creek so it seems like I left the forest and headed toward the pavement a few yards away. There is a small park there with a cement basketball court and the dogs would lose my scent at the edge of the pavement." Will dropped a piece of raveled thread from the sleeve of his shirt that had torn during his crawl through the valley as he stepped to the edge of the court. The park was hidden from the trail he had taken by the trees and foliage at the edge of the woods. He darted back into the woods and leaped into the creek. By the time he came to what he thought was the small path that led deeper into the woods and the bombardier's tree house, he couldn't feel his feet anymore. They were numb from the icy water. He was numb inside, hungry, angry, frightened, and alone. Stumbling over branches and his own frozen feet, he finally reached the old oak tree, grabbed the tether from the pine and pulled down the rope ladder. As fast as he could, every muscle aching, he climbed to the porch of the tree house, pulled up the rope ladder along with the tether, opened the door and closed it jamming the wedge between the bottom of the door and the floor. He lifted the cooler and put it in front of the door, turned on the small heater, closed and locked the shutters to the window and collapsed on the overstuffed pillows. He kicked his soggy tennis shoes off and propped his frozen feet next to the whirring fan of the heater, covered himself with the blankets. Just before he drifted into oblivion, he put a fresh load of pellets in Bill Tracoti's pellet gun and buried it under the blankets with him and his shaking body. 10:35 P.M. The moon sprouted wings and drifted in between the openings of the shutters of the playhouse. A gentle breeze encouraged whispers from the trees surrounding Will's hiding place. His tears dried on his face as he drifted into a fitful sleep.

Chapter Two

Casey

The hurricane season attacked the East Coast with a vengeance that August; towns and cities along the Carolina shore were hit the hardest. Despite preparations to steel themselves and their homes from the one hundred and twenty mile an hour winds predicted, evacuations inland were mandated. Jesse and Carolyn Peterson and their two boys, Jake and Charlie, were among those who wanted to hold out until they absolutely had to escape. They loved their home just thirty minutes from the ocean and all the fun it brought to their very athletic family. Jake was sixteen and loved everything about the shore. He had received his first surf board at the age of ten and every day after school and all summer long he would hone his balancing skills, challenging the giant waves of the Atlantic. The first time he rode the curl with the salty mountain of water arching above his head and his feet moving back and forth on the surf board he fondly called "Elmo," he knew that was how he wanted to spend his life— in the curl—heart beating like a drum in his chest and the sense of excitement beyond anything he had ever experienced—even his first kiss by Mary Ellen Finch could not hold a candle to that moment with the echo of the ocean's cave in your ears, the taste of salty water pouring on your face and in your mouth and realizing you were still upright. Charlie got his adrenalin rush from the basketball courts. He was destined to be a tall string bean from birth. His mother said it took an extra two hours in the labor room for all of Charlie's twenty-six inches to extricate him from her womb. Jake had to literally look up to his little brother from the time Charlie surpassed five foot two inches when Jake was eleven years old and Charlie was nine. Charlie topped five feet nine inches at age twelve. Jamison Junior High bred champions in basketball and baseball. They had several of their star athletes go on to college teams and several to the Pros. Maintaining good grades and attendance was a prerequisite to remaining on any team at the school as it was in most colleges along the East Coast. Though he towered over most of his classmates, Charlie had to climb obstacles from dyslexia to attention deficit syndrome to keep his grades at the passing mark so he could stay on the team. Jesse and Carolyn took Charlie to doctors and therapists, specialists, and tutors, spending hours with him managing medication and repeating exercises to retrain his brain. Jake had not inherited the disturbed synapses in his brain that Charlie had. His I.Q. was close to that of a genius. The confines of the classroom bored him and often got him into trouble as he tended to doze off during what his teachers felt were extremely important lectures. Even Mary Ellen's rubbing shoulders with him in the hallway and passing suggestive notes during class could give him the "high" that he needed.

Carolyn Peterson worked the day shift at the Madison Memorial Hospital, a few miles from their home. She would see the results of surfing the curl in the Intensive Care Unit where she worked. Head injuries and broken bones, near drownings, and drug abuse made her less than enthusiastic about Jake's prowess on the waves. Though she outwardly cheered the sight of his tan, muscular body balancing confidently on top of a wave, she would panic when he and Elmo disappeared under the pounding surf not to be seen for what she felt was a frightening amount of time. Jake didn't need her care taking. That was her calling both professionally and personally. She dove into the defects of her younger son not only because he needed her, but because she needed to be needed. Her childhood had been as disheveled and full of insecurity as one could imagine. An abusive father who only showed up to take out his anger on his wife and children then leave for weeks at a time on the big ships and a mother who was mentally ill, living much of her life in institutions and stoned on psychiatric medication when she was released left Carolyn to care for her brother and sister until they were finally separated into several foster homes. Carolyn had worked her way through nurses' training in the hospital as a nurse aide and waiting tables part time at a local restaurant. She had met Jesse at an Intern's party and tried very hard to thwart his persistent courting as she had heard about the nightmare marriages to doctors from nurses and friends and the gossip chain in the hospital. Jesse would show up in the I.C.U. even when there were not patients for him to see. He would call and leave pleading messages letting Carolyn know that he was different from his colleagues, raised in a good Catholic family, heady with ethical fortitude, and wasn't about to give up the race with several other men wanting to date the smart, pretty brunette with a good job and beautiful green eyes. He won the race, not so much from his persistence but from what she saw in him when they wound up working together on the Life Flight rescue team. Carolyn had signed up for the training to be one of the nurses that pulled mangled people from motor vehicle accidents, boating disaster, explosions, and hurricane debris. She had passed the course and was surprised to see Jesse as one of the doctors on the team. She not only was impressed by his ability to make quick decisions and medical skills, but also by his gentleness and real empathy for the victims and their families. They were married one year after working together as it was evident that the closeness they felt in the intensity of their work was more than just professional.

Pepper was just four weeks old when she joined the Peterson family. Charlie had named her Pepper Penelope Peterson (say that fast ten times!) just to show off his ability to repeat words with similar consonants easily. Pepper went everywhere with Charlie. She would wait outside school wagging her tail excitedly when her buddy would come running up to her scratching her soft droopy ears and accepting her big wet kisses all over his face without wiping them off. Jake tolerated Pepper as one of the family but would run to the ocean every chance he could get. Unlike most Labs, Pepper for some reason was not enamored with the water, especially the crashing sounds of the waves hitting the sandy beach. The first time the family took her to the beach and she ventured toward the edge of the tide, a huge wave grabbed her and tossed her around in the salty water. She drank quite a bit of that water and came up gasping for air. When Jessie rescued her drenched self, her eyes were bugged out like she had seen a lion and she proceeded to throw up her dog food, a biscuit, and part of the Atlantic. From that day on, Pepper sat sentinel style quite a distance from that noisy, salty, scary monster Jake loved to dive into each time she accompanied the family or Charlie to the beach. Pepper was quite aloof when Carolyn thought it would be a good idea for her to have a litter of pups before getting neutered. Carolyn had read somewhere in a pet health magazine that female dogs had less chance of cervical cancer if they had at least one pregnancy. Pepper did not share her mistress's opinion and would have nothing to do with the well groomed chocolate Lab male gigolo they put in the kennel with her at the veterinarian's. She would sit on her haunches every time the poor sucker would attempt to mount her and she would look over her shoulder with as much disdain as a canine can muster. Carolyn gave up after several vain attempts and was even contemplating insemination as a last resort. One day as Charlie was running with Pepper at his side she saw the most handsome, virile, spirited male. She had encountered nothing like this in the past several frustrating months at the vet's. He was rummaging through a can of garbage as they ran past and she had to stop and show off her best pro-file taking the stance of some of the show dogs she saw on Animal Planet. Charlie didn't notice Pepper was missing until he rounded the corner to head toward his house a block away. Charlie doubled back searching all the driveways and lawns he had passed to see if his best buddy had decided to relieve herself on someone's lawn or role in something smelly. There she was in the Porter's front yard next to a can of dumped garbage, a smile on her face, glazed eyes, and a strange dog on her back going at it without shame right there in front of the world and the Porter's who had come out to pick up their scattered garbage. The stray dog was having way too much fun to bark at the kid in the running shorts approaching him. When he finally was emptied, he dismounted and proceeded to let go with a low warning growl that sounded more like a lion than a dog. Slobber dripped from his joules as they rose to show yellow stained teeth. Charlie, the Porters, and a dazed, panting Pepper froze as the large disheveled hound headed toward Charlie growling and barking angrily. He crouched low and appeared to be readying to attack when Pepper came to and realized that her best friend was in danger. She leaped onto the sinister attacker and sunk her teeth into his side. The dog yelped in pain as Pepper's teeth hit soft tissue beneath the snarled fur. Charlie wanted to help his defender in the worst way but remembered that it would be senseless to come between two fighting dogs. Mr. Porter had run toward the house and came back to the street dragging the garden hose with him.

He aimed the hose at the battle scene, pressed the handle of the nozzle and let her rip. Yelps and snarls, retreating stray dog and an injured Pepper lying on the pavement, her sandy hair matted with blood and water...Charlie picking up his beloved pet running down Ashland Avenue faster than he ever ran in his life...running through the door of his house—Carolyn wrapping Pepper in a blanket and calling to her doctor husband—Jessie running into the house pouring antiseptic on the multiple bite wounds around Pepper's abdomen and back—Charlie sobbing as he frantically dialed the emergency number for the veterinarian......a quick note to Jake who was surfing with Mary Ellen—breaking the speed limit racing to the animal hospital—Pepper barely breathing—in shock...all of them crying—even Dr. Jessie who had seen much worse than the dog's wounds......but somehow this was worse.

Pepper spent two weeks in the animal hospital having intravenous antibiotics, debridements of her many infected wounds, seizures from high fevers, and, to top it off, the malaise of pregnancy. She was with child from a four minute encounter with a stray and a beating when she could have had her choice in purebreds like herself resulting in a child with several impressive names. Instead, she was to have a something or something's mutt, hopefully without the father's temper. Pepper had been a part of everything in Charlie's life. She had even attended his basketball games watching his buddy run up and down the court as though she knew what he was doing. She seemed to sense when the team had won, jumping around in circles like a trained circus dog. When they lost (which was rare), she would lay on the floor while the guys changed silently to their street clothes offering a paw or a wet kiss to those who bent to pet her as they left. Doctor Ames, the veterinarian, didn't think the pregnancy would go to term because of Pepper's condition and all the medication she had to be given, but she carried one fetus (per the ultrasound) to two weeks before she was due. The premature pup was born limp and lifeless. Pepper licked and pawed at her only child until he gasped and began to breathe on his own. Pepper bit the cord in two and devoured the placenta. Charlie and Jake had to turn away from that one but had been mesmerized up to that point as they observed their first birth.

Casey. They named him Casey. They all agreed he was a sad "case" indeed. No father. An injured mother. No brothers or sisters. An odd shaped head with the flattened nose of a Lab and the ears of a Retriever. Pepper tried to force her engorged nipples into the pup's tiny mouth but Casey had trouble grabbing hold and sucking so Carolyn (caretaker of the year) mixed up bitch milk, sucked it up into a medicine dropper, and fed Casey every hour rubbing his swollen belly to stimulate him to urinate into the diapers she wrapped him in for each feeding. After a month or so, Casey started to grow hair and could nurse and urinate on his own. The hair stuck out in all directions no matter how much product was used or even after multiple brushings. It was a muddy brown with a few scattered sandy patches. It looked like one of those wigs clowns wear—a real bedhead hairstyle. The ears grew longer than most blood-hounds would boast and the Lab nose expanded so it looked like Casey was grinning most of the time. His joules drooped below his lower jaw and one side would get caught in his mouth so his grin was often crooked. He was a clown. He discovered that appendage called a tail around his third month here on earth and chased it around in circles several times a day. The whirling dervish brought on a lot of laughs at the Peterson's especially after the spin when Casey would walk like a drunken sailor. Pepper loved her pup. She walked with a limp and had lost a lot of her playfulness which was replaced ten-fold by Casey's antics.

Casey was lying next to his mother as the family listened intently to the reporter trying desperately to stand up as the wind tugged at his drenched raincoat and microphone. It was north of the Carolinas. Hurricane Helen was out at sea just a few miles off shore. The epicenter was massive and everyone for one hundred miles down the coast and fifty miles inland were being ordered to evacuate. Jessie was literally restraining Jake from running out into the approaching storm with his surf board to head toward the erupting ocean. Charlie just shook his head at his insane brother. Charlie was the sensible one. He could see the worry on his parent's face as they gathered clothes and shoved water bottles, energy bars, first aid items, and clothing into duffel bags. Carolyn stuffed some blankets into plastic trash bags, grabbed cell phones, and a couple of flashlights.

"Jake, leave Elmo, we don't have room in the van. Grab some pillows from the bedroom and start loading...now! Charlie, leash up the dogs and bring a bowl for their water," Jesse yelled as he slammed the shutters against the windows locking them in place. The sky was an odd color of gray and yellow. Dark ominous clouds moved across the ocean in the distance. The wind had not reached them in full force. Estimates were seventy miles an hour and accelerating rapidly. Some of the shingles from the house next door had ripped away and slammed against the side of the house. The humans were rushing in and out of the door with their emergency stash when the shingles hit with a bang. Pepper heard them and leaped from her place on the floor, ran out the open door toward the deserted street. The family piled into the van as it rocked in the accelerating wind.

"Everyone buckle up." Jesse ordered keeping his voice as calm as possible. "Do we have everyone?"

Charlie was attempting to pull the van's back doors shut as the wind grabbed hold of them and battled with its powerful anger to rip them from

Charlie's grip. Charlie managed to win the battle as the doors slammed shut and he fell back into the bags of possessions rescued from the house. The engine of the old nineteen ninety Ford growled back at the wind as Jesse pushed on the gas pedal and began to turn down a side street that led toward town and the entrance to the freeway going inland.

Charlie and Carolyn peered at each other for a moment over the piles of clothes and rations.

"Jake? Where are you? This is no time to play games!" Carolyn pulled some of the bags and boxes aside to see if her crazy son was playing possum. He wasn't there. Pepper stuck her nose up from the pillow she had found to hide under in the back seat. She hated these storms. She hated any load noise and would hide under the bed, in the bathtub behind the couch anywhere she could drown out the noise that would make her heart race and cause this panicky feeling. She rooted and sniffed looking for Casey, but he was not in the van either.

"Jesse! Stop the van!! Jake and Casey are not here—my god...you don't think...oh, my god, Jesse...he went to the ocean!" Jesse put on the brakes so forcefully everyone lurched forward. "Dad, you and mom go on. I'll go back and look for Jake and Casey. They might have gone back into the house. Jake is wild, but not stupid. The wind is getting stronger. We'll go to the basement or see if there in someone we can hitch a ride with." Carolyn and Jesse were shaking their heads.

"Charlie, we can't leave you here. You have to go with us." A large tree branch flew like a missile behind the van and crashed into the porch of a house. "My god, Carolyn, we have to get out of here or none of us will be left in one piece.! What was Jake thinking? Oh...Jesus......look at that!" The ocean had been scooped up as though a huge ladle had dug deep into its depths and was throwing it against building, houses, and the few vehicles still parked along the street. The wheels of the van squealed as they tried to find pavement to hold on to. Water oozed through the doors of the van as it frantically shook in the torrent of debris, water, and howling wind. Carolyn was sobbing and Pepper whimpered trying desperately to bury herself under the seat of the van.

The waves had exploded into grotesque claws attacking the shore and collecting piers, boardwalks, and buildings like a professional gambler selfishly pulling all the poker chips away from the losers. Jake dodged flying objects and stepped over remnants of furniture and around partially collapsed buildings grabbing hold of pieces of wood and metal to keep him upright as the wind tugged at his body and tried to extricate Elmo from the death grip he had on his precious surf board. Part of him was terrified and another more primitive part beckoned to him and mesmerized him. He knew he should have jumped into the van with the rest of his family but the sound of the waves crashing into the land in the distance called to the infallibility young people feel and to his compulsive drive to conquer the "big one." As he strained against the howling wind, the roar of the angry ocean grew so load that he could no longer hear his labored breathing or the pounding of his heart. The sand and splintered wood cut into his face and arms. He could barely see anything ahead of him. Suddenly the part of the boardwalk that was still intact gave way and along with Jake collapsed into the wet sand below him. He laid there for a moment underneath a portion of the boardwalk that now deflected some of the torrent and flying debris away from him. He had managed to hold on to Elmo and he pulled himself onto his pal to get out of the cold wet sand. Looking toward the ocean, he saw it building with a savage furry some distance away from where he laid. A wall of dark green and brown sea water almost forty feet above him grabbed Jake and Elmo and tossed them into her bowels. Jonah's whale would have been a guppy compared to the jaws of Helen as she gobbled up that portion of the coast, the young adventurous boy, and his surfboard.

A completely disoriented and drenched puppy shook tremulously as he dug with his aching paws in the mud under the pile of wood and tree branches that once had been his home. Casey had run back into the Peterson's empty house just as Helen's blood curdling howl blew the post of the porch down Porter Boulevard. The roof groaned and fell, covering the front of the house completely. Water had poured into all the rooms and Casey tried in vain to find Pepper or any one of the humans he felt responsible to protect. He was wounded by flying debris, but still conscious enough to know he had to bury himself in a low place. That's what he had seen his mother do at the beach when she had that dazed look in her eyes as the ocean surf laughed at her. She would dig and whimper trying to hide from the frightening sound while that lady human would stroke her raised fur and make those sounds that humans make to settle you down. He managed to make enough of a dent in the mud to fold up into a ball underneath an overturned refrigerator leaning against part of the building still standing. The door had blown partially off its hinges and had been buried in the mud creating a tent like barrier from the increasing velocity of the wind.

The van shook violently. Jesse clutched the wheel trying to stay on the road. The water poured over the defenseless terrain and the van disappeared under the onslaught. The last thing Charlie remembered was the sound of metal breaking apart and screams…horrible screams. The world went black as he felt his back and head smash into something immovable. His breath exited from his lungs and suddenly there was no sound, no light, nothing.

Chapter Three

The Signal

Will heard someone calling his name. He buried himself deeper under Mrs. Swanson's blankets. He clutched the BB gun as though it was a canon, and tried to hold his breath. All of his senses had come alive and he listened as the voice called in a forced whisper. "Will...it's me, Ted...I know you're up there. Please let me come up and help you." Will crawled hesitantly still balancing the gun on his forearms toward the small crack in the tree house floor where the boards did not meet. He closed one eye and tried to focus the other to see if it truly was Ted or one of those awful men trying to trick him. He could see a small part of a tee shirt that had some letters on it. He could only make out two of the letters...MB...then the red hair of the person wearing the shirt. It was Ted. Will pulled the wedge from under the door and crawled onto the porch. He leaned over the edge just enough to confirm no one was with his friend. He still was wary so he called in the same forced whisper his buddy had.

"Ted. Tell me there is no one with you. Tell me you didn't tell anyone where you were going and I'll let you come up."

Ted looked up into the swollen eyes of his friend peering over the edge of the tree house porch and he could barely recognize him, at least that part of him he could see. "No one...I'm alone. No one knows I'm here. They think I went into town to join the search party. They have everyone looking for your family, Will. Let me up there." Will looked around the thick woods and towards the stream he had traversed and listened for dogs barking or any voices in the distance. Hopefully, the dogs had taken the turn away from the woods that he had attempted to create by planting his scent on both sides of the cement basketball court making it appear he had run away from the woods and toward town. He dropped the rope ladder toward Ted and barely gave him enough time to navigate the last rung before Will threw it and the top part of Ted onto the porch.

"Get in here and wedge the door!" Will growled to his recovering buddy. Ted scurried into the tree house, secured the wedge firmly under the door, and leaned against the wall opposite Will who had scooted the cooler up to the door and backed into a corner where only a small portion of the dim light from the whirring space heater outlined his trembling body.

"Will...what in the heck is going down? The explosion is all over the news and they couldn't find any of you! What in the hel...."

Will slid to the floor in that dark corner and began to sob. He didn't want to. He wanted to act like he could handle all this. He was in charge when his father was away. He had to be brave but he felt small and frightened and vulnerable. He was hungry and his chest felt like someone was sitting on it. The crying relieved some of the pain, but only a little. Ted stayed where he was and felt the empty place he had tried to fill with toughness and arrogance since his father had died open up. He knew that it wasn't manly to cry, but in his room alone or in the tree house the manliness gave way to the pain that would not disappear with the macho exterior. After a few moments Will swallowed the halting breaths that accompanied his tears and stood up in his mud covered clothes, glanced at his friend with eyes that had seen much more than any twelve year old should have, reached into the cooler and grabbed two semi-warm colas. Handing one to Ted, he dropped his weary body onto one of the pillow seats and related the day from hell to his fellow bombardier. Ted's eyes were as wide as the owl's he and Will tried to scare out of the tree near Ted's house, just to see the bird's amazing wings spread to their full four foot span as it soared to higher branches away from the pesky predators. Will ended with the question he would ask himself over and over again.

"You said they couldn't find any of my family? No...bodies. Did they find my dad? He was not here. He was out of town in..." Will reached deep into his brain to extract the conversation he had heard the night before his father had left. "Mom said...leaving for...new...something that began with 'new'."

Ted said the newspaper and the TV reported the police and FBI were stumped by the lack of evidence anyone was in the house at the time of the explosion. Pictures of Robert, Emily, Toby, and Will were all over the news, on posters, on the TV. They had gone to Will's father's office address but there was nothing but an empty desk and chair in the room. No one in the building knew of anyone following the description of Robert West. Will's father went to work at that office when he wasn't out of town and talked about people there, getting into betting pools on ballgames, playing practical jokes on each other. Why would he tell a lie? Where was he? Why did they have to move so many times? Why was his mother always hesitant to go places other than the grocery store and church? Will began to wonder why his family never had any neighbors or friends over their house like other parents did. They rarely bonded with or talked to neighbors other than to wave a brief hello and then barricade themselves in the now destroyed house. They never took vacations or even took drives in the country like other families did. Will never thought too much about it until now. They weren't at all like other families. Why didn't his father let him know what was the real story if he was supposed to be in charge when his dad was gone? For a brief moment he was angry with his missing family but that turned into the pain in his chest and the loneliness and fear that he would never see them again. He looked down at his torn blue jeans and mud caked shirt. Out of the corner of his eye he saw something red under the blankets. He pulled his race car from the blankets where he had collapsed the day before. It had lost two of its wheels and a portion of the frame was pulled away from the chassis. Most of the paint had been chipped away but the remnants of red reminded him of those last moments before the two men had walked up to his house and changed his life completely.

"What's that, Will?" Ted asked as he reached across the pile of blankets toward the model Will held tightly in his hand.

"It's a model race car dad and I had put together. My birthday…before the explosion…I was painting it…when…when…." Will's eyes filled with tears but he wiped them on his shirt sleeve. "Can't cry. Have to be tough if I'm going to find those guys and make them tell me where mom and Toby are. I know they are alive. Never found any bodies. That's what the news said."

Will had handed his precious race car to Ted. Ted loved fixing things so he was attempting to straighten the bent chassis when he suddenly scooted back against the wall dropping the car on the floor.

"Jeez! It gave me a shock…like when we put a knife in the toaster last year while it was still plugged in."

Will picked up the car as he chuckled for the first time in quite a while watching his macho friend cower against the wall a short distance from the race car. "You probably scooted across the wool blanket with your big butt when you were playing with this thing." All of a sudden Will dropped the car as he yelped shaking his hand in the air. "Yikes…that stings! What the heck is in there?!" Will picked up the pellet gun and pushed the attacking race care toward one of the blankets. He picked it up with the blanket between the car and his bare hand and turned it over to look at the bent frame. He could feel a vibration through the blanket. It pulsed irregularly—two pulsations, then four, then two, a pause, then five. As he held it to his face as close to the frame as he could get without touching it, he noticed the sequence repeated itself. "Ted, it's like Morse code! It's like someone is trying to send a message over and over again. Do you know anything about Morse code? We should've listened in history class." The pulsations stopped. Ted watched Will gingerly pull the blanket away from the race car.

"Ted, see if we have a screwdriver or anything I can pull the frame up a little." Ted rummaged through a coffee can of the Bombardier's treasures and found a putty knife they sometimes used to spread peanut butter on bread one of the guys pilfered from a kitchen. Will cautiously wedged the knife under the car frame and saw something shiny with a small green light blinking. He pried a little more. It was about the size of a nickel and seemed to have been glued or cemented to the bottom portion of the car. Will tried to find a place to wedge the putty knife between it and the flat surface of the car to no avail. He remembered counting seventeen parts to match the schematic when he and his father were preparing to assemble the car. He remembered the warmth of his father's arm when he put it around Will to assist in placing the parts together in just the right order. He remembered every part. The disc with a green light was not on the schematic nor was it one of the parts he had counted.

They heard them barking. Frantic, surly, deep guttural warnings in the distance. Will forgot about the disc with the eerie green light. He grabbed the pellet gun, the faded red race car, stuffed a couple of cookies, and the money from the Bombardiers' dues in his shirt pocket. Ted promised with a bombardier handshake that he hadn't seen Will for days and if anyone asked, he was mourning the loss of his friend who he thought had been lost in the explosion. With Ted hanging over the side of the tree house porch Will slowly hung onto Ted's arms until he was hanging about twenty feet from the ground.

"Let me go now!" he whispered as Ted grudgingly loosened his grip on Will's arms. Will fell into the pine tree next to the tree house. The pine needles pierced his skin as he swung from one tree to the next until he was about fifty feet away from the old oak tree. Ted had climbed down the ladder and was running around in crazy circles, rolling on the ground in an attempt to cover Will's scent. The barking grew closer and closer as Ted walked slowly out of the woods toward his home. He didn't look back. His eyes stung with tears for his friend as the pain from his own loss surfaced from the place he thought he had buried it.

Chapter Four

The Aftermath

Charlie laid against a portion of a roof that had been extricated from one of the houses Helen flung about in her furry. There was no sound, no wind, a piercing emptiness. No birds chirped, no human voices, just silence. He was dizzy and confused. The back of his head had a large gash and he saw his dried blood on the boards of the roof and on the ground. He must have lain there for quite some time, as his consciousness cleared he remembered it was early evening when he and his parents left in the van.

"Mom, Dad, Jake…the dogs! Oh, my god! We were in the van and that wave……" He frantically looked around at the chaos surrounding him. There were no houses intact. Cars had been thrown on top of debris and there was no van that he could see anywhere. No mother, father or brother, no dogs. He tried to stand but the throbbing in his head and dizziness made him stumble and fall. He was lying near some twisted metal and then he saw it. An arm, pale, twisted protruding between the metal. He crawled over to the ghostly appendage lifting up the sharp metal that partially covered it. The face of a woman filled with cuts and bruises stared back at him. The eyes were open and frozen in an empty stare. Charlie had to look away. He sat up and tried to capture his equilibrium. His trembling hand reached for the eyelids of the woman and gently pulled them down to partially close them. He knew she was dead from the icy feeling of her skin. He sobbed. There was no life anywhere in site. How did he survive? He had to search for his family. He had to know if they were buried somewhere under the twisted piles of houses and cars.

One block away, Casey inched his way out of the mud and refrigerator that had protected him from Helen's worst furry. His right paw was bent outward and when he stood he yelped as the pain shot up to his shoulder. He tried to lick the paw back into position to no avail. He was thirsty and his stomach was empty. None of the humans were around to feed him. No one was around. Driven by hunger and thirst, he got up once again and held his injured paw off the ground. Not in any way adapted to walking on three legs, he fell a few times before he was able to balance himself. Sniffing at the piles of splintered wood and metal, wires snapping in the street from poles leaning topsy-turvy, the smell of ruptured gas lines, downed electric equipment, and ozone burnt his nostrils. As he came around a huge tree that had been up-rooted, he saw something moving a short distance away. It was a human sitting on the ground his face in his hands. The human's shoulders were moving up and down. Casey limped cautiously closer but he stepped over a pile of wood that gave way, making a small groaning noise. The human looked toward the sound and couldn't believe his eyes.

"Casey...Casey is that you, buddy?" Casey ran as fast as his three legs could travel toward Charlie. He knocked Charlie over as he buried his muddy self into his best friend's chest. He licked Charlie's face and the salty tears. He began to lick the wound in the back of Charlie's head instinctively attempting to heal it. The two victims tousled around on the wet ground for several minutes. When the greeting ritual was completed, Casey laid in Charlie's lap licking his hand and making grunting noises as if to show his joy at finding his favorite human. Charlie noticed the bent paw.

"Got to fix that up so you can walk. We've got to search for the rest of the family, Casey. I can use your sniffer real bad right now" Charlie pulled out a small stick from the wreckage, tore off the sleeve of his shirt and fashioned a splint for Casey's paw. He had spent time with his mother at the hospital and had seen appendages relocated in the E.R. He gently stroked Casey's mangled fur and put his foot against the dog's body, pulling the paw toward him in the opposite direction it was bent. Casey howled in pain. He sensed that his buddy would never hurt him, but growled at Charlie just for a moment. Charlie whispered softly to his friend. "It's all right, Casey. I'm sorry...had to do it."

Charlie splinted the paw with the stick wrapping it and the paw with the shirt sleeve. Casey learned quickly that he could walk using his right leg again, but jumping was out of the question. The sun peaked through the clouds bathing the macabre scene like a searchlight. Charlie pulled boards, pieces of furniture and metal as he walked over demolished homes digging into piles of wet sand and calling his parents' names until his voice became raspy and weak. Casey wound around the piles of sticks, sniffing and snorting. He probably was looking for food more than bodies but he stuck to his friend's path regardless of finding nothing to eat. Charlie was sure that Jake had been drowned if he indeed had headed toward the beach. He was angry with his brother at the same time he was sad. If he hadn't been too crazy to take off in that storm, maybe the van would have gotten farther inland and his parents and Pepper would have been safe. The destruction went almost ten miles inland so that the few moments they hesitated would not have made a difference. Charlie had to hold on to any hope that some miracle might have saved them. He had lived through it, why couldn't they?

A helicopter flew low over the beach and began to turn toward the town that had been destroyed. Charlie waved madly and Casey barked at the big bird. It suddenly changed course and headed out to sea. The exhausted, frightened, starving boy and dog slumped onto a broken cement piling and tried to collect themselves.

"The hospital…Casey. We've got to get to the hospital and see if mom and dad…oh, of course, Pepper are there!" The two orphans crawled over the piles and piles of rubble scanning and sniffing for any hint of life as they headed away from the beach, their home, their life. The hospital was several miles to the east of their one time home and the hurricane had swirled west causing less damage to the towns along the coast. Casey whimpered as his paw began to swell in its splint. Charlie stopped several times to loosen the shirt that held the splint. His head throbbed and his mouth was dry and aching. The pressure in his chest came and went as the fact that his family might be gone seeped into his consciousness. They passed some houses that were partially standing but desolate. Charlie stopped in front of what used to be a two-story house. The entire side of the house was sliced off, which made it look like the doll houses he had seen girls ogling in the department stores. The refrigerator was still standing and curtains hung in shreds from the window. Charlie and Casey called out to see if anyone was still inhabiting the house, but there was no answer. They climbed into the kitchen and opened the refrigerator. The smell was less than appetizing. There was a pitcher of juice and some oranges that Charlie thought might be safe to eat and drink. He found a bent pot and poured some of the juice into it for Casey. Despite the unusual taste Casey lapped it up with enthusiasm as Charlie polished the rest of it off almost drowning himself guzzling it down. Casey chewed on the orange slice Charlie handed him then promptly spit it out while shaking his head in rejection. He felt weird and ashamed taking things from someone's home. His parents had taught the boys to be honest and respectful of others. Tears began to well up in Charlie's eyes as he thought he may never see his parents and Jake again. He bent down and buried his head in Casey's muddy fur.

"You lost your family too, boy, but we're going to find them if we have to look all over this state. We're going to find them, Casey." Casey barked agreement as if he understood his best friend. He sat up with that funny grin on his face which made Charlie's tears turn to laughter. Charlie looked around and noticed some clothes lying on broken furniture and on the portion of the floor that was left. He looked down at his muddy, blood caked jeans and shirt and decided that he would make sure to return them to the owners someday. He wondered where they were and said a little prayer for them and his lost family. He found some small boxes of cereal and some canned goods, silverware and a can opener, a couple of towels and some soap in the undamaged cupboards. Stuffing them in a laundry sack he found in the broom closet along with the clothes, he and Casey set out in the direction of the hospital. The sun was setting and he figured it was about six o'clock.

Chapter Five

Jamie's House

Will jumped down from one of the pine tree hiding places onto the pine needle covered ground. He looked at the sun that kept peeking in and out of the clouds and figured it was about three o'clock. There was a little chill in the air and he wished he could have stayed in the tree house with Ted longer to work out a plan. He took out the race car from the small bag of items he had brought with him. It wasn't vibrating and the green light on the disk embedded in the frame was dark. He was puzzled about almost everything including the message the disc seemed to try to send. He started to run as fast as he could toward a nearby town where he and his family used to go to deliver Christmas baskets to the poor. Circleville was approximately six miles from his house. He loved memorizing numbers and was always watching anything associated with numbers, including the speedometer in their car. He had excelled in math in school and his teacher was considering having him take junior high classes in algebra and calculus early. Many of the people in Circleville were very poor. The men worked in the forests to fall trees for the sawmill in town. It was a grueling, dangerous work and many lost a limb or a life when equipment was overused and unsafe. There was a homeless shelter at the edge of town–Will recalled that the shelter supervisors might offer him a bed, a shower, some clean clothes, and, most of all, food. One of the few things the family did outside of their home was offering their help with charitable projects sponsored by their church. Emily cooked many meals for the kitchen in the shelter and brought old clothes there for the needy. The thought of his mother brought that pain back in his chest which he shook off quickly. He had to stay strong—a soldier on a mission—a dangerous mission like the ones his grandfather Will used to tell him about. He glanced back at the forest to see if anyone had followed him and began to run faster.

"No sense lookin' back at somethin' that's finished. Just a waste of your time and you might trip. Just keep lookin' ahead one step at a time. Let God hold you up until you can stand on your own." Will recalled his grandpa's gruff voice giving him one of his lessons about life. He used to impatiently wish he was somewhere else when his grandpa would get on his soap box giving advice. Will wished he had paid more attention now because this was life at it's worse and he could only hold on to what he had learned in his few twelve years in order to survive.

Will stopped several times on his journey to Circleville. He passed by a neighborhood were the residents had put out their trash for pickup. An old suitcase with a zipper stuck so that you could only open it a tad—a pair of old tennis shoes just about his size, some rusty tools, and a ball cap with the letters "MPM" on it were scavenged. He was so thirsty that he found a bottle of dead Sprite that was half full and drank it down so fast he didn't have time to taste it. The lights were starting to come on in the small shanties on the outskirts of the village. The main street in town took visitors to the more affluent homes on the hills surrounding the town. Those homes belonged to the bankers and the owners of the lumber companies. Their richly decorated porches and windows covered with custom-made draperies looked down on the shanties of the workers ostentatiously accentuating the vast difference in their two lives. Will walked with his survival kit past the homes of the workers and their families and envied them. Despite their economic situation, some of them still had each other.

The shelter was an old schoolhouse that had been abandoned for years and needed multiple repairs. A social worker, who was working with families who had lost their meager homes when work wasn't available, had invested his own money to purchase the schoolhouse. In exchange for food and a place to sleep, the residents painted and repaired what they could, just enough to barely pass inspection from the local health department. James Shepherd, "Jamie," as many people called him, took the project on and stuck with it for the past four years. He had no trouble begging for donations from the rich folks. It always amazed him that the people who worked in the stores in the town and in other towns, the middle class, were more generous than those that had much more to give. Surrounding towns heard of the shelter called "Jamie's House" and would bring clothing, furniture, beddings, and food routinely to help him with his cause. Someone had donated a couple of television sets, some board games, and a radio. A friend of Jamie's who was a nurse donated her time to the shelter once a week to check on the residents and try to help with medication needs. Maria loved her job as a nurse at the hospital in Clover City, but her time at the shelter filled a place in her heart that none other could. She had even setup a small class for some of the women in the shelter to learn to be nurses' aides. There was some talk around town that Maria and Jamie were an item, but they both denied it vehemently. If you watched them working and laughing together though, there was chemistry there that bonded them.

Two columns held up a marquis above the school. The letters on the marquis were barely visible as time and harsh winter winds had scrubbed them away. One of the more artistic residents had taken the rickety ladder they had confiscated from the dump and climbed up to the ledge in front of the sign and painted "JAMIE'S HOUSE" over the faded "CIRCLEVILLE ELEMENTARY." Will sighed as he dragged his weary body up the four cracked cement steps to the door of the shelter. There was a small sign that read:

"YOU ARE WELCOME TO TAKE SHELTER WITH US. PLEASE RING THE BELL AND SOMEONE WILL HELP YOU." Before Will could reach up to ring, he heard the sound of footsteps behind him. With barely a few hours' sleep, no food, and frightened, he backed away from the door and crouched in a dark area of the entrance.

"Is someone there?" A deep but kind voice asked. "You needn't be afraid. There is no one here that will hurt you. I could use some help with these grocery bags."

Will inched out of the shadows holding tightly to his precious suitcase with the broken zipper.

"I'll help," Will offered in almost a whisper. "I need a place to stay and don't have any money (he wanted to save the few dollars he had taken from the Bombardier's treasury) but I can sure work…that is, if you don't ask any questions." Will could see the stranger in the dim lights on either side of the door. He was about six feet tall and had hair that needed attention. The stubble on his chin wasn't quite a beard yet, but had a good start. His eyes were kind and his face was that of about a thirty-something man. Will grabbed a couple of the paper bags and could see that the man wore a coat that was way too small for his muscular frame.

"Come on in, son. We've got a couple of empty beds. No one pays here. We all have our chores and there is always something breaking that needs fixing." Will followed the stranger down a hallway into a large kitchen. Though its appliances were the worse for wear, it was spotless and neat.

The walls had some cracks and some of the plaster was missing in places but they were painted with bright yellow paint that bounced off the bright florescent lights hanging from the ceiling. Will could see the man much better in the light and he guessed he was right about his age. He had jeans with holes in them and after he wrestled with the too small jacket laying it gently over one of the unmatched kitchen chairs as if it were a mink coat, Will could see that he worked out from the biceps bulging below the tee-shirt he wore. They both began putting the groceries away in the tall cabinets surrounding the kitchen. Several gallons of milk, large boxes of oatmeal, several kinds of fruit, hamburger buns, and several pounds of ground beef were put in their respective places with only a few "Not there's…" and "Yup, there's…" from the man. Will wondered if this was Jamie or one of the residents helping with the chores. He had never met the philanthropic social worker on trips with his mother. She and Maria had become friends and Emily would try to bring her donations on a day she knew Maria would be working at the shelter.

"Follow me…um what should I call you?" the man gestured to Will to walk with him back down the hall to several doors that looked like they used to open into classrooms. Beside each of the rooms there were old metal lockers. Some of the doors were barely attached and some had no doors at all.

"Max. My name is Max." Will didn't want to give his real name so he remembered the initials on the ball cap he had taken from the trash and promptly plopped on his head.

"Good name, Max. Mine is Jamie." He guided Will, alias Max, into one of the rooms. There was a rug on the floor in the middle of the room. It had the hint of a floral pattern woven into its worn threads. Along the walls and down the middle of the room, there were cots and beds of every type. Nothing matched including the sheets and blankets on the beds, but all were neatly made. Some of the beds had small tables, end tables, antiques, folding tables, and camping tables with small lamps on them or a flashlight. Between the beds along the walls were clothes racks—some full of clothes, others were empty. There were boxes beside some of the beds with toys, treasures rescued from homes, keepsakes, clothing, and other miscellaneous remnants of someone's life.

"There are two bathrooms outside this room down the end of the hall. They have showers. Looks like you could use one right now. Where…" Jamie stopped before he asked a question. He respected Will's request not to ask questions, but this boy was just that, a boy. Maybe twelve years old, though his eyes looked much older and wiser than any twelve year old he had seen. The boy had deep dark circles under his eyes and his hair was sticking out from his baseball cap like a clown wig. His face was covered with dirt and some scratches and his clothes were stiff with mud and tattered. He held an old black suitcase that looked like it had been through the same war he had. Jamie noticed he didn't put it down while he was showing him around as though there was something very valuable inside. Will followed Jamie to two doors marked "RESTROOMS AND SHOWER" on the doors. Will wanted to rip off his matted clothes and turn on the water to the shower as hot as he could. He wanted to wash away these past two days, let it all go down the drain like his life had suddenly done.

"Let's get you some clean clothes and some towels. I'll bet you're pretty hungry. Most everyone went on a bus to the movie in town. The owner of the theater invited everyone at the shelter to see *Pretty Woman, Star Wars*, and free popcorn! They were so excited they almost ran over each other getting to the bus. That was sure nice of him. There are a lot of nice people in this world."

"Some aren't so nice. Can I take a shower now?"

"Sure, Max. I tend to talk too much sometimes." Jamie opened a big cupboard just outside the bathrooms. There were shelves full of folded clothes all organized according to size. There was one shelf full of towels, wash clothes, and other linens. "This is the guys' closet. The girls have the one at the other side of the bathrooms. Help yourself and then come back in the kitchen and I'll wrestle us up some burgers. I'm a little hungry myself." Jamie winked at

'Max' and walked down the hall. Will watched him turn the corner and finally released his death grip on his suitcase. He looked through the shelves until he found some underwear, a tee shirt that had "Go to Winky's for the Very Best Twinkies" inscribed on the front and back and a dark green sweatshirt with a hood. The bathroom was scrubbed and smelled a lot better than he did. He turned on the shower until the steam filled the room. There was a small sink with a mirror and a box on a stand with toothbrushes still packaged in their plastic wrappers. Three tubes of toothpaste, a box of combs and brushes covered in plastic, and shaving equipment. Small sample bottles of shaving lotion, men's cologne, and shampoo were also in boxes on the table. A sign above the table next to the mirror read:

"IF YOU NEED TO USE SOMETHING, REMEMBER BE FAIR
ONLY TAKE WHAT YOU NEED AS OTHERS ARE HERE."

Will took off his cap marked "MPM" thinking how clever he was to use another name that began with those letters. He pulled off his wrecked clothes and put them in a pile on the floor. He looked into the mirror and for the first time in days saw himself. He took a deep breath as he could barely recognize the person staring back at him. He had aged. His eyes were sunken and dark circles surrounded the sadness in those eyes. The memory of the evil man with vacant eyes flashed through his consciousness and he turned away. He stepped into the steaming shower and closed the curtain. He wanted so to close the curtain on the whole mess. He wanted his family back. As he scrubbed the dirt away he became angrier and more determined than ever to find them and to find the men that had done this.

Will with the borrowed name, dressed in his borrowed clothes, doused with borrowed Old Spice cologne, teeth brushed with the borrowed toothbrush and toothpaste, sat in the kitchen on one of the unmatched borrowed chairs eating burgers that tasted like steak to him with Mr. Jamie. They didn't say too much at first.

Will, alias Max (for the big "M" on his hat), liked the man sitting across from him at the borrowed kitchen table. He didn't ask him any questions. He seemed to know there was something awfully wrong, but didn't pull at the bandage over the wound. He let Will, alias Max, be Max for now.

"There are washers and dryers in the basement. When you are done, I'll show you your bed and take your stuff downstairs and throw them in for you. You look pretty tired. How are the burgers? Whoops...I wasn't supposed to ask any questions, was I?" Jamie jabbed a little. He noticed that Max had brought the black suitcase with him and set it guardedly next to his chair.

"They're super. I was so hungry and I am a little tired. Thanks so much for all this. You've been really kind. I'm sorry I can't tell you anything, just trust me I have to take care of myself. I know how. My da..." Will stopped mid-sentence. He needed a friend...He needed one desperately, but he didn't want someone to try to take care of him because he was a minor alone or an orphan probably. So with his mission in mind, he held his ground. Jamie being a social worker had seen kids younger than Max scrounging for food, sick with disease, lost, and apathetic. He had seen them during his time with the Peace Corps not only in foreign countries but also in the United States. Max was healthy and seemed to have had parenting where many of the children had no parenting, just abuse. Jamie had looked through the files in his office while Max was cleaning up and found no lost child with the initials MPM. Only one file for a "Max" who had been lost for two years. Lots of missing children and teens. Jamie wished he had the means to adopt some of the ones that came through the shelter yet alone those hundreds of lost souls, wandering somewhere, or totally lost.

"My friend, Maria, is a nurse and comes here on Tuesdays each week. Maybe she should look at those scratches on your arms. They are pretty red and might be infected. Can you stay until then? I'd like you to meet her. She is super and all the residents love her."

Will shook his head as soon as he heard the name of his mother's friend. She had met Will before when he used to come with Emily to the shelter. He never stayed long while she visited as he loved sledding down the hills nearby or shooting hoops with the kids from the shelter and the shanties on the playground next to the former old schoolhouse. "I have to be gone by tomorrow afternoon," he said without explanation.

Jamie didn't have time to wonder as the bus pulled up in front of the shelter and the twelve adults and six children, some asleep on their parents' shoulders, came through the door shouting how great the movies were and what a wonderful time they had. Will looked at them briefly, nodded, and whispered to Jamie. "Can you show me my bed now, please?"

Jamie hugged everyone and pointed toward Will who was trying to steal into a secluded spot somewhere with his beloved suitcase. "This is Max. He's going to stay with us tonight."

Jamie extricated himself from a cute little blond girl's grip on his neck and led Will to a bed in the far corner of the sleeping quarters. This bed had an end table and lamp. Will placed the black suitcase on the bed and turned to thank Jamie again.

"If you ever want to talk or need anything, here's my card with all my numbers on it, Max."

Will took the card and put it in the back pocket of his borrowed jeans. He reached out his trembling hand and shook the warm hand Jamie extended to him. The voices of the enthused residents faded as Will looked around the room before he reached cautiously into his suitcase. He put the suitcase beside the bed and eased his weary body under the comforter folded neatly at the bottom of the bed. He took the flashlight from the end table that had a small doily on it and a book of prayers lying open with a faded cloth marker separating the pages. He held the race car in his hand covered by the sleeve of his green sweatshirt in case the vibrations would magically begin. The dim ray of light from the flashlight illuminated the bent frame of the race car. Will tented himself and his treasure with the comforter and slowly lifted the corner of the metal frame awkwardly balancing the flashlight between his shoulder and cheek. He jumped slightly as the tiny green light flashed two times and the staccato vibrations made it difficult to hold onto the chassis of the car despite the cloth protector.

"Buzz, buzz......pause......buzz, buzz, buzz......pause...five successive buzzed......pause......buzz, buzz." The green light had shone corresponding with the signal. It repeated itself three times as it had in the tree house then grew silent and the green light faded. "It had to be dad that put this metal thing in here. No one else had this car except me and him." Will tried hard to focus on every moment of that day. The only time he and his father had not been together was when they were interrupted by his mom opening the garage door leading into the kitchen to tell his dad there was a phone call. He suddenly remembered the look on his mother's face as she whispered something in his dad's ear as he walked into the kitchen to take the call. It meant nothing to Will at the time as he was lost in the task of making the race car whole. His dad had taken the car with him into the kitchen but had returned within a few minutes with the model in his hand. He remembered now that the rest of the time they were together completing the project his father silence. Will was so fixated on the project itself he really hadn't even noticed the change in his father's demeanor. He also recalled muffled exchanges behind his parents' closed bedroom door when he went to bed that night. His father was gone by the time Will awoke the next morning. Gone again. Gone to New...new......New Brunswick! That was where his mother had said his dad was going......New Brunswick!

He closed his eyes as the model car continued to vibrate the same sequence in his hand. New Brunswick is in what state? He had to try to remember his geography—not his favorite subject though he wished at this moment he had paid more attention.

The vibrations stopped and Will jumped out from under the comforter as he heard, "Max are you okay? Just wanted to bring you your clean clothes."

Jamie was standing over the bed holding Will's clean and folded clothes. There was a paper bag bulging with something lying on top of the clothes as Jamie laid them on the disheveled bed.

He looked straight into Will's eyes as if he was trying to see the story behind them. "You better get some rest if you are leaving in the morning. We have breakfast about seven A.M. Everybody pitches in if they don't have to leave for work, the few that still have jobs I mean, or have to get in line at the welfare office. Do you have any money to get home? I...I was guessing you're trying to get home, son...aren't you?"

Will looked away from Jamie's intense gaze. "Yeah, home. I'm going home." His voice cracked at the word home. He didn't have a home anymore. He wasn't sure if anything was left from the life he thought he knew. He wasn't sure if the life he knew for twelve years was real or just a play with another secret life being led behind the scenes. Were his parents spies or criminals hiding from the law? Had they had plastic surgery to change their faces like the hoodlums and snitches in movies he had seen? Why would they put their children in harm's way? Were they really his parents? Was Toby really his brother?

"Thought you promised not to ask any questions" Will said to Jamie as well as to himself.

"I'm sorry, Max. Just worried about you. That's the way most social workers are. We worry. We care. Sorry. Let me know if you need anything. See you at breakfast." Jamie turned and walked away toward the hallway. People were quietly tiptoeing into the dorm room. Their silhouettes painted shadows on the wall making the room look like it was filled with ghosts growing and receding as they moved in and out of the dim light from the hallway. Shadows of men, women and children, thankful for the shelter, comforting, and food, yet yearning for the ability to stand on their own again.

The child in Will wanted to run up to any one of the families and unload the horror of the last few days. He wasn't ready to be on his own, to grow into a man before his time, to go out into the world to search for a family he may never find, to fight a terrifying enemy with hollow eyes and confusing disguises. He wasn't ready to be an orphan.

Chapter Six

The Hospital

Charlie's legs were wobbly and the orange juice and orange he had eaten in the vacant house had been burned up walking over debris and through mud up to his calves. Some of the houses and businesses were still fairly intact as he headed inland toward the hospital. Ambulances and rescue crews began to appear along the roadway. There were tents and people with various injuries lying or sitting on cots. The air smelled of broken gas lines, human excrement, stagnant water, and garbage. The contrast with the blue sky dotted with fluffy white clouds and the disaster scene grew as he and the limping Casey weaved unnoticed around equipment, rescue personnel, lost humans looking desperately for loved ones, injured and dead. He noticed a gray-haired woman in a torn house dress with a large bruise on the side of her face and her right arm in a sling singing to a small group of children sitting on an overturned car. The children were smiling and he suddenly felt a little hope that he and Casey would be all right, no matter what. He had been knocked down many times during a basketball game, shoved and cursed at, but he always got back up or recovered, ignoring the insults and sometimes running full court to make a basket.

Madison Memorial Hospital had lost a portion of its Emergency Room when the huge sign directing people to that area had blown against the entrance destroying the waiting area, reception desk, and several of the patient cubicles. Water had flooded much of the main floor of the hospital and power was nonexistent for several blocks surrounding the hospital complex. Emergency power was being diverted to the three functioning operating rooms, the Intensive Care ventilators, and the Intensive Care Nursery. Battery operated equipment, headlamps, and flashlights were brought to the radiology area on the second floor. Wheelchairs. stretchers, IV poles, and other equipment on wheels had been gathered in what was left of the hospital cafeteria on the mezzanine as there was a ramp leading down to the first floor delivery entrance that had escaped the mud wash that followed the flooding. Emergency canned foods and staples were assembled at the back of the cafeteria, counted and rationed to the most needy. Back-up battery powered refrigeration trucks were being filled with the perishables stored in the huge freezers and refrigerators in the kitchen area. Helicopters were landing and lifting off carrying the most seriously injured to other more functional hospitals up the coast and inland. Volunteer nurses, doctors, lay persons, Red Cross volunteers, Homeland Security personnel and National Guardsman bustled about performing their magic in a world filled with chaos and sadness. There were many injured and dead, but thankfully most people living in the area had heeded the warning to evacuate and the amount of casualties that could have occurred were diminished.

Charlie searched every cot, chair, tent set up outside of the hospital. None of his family was among the victims or the rescuers. He didn't even see any of the nurses or doctors he had been introduced to that worked with his mother and father. When he tried to enter the hospital through the front entrance, he was stopped by a young Guardsman who looked about Charlie's age.

"You can't come in here unless you have a volunteer badge or are a doctor or nurse," he said in the most authoritative voice he could muster. "No animals allowed at all," as he looked at Casey who tried to offer his most pathetic expression to the soldier.

"My mother is a nurse in the ICU and my dad is Dr. Peterson. I'm here to help and was told I don't need an ID." Charlie figured it really wasn't a lie except for the ID part.

"I guess you can go then, but the dog stays here," the Guardsman said with a frown directed to Casey who was smiling up at him even though his paw was throbbing.

"Casey is a rescue dog. One of the best. He has to come with me." Charlie embellished a little trying not to chuckle looking at the goofy half smile of his "rescue dog".

"I have to ask my Captain about that. You stay right here."

As soon as the Guardsman turned to walk out the door, Charlie and Casey ran to the stairway leading to the upper floors. The stairs were covered with linens and cans filled with damaged equipment, pieces of glass, and soggy papers. Charlie remembered the Intensive Care Unit was on the second floor as he stepped around the debris and came to the door marked "AUTHORIZED PERSONNEL ONLY–MEDICAL AND SURGICAL INTENSIVE CARE UNITS." He ordered Casey to sit and stay in the stairwell as he cautiously opened the door. He was not prepared for what he saw. Beds and stretchers were lined up with very little space between them. It looked like the movies he had seen about war and the infirmaries with rows of injured and dying soldiers. Most all of the beds and stretchers were occupied by men, women, and children. Blood, both fresh and dried, marred some of the sheets and blankets covering the patients.

A forest of poles with intravenous fluids and blood stood sentinel beside most of the beds and some of the stretchers. Several of the stretchers held bodies covered completely with sheets and Charlie knew that those were victims that didn't survive. The faces of the nurses, doctors, and volunteers were filled with compassion and weariness. Mixed with the murmurs of the voices were the heart wrenching cries of babies and adults—some crying in pain, others from hunger, and the most agonizing were the sobs of loved ones as they clutched the icy hands of the dying and the dead. Charlie frantically looked at the faces of the injured and the workers. They glanced at him but quickly returned to their own world. Charlie even lifted the sheets covering the cadavers holding his breath not only because of the smell of death but also in fear that one of them would be his mother, father, or Jake. There were cubicles surrounding the nurses' station at the far end of the area filled with beds, equipment, and stretchers. A man with disheveled hair and a wrinkled lab coat motioned to Charlie as he passed one of the cubicles.

"Hey, son. Could you please help me with this patient. I need someone to hold him while I take this piece of metal out of his arm." Charlie tried to act like he did not hear the plea but his conscience told him to do the right thing.

"I'll help. What should I do?" Charlie looked into the pleading eyes of the young man on the bed and smiled at him. "My name is Charlie. I play basketball at Jamison High. You look like an athlete. What's your sport?" Charlie grasped the shoulders and right arm of the patient as the doctor tied the injured arm to the bed rail. The arm was covered with blood and cuts with a large jagged piece of metal protruding from the upper part of the arm.

"Football. I...I...played...play quarterback at Miami State. I......" The scream exited from his clenched jaw as he tried hard to stifle it. It was more of a growl than a scream. Charlie closed his eyes and pushed down on the shoulders and arm as the young man's body arched in pain.

"Got it!" The doctor exclaimed as he applied pressure to the gaping wound left by the metal piece. Charlie loosened his grip on the young man as the doctor patted him on the back. "Thanks. You were great, son." He gently wiped the sweat dripping from his patient's face. "So did you. I'm sorry I had to hurt you. We ran out of anesthetic hours ago. I'll be right back." The doctor wrapped a cloth around the wound and turned to exit the cubicle.

Charlie began to follow him to see if he was from the hospital and might have known his mother. He turned back to the young man who was staring at the ceiling blinking back tears.

"You got my name but I didn't get yours." Charlie moved back toward the bed pretending not to notice the tears.

"Eddie...Eddie Munroe. Thanks for asking. You made it through the storm. I was visiting my parents and had gone to pick up some gas so we could travel inland when they called for the evacuation. The line-up was unbelievable so I called mom and dad on my cell and told them to go ahead and I would follow. As I waited in line, the wind picked up to a howl and then everything went black. I went upside down in what used to be my car as it smashed against a brick wall. The gas station was destroyed and there were bodies and smashed cars everywhere. I passed out and next thing I knew I was here. I don't know if mom and dad made it in time. I've asked if there are any phones but only the special lines and walkie talkies work and that is for the emergency persons."

"I've lost touch with my family and our dog. I was in our van heading inland and the next thing I knew I was laying outside with a big gash on my head. Everything was smashed around me and there were no people except..." Charlie thought it would be better not to mention the corpse of the young woman he had seen. "My mother worked here as a nurse and I thought there might be a slim chance she made it here." Charlie looked away from the boy on the stretcher scanning the room for any familiar face. The faces reminded him of the ghosts in a horror film he had seen—hollow, painful, lost, exhausted, and tearful. The doctor returned and Charlie asked if he had seen his mother or anyone that looked like her but the doctor turned out to be an EMT from the next county that had volunteered to help in the disaster zone. Disappointed and suddenly remembering Casey and how ravenously hungry he was, he shook the uninjured hand of his first patient ever and both promised to pray they found their loved ones. Casey was sleeping when Charlie opened the exit door. He panted and whimpered a cheery hello as Charlie bent down and buried his face into Casey's thick, matted fur, rubbed his floppy ears, and tried to think of what to do next.

* * *

Will waved to Jamie standing on the porch of the transformed schoolhouse. He had no idea where he was headed. He had no idea where New Brunswick was, if any of his family was alive or safe or dead or imprisoned. He had no idea whether the two men who had invaded his life four days ago were anywhere nearby, were friend or enemy. He had no idea if there was anything real about his life before the explosion or if his parents had told him anything about themselves that he could believe. His grandpa's words gathered his thoughts and reminded him that he did have a plan. He just had to focus on how to find his father, how to get to New Brunswick. That was what he overheard his mother saying the night before his father left.

Chapter Seven

The Black Box

Two men were in the cheap motel room just off Route Seventy. One man sat at the small table covered with maps, a couple of heavy pistols, beer cans and a half eaten sandwich, cigarettes stubs in a ceramic ashtray, a laptop computer flashing lists of strange symbols and numerical codes, and a small metal box about the size of a radio that lit up red and green buttons intermittently with the same sequence. Two flashes…four flashes…two flashes……a pause…then five flashes. The other man was intently watching the news on a fuzzy TV screen as it reported the current events.

"Hey, here it is, Joe. The kid. The picture of the kid." The man motioned to the man who was sitting gazing at the computer as it continued to display the odd symbols and numbers. Joe extracted the cigarette from his mouth and pulverized it into the ashtray as he pushed the chair aside and walked over to the TV Will's face flashed across the screen. The recent seventh grade photo showed a smiling young man with his spiked hair and new blue shirt he had begged his mother not to make him wear as it wasn't the cool tee shirt he wanted to show off. The newscaster was repeating the mysterious explosion and the fact that no bodies had been found at the scene. He said that there was evidence that Will had been tracked to the edge of the woods near the disaster and then the tracks disappeared. They were picked up again headed toward town, but no one had seen or heard from the boy. An eight hundred number ran across the screen.

"If you have any information on William Edward West Jr. or any of the West family, Robert, Emily, or Toby, please call this number." The newscaster pleaded and then the picture dissolved as the reporter was moving quickly to the national headlines about conflicts, accidents, and corruption throughout the world. Joe turned his hollow eyes away from the TV without commenting.

His expressionless face was marred with two jagged scars that started at the top of one cheekbone and extended down his empty face to the lower jaw. He wore a vest with an emblem near the right upper chest and his shirtsleeves were rolled up showing off hairy muscular forearms. One arm had a tattoo of a man kneeling cutting open the carcass of a deer. The man's face was hidden by a large wide brimmed hat and his hands and arms were covered with the dead animal's blood. He walked toward a cot in a darkened corner of the room and bent over a figure lying under a blanket on the cot. The figure moved slightly and the man with hollow eyes reached into a pack hanging from his belt. The dim light caught a flash of something metallic as he pulled the object from the pack. He reached under the cover and wrapped a tourniquet around a lifeless arm, held the object close to the arm for a moment, the released the tourniquet, walked back to the table and resumed his gaze at the symbols flashing across the computer screen. The metal box flashed red lights. Two…four…two…pause…five. Two….four…two…pause…five. Joe grabbed the metal box and nervously attempted to connect a cord dangling from the box to the one of the computer ports. He motioned to the man still standing gazing at the TV screen while drinking a beer. The man moved toward the cot in the darkened corner of the room and grabbed the rag doll figure from the bed and dragged it to a chair near Joe. He grabbed a beer and threw it into the face of the figure in the chair.

Will felt a chill and pulled the hood of his loaned sweatshirt over his head. The sun peaked in and out of the clouds as he headed toward the library in town. He knew libraries had computers and for a small fee he could access the internet to search for New Brunswick. He mirrored the way his mother used to scan the streets and shop fronts whenever they would leave the house. What was she looking for or running from? He opened the double doors of the library and quietly stood in front of the librarian's desk. There were only a few people scattered in chairs around tables filled with stacks of books and newspapers.

"Hello. Ma'am, Miss Librarian. Do you have a computer I could use? I need to look up some information for a school project," he whispered sheepishly. Will wasn't very good at telling lies, but he was getting better at it.

"We do have computers, young man. If you or your parents have a library card they are free. If you don't have a card then it will be one dollar and fifty cents for one half hour," the spectacled, hair in a bun librarian with a polka dotted dress and a suspicious eye reported authoritatively to the boy with the ball cap with "MCM" on it. She thought to herself, "Young people don't have manners anymore. He could at least remove his cap!" Will kept his head down toward the library floor hoping not to be recognized as his picture and those of his family were probably all over the TV. He reached into his pocket and laid a crumpled dollar bill and coins on the desk. The librarian gestured to a row of three computers two of which were occupied.

"Thirty minutes. Just use this sign on." The librarian tried to peer under the cap at the face that quickly turned away from the desk. She had handed Will a paper with a sign on code and password. He mumbled, "Thank you," as he turned and sat quickly into the vacant chair in front of the desktop. He did not even glance at the person sitting next to him and proceeded to log on as fast as his fingers could type. He Googled New Brunswick and found there were two places. One was a town in New Jersey on the East Coast and another a province in Canada. He couldn't imagine that his father would have any reason to go to Canada, but then he couldn't imagine anything that had happened in the past several days. He noticed that the town in New Jersey was near an army ordinance depot. He recalled some whispered conversations between his dad and mom and also on the phone with the word "weapons" buried in the conversations almost imperceptibly. He wondered if his parents were part of the secret service or hopefully not an enemy country. They always seemed so righteous and patriotic so he shook that last thought right out of his head. He hit the print button and grabbed directions to both the New Jersey town and the province. Before he left, he also searched for railroad and bus stations close to Circleville. He found a lumber transport leaving at six thirty after refueling at the railroad yards about one mile outside of town. Those cars were headed to upstate New York and had stops along the way in East Pennsylvania, about thirty two miles from New Brunswick. He glanced at the clock which read five fifteen P.M. He had less than five minutes left of his thirty minute allotment on the computer. One last search. He typed in "emblems – military or police" in the search box. Hundreds of emblems appeared but he knew what he was looking for – an eagle perched on the world with a branch of some kind in its beak. Two emblems similar to the ones he recalled seeing on the vest of the man with dark glasses standing outside his ruined home. The first represented the World Peace Corps which he readily discounted – no peace surrounded that man. The second belonged to members of the Federal Communications Bureau of the United States of America. He quickly printed off information about both and closed down the computer, glanced once more at the clock whose hands had moved to five twenty five. He quietly gathered his suitcase, bag and printouts and moved toward the door of the library. Then he saw him. Jamie came breathlessly through the door as Will ducked behind a rolling bookcase.

"He must have seen the news and found out I wasn't Max." Will thought to himself. "Got to get out of here somehow without him seeing me."

As Jamie stood across from the librarian with the polka dot dress his back was turned away from Will. Will slithered between the desks and through the door just as the librarian was pointing to the row of computers in the far corner of the library. There was a young man who had been sitting next to Will at a computer who had a ball cap on as he glanced from a book on the desk to the computer screen. Jamie rushed toward the young man and grabbed his shoulders at the same time saying, "Max…Will let me help you." The startled young man with the ball cap jumped up drawing his fist back ready to deck his attacker.

Jamie backed up as soon as he saw it wasn't Max (Will). "Jeesh, fella, I am so sorry. I thought you were someone else. Did you happen to see a boy about twelve years old here?"

"Man, you are lucky. I didn't deck you! Yeah, there was a kid here just a few minutes ago but he left. He was looking up railroad, bus stations, and some kind of emblem. I couldn't help noticing since the computers are so close together. He was writing things down and probably noticed I could see his searches so he turned the screen away from me and moved his paper to the other side of the desk. I thought maybe he was doing something for school and really didn't pay too much attention." Jamie was already heading toward the door when the young man mentioned the railroad yard and the bus station. It was fall and the sun was low on the horizon allowing the crisp coolness of the evening to wrap itself around the small town. Jamie buttoned the two remaining buttons on his used, poorly fitted coat and headed in the direction of the bus station.

Will threw his few belongings in the dark railroad car marked "PACIFIC LUMBER". He crawled into the car that smelled of freshly chopped wood that reminded him of the comforting fireplace in the living room of his home. He zipped the borrowed sweatshirt and pulled the hood over his head and the ball cap with his new identity stamped on the front. It was cold and damp in the dark corner of the half empty rail car and he prayed his "Angel" prayer as someone closed the metal doors with a bang and the darkness became impermeable. He could see nothing but the flashing lights through a crack where the metal doors didn't meet perfectly. The car jolted forward as the big engine pulled its load eastward.

Jamie questioned the few people awaiting transportation. No one at the railroad station had seen a boy fitting the description of Max or Will or whoever he was. He had seen the newscast on TV while he ate a sandwich shortly after Will had left the shelter. He was focused on the newspaper in front of him and glanced up just as Will's seventh grade picture flashed on the screen. The paper fell to the floor as he rushed over to turn up the volume on the old TV set. The sandwich was left half eaten and the newspaper lay on the floor as he grabbed his coat from one of the coat hooks next to the front door and rushed out in the direction he saw Will traveling. He surmised that Will would be looking for his family and would need to get information. The library seemed to be the most natural place as it had computers and maps. "I knew the kid seemed lost and frightened. I should have pressed for more information. God, I hope I find him before he gets into trouble. He's only twelve years old. What a mess!" Jamie ran from the bus station to the railroad yard just as the last car disappeared over the hill leading out of town. He walked to the station a few yards across the tracks and tried to find out where the last group of boxcars was headed.

"They're headed to upstate New York with a few stops for refuelin' along the route. No, didn't see anybody around the cars before they left. Kids don't do the stuff we used to…too busy with gadgets and TV to have kid fun."

"Thanks, anyway. This kid wasn't having fun." Jamie said as he looked down the empty track headed east.

Chapter Eight

The Search

Charlie and Casey exited the hospital and the parking lot jammed with Red Cross vans, volunteers, injured, and dead. They both were lost as to what to do or where to go next. Charlie remembered his mother had a sister who lived in North Jersey—his Aunt Kathy. A slim chance that his family had migrated that far north, but he didn't have any money or a way to search for his parents among the thousands that had left during the evacuation. He didn't even know where to start but he knew he needed someone to help him. He headed toward one of the Red Cross vans that were serving rolls, fruits, and warm drinks to anyone. The young lady who Charlie was not too tired to notice had kind blue eyes and a pretty face with long brunette hair pulled back into a pony tail handed him a roll, a banana, and some hot cocoa.

"Thanks, ma'am. Do you think I could have a cup of water for my dog and another roll?" Charlie looked down at Casey who conveniently had caught one side of his joule under his teeth and was smiling with the droopiest expression up at the pretty young volunteer.

"Oh, what a cute dog! He looks like he is smiling," she chuckled as she reached for a large cup and poured water from a jug into it. She handed it to Charlie who couldn't help staring at her blue eyes. Charlie almost spilled the water as he set it on the ground lost in a teenage trance by this gorgeous creature. Casey attacked the water like it was his first drink ever forcing his nose deep down in the cup in order to get the last few drops into his thirsty belly. The cup wound up stuck on Casey's snout and Charlie and the young lady volunteer laughed so hard they ended with taking a deep sigh at the same time which made them laugh even harder. It was easy to lose it over most anything when neither the two young people nor the pooch had slept in days.

"Can I pet him or her?" She asked as she exited the van through a door in the back. She wore blue jeans which hugged her perfectly rounded firm bottom and slim shapely legs and a tee-shirt that had "Red Cross Volunteer" with the big insignia cross on the front outlining a very shapely bosom and tied at her tiny waist. Charlie was taller than she as she bent down to stroke the matted fur of Charlie's best buddy. Her pony tail fell across one shoulder and Charlie could see she didn't have any rings on her fingers. He was almost fourteen and was starting to feel those amazing feelings one gets when testosterone enters the blood stream in its initial rush toward manhood. For a few moments he forgot his situation, the bedlam around him, the possibility of never finding his family, the loss of his home, the hunger, and the fear. For a few moments, he was a young man experiencing the beginnings of the mating dance. He sipped the warm coffee like it was the nectar of the kings and bit into the soft jelly roll that tasted better than a prime rib dinner he loved so much. A little jelly oozed down the side of his mouth and the young lady stood up from her petting, took a napkin from a holder on the ledge of the van and gently dabbed the jelly away. Tingles and chills ran up and down Charlie's arms and legs and a pulsating feeling in his groin made him blush.

"You look like you've had a pretty rough time, you and…what's the dog's name?" She said in a voice that sounded like the sexy announcer on the radio station his parents used to listen to.

"Casey…his name is Casey."

"And yours is?"

"Charlie…Charles Peterson. You are…?"

"Amanda……Amanda Murphy…Red Cross Team Leader."

"Hi Amanda. Thanks for the water and food. We were starving!" Charlie collected himself enough to be polite and also to give Casey one of the rolls since the poor dog was drooling copiously staring at the delectable treat in Charlie's sweaty hand. As Casey devoured the roll in less than three gulps Charlie asked Amanda where he could get information on evacuees. She pointed to a tent at the far end of the parking lot.

"They have some laptops and radios trying to locate information for people who have lost track of one another. This is one of the worst disasters I have seen and it is so difficult trying to locate people since we have shelters all over the states and can barely keep up with identifying the injured and the dead." She saw the painful look in Charlie's eyes when she made the last statement. "Are you looking for your parents? You look about fifteen of sixteen." Charlie straightened up as tall as he could, puffing out his chest like a pigeon in heat.

"Yeah, just about. I am looking for my parents and my brother. We were all in a van headed inland when this monster wave came and the next thing I knew I was laying on the ground and everything was……gone…no van, no parents, nothing. Then Casey appears out of that mess with a broken paw. My mom is a nurse here at the hospital and my dad is a doctor, so I knew how to fix his paw temporarily. I got a gash in my head but it is okay." Amanda turned Charlie around to look at his wound.

"Let me clean that up and put some antiseptic on it. You're lucky it isn't infected. Are you having dizzy spells or headaches?" Amanda had stepped back into the van and returned with a bottle of peroxide, antiseptic, and gauze. She motioned Charlie to sit on the step of the van while she gently cleansed his wound and applied the antiseptic. "Here are a few antibiotic pills. You aren't allergic to anything are you?" Charlie shook his head "no" and petted Casey as Amanda tended to his head wound. "Take two a day for three days."

"Thank you. Casey, thanks you. I have to find my family. Hope I see you again." Charlie reluctantly stood and started to head toward the information tent. He knew Amanda was quite a bit older than he was even at his supposed age of fifteen or sixteen, but he really didn't care because the feelings were so much better than those he had ever felt—even making the winning point in a championship game couldn't hold a candle to the ones he had just experienced.

At least fifty or more people were huddled outside and inside the "Disaster Information" tent. Soldiers dressed in combat uniforms and boots wrote down information and turned to computers and radio transmitters located along long tables in front and behind the soldiers. They were part of the National Guard communications team feverishly trying to connect people with their families and friends. It became a near impossible task even if people registered with the shelters set up across the region, there were those who were injured and those dead or missing with no identification and some unable to offer any information. Charlie waited with Casey lying on the ground licking his swollen injured paw. He heard the sobs of those who found they had lost a loved one or several loved ones. Some people fell to the ground in anguish and disbelief. Others tried to comfort them as they themselves feared the same could befall them. Others sobbed joyfully as someone they feared was lost was found and they were directed to buses and vans assembled for transport to reconnecting points.

Charlie looked back every so often to the Red Cross van that held Amanda Murphy. He sure wouldn't forget that name. The lines moved slowly and he was soon inside the tent where he could hear the radios static and occasional voice breaking through reporting locations and names of the persons registered there. Shelters in schools, arenas, churches, and hospitals all over a three state region had been set up by Homeland Security, the National Guard, and the Red Cross. Supplies and volunteers from all over the U.S. were being flown or driven in to the disaster victims. Heavy equipment to begin the endless clean up of wreckage was being airlifted by huge military and commercial cargo planes to airports that had received the least damage.

"How can I help you, Sir?" The young guardsman asked when Charlie and Casey finally arrived at the table inside the tent. "Are you here to report missing persons or to give information on someone?"

"Both," as Charlie remembered the girl he uncovered in the debris not far from where his house once stood. "I need to find my parents and my brother and I found a dead lady in a pile of boards near my...home."

"Fill out these papers describing your family members, where you last saw them, what they were wearing, driving...everything you know about them. If you remember their social security numbers or any other statistics, that would help a lot." Charlie remembered lots of numbers. His dyslexia was an impediment but also allowed some part of his brain to overachieve in the area of numerical recall and calculations. He quickly wrote down everything he knew about his parents and Jake. He recalled all their social security numbers, the license number of the van, the security numbers on the hospital badges his parents wore to work, the registration numbers of the van, even the license number on Pepper's dog collar. He remembered the exact time just before the huge wave enveloped the van and the mileage on the van speedometer as it attempted to turn the corner to escape the storm.

"You've got quite a memory there, son." the guardsman commented as he looked over the paper filled with much more information than most could remember. "Most people can barely remember their own social security numbers and even their addresses they are so shook up." The guardsman turned toward the laptop and began to type in the information to a central processing unit in upper Florida. "This will take a little while. You look pretty whipped, you and your dog. There are some benches over there under the trees if you want to sit and wait. Help yourself to some water outside the tent. There is a bin of water bottles out there." Charlie thanked the guardsman and grabbed a couple of water bottles as he and Casey walked toward a bench a few yards away. He found an empty milk carton and tore a portion of it open fashioning a dish where he poured one of the bottles of water for Casey. The dog gulped it down and dripped water from his wet joules on Charlie's pant leg as he rested his head looking up at Charlie who rubbed his floppy ears and mangled fur.

"What would I do without you, buddy. What would we do without each other?"

After what seemed to be hours the guardsman came over to Charlie and Casey. Charlie could tell by his stooped shoulders and solemn expression that he wasn't bringing them the news Charlie prayed for—that his parents were alive and safe, Pepper was anxiously waiting to see her only pup, and through some amazing miracle they had found Jake and Elmo totally cured of surfing. That wasn't the news the guardsman handed Charlie. The words screamed at Charlie from the paper printed from the computer.

Purple Ford Van
Florida license M60794
Registered to Jesse Peterson, M.D.
Two adults and one Labrador canine
License G213
Found in overturned vehicle, no pulse or respirations
Mortal injuries

September 24, 1998
Extricated from vehicle and transported to Atlanta, GA Emergency Triage
Unit Fort Ulysses Air force Base

"It's a mistake! It has to be a mistake! Oh, God...please, please. You have
to try again! They can't be all..." Charlie grabbed hold of the guardsman crum-
pling the paper as he shook him and finally buried his head in the young man's
shoulder. The guardsman stood erect and held the sobbing boy as he lowered
himself to the ground. Casey limped over and pushed his nose into Charlie's
arm. Charlie grabbed the dog and wrapped his trembling arms around him
rocking back and forth on the damp ground as the guardsman knelt down
beside the two and said, "Is there someone I could help you contact? A relative or friend? We have transportation that can take you most anywhere. I have
a kit with some dry clothes, passes for transit on trains and buses, and some
rations we are giving to evacuees. I'm so sorry. How old are you?"

Charlie wasn't one to lie but he needed to be older than thirteen going on
fourteen. He didn't want to be placed with other orphans to wait to be chosen
by a family he didn't know. He didn't want anyone but his own mother and
father. The pain he felt was numbing and icy. His mind could not rid itself of
the imprint of the words from the printout. He needed to get to Atlanta and
see for himself before he could even assimilate any of it, let alone believe it.
Maybe he was still in a coma from being injured in the storm and this was all
a nightmare—a horrible nightmare.

"I'm fifteen, almost sixteen. I have a relative in north Jersey, my
m...m...mother's sister. If you can get me to the Air Force Base in Atlanta so
I can say good-bye to my parents...I...I can get to her from there. I'm fine. I
will be fine." Charlie straightened up as tall as he could and spoke in the
deepest voice he could imitate. He was just starting to get his man voice at the
beginning of the school year. It would go from soprano to alto at intervals
sometimes sounding like he was yodeling. "It would help if I could have one
of those kits you mentioned." The guardsman looked somewhat suspicious of
the fifteen going on sixteen part but felt so bad for the kid, for so many tragic
printouts he had to give out that day and the days since the hurricane. He motioned Charlie with Casey limping behind him toward the back of the information tent where a truck stood with the insignia of an eagle sitting on the
world with a branch in its mouth painted on its doors. The guardsman opened
the doors and handed a backpack with the same insignia to Charlie and then
led him to a row of buses. Charlie and Casey shook hands with the guardsman.
He saluted them and wished them luck as the bus pulled away.

* * *

The freight train slowed and the screeching of the wheels as the engineer
applied the brakes to the long line of cars hooked behind his trusty engine
startled Will from his stupor as he huddled in the corner of the freight car. At

first he wondered where he was and as the cobwebs cleared he remembered the nightmare of this past week. He searched in the darkness for his bag and found it wedged against some planks stacked near him. Frantically he reached inside the opening left by the broken zipper and felt for the plastic and metal of his treasured, mysterious race car. He blinked his eyes as hard as he could to try and see the bent part of the chassis under which the strange metal disc with the Morse code messages was hidden. He peered into darkness holding the car with one of the shirts Jamie had given him at the shelter. The green light flashed and Will could feel the buzzing vibrations as the light flashed in time with the message. Two————four———two——pause——five—no light; then it repeated two——four———two——pause——five. The code repeated itself four times then a group of single flashes, one red flash, then silence. No more light. No more codes. Will knew it had to be his father. No one, not even the two evil men that had visited that day had anything to do with that race car except......except...the man with the hollow eyes had reached for it and held it upside down for just a few seconds before Will grabbed it back. "That couldn't have been long enough for him to see anything and anyhow it was still in one piece." He wrapped the car in the tee shirt and carefully placed it back in the suitcase. The train had been still for several moments. Will crawled over to the doors to see if he should see anything that would tell him where they were. The computer had said this particular freight train made two stops before it reached the eastern Pennsylvania border and began to head north to upstate New York. He wondered if this was the first or second stop or if he had slept through both of them and this was his destination point. As he peered through the opening between doors, he could make out rows and rows of railroad tracks some with freight cars others with engines. At the far side of the tracks, he could make out a brown building and there was a water tower that read "DAYTON" on it. "Darn, I wish I had paid attention in geography class! Dayton......I think that's in Ohio, not Pennsylvania. Dayton...that's near Cincinnati...dad's favorite team!" The thought of his father and the rest of his family made his heart thump in his chest and the ache come back that he knew he had to push away. The train jerked and Will fell backwards onto some lumber stacked in the freight car. Will chocked down a yelp as the boards fell against his back. The pain shot through his lower back and down his leg like a hot sword riveting his spine. He rolled away from the lumber as the train moved forward and picked up speed. Will crawled slowly to the corner where his few possessions lay. With every movement he stifled a cry as the pain shot from his spine to his right leg. Finally reaching the corner he sat with his back against the wall of the freight car. Tears ran down his face and he bent as far forward as he could stand until the pain in his leg subsided. He rubbed the skin on his lower back where the lumber had hit the hardest. There was no blood, just pain. He could handle pain. He just didn't want anything like blood to make people he might encounter on his journey ask questions. He reached into the paper bag Jamie had given him when he left and found a bottle of water, an apple and a peanut butter and jelly sandwich.

While scarfing the lunch down ravenously he thought, "That Jamie was really a nice guy. I feel bad I had to lie to him."

Chapter Nine

Something Evil

Jamie rushed back to the shelter from his near miss trying to find Max, or Will, whatever his name was. It was Will. He had seen it on the television. The whole story about the explosion and not being able to find and bodies, none of the West family. It was as though they had vanished. Jamie recognized Will as soon as he saw the picture. Though Max looked older and much more sullen, Jamie had rushed from the shelter to try and help the kid. He frantically began to dial the eight hundred number they had flashed at the bottom of the screen. A banging on the front door of the shelter interrupted the call. One of the residents, Walt Calhoun, who just returned from his daily lineup at the logger's union hall to see if there was any work for him, stood at the door talking to two men dressed in suits.

"Walt, who is it?" Jamie asked.

"It's some detectives, Jamie. They are looking for a kid named Will."

Jamie looked at the two men who had entered the foyer as Walt opened the door. One was about Jamie's age and had a scruffy day old beard. He scanned the entrance to the shelter as though he was looking for some hidden clues. The other man had salt and pepper hair and smelled like Old Spice. He had a craggy face and piercing no nonsense eyes. He flashed a badge in a leather holder that Jamie could see had FBI etched into it.

"We think you had a guest here the last couple of nights that everyone is looking for. You might have seen him on TV William West is his name and he's the only one left from his family after a terrible explosion last Sunday at his house." The man that smelled like Old Spice said in a no nonsense voice. The agent moved farther into the foyer and started looking into the kitchen and the other rooms where the doors were open. A few of the other residents, mostly females with some kids tagging along, came to the doors to see what was happening. Walt was a big man from the last twenty years felling huge trees and hauling lumber. He stood between Jamie and the two agents like a protective wall. One look from Walt and the women and children retreated to the bedrooms.

Jamie wondered about something the older agent said and also the way he just moved past him looking into rooms without asking permission. What little Jamie knew about the law he was sure that an FBI agent would not have began a search without permission or a warrant. Walt had not met Will, alias Max and Jamie had a eerie feeling about the two men who pressed for an answer.

"We get a lot of folks in and out of here. Are you talking about the kid on the news?" Jamie asked innocently. "We've only had little kids come with their parents this week. No one named Will."

"Are you sure, mister? His mother used to bring clothes and food here and she was friends with a nurse that helps out here." The agent with the five o'clock shadow urged.

"Sorry, can't help you there. There is a nurse that comes here during the week but I never saw her with anyone like you describe." Jamie thought of Maria and felt warm inside. He knew he loved her but has been too shy to let her know. He would someday. He knew he would. He also was beginning to become more suspicious of these supposed agents. The man had said that Will was the only one left in his family but the news said they had not found any bodies. "I'll keep my eyes opened for anyone like that."

Jamie smiled his most congenial smile as he began to usher the two men out of the shelter. Walt got the message that Jamie was not too sure of these guys and he moved his massive self next to Jamie.

"Okay. We might be back if we need some more info." The man with the start of a beard said gruffly as he sneered at Walt. Jamie closed the door and locked it for one of the first times since he had opened the shelter. He thanked Walt for his help and rushed back to the kitchen, picked up the phone and began again to dial the eight hundred number. 1-800...two shots ripped through the window near the kitchen and into the side of Jamie's head. His brain exploded and he fell in a crumpled heap to the floor. A computer voice on the phone laying in the social worker's hand kept repeating

"If you'd like to make a call, please hang up and try again...If you'd like to make a call...

* * *

Will felt a chilling sense of foreboding as the train moved along to the next stop. He hid himself behind some of the lumber in the corner farthest from the metal doors. He nibbled on some peanut butter crackers Jamie had put in the bag along with two bottles of water a sandwich, and a box of raisins. He had seen it was 6:00 P.M. on a clock tower near the small building across the tracks in the town they had left. If he calculated correctly the next stop would be the one nearest the Pennsylvania New Jersey border and it would be dark when he exited the train. Since it had been almost a week since the explosion, he figured the news may have put his story on the back pages and the less people who saw him the better. Maybe the story was not even news worthy this far away from Ohio so he took a deep breath and tried to formulate the next part of his plan.

Chapter Ten

Painful Discovery

The bus stopped at the Ulysses Air Force Base and several of the passengers dragged themselves and their sparse belongings off and headed for the base hospital where cadavers from the disaster were being held until they could be identified. Charlie shivered and the feeling of nausea stuck in his throat thinking that his parents were in a box frozen and lost to him forever. National Guardsman, military personnel from the Base, some reporters from local and national newspapers, and radio and TV stations hovered about the drop off area just outside a massive chain link fence with its talons grasping foreboding barbed wire and a gate with warning signs boldly shouting their message to halt, retreat and scatter unless appropriate identification was shown. Two soldiers with orange vests covering the camouflage uniforms complete with belts weighted with guns, knives, walkie talkies and grenades searched meticulously through papers the bus driver handed them. The passengers were herded into a small cement block building where their belongings are placed and they were scanned thoroughly with infrared wands, x-ray equipment and patting down by both female and male security staff. After all were cleared, they were transported by a shuttle to the Base hospital that had been converted to one huge casket. None of the passengers spoke unless they needed to respond to one of the security guards' questions. It was as though any levity or negativity might be inappropriate during the transition from hopefulness to reality. Suspended in the moment like waiting for the parachute to open, they dared not project any emotion. Charlie looked at the faces of his fellow passengers. Some were very young like himself. Some were accompanied by an adult and a few others pretended, like himself, to be with an adult conveniently sitting next to someone older during the ride.

"Maybe the van the guardsman hesitantly reported belonging to my parents was a mistake and the people they thought were Mom and Dad were lying nearby were some other victims. Maybe they made a mistake and they are only injured or in shock and have no way to know I am okay. Maybe...just maybe..." The shuttle stopped with a jerk and a squeal of its breaks jolting Charlie and the rest of the passengers out of their thoughts as it parked itself in front of a large building with the marquis announcing their arrival at Ulysses Hospital and Trauma Center. No one stood up from their seat. Barely moving or breathing, they waited praying all of this was a bad dream...It was as though to move, to breathe would be an insult to those lying in silence beyond the electronically monitored doors of the hospital. A middle aged man in fatigues and what at one time may have been a white lab coat stepped onto the shuttle and introduced himself and Colonel Gregory Adler, M.D., Coroner. The title of "Coroner" settled on the ears of the passengers like a steel door slamming shut on any hope that some miracle could breathe life into the lifeless. His instructions were concise and offered in a monotone so opposed to the emotions emitting from the living frozen in their seats. They were led off the shuttle, through the doors that buzzed loudly announcing security had been broken. The lobby floor was covered immaculate Terrazzo flooring, with green and blue swirls of color mimicking the ocean. Two marble desks with uniformed men sitting in swivel chairs greeted the group of solemn visitors and returned quickly to the bank of security screens and computers before them. Dr. Adler explained that those passengers that were together should identify themselves so the entire unit could attend the viewing. One person from each group was to be chosen to complete the paperwork if indeed the corpse was identified. Tissues and water would be supplied and an attendant would be available should anyone feel faint or have other symptoms requiring first aid. Charlie thought they all had seen so much death and other tragedies it had all become a part of their duties that did not allow emotion to sway their judgment and efficiency. He was sure that there must be moments when the wall crumbles and they felt the sadness of others. The groups were ushered individually down a hallway. There must have been an exit after the viewing at the other side of the building as the groups never returned. No sobbing or cries of despair were heard—only the footsteps of the soldier elected to usher the anxious participants down the hallway and beyond and the clicking of the keys of the scanners and computers as the two robots behind the desks filtered information from the screens barricading them from the suffering just a few feet in front of them.

Three young people remained sitting in the chairs to the left of the hallway. One of them was a girl about sixteen, Charlie guessed. She was about five feet tall and somewhat plump with a china doll complexion contrasted by large hazel eyes. Her hair was auburn with curls framing her Precious Moments face. One of her arms was in a cast with no signatures as would have been the case in other circumstances. She wound the shoulder strap of a tiny purse around the bottom portion of the cast nervously. Every once in a while, a smacking sound would emote from her mouth as she chewed a large wad of gum. The other young man with the trio wore a flannel shirt much too large for his small frame. He sat on the edge of the chair holding his head in his hands every once in a while looking at a watch on his wrist as though time really mattered. The third was Charlie and his faithful Casey who had been allowed to accompany Charlie on this frightening mission by grinning his most mesmerizing grin and looking as sad as he possibly could at each checkpoint.

The silence was broken by the girl with the cast. "Can I pet your dog?" She whispered in her best hospital voice.

"Sure, he's really gentle. His name is Casey" Charlie clicked a command to the sleeping hound as they both moved toward the young girl. She bent down and made those baby noises Charlie's mother used to make as she rubbed Casey's favorite spot with her uninjured hand. Casey licked her Precious Moments face requesting more ear-scratching the only way he knew. The girl giggled and wrinkled up her nose as the dog slobbered and licked and slobbered some more. The young man who had been holding his head in his hands looked up and came over to assist in the dog petting. Casey was enjoying every minute of the attention and the back and ear scratching.

"My name is Charlie."

"I'm Tom from Miami."

"Jessica Catherine, but everyone calls me JC."

The three of them awaited their turn to look for their loved ones and talked about the nightmares that each had encountered the past few days since the hurricane blew their lives apart. They all had been separated from their families. Tom was in Maryland at school when he found out his brother and sister-in-law and their kids had been evacuated but could not be located. JC was working at her uncle's tool and dye shop trying to save some money to go to school to become a park ranger. Her parents were divorced and she had not seen her father in several years. Evidently he had chosen alcohol and drugs over his kids and wife and had lost contact with life and his family. Her mother had just spoken with her daughter a few hours before Helen unleashed her rage on the coast. Her boss at the restaurant where she worked ten to twelve hours a day ordered the staff to gather up some food and the emergency bags stashed in the basement. There was not time to go home as the small town of Pleasantville was just north of Fort Myers and directly in the path of the most vicious part of the storm. They piled into their cars hugging each other as they exited the parking lot, their cars and the passengers trembling in the wind. Pamela, JC's mother's last words to her were, "You stay where you are. I will be there as fast as I can." JC's uncle's shop was twenty miles inland and there were only two other people working that day. JC waited until everyone had left and her uncle dragged her toward his truck.

"Dammit, JC! The place is going to fall on us. Your mom probably had to head wherever the police directed the traffic. She's not coming! We've got to get..." his screams fell silent as a telephone pole crashed in front of them one of the cleats holding the wires hitting JC's arm so violently her radius and ulna snapped and a portion of one of the bones exited through her skin. Blood spurted from the wound and JC collapsed onto the rain soaked ground. Her uncle dragged her to the truck as pieces of rooftops and siding crashed against the old Ford. He was able to make it to the highway that ran near his now demolished factory. As the truck merged into the serpentine lineup of cars slithering through the blinding rain and wind out of the town he glanced back at his injured niece who was lying on the floor of the truck be against a pile of tools that had dumped over onto the floor. She moaned in pain as she came to and tried to move her grotesquely bent arm. Her face was pale and she had blood dripping, no longer spurting from the wound. She wretched and then vomited onto the sleeve of her jumpsuit.

"Uncle Phil. Where are we? My arm...where's Mom? Where...." She fainted collapsing onto the floor covered with her emesis and blood and the cold hard tools she had helped to fashion. The traffic had stopped and the old Ford was trembling as the wind and rain sporadically grabbed hold of the cars and played with them. He stepped into the bed of the truck, took off his drenched shirt and wrapped it gently around the wounded part of JC's arm. He tied the two sleeves around her limp neck like a sling and moved her away from the debris and tools to some foam padding wrapped in plastic on the opposite side of the truck bed. JC groaned as he moved her as gently as he could. He shivered as he slumped back in the driver's seat as the traffic began to inch its way inland. Police cars and military trucks separated groups of vehicles leading some of the groups to exits where shelters had been set up for the injured and the evacuees. Phil was on his flashers as he was motioned on to the next exit by soldiers or guardsman standing along the roadside next to their vehicles. He rolled down his window yelling above the wind and rain pelting him, "I've got a badly injured girl in here and have to get somewhere fast or she won't make it!" One of the soldiers who heard him motioned him to pull out of his group onto the exit he had just been ordered to pass. Phil backed the truck along the berm and proceeded to move with the other cars exiting toward the town, where a military hospital tent had been set up next to an elementary school. There, JC was placed onto a gurney and rushed to the operating cubicles. Phil was ushered to a cot and given some hot cocoa and warm dry clothes. He tried hard to stay awake so he could find out how his niece was doing but his weariness won and he sagged onto the cot with his cocoa still sitting on the floor next to it. When he awoke he frantically questioned everyone until he found that JC had been taken to the Air Force Hospital in Atlanta. There, an orthopedic surgeon worked for several hours to repair the injured bones, torn blood vessels, and damaged nerves in order to save her arm. She had no feeling or movement in her thumb and index fingers at the end f the procedure. The surgeon doubted if the function and sensation would return, but he didn't know JC. She was tougher than most girls and determined to beat the odds. Charlie found out she was eighteen though her cherub face made her look much younger. Tom was in college and had lost his mother to cancer while he was just entering high school. His father was in the service as a helicopter pilot over in Afghanistan. He needed to find his brother and his family as he had no one else. He couldn't imagine losing them, too. He missed his mother whom he had cared for during the three years she battled cancer. His father was allowed to come home twice during those years and for the funeral. He tried to get more time with his grieving son but they needed his skills and the military expected he would put them first as he had so often during his career.

"Charles Peterson." The usher called. Charlie hugged JC and shook Tom's trembling hand. They rubbed Casey's ears as Charlie followed the usher to the dimly lit hallway. He entered a room with white ceramic walls. There were two forms lying on drawers pulled out from boxes lining one wall of the room. The forms were covered with white plastic sheets. There was a lady in a lab coat standing near the forms. She looked exhausted with dark circles under her downcast eyes. There was one wooden chair and a cart with tissues and some other items sitting just inside the door. When the door closed behind Charlie the hollow sound echoed like the ocean sounds in a conch shell in his ears.

The lady cleared her throat and read from a card held in one of her gloved hands.

"Charles Arlan Peterson. Son of Jesse and Carolyn Peterson?"

"Y…yes, ma'am. I'm Charlie Peterson." his voice was shaking and it too echoed against the walls.

"Please let me know if you can identify either or both of these patients," the lady called them patients. If only they were patients that could be healed he pleaded. She pulled back the plastic sheets one by one. Charlie stared into the ashen faces and blue lips. The clock on the wall moved its hands to 6:00 P.M.

* * *

The two men snarled at the person they had dragged from the cot. She was bruised and her red hair hung in damp tangled strands around her swollen face. Her head bobbed loosely her chin almost touching her chest as the men roughly tied her wrists together behind the wooden chair. Her shirt was torn and there were dried blood stains evidently from a gash in the side of her neck that was angry red and oozed a yellow liquid.

"Listen. The code……we need the code! We need it now or we will get rid of you!" Joe placed his scarred face a few inches from hers as he pulled her hair to raise her face to his level. His breath stunk of old beer and cigars and his eyes were frightening, blazing with fierce anger.

Her parched lips were wrinkled and some of the skin had pulled away from her lower lip. "I told you I don't know what you're talking about…I don't know anything about a code. Where am I? Who are you…" Before she could utter another word the second man who was big as an ox and almost as ugly grabbed one of the guns off the table and held the barrel against the woman's head.

"Joe, she don't know nothin! Let's just get rid of her and get on with it." He cocked the pistol. The tiny click echoed in the woman's ear like a bell tolling mass. Her whole body trembled and she closed her eyes waiting for the end of what at one time seemed a very stable and charmed life. Joe knocked the pistol out of the ox's hand just as the bullet entered the chamber and exited toward empty space. The captive took that moment to stand, turn and slam the chair into Joe's legs, grab the gun left lying on the table with her hands still tied behind her and shoot "Ox" in the chest. She wheeled around and delivered a shot to Joe's head as he was attempting to stand. Ox was crawling toward the gun Joe had slapped from his hand, blood running from the corner's of his mouth and wounded chest. The events in the next few moments appeared in slow motion as the woman turned away from Joe who lay unmoving on the floor. Ox had reached the gun and rolled over on his back. Slowly raising his hand, he aimed at the back of the woman. The bullet headed toward her spine as she turned just as she heard the sound of the gun going off behind her. She fell to the floor and the bullet hit the soft tissue of her shoulder. She fired two rounds into Ox's head. All three laid very still for what seemed to be a minute. The woman stood up, wincing slightly from her injured shoulder. Smashing the chair against the wall she extricated herself from the ropes that bound her arms. She ran to both bodies to make sure they were both dead, picked up both guns and moved toward the computer which continued to display rows of numbers and symbols. The box attached to the computer flashed red and green intermittently in numerical sequences across the display panel. She pressed a glove that was lying on the table to the wound in her shoulder. Blood oozed onto the glove and between her fingers. She took a piece of the rope that had bound her to the chair and secured the glove to her wound with it. Her head was swimming from the injection Joe had given her and from the adrenalin rush of the last few moments.

The code. E 7…send the code should anything go wrong. Her brain sifted through the haze similar to the computer's drone of endless numbers, sequences, and symbols. She reached for the keyboard with bloodstained fingers and entered 704:993-6 after she unhooked the flashing box from the computer making sure it had not connected to the sequences on the box. A message began to type itself onto the screen as though it was being sent in real time to the woman. Her body straightened and she brushed her disheveled hair away from her face. She took the box that she had detached from the computer. It's display now only flashed a green signal Two…four… two…pause…five.

She walked toward the door of the motel room, lifted her tattered skirt, pulled a strip of tape from the lining of her panties, pulled off the clear plastic strip from the middle area of the tape, pressed it against the door, closed the door carefully and ran through the parking lot to a green van. She closed the van doors just as the explosion erupted and the van sped down the road heading east. It was 6:12 P.M.

Chapter Eleven

Chance or Fate?

Charlie opened his eyes to a bright light overhead and someone calling his name softly. He was lying on a gurney with a blanket covering his aching body. The vision of his parents' faces, his father's etched with slashes from the splintered glass of the crushed van and his mother's beautiful face unmarked, frozen, white, the lipstick of death…blue/gray/purplish and immobile; the lips that had kissed him goodnight, had taught him about life, had shouted cheers for him at all his games, win or lose. His father, the doctor, the healer, the man who made him laugh, the man who had taught him how to be tough and gentle at the same time; the man who played hoops with him anytime he asked so he could become a better basketball player. The man, the woman…bodies…just bodies. He sat up frantically looking around him and the room slowly closed down like a lens on a camera. His head swirled with dizzying confusion and agonizing pain and he fell back onto the cardboard pillow.

"Mom…Dad…I need you! I'm just a kid! You can't be gone! What will I do? God, please help me…God, please…." He turned his head into the cardboard pillow and sobbed, gasping in between each heart wrenching cry. He felt someone touch his shoulder and bend down next to his face.

"Charlie. Someone wants to see you. We are so sorry for your loss." Charlie opened his tear filled eyes and saw a woman with her brown hair pulled back under a cap with a Navy emblem on it. Her dark brown eyes almost matched her hair and she gently pulled Charlie into a sitting position on the stretcher with his legs dangling off the side. She smelled like a combination of bleach and apples as she stood holding him making sure he was not going to faint again. She seemed about his mother's age, wore no make-up, and had that all-knowing look that nurses have—the one that says "I have seen most every kind of sadness and pain possible, but also life's joys, beginnings, and quiet endings."

"I am Staff Sergeant Anna Michaelson," as she loosened her grip on her patient at the same time clicking her heels together and standing at attention. "This guy was panting and whimpering outside the door. I think he was worried about you. I know this has been the most horrible moment in your life and it will take time to put it into perspective. We have people who can help you. If there are relatives we can contact for you, we can do so and even arrange for transportation to their location." She helped Charlie slowly stand next to the gurney. His legs felt as limp as noodles and tingly. A hammer pounded inside his head with the rhythm of his heartbeat as he bent down to his faithful Casey grinning his silly grin and the usual drool dripping onto the floor. Charlie buried his head in Casey's bedraggled fur. Casey licked the tears from Charlie's face and pushed his head under his armpit giving Charlie his biggest "dog hug". Sergeant Michaelson looked around the room to see if there was anyone else in the room. Seeing the coast clear, she bent down beside Charlie and was greeted with "dog hugs and kisses" as well.

"They seem to know, sometimes better than humans, when we need them the most, don't they?"

Charlie's voice was hoarse and he had to swallow the huge lump in his throat before he could answer. "His mother, Pepper, was in the van with my...Mom and Dad. I didn't see anything in the report about a dog." Tears burned in Charlie's eyes as he realized Casey and he were orphans...for sure now they were orphans.

Sergeant Anna Michaelson retreated into her military pose as she stood up brushing Casey's hair remnants from her fatigues. "No, sir. I do not recall their finding a dog at the scene. There was so much debris that it will take a while to uncover all the victims and identify them," she reported. A tear ran down her cheek as she tried to speak in the most official, disconnected tone she could. She was only twenty-two years old, but in the last two years in the Navy Medical service, she had seen more suffering, broken bones and lives, death, and destruction than most see in a lifetime. She knew she had to steal herself from her feelings. Stay detached, but caring; efficient, but empathetic; focused, but flexible they had told her in training. She was a nurse. She became a nurse because she cared and needed to do all the above. Without sleep, missing meals, dealing with extreme conditions and only a few moments when she felt she was helping these victims, the emotions overtook the regimentation. Charlie and Casey followed her to an office where several other people sat across desks of military personnel filling out paperwork to finalize their loved one's farewell. Some of the people were bandaged from injuries they had incurred. Their faces all resembled Charlie's—empty, hollow swollen eyes framed by dark half circles. Eyes that just had seen the face of death of those they loved and shared daily life with just one week ago. Time heals all wounds, they say, but the healed skin of such a large wound is always tender and more easily scraped away then healthy skin. Charlie wasn't sure what to do with his parents' "remains," as the Ensign that Sergeant Michaelson had directed Charlie to so aptly put it. He sat there staring at the list of disposal suggestions numbed by sorrow and loneliness, angry with his brother, God, even his parents for leaving him. He had only met his mother's sister one time when there was a family reunion about four years ago. Everyone seemed shocked that she showed up. Even Charlie's grandfather, the two girls' father rarely spoke of Aunt Kathy as was the case with most everyone in the family. No one said anything really bad about her, just that she kept herself separated from the family members and rarely even communicated with them since she was sixteen and had left home to hitch her way across the country with just one hundred dollars, a duffel bag with her clothes and some toiletries, a carton of cigarettes, and her stuffed frog named Mr. Peepers. She was a throw-back to the sixties, her long red hair tied in a pony tail, her jeans tie dyed and a camouflage shirt thrown over a tee shirt with a faded peace sign stamped on the front. She had taken karate lessons since she was nine and held a brown belt, soon to earn a black belt. She preferred motorcycles, drag races, and rock climbing to dances, dresses, and hairdos. She had a boyfriend once it was told but he escaped with a bruised chest and ego when she drop kicked him for shooting a deer during hunting season. She lived somewhere in New Jersey and rumors circled that she was a hitman for the mafia. Charlie had no address or phone number. The only reason he remembered her last name was that she had married and divorced keeping the last name of her ex-husband, Capute. As their marriage was "kaput," the name stuck in his mind. When she made her grand entrance to the reunion wearing the lowest cut dress exposing the largest breasts he had seen, except for the ones in the confiscated Playboy magazine he and his buddies slobbered over at one of their houses, and her long red hair falling over one side of her amazingly beautiful face, a hush fell over the family and friends gathered in the Knights of Columbus Hall. She smiled demurely and headed immediately to the bar where the ogling bartenders over filled her martini as she leaned over placing those two immense breasts on the bar. She turned with her glass held in one of her perfectly manicured hands and shouted, "Hail to the Peterson clan! The Prodigal's daughter has returned!" She began to mingle and it was fun watching the wives huddle close to their husbands or drag them off to a corner as she approached. Charlie wanted to talk to her, to find out where she had been and what she had done. He loved adventure stories and spent hours reading about people who took risks and lived on the edge when he wasn't practicing his hoops or studying. He wasn't sure which "edge" Aunt Kathy lived on, but her sure was going to try and find out. Being barely nine years old, tall and skinny, somewhat shy and "geeky," he made several halting attempts to approach her, but there always seemed to be someone careening in his path as he almost tiptoed toward her. She sat with her long legs crossed exposing just enough of her trim thigh to make men imagine what was hidden by her beaded dress. The green gem like beading on her skimpy dress was a beautiful match for her green eyes and contrast to her wavy red locks. She had morphed from a tomboy caterpillar to a striking, confident sexually attractive butterfly.

Carolyn Peterson, Charlie's mother, hardly knew this cosmopolitan fashion model. She had tried many times to locate her sister from the time Kathy had left home. Letters sent to addresses that had once been viable were returned during the first two years. Kathy wrote sporadically with just a few brief scribbles about the sunsets, the mountains, and a few of the people she had met in her travels during those years. After the last letter almost two years to the day after her departure no one heard from her, not even her ailing mother and abusive father. When their mother passed away, Carolyn searched the Internet, wrote letters to people who might have seen Kathy, but to no avail. How she found out about the reunion no one could figure out, but there she was, in all her splendor. Her father would not talk to her that day. Charlie's grandfather remained on opposite sides of the hall glancing occasionally her way but lowering his head or turning away when she would catch him looking at her. Charlie finally put his hands in his Sunday suit pockets and marched up to his mysterious aunt.

"I'm Charlie, Jake's brother, your nephew. I'm nine years old and I love basketball. What do you like?" He looked into those green eyes and then down at those amazing breasts. They moved as she breathed and the sparkling green necklace with a small green cross moved with them. There was something in those eyes that made Charlie feel sad for a moment, something not at all like the rest of her, something lost and lonely, not confident and haughty like she appeared to be.

"Hi, Charlie. I'm sorry I haven't met you before. I'm terrible about keeping in touch, especially with my family. I know lots of them are mad at me and they certainly have the right to be. So you love basketball. I got to meet the New York Knicks once. They were amazing guys and I felt like a midget next to them. Do you play on a team?" She pulled a sweater from her very large beaded purse that also was green and sparkly and put it around her tying the sleeves over her breasts. Charlie really wished she hadn't done that, but it seemed easier to talk to her after she covered them.

"I play for the YMCA on Saturdays and at school, when I get into high school I'm going to try out for the team. I read a lot of books about people who have traveled across countries. Can you tell me about the time you hiked across the country? Mom told us some of the things you saw when you wrote to her, but I'll bet there's a bunch more." Charlie liked her right off. She seemed to be really interested in him. Jake was the one who usually got most of the attention, especially from girls but he was showing off his new surf board to a bunch of the cousins and friends. This time Charlie had the floor.

"Well, Charlie, I have been to both oceans, the Grand Canyon, Washington, D.C., up the west coast all the way to Alaska, across the seas to Europe and Russia, have seen the Eiffel Tower, the Coliseum in Rome, the bullfights in Spain, more than I ever dreamed I would see. The one thing I have missed is having a family, a home, a garden, kids, even a dog. You have so much to be thankful for, young man. Treasure it. Yes, dreams of adventure are amazing, but not at the expense of loved ones, not at all." Charlie saw the sadness in her beautiful green eyes and wanted to give her a hug. He still yearned for the adventures and excitement of blazing new trails and all the things he read about in books, but his life was good. He gave her a hug and she kissed him on top of his fuzzy new buzz haircut, sighed and walked over to Charlie's mom and dad. She whispered something in Carolyn's ear, blew a kiss to her father who turned away. Her shoulders slumped for a moment at his rejection. She straightened quickly and smiled at the stares from the folks she passed as she exited. Charlie never saw her again and only knew that she had a home somewhere in New Jersey not too far from New York City. All of his grandparents had died and he barely knew any cousins or other relatives. He signed the papers to have his parents cremated and asked that the ashes be put together in one container. Since he was a minor, the Private on the other side of the desk said he would try to locate Charlie's Aunt Kathy. There were some barracks near the hospital and Charlie was directed there where he was given some tee shirts and pants, meals, and toiletries. Casey was given a much needed bath and some dog chow which he gulped down without chewing one morsel. He slept and dreamed of his home, his friends, playing ball, and going to the beach to watch his brother surf. He awoke, sweat drenching his shirt and his heart pounding. His brother. His parents, Pepper. Everyone…gone. His whole life was gone with the wind, totally changed. He bent down and wrapped his arms around the only part of his world that was left……Casey groaned as Charlie rocked back and forth holding him and sobbing until there were no more tears. There were several other people in the barracks, but they all were lost in their own situations, tragedies, and pain. No one had located Jake. Since the last he was seen was headed toward the shore at the peak of the storm it was assumed he had been swallowed up by the enormous waves Helen produced. Charlie couldn't give up hope that his crazy brother might have just conquered the most awesome wave and had survived. The thread of a chance that his brother might still be alive gave him the courage to push aside the sorrow and move on. He would find Jake. That was his plan. He would find his brother no matter what.

At 5:00 A.M. Charlie shushed Casey as he woke him and packed the rations, clothing and his few other belongings into the pillow cases from his bunk. They had told him his parents' ashes would be in a marked box in a building next to the barracks. He entered the dimly lit storage room that smelled musty and was lined with tables with plain white boxes marked with typewritten labels. He walked quietly as though he were in church and late for mass looking at the names of those that had lost their lives in the storm. Very organized, neat rows, alphabetically arranged…Is that how they stand waiting to get into heaven, in neat rows, alphabetically arranged? Charlie asked himself. He had no more tears left, just a hole in his heart that would take years to heal. L…M…N…O (just two O's)…Pa…Pe…Peterson…Jesse Peterson, M.D., Carolyn Peterson…They didn't put the R.N.…why didn't they put the R.N. after her name? She was a wonderful nurse. Charlie picked up the box noticing it was quite heavy. There was a sign out sheet and a pen. He wrote "R.N." next to his mother's name in his best cursive writing, placed the box in one of the pillow cases, slung them over his back and walked toward a group of buses lined up across the field. The sun was just coming up over the buses. He climbed on the bus whose marquis read "New York". JC looked up from the box she held lovingly in her hands. Tears fell on the box marked "Linda Rutherford". Charlie took the seat next to her pulling his white box from the pillow case. They never said a word. They held tight to their boxes and each other's hand. The bus sputtered and belched as it headed north.

Chapter Twelve

A Diner in the Rough

The train started to slow as it approached Philadelphia. The city lights pushed their way through the smog leaving an eerie glow over the tops of the sky-scrapers. Will peeked out from his hiding place behind the stack of wood and began to gather his few sparse belongings. He checked carefully to see that he had the maps he had printed at the library showing the routes from Philadelphia to New Brunswick and that his race car was wrapped in one of his borrowed tee shirts stuffed in the bottom of his suitcase. He was not at all sure how he was going to get the eighty two miles to the city where he last heard his father was headed, nor was he at all sure what he would do when he got there, but it was the only plan that made any sense to him. He waited until the train had stopped and he saw no one around the box car. After jumping down into the stones near the track he ran toward a station house nearby just as the engineer jumped down from the engine and started to make his rounds checking the connections between the cars. Will hid behind the building barely breathing until the engineer walked back toward the front of the train to su-pervise the refueling. He noticed a news stand that held a paper but it was turned away from where he was hiding so that he couldn't read the print. There was a single light hanging from a rusty tin shade with spider webs veiling its dim wattage. He looked both ways and sneaked around the oppo-site side of the building. From that vantage point he could read the header The Philadelphia Town Crier. He could only make out a few words of the headline, "Iraq...Oil...Embargo" meant nothing to him. He was relieved not to see his or his family's names, nor his picture on that front page...at least the part he could see through the smudged glass and bars holding the papers. He knew he had to get some money in order to get a bus to New Jersey so he began to walk toward town. The railroads yards were not in an especially good part of Philadelphia. The streets were dark and littered with broken bottles, papers and sewage. Many of the old buildings had been burned. The carcasses of staircases and wires dangling from caved in rooms. A few of the houses had lights in the windows that projected shadows of people in the rooms, but no people sitting on porches or in the streets which even made it more creepy. Will bit his lip and jumped a few times when he heard a can tipped over in an alley and a cat hissed at him from an overturned cardboard box in one of the weed covered yards. He had a death grip on his suitcase wishing there was a better way to hide it so it didn't look like he had anything of value. He thought he heard footsteps behind him and he started to run his heart pounding and his eyes blazing with fear. He saw a diner about a block away. The lights flashed on the sign missing quite a few of the letters. "Oupy's Ood Foo," it flashed and to Will it looked like the Statue of Liberty. He rushed into the door as a bell announced his entrance. He was panting and felt like he could wet his pants.

"Well, ain't you the sight! What's a kid doin' out at night in these parts?" She said as she came out from the kitchen to see who rang the bell. "You ain't from around here are ya cause ya don't look like a gang memba' and ya look like ya jest sawr a ghost." She had brassy blond hair pulled up into a knot on top of her head. Her nose was way too big for her face and the bright red lip-stick painted way over her lip lines made it even look bigger. She had false eyelashes that curled up into her arched eyebrows. She blinked them often as she spoke in her Philadelphia brogue and they looked like spiders dangling their multiple legs over her eyes. "C'mere, kid. I ain't gonna bite ya."

Will walked cautiously over to the counter that was empty except for a few used dishes sitting at the end and the usual sets of sugar holders and greasy looking menus. "I need a job for a few days and a place to sleep. I'll pay for anything I eat. I'm a hard worker. I don't eat much. Just don't need anybody asking questions." Will said in his deepest, toughest, most confident voice.

"Ain't yer folks wonderin' where you are?"

"Don't have any folks." Will tried to sound unfeeling

"You can do dishes. Jest lost my helper, he was a druggie, damn cheat! There's a cot next to the cooler. You can have any left ovas that are left in the pots." She waved Will toward the kitchen and handed him a dirty dishrag, some soap and led him to two beat up sinks filled with dishes that had food remnants stuck to them for some time. The water that came out of the faucet never got above lukewarm so it took a lot of scrubbing and chiseling to get the dishes somewhat clean. His legs and arms ached and his stomach growled hungry sounds. He gagged a few times from the smell of the rancid food left on the dishes and in the garbage can that was overflowing next to the sinks. He had slid his suitcase under the cot that looked more like a pile of old rags laying on a bent rusty frame. "A buck fifty an howa, dat's awl ya get plus the left ovas." She laughed as she wiggled her more than ample butt toward him and walked into the main part of the restaurant lighting up a cigarette on the way. By the time Will collapsed onto the rag cot it was 7:00 A.M. and the sun was pushing the hazy glow of night away from the towering buildings of the big city. Will stayed three days and two nights working almost all of that time. Though the lady was tough and brash, she never asked any questions and she paid him fifty-one dollars for his hard work. She bantered with the customers and swore like a sailor, but there was something good about her, something good about most everybody…that's what his mother had taught him to look for. He wasn't sure there was anything good about the two men who had destroyed his life almost two weeks ago. He thanked her. Her name was Tess and her advice to him was "Stay outa da places dat have nude pictas of guys and gals. They'll see a good lookin' kid lie yous n' use ya, kiddo." Will had no intention of going near any place like that. He asked her for directions to the bus station and started to head toward downtown.

The black van pulled up in front of the diner just as Will was about to make his exit. He almost knocked Tess over backing up and running to the kitchen. Two men dressed in suits and wearing dark glasses got slowly out of the van and headed toward the diner. Tess didn't ask any questions. She opened the door of the cooler and pulled the trembling Will into a corner, quickly moved some boxes of supplies in front of him and winked at him. He sat on his suitcase and held his breath as the door closed and all went dark.

"Watcha want, fellas?" She looked the two visitors up and down paying close attention to see if she could see any telltale signs of weapons. "We got a special on apple pie…50 cents a slice."

"We're looking for a boy about twelve years old who we think jumped a train last night and may have come this way." One of the men took off his glasses and stared so coldly through Tess that even she had to shiver a little. The other man started walking around the counter toward the kitchen.

"Hey, mista, are yous some kind of cops? Ya gotta have a warrant or somethen' don't ya?"

"I ain't seen no kids in heya fer a long time, they hang out at McD's down the road." The second man had entered the kitchen and was moving things around. "His parents are real important people. Probably would pay a reward for him to be returned safely." Tess wrestled with that one, but something just didn't seem right. She had seen enough TV to know that the FBI only gets mixed up in kidnapping cases and missing political figures. She also was street wise enough to sense when there was danger. Anyhow, the kid seemed a lot different than most runaways. He was polite and courteous and a hard worker. The man at the counter held up a picture of Will, not the disheveled, frightened one she had seen the past few days but a smiling clean cut contented kid with a shirt his mom probably made him wear for the picture. Will shivered in the cold damp darkness of the cooler. How did they find him? No one knew where he was going. Jamie? Did Jamie find out something in the library? The acid from his aching stomach burned his throat and he tried to catch his breath just as the door swung open to the cooler. Light from the kitchen florescent overheads streamed into the cooler as the agent who was searching the kitchen moved into the room. Will could hear him breathing as he started to move some of the boxes from the opposite side of the cooler.

Someone shouted to the man just as he was moving toward the corner where Will was attempting to shrink into the cold immovable wall. "Jesus! E-7 escaped with the box! Joe and Ox shot. Motel blown up! Forget the kid! Got to get new plan!" The man ran from the cooler, from the kitchen and into their van like rabbits being chased by a hunter. Will said the angel prayer and included whoever E-7 was for doing whatever E-7 did to make them run. He slowly stood up from behind the boxes of creamed corn and niblets. He picked up his suitcase with the broken zipper and looked around for Tess. She was plastered up against the front door lashes blinking frantically trying to light a cigarette with her shaking hand.

"What the hell are you into, boy?" she stammered as she starred at her dishwasher slash "most wanted."

"I'm not sure at all, ma'am. Thanks again for covering for me and all your kindness." Will answered.

As he walked past her he shook her other hand and ran toward the bushes at the side of the road.

"Nice kid," Tess said as she shook her head and walked back to the kitchen.

Whatever was going on was a lot bigger than Will could even imagine. Bigger than anyone involved could imagine. There were only two people who knew the clock was ticking on an event that could not be stopped if it reached a certain point. An event so frightening it only could have been devised by demons without any morals or regard for human lives. In Will's suitcase wrapped in a tee shirt and stuffed under his few belongings, the small disc flashed it's red and green light in the sequence it had from the moment it was placed there.

* * *

Raritan Ordinance Depot had been closed for twenty years. It used to house weapons from previous wars in a museum open to the public on occasion. This was one of several arsenals that kept track of the weapons used for defense and wars, cataloged them and tested them before they were authorized to be used in theaters around the world and to protect the country should it be attacked. In the late '50s and 60s many of these were merged into just five arsenals across the country when the advancements in technology and computerization, ground fighting had changed, and the need for certain weapons was diminished. Nuclear weapon production and design were relegated to desert areas away from large populations. Edison, New Jersey, home of Raritan Ordinance Depot, now a park near the town, is situated not too far from New York City, Philadelphia, Washington, D.C., and other large cities. A quiet town with artsy theaters and old style New England buildings and hotels, it offers a taste of the big city mixed with a country home flavor. Many years ago, a man named Dr. Gregor Olmstead from Germany had migrated to the United States to more easily use his mathematical genius without the government hounding him and directing him. He and his family settled in New Jersey and he began to work at Raritan Ordinance Depot. He worked in the engineering section and was highly respected for his ability to create alloys of metallic substances that had amazing strength but were light and malleable. He loved experimenting and was allowed to use the laboratory after hours to play with his chemicals. One of those nights he discovered that by manipulating three chemical compounds he could multiply the power of a weapon four times its original strength. The process could not be reversed once he had added it to the original explosive. At that time there were three nuclear bombs buried in a huge housing underneath the Depot. He had inadvertently allowed his compound to fill the ignition housing of the bombs. Terrified, he devised a code attached to a computer calculation that would block the compound from igniting the bombs and reported the error to his supervisor. He stashed the black box with the settings in his home. In recent months he began to show signs of dementia that could not be explained by the physicians sent by the agency to test him. CAT scans failed to show any ischemic events or atrophy. In order to protect him and to relieve him of his duties, he was housed in a sanitarium in upper New York. His wife had since died and when the family was cleaning out some papers from his old office attempting to find out where he might have gone, they discovered the drawings and plans, the calculations and notes that frightened them enough to get in touch with Homeland Security. A special team of technicians, secret agents, and security officials searched his entire home, even used metal detectors and x-ray equipment to find the black box that he referred to often in his most recent papers. Should the box and the code sequence be found, the code could possibly be broken and the bombs would be detonated. Three nuclear bombs each with four times its destructive power would erase North America and parts of Central and South America off the map. The subsequent tidal waves, migration of nuclear fallout, and economic chaos would have disastrous results on the entire world. The team knew there was a black box with digital components sequenced by a computer formula. They were told to find it and protect Dr. Gregor Olmstead at all costs. The government named the investigation 'Project BBX42' and gave it a top secret status. All the notes, papers, manuals, even sticky notes were labeled top secret and taken to a special vault at the office of Homeland Security. The eagle perched on top of the world holding an olive branch in its mouth symbolized a branch of the secret service called the 'Red Dragons'. These were men and women highly trained in communications, combat, espionage, and undercover investigative techniques and languages. They were hand-picked by the President of the United States and worked with all Federal Agencies and the United Nations. They usually lived as regular citizens, maintained their physical fitness, endurance, and expertise at secret locations across the U.S. and in Europe. They knew that they could be called into action at any moment with little warning when their Commander felt America might be in danger.

The President knew after researching Dr. Olmstead's papers that should the black box fall into the hands of radicals or aliens along with the only man who knew the sequencing, that could unleash catastrophe that the clock might be ticking towards doom's day. One person had been contacted to find the box and protect Dr. Olmstead and was informed of the gravity of the situation. A code sequence was downloaded into a microchip that was similar to the last code in a journal found among Dr. Olmstead's papers. As long as the microchip was safe, the black box would answer the code and might be able to be tracked to its whereabouts. The nuclear bombs that were buried at Raritan were to be deactivated. As far as the agency knew the detonators had been unearthed and destroyed. They were not sure if the chemical that Olmstead had allowed to enter the reactor could possibly be detonated despite the activators being destroyed. What they didn't know was that a terrorist cell had infiltrated some of the departments associated with Homeland Security and had altered the security paperwork that claimed the site had been secured and the activator components eliminated. The terrorists had aborted the mission and the bombs were still alive. So far the disc was tracked moving east toward Pennsylvania. Agents believed that the disc had been confiscated when they lost track of Robert and Emily West and their family. At first they were sure the family had been eliminated by the terrorist cell until they heard no bodies had been found in the wreckage. Satellite computers picked up signals from various locations that possibly could be the microchip or the black box. It was confusing as signals were similar but coming from different locations at the same time. When E-7 sped away in the van after escaping from the motel, she seemed to have disappeared as well. Signals were picked up from a device the agents thought might be the black box, but soon disappeared about thirty miles north of the motel explosion assumed to be the last place E-7 contacted the agents. Since it was deduced that decoy boxes emitting traceable signals had been planted at various locations along the east coast, the only reliable signal would be coming from the microchip.

Will had no idea that everyone, the terrorists, Federal agents, the police, the FBI, impersonators from these agencies, and perhaps even his parents were trying frantically to find him as he was trying frantically to avoid the bad guys and find his family. Will did not know that Jamie had been shot and was lying in Intensive Care at the Mayo Clinic Hospital. He also did not know who he could trust and why the man who had shot the lock off his front door was talking to the police the day after the explosion. He had no idea what his parents really did for a living but he believed it has something to do with secrets everybody seemed to want. The metal disc that flashed codes intermittently in the bowels of his race car had to have been placed there by his father. There was a slim chance that when the man with the hollow eyes picked up the car that he could have slipped the disc under the frame, but that would have taken a magician's slight of hand as the man barely held it for a few seconds. Will wasn't sure if any of his family was alive or dead, whether they knew he was alive, and whether, if they were alive, they were able to try to find him. He also wondered how the men who were following him knew where he was. Maybe it's that disc thing. Maybe they have a way to track that disc. Will wondered if he should bury his race car so that he couldn't be followed, but if that was the only way his family could find him he would be untraceable. Because it appeared that his father trusted him with this disc by putting it in Will's possession, then he would hang on to it hoping that he made the right choice.

What he did know was that New Brunswick was about eighty miles from Philadelphia, that was the last place he thought his father had traveled, that he had just enough for bus fare, and that he kept looking behind him as he dodged in and out of trees and behind buildings along Route 70 toward 95. He passed what was left of a motel that looked very similar to his destroyed home and a chill ran through him and he felt the loneliness and confusion more acutely. When he arrived on North Broad Street he realized how small he must look to the throngs of people passing him on the busy city street. Hardly anyone even glanced at him or seemed to care that there was a young boy with one pillow case and a torn suitcase holding his belongings alone in the midst of this big city. According to the directions Tess had given him he would find the bus terminal about three blocks down North Broad Street. It seemed like an eternity before he saw the greyhound in its racing pose just below the sign that read 'Bus Terminal'.

Chapter Thirteen

No Questions

The bus trip was long and tiresome. Charlie and JC got to know each other pretty well during the ride as Casey laid on the floor enjoying a long snooze. Both kids had lost their parents. JC said she did not even care to locate her estranged father as he had not contacted her mother or her since he left many years ago. Charlie was going to try to find Aunt Kathy but had little more to go on except the last address he saw on a letter his mother had him take to the mailbox almost a year ago. JC was going to see if she could get help from the government to enter college and move on with her life. She had saved some money which she had pinned to the inside of her duffel bag and felt that communing with nature would push away the pain. Every once in a while Casey would look up at the two with his joule caught above his teeth in his very own smile and they would laugh rubbing the silly dogs ears as he groaned his approval of the petting. After many stops and almost twenty hours the bus pulled into the Greyhound Bus Station in Philadelphia, Pennsylvania. There would be an hour before the bus would resume travel north on I-95 towards Newark. JC agreed to share a cocoa with Charlie and Casey before she set out on her own in the big city. She planned to find shelter at one of the YWCA's that were listed in a services book the Air Force personnel had included with some other materials. The two orphans vowed to keep in touch as they had become friends the past few days. JC kissed Charlie and Casey good-bye and they both watched her move out into the busy streets only turning back to smile and wave a couple of times.

Coincidence is an accidental and remarkable occurrence of events, ideas, at the same time, in a way that sometimes suggests a casual relationship. Fate is the power supposed to determine the outcome of events as they occur. What happens to these 'orphans' from this point forward could only be described as a combination of both.

Charlie finished his cocoa and set the saucer on the floor for Casey to lick clean. As he bent down to retrieve the shiny saucer someone rushing past his table accidentally kicked the saucer a short distance into the isle and Casey jumped up and bounded toward the delectable dessert. The young boy's attention was on the clock hanging over the ticket booth and not on the saucer or the salivating canine careening across the aisle. Will's legs connected with Casey and he landed face down in the aisle. Casey recovered and proceeded to lick the saucer clean before he turned his attention to the body lying next to him. Because he saw himself as a professional rescue dog from his intensive training these past two weeks since the hurricane, he began licking the face of the stranger with vigor. Charlie had exited the table as soon as he heard the thump as Will hit the floor. He and a few other customers gently turned the boy over to see if he was conscious. Casey kept trying to push through the group hovering over Will attempting to continue his rescue attempts.

"Are you okay?" Charlie asked as he asked the spectators to back away so the boy could breathe. "I'm sorry about my dog. He gets in the way sometimes but he's a great dog." Will began to sit up and rub the expanding lump on his forehead. "You should lie down, um......MP." Charlie directed placing his sweatshirt under Will's head as he helped him lay back on the floor.

Will resisted Charlie's grasp on his shoulder, "Got to get a ticket......can't miss this b..." as he felt the room begin to spin and his head throbbed especially where the lump was located. He stopped resisting and laid back against the sweatshirt. One of the counter clerks who had seen the incident and had filled a plastic bag with ice came rushing over and placed the ice over the now golf ball sized lump. The ice aroused the woozy victim and he tried once again to sit up a little slower this time with the counter clerk and Charlie steadying him.

"Just sit here for a minute. I can get your ticket for you. Where are you going?" Charlie looked toward the clock which indicated he had about nine minutes until his bus would be pulling into the garage parking lot.

"New Brunswick. I...I am visiting family there." Will offered. Not really a lie as he hoped he would find someone from his family.

"Hey, that's the same bus I'm taking and I have a pass from...from a friend you could use." Charlie offered as he looked into the young man's eyes and felt a funny connection, a sadness, and some fear that he felt as well. Water dripped from the plastic bag filled with melting ice onto the floor and Casey began to lap it up. He looked up from his job with slobber dangling from his joules and one of the lips caught under his teeth giving the impression that he was smiling. Will, Charlie and the few customers who still remained curious laughed at the pooch's clown face. "Here, I'll help you up. Sit on this chair. We've got a few minutes before the bus comes. Do you want some water?"

Will took the glass of water brought by the counter clerk and drank it down as his eyes searched the floor wildly for his bag with the broken zipper.

It had slid under one of the tables across the aisle along with the pillow case with some of Jamie's rations strewn across the floor nearby. Charlie saw the panicky look in Will's eyes and offered to look around for whatever Will was so frightened of losing. "It's just an old suitcase with the zipper broken and a bag with some food in it." Will tried to get up to look himself but the throbbing in his head forced him right back in his seat. Charlie and Casey, now assuming the role of a bloodhound, moved chairs and peaked under tables until they found the suitcase, gathered up the sandwich, cookies, and a small envelope with 'Max' written on it and brought it back to Will.

"Max. Is that your name?" Charlie questioned as he brought Will's treasures back to the table.

"Yeh, that's me." Another lie. Will knew he would be spending lots of time in the confessional, if he ever got out of this mess.

"Let's try standing up. I'll take your bag." Charlie barely got the words out as Will grabbed for the bag. Charlie quickly handed the pillow case he had stuffed the envelope and rations in noticing that Will wasn't trusting anyone with his stuff. "I think the bus is here, Max. You can ride to New Brunswick on this pass. Maybe we can sit together." Will looked at the pass Charlie handed to him. The words U.S. Navy screamed at him and the image of the eagle brought the danger of being followed by an unknown enemy back into his consciousness. Will looked around the station. His searched the faces of the few sleepy eyed passengers standing at the ticket counter and in the seats with a paranoia that made each one of them look suspicious.

Charlie couldn't help but notice the change in Max's face as he handed him the pass. He could tell that he was younger, maybe about eleven or twelve years old. He felt like he had seen him somewhere before but discounted that thought as Max had said he was from the Midwest. Maybe he's a runaway and his parents are going crazy looking for him. The thought of never seeing his parents again rose up in his chest like a tidal wave and the tears burned his eyes. He could blink back the tears but the pain felt like a dagger might feel piercing his heart. Charlie bent down and rubbed Casey's ears, allowing a few tears to escape into his best friends furry neck. Casey seemed to sense that his human was hurting and he buried his head in Charlie's armpit giving his very best dog hug. Will (Max) turned his attention away from his scanning of the station sensing that all three of them were frightened and had been through something awful. He bent down next to Charlie and joined in the petting, hugging frenzy much to Casey's delight. The joule caught under Casey's lip as he unburied himself from Charlie's armpit and gave both boys one of his goofiest smiles.

"Thanks for the pass. If we sit together you have to promise not to ask too many questions. Okay?" Will said as he stood up and heard the big Greyhound belching outside gate number three.

"Likewise, not too many questions about me either." Charlie agreed as he swung his sacks over his shoulder. "We'd better get going. The bus is supposed to leave in five minutes." He reached for Will's suitcase, but Will grabbed it.

"I can get it." As Will turned to follow Charlie and Casey a van pulled up near gate five about twenty feet away from the other gates. The trio paid little attention as three men exited and entered the station The boys were rushing to the bus when one of the men shouted, "That's him!" The other two men turned toward gate three just as the boys and panting dog began to enter the bus with the marquis that read New York.

"Stop!" the lead man wearing a cap, fatigues, and a vest with an emblem on the front shouted.

Will turned as he stood on the first step behind Charlie.

"Oh, my God...hurry up...bus driver close the doors...please." It sounded like one of those poppers used at birthday parties followed by a "ping" as the bullet hit the metal near the entrance to the bus.

"What the hell!" the bus driver almost closed Casey's tail in the doors of the bus as he slammed the doors shut and stepped on the gas. Will laid on top of Charlie as he had pushed him onto the floor just as the bullet hit. Casey barked his displeasure with the near loss of that furry thing that always followed him around and that he loved to chase. The bus careened to the left as the wide eyed bus driver turned his wheel sharply and barreled out of the parking lot. The big Greyhound answered the driver's foot jamming the gas pedal to the floor with a roar and wheels screeching across the damp pavement as it turned north on Madison Ave.

Al Blakely had driven over four hundred thousand miles in his career. He had been a soldier in Viet Nam for two years bringing home with him twelve pieces of shrapnel in his back and right shoulder from a landmine explosion, a persistent limp from nerve damage, and nightmares that awakened him, sweat pouring down his face and ghostlike remnants of bodies blown into pieces slowly melting away. He had lost his fiancé to one of his friends who did more than comfort her while Al was away. There were no parades for the men and women who returned from that war and very few jobs. For a while he spent the money he had saved to buy his Melissa an engagement ring and a down payment on a home on booze, hookers, and pot. He got into fights in bars and wound up in jail a few times. He never ran from a fight as the anger inside him erupted for the slightest reason or no reason at all. The weakness in his leg prevented him from running the anger off. The trophy for state championship in long distance track events at his high school was a constant reminder of what the war had taken from him. After several failed attempts at busing tables in a greasy spoon restaurant, sweeping floors at one of the cinemas, and sleeping in abandoned buildings he took a swig of the last bottle of cheap whiskey called AA, checked into a rehab and prayed for his life. Ten years. It had been ten years without drugs or alcohol. Ten years. The need to escape, the need to fight a faceless enemy had been replaced by this man who never missed a day of work, greeted his passengers with a smile exposing one gold tooth in a row of slightly crooked teeth and quietly took his place in a chair at his AA meetings, made coffee, helped put up and take down chairs, kept to himself most of the time in a small apartment staring at the TV that was turned on just for the noise, and polished his AK–47 until the metal glowed. Holding the weapon with the tenderness he had once held his Melissa, kissing her soft blonde curls, and feeling her heart pounding against his chest he felt safe from the enemy that lurked in his subconscious. Driving the bus kept his mind from its incessant state of anxiety and readiness to attack. His platoon of passengers obeyed his directions and did not ask anything of him other than to carry them safely to their destination, on time.

Al glanced at the faces of the two boys as they recovered from their leap onto the bus. Will bended over to pick up a tattered suitcase and a couple of plump laundry bags. Al didn't ask any questions as he looked ahead through the window of the bus and into both side mirrors. He maneuvered the big bus hound around the cars, bicycles, trucks, and city buses with the skill of a race car driver. The sound of bullets hitting metal squeezed the adrenalin into his arteries. His heart rate escalated and his senses heightened. The lights of the city were turning on and they whisked by the window like fireflies. The engine of his tank roared with a fierce growl and the mumbling of the troops sitting in their seats unaware of the attack that just took place grew louder.

Will and Charlie were petrified as they inched into their seats behind the bus driver. Charlie ushered Casey to a place on the floor in front of the seat. There was more space between those seats and the back of the driver's seat, just enough to put Will's suitcase and small bag and Charlie's bags. He had promised Max (Will) that he wouldn't ask questions but he felt strange men jumping from a car, shouting and shooting at them negated that promise.

"Max, do you know those guys? Geezupete! They were shooting at us. We could have been killed. Are you in trouble or escaped from somewhere?" Charlie whispered his throat dry and palms sweating as he rubbed Casey's ears.

"I don't know who they are, I swear. Sometimes I wonder if they are bad guys or good guys…I'm so confused and scared. I think they want something I have. I'm afraid they have got my parents somewhere or…I don't know. Since last week nothing is the same…nothing." Will murmured as he felt the weight of his situation pushing him deeper into despair. "I'm just a kid. All I want is to see my mom and dad and Toby. I don't care about anything else." Will reached over and shared in the petting. Somehow the dog with the crooked smile seemed to sense the two boys' feelings, like pets so often do, and he drooled on the kids giving one of his best hugs and smiling that crazy Casey smile. Charlie tried to see if someone was following them but all he could see were lights reflected in the side mirror of the bus. They looked like hundreds of eyes peering into the streets racing by them. Al could see the passengers from the third row of seats to the back of the bus in the rear view mirror, but could not see the two boys and dog who seemed to be in trouble.

"Probably a couple of deserters……chicken shit." Al thought to himself as he felt himself inching back in the jungle, lights all around him from the fires burning in destroyed villages. His vehicle carrying prisoners and deserters to a post just beyond the jungle weaved in and out and he caught glimpses of burned bodies, women and children inside the remaining huts. They glared at him with agony and fear. He had to get them back to the commander. Despite his delusion he kept on the route that led north to Route 95. Part of him was in the present but the gunshot had triggered a part of his brain that could not let go of the past - the horrible, frightening, traumatic past.

Charlie didn't ask the boy he thought was Max any more questions. It seemed like a crazy dream. His parents gone, his brother dead or lost, his home destroyed and now mixed up in some insane drama with an eleven year old kid he barely knew. He wondered why the bus driver never said a word, just kept driving. It was eerie. Most bus drivers rarely get shot at and have two kids on their buses without adults with them.

He never said anything about the dog either. It was as if he didn't even see Casey. Strange. Everything was super strange! Buildings passed and marquis flashed their messages to "Dine in Luxury," "Fantastic Jazz Quartet," "Greek Palace," and "Foot Long Hot Dogs" in a surreal dance. The faces of the passengers were cast in a staccato aria of light and shadow imitating a silent movie. Charlie had nothing to hide. He needed to pour out the caldron of heaviness and loneliness he felt to someone. Max stared ahead clutching the suitcase with the broken zipper every so often leaning down to touch Casey's fur. Casey yawned and snorted resting his head on Charlie's shoe.

"There was an awful hurricane. My brother, Jake, didn't come with us in the van. He loved surfing and I think he was crazy enough to head toward the beach just as the huge waves and wind hit the shore. Mom and Dad and Casey's mother, Pepper, were in the van with me. We were trying to get inland but we stopped when we saw that Jake wasn't in the van. My dad is…was…a doctor and my mom…my mom……" Charlie suddenly saw in his mind the sheet being pulled away from his mother's face. She looked like she was asleep except for the lack of color in her face and lips. How many times had she and his father pulled a sheet over one of their patients and consoled the sobbing families and friends. There weren't any tears in his eyes. He had cried them all. He felt like he was crying though. Inside there were tears melting his heart. "They're gone…they're all gone. They haven't found my brother…I have to believe he is still alive. My mother's sister lives near New York. She's the only family I have. She will help me, I know. I played basketball in school. Really was pretty good. Being tall helped." Charlie looked at Max who had turned to look at Charlie.

"My name isn't Max; it's Will. My picture was on TV because everyone was looking for me. I wasn't in the house when…when it exploded. It exploded with my mother and my little brother in there! They couldn't find them. Those men came to the house and asked for my dad, then they shot off the handle on the front door and I ran…Mom yelled, 'Run, Will, run' and I ran. The house exploded and I hid in the bushes. I saw one of the men the next day with the police. He had a vest on with the picture of an eagle with a branch in its mouth sitting…"

"…on top of the world! I saw that somewhere. On a van near the hospital. Max, I mean Will. It must be some kind of rescue service because a girl I met was helping people after the hurricane and she was with the van. She was really nice…and pretty." Charlie blushed a little.

"Why would good guys shoot off our door handle to try and get into our house and then be there with the police when they came the next day? What made the house explode? After I ran, the car the men drove was gone from the driveway when I looked back at the house and it blew up. I remember, now, the car was gone. Maybe they took Mom and Toby and set a bomb off in the house. Why would good guys who help people do that?" Will's voice had gotten louder as he tried to make sense of the craziness. The bus slowly pulled over to a pull off several feet from the entrance to I-95.

Al pulled the emergency brake and slowly scooted out of his seat, stood at attention and turned military style to face the confused passengers in the bus. His face had changed from the pleasant greeter that had ushered the passengers into bus number twenty-two to a stone like mask of indifference. His eyes looked at each of his 'prisoners' with cold contempt. The thumbs of his trembling hands pushed into his belt as he arched his back and straightened his shoulders in the stance of a commander. The passengers' muffled voices and anxious faces made him feel powerful and invincible. Will and Charlie starred at the driver who was standing rigidly just a few inches from their seats. Casey sat up and panted heavily as he sensed the tension surrounding them.

"Listen up, you degenerates." Al snarled at the 'prisoners and defectors'. "We've got a situation here that's going to require you all to follow my orders. The enemy fire when we left the base tells me they are tracking us and may not be far away. You have no weapons but I have one and am a perfect shot." One of the male passengers, a balding stocky man wearing a business suit, stood up from his seat and yelled.

"This guy is nuts! We are not in a war. We're passengers on a Greyhound bus headed for Jersey, for God's sake. What in the hell are you talking about— the 'base' and 'enemy'! C'mon people. I think we need to take over the bus and get to some help." Before the man could rally the other passengers to a mutiny, Al marched down the aisle and stood above the man glaring down on him with contempt.

"Sit down soldier…now!" He snarled through clenched teeth. What his deluded eyes were seeing was a Viet Cong combatant in a ragged uniform. All the dead eyes and faces of the comrades he had seen killed flashed before him and he felt the rage growing towards this 'prisoner' who probably had killed many Americans. "Sit down and button your lip…now!" he repeated. The man looked around at his fellow passengers who, by now were cowering in their seats. He began to laugh. That was absolutely the wrong response. Al applied his clenched fist to the man's midsection and another to his jaw. After an anguished expulsion of air and an attempt to get his breath, blood sprayed from his mouth and he slumped to the floor in the aisle. Blood had spattered on the side of the face of the young man sitting in the window seat and he began to gag as he tried to bury his face into the seat.

Casey watched the attack easing himself into the aisle at the front of the bus. Coming from a line of fighters on his father's side his instincts told him to attack the assailant. Before Will or Charlie could restrain him, Casey bounded toward Al. Foam was dripping from his mouth as he barred his teeth not in his usual cockeyed smile but in aggressive and primitive ferocity. Al turned just as Casey leaped onto him growling a low ominous growl and barking angrily. When he backed up to fend off the carnivorous canine he tripped over the bald headed guy laying on the floor and he fell backwards striking his head on the metal frame of one of the seats. The four women on the bus screamed and a couple of the men grabbed Al and pinned him to the floor. The young man who had been sprayed with his seat partner's blood ripped his belt off and yelled, "Tie him up! Give him something to tie him up!"

" I've got some duct tape!" one guy shouted toward the front of the bus.

"Here's the electric cord from my hair curler!" one of the women who had recovered somewhat shouted. "Is he still alive? He hit his head pretty hard." Women always seem to have that care taking side, no matter what.

Al was unconscious as far as anyone could tell. He laid on the floor in the aisle several feet from his victim. The passengers tied his hands and ankles with a mixture of duct tape, electrical cords and belts. The women who had asked about his condition had rolled a jacket into a makeshift pillow and placed it under Al's head. There was some blood exiting a wound just above his left ear and the area was swelling visibly. He was breathing. Charlie had retrieved his dog who pranced past the frightened passengers with the regal stance of a war-rior home from battle. He settled his weary self onto the floor in front of his humans and glanced up at Will with the look of puppy innocence. Will bent down to scratch Casey's ears, "Atah boy…good boy!" he whispered.

The woman who had shown concern for Al announced she was a nurse and she asked for help to lift the bald headed guy back into his seat. He groaned when two of the guys lifted him and deposited him, began to open his eyes and tried to speak. He yelped when he attempted to push words through his bruised mouth and swollen jaw.

"Don't try to talk. Can you hold up three fingers?" Baldy, whose name was Frank Goldman, held up three trembling fingers. "Here's a piece of paper and a pencil" Sarah Jackson, nurse at St. Francis Care Center pulled the items from her purse and gently asked Mr. Goldman to write his name. Frank wrote his name and a few words:

Frank Goldman, Attorney
From New York
What in the hell happened?

Sarah wasn't too sure she knew either but she tried to put together the last few moments of bedlam.

"I think the bus driver snapped for some reason. He said something about shots and the enemy closing in. We need to get both of you to a hospital but we don't have a driver anymore. At least, we don't have a coherent one." Frank Goldman tried to speak but yelped again after uttering a garbled "Don't......"

Several of the passengers had gathered in the aisle to take part in the conversation.

"I used to drive a school bus years ago." A woman with brown hair streaked with scattered gray strands and glasses with maroon rims offered. She appeared to be in her fifties and wore a maroon turtleneck sweater and fitted jeans. The eyeglasses and maroon sweater reflected in her blue eyes and almost matched. "Maybe the gears are similar and I could try to get us to a nearby hospital."

An older man with a Yankees baseball cap, a flannel shirt and baggy beige pants piped up "I gotta get to New Jersey. My wife is with my daughter who is about to have our first grandchild. If we're gonna do something let's get to it."

Brenda Rivera was going back to New Jersey to start a new job teaching in a small Junior High School in Summit. She had lost her husband two months ago to the ravages of diabetes. Many surgeries, countless infections, loss of one of his legs, the depression from living in a disease that overwhelmed his life took its toll. She needed something to fill the empty space he left and to utilize her care-giving nature. She had retired from teaching in order to care for him. Now she needed to return to her second love—teaching young adults about the intricacies of anatomy and physiology so they might gain respect for that awesome machine, the human body. She had no idea that she would be a part of a drama that far exceeded the confines of a greyhound bus, that she would even be driving a bus on a journey overshadowed by intrigue and entangled in imminent danger. She took the wheel, examined the gearshift and its corresponding settings, adjusted the seat that Al had vacated so her feet could reach the pedals. As she reached down to grasp the adjustment bar at the side of the seat she encountered a plastic bag with something hard and cold inside. She pulled it out of its hiding place and gasped softly as the bag pulled away from the AK-7 rifle. Its barrel reflected the lights from the interior of the bus as its polished metal glistened.

"My goodness! He had a gun...he had a g..." One of the passengers sitting directly behind Charlie and Will jumped from his seat and ran up to Brenda who was standing dumfounded in the aisle next to the driver's seat holding the weapon gingerly as though it might discharge on its own any moment. Her eyes were wide peering over her lavender rimmed glasses that had inched their way off the bridge of her nose. Adam Kresge had been a gunnery sergeant in the Marine Corps ten years ago and knew the power of the weapon Brenda was holding. He also understood the craziness of the man who had slipped mentally back into his foxhole now unconscious in the back of the bus. He too had seen men die in pieces and had suffered night after night with those scenes of war spinning in his brain. He had been paralyzed from an enemy's bullet lodged precariously in his lower back and had spent almost two years in therapy regaining the use of his legs and healing his confused mind. He was able to sleep through the night and continued to see a psychologist at the Veteran Hospital in New York City even to this day. He, unlike Al, was one of the few who recovered from post traumatic stress syndrome with medication and psychotherapy.

Adam moved slowly toward Brenda who was trembling riveted to the weapon and frightened beyond her own personal fears of being left to fend for herself. "Fend" had not included discovering her bus driver was "whako" and carried an arsenal with him.

"Ma'am, I can take that from you." Adam said gently as he reached for the gun she held "We're going to be okay. We really need to get going. So if you can drive this canine, let's get moving."

The gun felt familiar as he checked to make sure the safety was engaged. He guided the relieved school teacher, former school bus driver gently into the driver's seat. She looked at his deep gray-blue eyes and the strong visage of his handsome face smiling at her in a way that gave her confidence she could get these injured folks somewhere safe. She turned the key in the ignition and stepped gingerly on the gas pedal. The bus sputtered and roared as the gasoline woke up the engine and settled into a loud purr as she released the pedal to allow some warm up time. There were ten gears similar, from what she could remember, to PS 320 Gregory High School's big yellow school bus. Adam had returned to his seat. Charlie and Will strained around their perches to see the big gun he now held in his lap. Al lay unmoving on the long seat at the back of the bus. Frank Goldman sat holding the now warm ice pack to his throbbing head. Sarah moved back and forth between the two men, checking pupils and taking pulses. The man with the baseball cap settled down with the evening newspaper. The reading light flickering intermittently. Casey slept on the floor at Charlie's feet probably dreaming of a huge piece of steak as a reward for his ongoing heroism. The bus pulled onto the ramp headed north to Route 95. A dark blue van pulled away from the berm of the highway allowing several cars to pass between it and the bus. The two men inside had holsters with pistols hanging over their shoulders and across their chests.

Chapter Fourteen

Friendship, Duty, Family

Robert West awakened with perspiration drenching his pillow and his tee shirt. His heart raced in time with the faucet dripping into the rust-stained sink across the room from the bed. The gray haired man laid facing the wall of the dismal hotel room. Bent, dirty venetian blinds sagged from broken hinges across the smudged window letting in tiny rays of light. This was it for him. He was getting out. He fell to his knees on the floor the night before praying to his God that his wife and children were still alive and safe. Tears filled his eyes, so foreign to this tough ex-Navy Seal, this no nonsense agent with nerves of steel and an attitude of rigid confidence. They had gone too far. They had put his loved ones directly in the line of fire. Every mission before had placed them in distant danger, but not immediate. Emily and he had shared missions, dangerous ones. That was before their boys had expanded their family and they began questioning the paths they had taken. Emily had retired with a security watch present tracking her every move in order to ensure her safety. You never retire from the Service. They never retire from you. You always are considered their property needing protection despite the lack of espionage, assignments, and intrigue. She was mostly thankful that there would be somebody at her back as well as those of her kids. Robert felt compelled to continue until this last assignment was completed. Compelled by patriotism, the magnitude of the disaster should the mission fail, and the love for his family and his country he agreed to take the mission. Had he known the plan included risking his family's lives, he would have begged to be released. The gray haired man turned away from the wall and opened his eyes staring blankly into the dimly lighted room. His hair stood out in several directions and his flannel shirt was soiled and wrinkled. He began to cough and mumble something as he reached for a frayed handkerchief in the pocket of his shirt. His hands trembled as he tried to stuff the handkerchief back into the pocket. Robert walked over to a wobbly nightstand and poured coffee from a half filled coffee pot. He walked slowly over to the man whom he had known for ten years. They had met in Germany while Robert was on a dangerous assignment. Dr. Gregor Olmstead was not impressed at first by the young, caution to the wind, virgin agent. This upstart daredevil was sent to the guru to have a detection device installed under the skin of his forearm so the agency could track his whereabouts. 'Bobbie,' as Gregor eventually would dub him, often would detour from the agency plan to attempt raids on villains he felt deserved a lesson. This would cause furrowed brows and reprimands even though he often saved lives with his diversions from protocol. Bobbie grew to love and respect the gruff, brilliant scientist who shook his head and mumbled in German every time he had to rescue him. Gregor was fondly dubbed 'George' and eventually was romanced into coming to the states to work in the Defense Department's high security division. Robert had met Emily in Germany as well. Emily was one of the Service's top agents, posing in many disguises from hooker to courier. He was stricken with her beauty and her courage. She spurned his advances, calls, and bouquets of flowers until finally both shared an assignment that threw them to together clinging to each other as their lives hung in the balance. She grew to admire his fearless commitment to justice and his trim muscular body wasn't too difficult to take either. They married and continued to accept assignments until Emily became pregnant with her first child. They both had decided that children would have to wait until their tenure with the agency was enacted. That would make Emily thirty five years old when they would even consider an extended family. Accidents happen and the soon to be Will was just that. After an evening celebrating one of the agent's birthday at which they both sloshed down an excess amount of champagne, caution to the wind wound up in Emily's womb. They both knew they would have to make a real home for their child, one that wasn't on a ship, in a foreign slum, or a cabin far out in some unfamiliar country. You never really retired from the agency. Emily and Robert were given safer technical assignments and were both fitted with tracking devices. Their home was manned with every security device known at the time. George had his hand in all of this as he had grown to adore and respect the beautiful agent as much as Bobbie did. When Robert and Emily were told an attempt to abduct George from his hiding place they decided that Robert must go back into active status with the Agency to head Project RRX42. Robert had always suspected that someone had gotten to George while he was still working at the arsenal because the doctors had difficulty explaining the sudden memory loss and confusion without any physical or clinical signs of dementia. The early signs were insidious. When the operation to deactivate the bombs was taking place, the government relied on Dr. Olmstead to facilitate the process from the base. Forgetting phone calls, missing meetings, confusing security codes to gain access to the research center on the base were all excused with explanations of fatigue, late work hours and George's eccentricities. Though calculations and repeated security checks verified completion of the deactivation, it had been jeopardized by the mental decline of the brilliant scientist and false readings integrated into the security system by terrorists. As it sadly became more evident that George's memory was deteriorating rapidly, the agency located the sanitarium in upstate New York and set up what they regarded as a 'fail-safe' monitoring system to track their scientist as well as placing guards posing as clinical staff within the institution. Despite all of the precautions, the enemy was patient and resourceful. They had somehow broken the code that was supposed to alert the government agents posing as clinical staff of any changes in plan. The terrorists were sent disguised as replacements. They sought out one of the actual attendants whose background history had been somewhat shady and paid the attendant to add a low dose hypnotic to George's regular medicines each day. George began to demonstrate signs of increasing confusion and ataxia. The terrorists posed as physicians and arranged a transfer to a local hospital as a cover for a planned abduction. One of the nurses became suspicious when she caught the aide adding a small yellow pill to the Olmstead's tray. She called the Agency and George was abducted, not by the terrorists but by his good friend Bobbie. They had aborted a plan devised by a terrorist group known as 'Hatham' which stood for 'young hawk' in some Middle Eastern languages. Robert 'Bobbie' West had left his home shortly after his son's twelfth birthday. His son thought he was going on another business trip. Emily and Robert had wrestled with the implications of returning to active duty and the dangers that lay ahead, not only for Robert, but also for his wife and children. They had argued the night before Robert was to leave but both also felt compelled by the gravity of the situation and the bond between the two of them and their friend. If George still had the capacity to configure the formula to breach the deactivation of the bombs hidden under the old arsenal buildings the terrorists would stop at nothing to extract that from him. He had seen the kinds of torture used by his enemies both in the Navy and in his time with the Secret Service. There was no mercy. Death was an option but they kept their captives barely alive, healing them just enough to begin with another horrific and relentless interrogation. Unknown to all but the terrorists and three other persons was the fact that the bombs deactivation had been halted and no one was sure if there was still a potential threat of igniting them or of the level of power they possessed. Even the terrorists were not completely aware of the power the cards held by all involved. Robert had cemented a disc into the race car of his oldest son believing it was a tracking disc. The doctor had given the disc to him a few months before his declining mental state was noticed. What the doctor did not tell his friend was that the disc also contained a sequence of formulas matching those in the notes that had been secured in a vault in Washington, D.C. shortly after Dr. Olmstead was admitted to the sanitarium. If the disc was placed into a secret compartment of the black box, it would nullify the sequencing to the deactivation chamber and the process would begin to detonate the bombs.

"George," he spoke gently so as not to frighten the man who barely resembled the trim, distinguished scientist he knew. "Gregor (he thought perhaps his formal name would be more familiar) would you like some of this 'burn a hole in your gut' coffee?"

"Gregor" touched the part of his brain that appeared to have been clouded with poison and he looked up at the man holding a chipped coffee cup toward him. He wiped his eyes and reached for the cup spilling some of it on the stained carpet. He grasped the cup with both hands as he shakily put it to his parched lips and sipped the hot liquid, letting it run down his throat. He coughed and sputtered, some of the coffee running down the side of his mouth. He pulled the handkerchief out of his pocket to wipe it away.

"Bobbie......is that you, *mein kampf?*" He stared piercingly at Robert as if he was trying to pull memories from a nailed casket. "I...I can't seem to remember much of anysing. My God, where am I? My notes...I has to find my notes...something is wrong. I can't remember. I have to remember...it is bad, Bobbie. It is very bad!" Robert sat next to him on the bed and tried to calm him.

"We have your notes in a safe place, George. We think someone has been drugging you making it appear you have dementia. These guys are not kidding. They want your brain and a formula for an explosive or something. We have to get you to a safe place where you can get some treatment to reverse the effect of the drugs if..."

"You mean IF it can be reversed...if...if." The doctor's eyes clouded over like an apron of fog sweeping over the Bay. "Who are you? Vhat do you vant? Leave me alone..." He pushed Robert away and curled into fetal position facing the wall once again.

It would be the first time Robert West felt utterly helpless. He was responsible for the safety of this man who went in and out of lucidity, his home had been destroyed and he had no idea if any of his family was alive or where they might be. Most disturbing of all was the sixth sense he had developed warning him of some impending doom. He had been informed that another agent had retrieved the black box from a motel on Route 95. She had been tracked heading north toward Washington where agents were to transport the box to D.C. where it could be secured and formulas compared to Olmstead's notes. Somewhere about twenty miles from her rendezvous they lost track of her. It was as though she had disappeared. Agents were sent to the last sighting of her tracking device which led them to search a baron area with no buildings, only open fields and abandoned landfills. No van, no box, no Kate.

Chapter Fifteen

Following too Close

The bus moved along highway 95 North at a comfortable 65 miles an hour. It was 3:00 A.M. and some of the passengers dozed their heads bobbing as the Greyhound negotiated through the few other cars and trucks traveling north. Brenda Rivera noticed lights from a vehicle that was following closely behind the bus and seemed to make every lane change she made never passing but always staying just a short distance behind her. She purposely maneuvered from one lane to the other to see if the vehicle continued its suspicious tailgating. She was nervous enough just driving this canine which seemed twice as big as the school buses she had driven in the past. This definitely was more exciting than traveling thirty five miles an hour over the same route day after day with noisy kids shooting straws and spitting gum at her. Definitely more exciting......but absolutely more stressful. She noticed one of the boys sitting in the seat behind her was still awake staring out into the darkness. The lights from oncoming cars gave a staccato image of a young man who was in pain. Her heart melted as it always did when she sensed a child in pain. Adam Kresge was nodding off periodically his hands frozen in a death grip on the rifle.

Brenda tried to get Charlie's attention "Pssst...Pssst. Hey, mister!" Charlie thought he heard someone but it was difficult to hear over the hum of the engine and its occasional sputter when Brenda changed gears. Besides, he was lost in the confusion and loneliness of the past few weeks. He had no home, no parents, possibly no brother. It was he and Casey, that crazy crooked lipped, loyal, brave dog. He looked over at Will who was curled up in the next seat and Charlie realized this was a young kid who was running from a demon he did not know, didn't know if his parents or brother were alive or dead, and didn't really have anyone except him and Casey.

"Hey, kid next to the window, come up here please" Brenda whispered in her most authoritative school bus voice as she shone a flashlight towards Charlie aiming over her head while looking in her rear view mirror. Charlie shook his head and slithered past Will and Casey stepping down into the well of the entrance next to the driver's seat.

"What's your name? Pretty awesome dog you have there. Is your brother in trouble? You guys leaped into the bus like a lion was on your tail. The bus driver is crazy and now he's injured. Oh, my name is Miss......uh Brenda (no time for formal titles). I'm really just a school bus driver but I guess I know enough to get us to the first stop in Jersey. I think we're being followed...and I don't want to wake anyone up. I saw you were awake and I just needed to...I'm sorry. I always talk too fast and too much." Charlie's eyes must have been rolling as he tried to listen to Brenda's oration.

"I'm Charlie. Casey is the dog but Will isn't my brother. He is running from some guys that probably have done something to his parents and little brother. He's trying to get where his dad told him he was traveling to before his house blew up. He's scared and lonely like me. My parents are dead and I need to try to find my aunt......that's all I have." Charlie liked this school bus driver and probably told her more than he meant to, but he felt he could trust her. She kept glancing at the side mirror. She chewed a wad of gum, that by now was a wad of rubber, faster after she saw the same two headlights still following the bus. There were no other cars or trucks in either lane when she switched lanes once again to see what the stalker would do. The van stayed behind her within a few feet of the bus as though it wanted her to know they were being followed. Charlie looked through the window slats of the door and could see the headlights of the van in the right side mirror. He watched it mimic Brenda's maneuvers exactly and he became more anxious as he remembered the shots aimed at he and Will as they dove into the bus.

"I'll bet it's the same guys that have been chasing Will and shot at us before we took off."

"Shot at you! When did they shoot at you? I didn't hear anything! Shot! Giminy Crickets! What the heck are we going to do?!" Brenda swallowed her wad of gum and pushed the pedal of the big machine closer to the floor. "Maybe if I speed there will be a cop car and we can tell them what is going on! Where are they when you really need them?" The bus lurched forward as Brenda rammed the gear shift into tenth gear. The speedometer started to climb to eighty miles per hour.

"I think you ought to back off the pedal a little, Miss Brenda. Don't want to wind up in a field or a ditch with those guys after us." Charlie tried to use his most adult and calm voice even though his stomach was gurgling and he felt a little panicky himself. Will adjusted himself in his seat. His neck had been bent to the side and when he moved the pain woke him. He didn't notice at first that Charlie was not in his seat until some oncoming truck lights illuminated the empty spot. Casey sat up when Will stepped on his tail and started to whimper when he didn't see his human and also the pain in the tip of his shaggy tail. He began to nuzzle Will as if to say, "Where is my human?" pushing against Will's leg. Will scratched his ears and apologized for stepping on him.

"It's okay, buddy. He's around here somewhere." Will looked around the bus. Most of the ten passengers were sleeping except for Nurse Sarah and Frank Goldman. Sarah kept checking on Al who was still lying pretty motionless on the back seat of the bus. Frank kept looking toward the back of the bus where Al lay as though he needed to be ready to leap into action if the crazy guy came to. Will stood up and Charlie noticed his figure in the darkness.

"Will…I'm down here next to the driver. Come over here. We've got a problem," he whispered.

Will was getting used to problems. "I wonder, what's up now? This is just the craziest trip." He thought to himself as he eased himself next to Charlie in the entrance well.

"There is a car, looks more like a van or truck from the position of the headlights that is definitely following us. Miss Brenda has weaved from one lane to the other and in and out of traffic but they won't pass us and stay right behind us. It's like they want us to know they are following us." Charlie waited for Will to say something. Will was staring at the side mirror and the two headlights reflected there. His heart was racing and he quickly went back to his seat and grabbed the suitcase. When he came back beside Charlie the look of panic in his eyes was evident despite the darkness.

"What's going on, Will? What is in that suitcase?

Chapter Sixteen

Prisoners

Emily and Kate struggled to open the huge steel door that led to their prison. They were weak and dehydrated having been fed only small portions of rice and one glass of goat's milk a day since they had been captured. Emily's condition was worse as she had hoarded the milk for Toby lying listless in the corner of the old dungeon hidden deep beneath the floor of an abandoned foundry. Two weeks had passed since Emily had been dragged from her home with a death grip on her youngest son. She and Toby were stuffed into the trunk of a black car just as she had screamed to Will to run. Through the haze produced by the chloroform soaked handkerchief her abductors had clamped over her mouth she heard an explosion that echoed against the metal trunk and in her heart. Toby trembled as she pressed him closer to her bosom. She tried to hum a lullaby but her throat was so dry she could barely utter a tiny whimper. "Oh, God, please let Will be okay...Please help us. I know they can track us, but these horrible men have ways of blocking that. Please let Toby be safe no matter what happens to me. Please, God." The black limo made several turns, first to the left and then two turns to the right. The first turn occurred just a few minutes after she and Toby were stuffed into the trunk, then the explosion, about four minutes and the first turn to the right, then an agonizing thirty minutes until the first right turn. Though Emily, the mother part of her was terrified, Emily the agent took over and she memorized the faces of her captors, the route the car was taking, and the sounds she could discern from her cramped position in the trunk. Toby fell asleep with the hum of the motor so she could start to formulate a plan even though the odds were definitely against her. Not that she hadn't been in situations worse than this, but this time she had to protect not only herself but the child that was lying in her arms. She surmised they both would be used for ransom to lure her husband and the doctor into a rescue. She knew Robert, the agent would never take that risk, but she was not sure Robert, the father and husband wouldn't. When the sun shone in her eyes as the trunk lid was opened she tried to sit up despite the awkward bend in her legs and back from the position she had in the trunk which she surmised lasted about six hours. The hum of the motor and a lack of turns after the first four led her to believe they were on a highway. Calculating the amount of time multiplied by around fifty miles per hour, she thought they might be about one hundred fifty to two hundred miles from her home. She got a glance at a warehouse or some type of brick buildings with faded letters "NAT" on the face of the building before she was roughly dragged from the trunk and blindfolded. She held tight to Toby who continued to sleep in her arms. Her captors did not speak. She sniffed at the air to try to identify any smells and listened to the sounds as she and Toby were pushed along towards one of the buildings. Several odors lead her to believe she was in a factory district. The acrid smell of furnace burning metal or coal plus an occasional whiff of sewer gas combined with counting her steps until the odors changed to musty dampness and cool air hit her face calculated to around thirty feet from the car to the building. It seemed like her son weighed one hundred pounds and he began to stir moving his arms and legs making it even more difficult to hold on to him. His diaper was full of urine and some pushed out on to her blouse as she tried to hang on to him. A turn to the right and more dampness, down eight stairs into deepened darkness. She thought of the catacombs she had visited in Rome during one of the rare holidays she enjoyed as an agent. The steps were uneven and carved from stone similar to the ones she had just been forced to negotiate. The smell of ancient stone dampened with seepage from the soil surrounding it made her surmise this was an old building with a basement or wine cellar. The grating sound of a metal bolt startled Toby and he began to cry. Emily was pushed into a room landing on a cold wet floor. She had a death hold on her son whose whimper turned into a wail that echoed against the stone prison. She rolled as she fell the way she had done many times in her encounters with evil, but this was the first time she could not complete the roll that could prevent injury so she landed on her right elbow. Her humerus jammed itself into the cup of the clavicle that normally facilitated the rotary movement of her arm. The clavicle snapped and the pain forced a yelp from her that managed to frighten Toby even more. She laid on the cold floor with her right shoulder dislocated and her clavicle cracked in its mid portion. Her son rolled off onto the floor beside her screaming with all of his lung power. She ripped off the blindfold. Everything was blurred. She frantically reached for the wriggling figure she could barely make out in the darkness of the room. She tried to sit up holding the trembling child to her chest rocking him and making "shhhhhh" noises. The pain shot through her chest, right shoulder, and entire arm as it hung limply at her side. Toby finally settled into a soft whimper in between the sucking noises as he located his trusty personal pacifier. Emily turned on her right side bent her right leg against her chest. Grabbing hold of her foot she laid on that cold floor and pushed her leg forward forcefully to relocate her shoulder. She gasped as the head of the humerus snapped back into its socket. The knife like pain almost caused her to pass out as the humerus pushed against the end of the broken clavicle. She panted like she had when her labor pains ran into one long agonizing cramp seizing her back and pelvis like a vice. Her eyes cried and she started to adjust to the darkness. A tiny shaft of light filtered through a small opening at the upper portion of one of the walls. It must have faced the outside as she could hear some street noises coming from that direction. Toby wiped his snot on her blouse and whimpered "Da-da."

"I want your daddy, too, baby doll." Emily West whispered to her youngest boy as she rocked him back and forth sitting on that cold wet floor. "We both need daddy..." Tears ran down her cheeks and the agent part of her allowed the mother and wife to take over for a few moments. She knew she couldn't stay in that space so she brushed the tears away on her sleeve, searched on the floor for the blindfold and fashioned a sling for her injured arm and clavicle. Holding the baby with her uninjured arm she stood and moved around the edge of the room until she found a bench or some type of bin against one of the walls. She took off her shirt under which she just had a sleeveless top. Lying in the wooden object she hummed a lullaby as she gently place Toby in his 'manger'. She looked up at the small opening and saw stars beginning to push their way into the night. She said the 'Angel' prayer she always prayed with her boys when she tucked them in each night. Her voice cracked, but she swallowed the tears that wanted to push the agent aside. *Please protect my boys and my husband.* She silently begged. Exhaustion took over and she drifted off leaning against the wall of her prison holding the hand of her sweet son.

Kate was driving the van as fast as she could heading Northeast toward Washington, D.C. Her ETA was 1:00 P.M. at a roadside restaurant just outside the city. She was sure she wasn't followed as she had almost as constant an eye on her mirrors as she did on the road ahead of her. She had to get the box to the agents she was to meet and get down to Florida as quickly as she could. She had heard of the monster hurricane that had gobbled up most of the towns in the northern part of the state along the coast including the town where her sister and nephews lived. That was two weeks ago and she had tried every avenue she could to locate their whereabouts. She could only do this when she wasn't attempting to find the terrorists who had somehow located a black box. It appeared to be the one that Dr. Olmstead had devised to interact with the intricate computer program to release a hold on some bombs buried under the old arsenal site in New Jersey. The bombs were supposedly disengaged from the detonation device. The problem was that there was no way to confirm the inability of the bombs to explode and that the device that was originally put into the ignition system had the potential of increasing the explosive power of the bombs fourfold. The black box continued to display calculations and if downloaded into a computer system with the program running there was a statistical risk of the two programs marrying at some point which was supposed to negate the fail-safe device inhibiting the chain reaction. She had followed two men leaving the former house of the doctor and traveling to a cave deep in a forest in Pennsylvania. There they were seen exiting with a box which they loaded in their van. She followed them to the motel just off Route 95 and signaled for assistance in storming the motel. Before she could give her location, she was attacked and the next thing she knew she was inside the motel bound, gagged, drugged, and thrown on a bed in the corner of the motel room. While being interrogated as to the whereabouts of the West family, she managed to free herself, grab the box, and destroy the room.

Kate had never met Robert or Emily West but knew their reputations and history with the agency. What she did not know was the fate of her sister and the children and the danger Charlie might be in traveling with Will. She had her orders and was in the van before the explosion occurred. As soon as she could unload the box to the Washington agents, she would be on her way to Florida. The Hatham had other ideas as they lost contact with Ox and Joe. The van was tracked by a device whose signal should have only been able to be seen by the U.S. agency. The terrorists were technically a step ahead of U.S. computer tracking systems and were able to reroute the signal to their central communications. Kate had driven about sixty miles north east of Route 95 when she was halted by a road block placed by the terrorists. Before she could begin to question and escape, she was paralyzed by a dart shot at close range whose capsule containing a chemical agent similar to those used by natives in Africa to paralyze their pray. Doxacurium chloride, normally used as a skeletal muscle relaxant in surgery immediately rubberized Kate's body as soon as the capsule was released in her system. Her abductors used a chloroform soaked handkerchief to muzzle her protests as she was dragged from the van and thrown into a black limo. She was blindfolded and stuffed on the floor of the back seat. Kate was roughly dragged from the limousine after several hours in a fetal position on the floor of the car. Someone held a big foot on her back making it difficult to try to change her position even slightly. Kate tried to concentrate on anything she could hear as they traveled, any sounds at all as well as the amount of time lapsed and the direction the limo was traveling. They finally stopped and she was almost thankful to be dragged out of the ve-hicle and made to stagger toward the smell of burnt metal and sewage. The grate of metal on metal, a heavy door making inner sanctum sounds as it was opened, and that foot pushing her onto a cold, wet cement floor. She heard a noise. Her hands and feet were bound and she could not remove the blindfold. It sounded like a baby's whimper. Suddenly there was someone stooping over her and she felt this might be the end of her crazy life except she did not feel the cold steel of a knife at her throat, nor the barrel of a gun to her head as she anticipated, she felt a hand untying the blindfold and moving to release the ropes that bound her hands and ankles, then the person moved away from her. Her eyes slowly adjusted to the darkness and she frantically searched the room for the person who released her. She heard a woman's voice whisper.

"Shhh—I'm over here against the wall."

"Are you alone?" Kate whispered at the same time covering her mouth and feigning a cough.

"In the corner but don't come to us. My son is a baby and I will die to protect him." Emily whispered.

"Okay." Kate stumbled over to the opposite side of the room. Her legs were weak and rubbery. She was still dizzy from the chloroform and the muscle relaxant. She leaned against the cold cement wall to ease the pain in her back and fell into a restless sleep haunted with toothless demons, hawks with razor sharp teeth, and the image of her sister being carried off screaming her name. Kathy was always restless even as a child. She was nothing like her level-headed, quiet, obedient sister, Carolyn. Her father's stubbornness mixed with alcohol and her determination to do things her way and detour from the norm caused raucous confrontations and hours of punishment that Kathy, better known as Kate, deemed as unfair and thwarted with little guilt. She and her father were so much alike in the way they viewed the world that they constantly were trying to prove whose way was best. Kate escaped to wander the country when she finished high school one year early at the age of sixteen. She worked anywhere she could get hired for any amount of money, waiting tables, laundromats, picking produce on farms, washing dishes, pushing gurneys and wheelchairs in hospitals, cleaning toilets—nothing was too repugnant or demeaning as long as she had enough to keep traveling. She lived in campgrounds, sleazy motels, peoples' homes that would take her in, missions, half-way houses, public bathrooms, wherever she could doze off for a few hours. She was almost raped, beaten up, robbed, rejected, accepted, driven, frightened—all of these had toughened her and honed her street-wise skills. At age eighteen, she signed up for the navy and toured the world as a communications officer and gunnery expert. It was in the navy she met Ensign Jeffrey Porter. He was handsome, especially in his dress uniform, hell bent on becoming an admiral, and almost as wild and carefree as Kate. They latched on to each other in basic training and battled for the top rankings in target practice, field drills, and grades on technical exams. Both were extremely intelligent, competitive and fearless. They fought, drank, excelled and made love passionately with complete abandon. When Jeff was promoted to Corporal in the Navy Seals, he had no qualms about putting himself in harm's way if it meant protecting his men and women. Dangerous assignment after dangerous assignment continued to elevate his stature and brought him closer to his goal. Kate worried about him but was forging her destiny by becoming an expert in clandestine communication techniques and sharpshooting expertise. She worked out every chance she got in between her schooling, assignments, and gunnery practice. Her body was sinewy and agile. She had inherited her mother's ability to bend her limbs in almost grotesque positions that gave her the ability to crawl through small openings and narrow passages as though she had no bones at all. She thought like a man, rarely cried, and dispelled the amenities of keeping in touch with her family and friends as inconsequential. The family tried to keep track of her and communicate with her but finally gave up. Carolyn persisted and had found an address in New Jersey where she sent letters that were never answered. She just kept sending them. They had seen Kate one time in fifteen years at a reunion a few years ago. Jeff's final mission was to infiltrate the Vietnamese northern camp and capture two key leaders of the Viet Cong regime. Unaware that there were mines set around the post, he was mortally wounded when he sensed one of his men moving toward an area in the brush that appeared to be freshly transplanted. He dove toward him just as Peter Marshall, aged twenty four, was about to step on the charger. Jeff landed on the mine and quickly rolled away just as the charge ignited. His entire right side exploded along with the mine and a large piece of metal pierced his lung and entered his heart. Pete lost his right leg below his knee. Jeff lost his life. Kate cried choking her guttural sobs into the bunk pillow for several hours, sat staring at the duffel bag with Corporal Jeffrey Porter inscribed on the dog tags draped over it lying at the end of her bunk for two days. She did not eat nor shower. Other than a few trips to the head, she did nothing but sit and stare. The third day she stopped staring, took the duffel bag and dog tags to the mail room to be sent out to Jeff's family, showered, donned her fatigues and returned to her post and classroom. Her heart grew a covering of steel so that it would not allow any pain to enter and any empathy to leave its chambers. She signed up for the Secret Service Espionage training program when she left the service and became one of the most feared agents by enemies that the United States had ever produced. She had been married, divorced, and had men in her life but never allowed a breach in the steel to afford compassion and forgiveness to seep into the softer tissues of her heart.

Kate had heard of Emily and Emily had heard of Kate. The only difference between the two was that Emily had allowed her children to melt a small segment of her frozen heart, but Kate had not. Toby whimpered and Kate peered into the makeshift crib. A twinge of tenderness slithered in from the cold prison that encircled her heart at the sight of the child lying limply wrapped in a soiled shirt. She looked away and directed her focus on the room the imprisoned her and her fellow agent, avoiding the prison that surrounded her countenance as a woman. In the dim light filtering through the two by two opening at the far side of the room, she could see cement block walls dripping with moisture. There was a single drain in the middle of the room that was doing a poor job of draining the water that lay on the cement floor in small puddles. The steel door had a tiny access door through which their captors would shove cold lumpy porridge and goat's milk, one piece of moldy bread for each of the captives twice a day. Nothing was made available for the baby even with Emily begging for a blanket and some diapers and milk for him in exchange for her ration.

Kate spit into the drain in disgust when Emily showed her vulnerability when it came to Toby. She knew the terrorists had found the weak spot in her and were ready to toy with it to render her skills as a feared agent impotent. The room was about ten feet by twelve, Kate calculated. The only item in the room was the wooden bin that housed the kid and a six inch chain dangling from the single opening. Emily and Kate had pulled with all their might on the chain hoping to pull the metal grate away from the opening, but to no avail. Kate marked the hours the ray of light moved on the concrete floor with a chunk of cement block that had cracked from the dampness. It was jagged and could be used later as part of an escape plan. She hid it by putting it back into the block. Kate shared her rations with Emily as hers were given to Toby. They hid parts of the moldy bread in their bras so they could keep up their energy between meals. Both women did push-ups at night when they felt they were not being observed. They had both felt around every inch of the walls and floor they could reach to detect a monitoring device. There movements seemed to go unnoticed except for the times when rations were delivered by a man with a shaved head, dark glasses, and a scar across his right cheek. Every time the surly guard delivered the so-called meals, he peered into the room and yelled in a foreign language at the three captives. Kate and Emily knew enough languages to understand the curses and threats being sprayed from his foul mouth. They also knew they all were being used as bait to lure Robert and the deranged doctor into their clutches. Emily shared with Kate that Robert had been called back into active duty to protect their friend, Dr. Olmstead. Kate shared with Emily that she had rescued this black box only to have been tracked in some manner by the terrorists who would stop at nothing to capture the doctor and the box. Neither of them knew the entire story, nor what had happened to the rest of their families. They knew that project RRX42 was high priority and top secret and that they had to find a way to warn Robert and reclaim the box.

Chapter Seventeen

Jake

The doctors in New York Metropolitan Hospital had attempted to contact someone in the young man's family. Jake had laid in a coma on a ventilator for the past two weeks. He had been found by a rescue helicopter impaled on a jagged piece of fencing several miles down the coast from the towns destroyed by Helen's ferocious onslaught. He was barely breathing and his pelvis, right arm, and right femur and ankle had been shattered. He had lost a great deal of blood and was bloated from the hours he was tossed about in the cold waters of the now subdued ocean. The surgical team worked through the night removing the fence that had somehow missed his aorta and spinal column. Four surgeries had been performed since he was found and placed on a ventilator. Two repaired the fractures in his thigh replacing the hip joint with prosthesis and the ankle with pins and plates. A colostomy was fashioned on his abdomen as a large section of bowel had been severed when was thrown on to the jagged fence post like a horseshoe around the stake. The third was a tracheotomy to open the swollen windpipe to allow the ventilator to pump oxygen into his lungs that had filled with sea water. The fourth surgery was an attempt to realign the crushed bones in his right lower arm. The pneumonia had improved and the leg and pelvis were healing well. An electroencephalogram showed brain activity close to normal that the neurologists working on the case could hardly believe. They assumed the icy salt water had lowered Jake's body temperature enough to lessen his organs' requirement for oxygen and also had acted like a saline irrigation to what could have been a mortal wound, thus preventing infection. The ocean that was Jake's most treasured toy had attacked him like a dog that once was a pet turned into a mad ravenous beast. It seemed to later want forgiveness bathing the wounds it had inflicted with waves of the Master's own saline. Several yards from where Jake was found pieces of his surf board 'Elmo' were picked up by search parties looking for other victims about a week after he was found. One piece had some lettering that was barely visible—Jake Peterson, Elmo the magn...The rescue crews took the piece of Elmo that might have belonged to the young man they had found lying on a rock pile caressed by the now languid sea and held in place by a bayonet of wood that ran into his abdomen and exited just below his lower rib. It took almost a week for specialists could treat the wood with chemicals that brought out the muted lettering. The newspapers, radio, and television began to flood the airways and clients with the inscription. National news was preoccupied with a missing young man and his entire family as a result of an explosion at their home in Ohio. That story became old news as no clues were found as to any of the family's whereabouts. Jake's story appeared on some national news stations while Charlie was on a bus headed for New Jersey. The ventilator was removed as Jake's lungs healed and he was to start physical therapy soon to regain his strength.

* * *

Brenda Rivera had a spicy temper that she held at bay while she was teaching or driving kids to school. It would rear its ugly head when kids would talk back to her and test her patience once too often. She had been counseled a few times when she would grab the offender by the arm and escort him or her forcefully out of the classroom or off the school bus. The headlights from the vehicle that evidently was pursuing 'her bus' were getting on her last Cuban nerve. Charlie and Will had decided to let Adam Kresge in on the story because he seemed to know about guns and appeared more level headed than some of the other passengers. Brenda's jaws kept tightening as she clenched her teeth trying very hard not to slam on the breaks and allow the 'asshole stalkers' to smash into the back end of the bus.

The van moved so close behind the bus that Brenda could no longer see them in her mirror. Suddenly a bullet smashed the mirror on Brenda's side of the bus. Glass splattered against her side window as she floored the gas pedal startled by the explosion. Brenda spontaneously lurched forward and hid her face with her right arm. The greyhound leaped forward and the tires screeched as the bus attempted to find gas enough to keep up with the grounded pedal without being shifted into high gear. The fire inside Miss Brenda boiled over and she slammed on the brakes. Passengers, belongings, and bus spun around with the centrifugal force of a space ship launch. The van with its two occupants hit the back of the bus and went airborne landing on top of a car several feet behind it. The car and van were knocked off the road by the spinning metal canine.

Harry Fondessey sleepily negotiated his sixteen wheeler into the left lane to pass the car in front of him. He was listening to his favorite country station and reminiscing on lost lovers when he was jolted awake by the scene in front of him. He was bound for New York with a load of steel pipes and a much needed sleep over as well as a big dish of stew washed down with Aunt Hattie's apple pie at his favorite truck stop just a few miles ahead. The car to his right ahead of him was hit by another vehicle that flew on top of it and it careened into his lane. A bus came spinning barely ten feet in front of Harry's truck as he stood on his brakes and down shifted frantically. The steel bands holding the pipes in place snapped as the truck jackknifed. The pipes shot through the cab of his truck partially decapitating Harry and flying like missals onto the highway. The bus hit the pipes and rolled several times just missing an impact with the jackknifed truck. The few cars some distance behind the disaster did not see the pipes in the road until they were upon them. Several crashed into one another like dominoes as they tried to avoid hitting the pipes. The smell of gasoline and crushed metal, the tinkling of glass, and the screams and cries of those still alive and injured filled the few seconds of ghostly stillness that occurred when everything stopped moving. Inside the bus, Brenda's limp body was draped over the macerated steering wheel. Casey, Will, and Charlie had been thrown from the bus on the initial impact with the van as the door to the bus bent into pieces and was ripped from its hinges. Adam was pinned under one of the seats that had bolted from the floor and landed between the caved roof and the floor. The only reason he was alive was because of that seat which acted like a jack protecting his body from the roof crushing him. The bus laid on its side near the woods where it had rolled several yards from the highway. He listened for any human sound coming from the bus but could only hear the screams of those on the highway and sirens approaching in the distance. He felt a warm trickle of what he assumed was blood running down the side of his face. His head pounded with every beat of his heart and his legs were pinned under the top part of the seat. He tried to push up on the seat to extricate his legs to no avail. Then he heard it. It sounded like a frightened child but not human. The rifle was lying a few feet from where he was trapped and he stretched as far as he could arching his back in order to reach it. The blood from the large gash in the left side of his head trickled into his eyes. Wiping it away and straining to reach his only protection from whatever was out there his fingers trembled as he located the nose of the gun, stuck his finger in the hole and eased it toward him. Two eyes glistened in the moonlight peering through the opening that used to be the entrance to the bus just a few feet from where Adam waited breathlessly praying he could somehow scare, kill, or injure whatever it was approaching him in the darkness. He heard breathing and a low growl as he tried to cock the rifle and shoot. As he arched his head back to orient himself the blood gushed from his head wound and his arms went limp. The searchlights from the rescue crew sifting through the gory scene on the highway filtered through the openings in what was left of the greyhound just as Adam's consciousness drifted into oblivion and the eyes stared eerily at the limp figure, its hands wrapped tightly around a rifle.

Chapter Eighteen

Masterminds

One of the cardinal rules of espionage is to never let two agents or crooks be in close proximity to one another. Though Dr. Olmstead was in a confused state, there still was a mastermind somewhere beneath the portion of his brain that had been drugged by the Hatham terrorists. Robert West's faculties were totally intact and his incentive to protect his friend was heightened by his need to locate his loved ones. The adrenalin that shot through him sharpened his wit, his hearing, and his perception. He was sure that his enemy would try to set a trap for him by allowing him to think they were holding his family for ransom. His enemies also knew him well enough to know that he couldn't be lured into a compromising situation easily and without backup. He had heard about the explosion at his house and was worried that Emily and his two boys were injured or worse. That was the father and husband part of him. The agent part, the part that could get him through this nightmare assignment, had confidence in Emily, the agent, to be alert and protect her assignment as a mother with all the tools she had gathered as an agent. Robert knew that he had to separate himself from his need to find his family and keep George safe and secluded at the same time. One large impediment would be Dr. Olmstead's labile state of mind effecting Robert's ability gain the doctor's trust and to have him understand the seriousness of the situation.

"George......Gregor," gently touching the shoulder of the sleeping doctor, Robert whispered earnestly. The body of his friend stiffened and rolled on its back as his eyes starred at his friend with fear and confusion.

"Vhat do you vant? Who are you? Don't I know you...you look familiar but..." Gregor grabbed hold of the hand extended to him and sat unsteadily on the edge of the cot. Robert sat next to his friend and allowed a moment for both of them to collect their thoughts. The late afternoon sun filtered through the tiny window and cast the shadows of the two men sitting next to one another onto the wooden floor of their hideout. Dr. Olmstead had dreamed while he laid facing the wall starring at the peeling wallpaper with some kind of faded flower arrangement. He drifted off to sleep and a woman walked with him in a park. Hills dotted with a white church and small cottages framed the background of his dream as he seemed to be comforting the woman whose face was both familiar and not familiar to him...if that was possible. She seemed to be trying to implore him to do something but her words were muted and distant. He kept shaking his head "no" and she almost appeared to be crying. Suddenly, she turned into a hawk. The bird's eyes were yellow and evil and it kept pecking at him as he tried desperately to protect himself. Series of numbers began rolling past him on the walkway as he tried to escape the ferocity of the beast. As he was about to reach a cliff with no escape but to leap, the hawk turned into the woman and she rescued him at the same moment he felt a hand gently shaking his shoulder. He could see the outline of the man standing over him as he tried to focus and erase the terror and confusion left in his chest from the dream. There was something comforting about the hand that helped him sit up and the man who had taken a spot on the bed next to him. The cot sagged pushing them closer together and Gregor leaned on the man's shoulder to steady himself.

"George, it's me, Bobbie, Emily's husband...your friend...the pain in the butt! You have to remember, George. I know you can come out of this. Emily...you couldn't have forgotten Emily." Robert put his arm around George and stared into that face that had often frowned when he asked for some ingenious do-dad to block or send communications, detonate bombs, or intercept messages. He saw a hint of the sparkle George had in his eye when one of his inventions worked perfectly and a mission was accomplished.

"Emily...Emily. She vas in my dream. I remember Emily. She married you...ze poor sing!"

"George. Gregor. You are in there! Keep trying to remember, that will help bring you out of this. Yes, I did marry her and if we can get started, if you can trust me enough to do exactly what I say, we may be able to save her."

"Save her! Is she in trouble? Vhat kind of nonsense did you dream up now!" The fog had lifted for a moment and the old worries that haunted him whenever Bobbie revealed a "plan" began to come back into his consciousness.

"Believe it or not, it wasn't me this time. We had retired to raise our family with some level of normalcy when......" Robert took a chance that the fog had cleared enough for his friend to absorb the details of the agent's new assignment. He hoped that somehow remembering his favorite lady agent had opened a door that could lead to preventing a disaster and also to reuniting with his loved ones. So much at stake, so little time. He recalled the prayer that Emily would say with their boys as she tenderly covered them at bedtime. Though he couldn't recall the exact words he knew it was asking your own personal angel to guide you and protect you. Having very little religious background of his own Robert West, the big tough fearless agent had been sprinkled with some of Emily's faith and it had helped him see aspects of situations and people that he had never been able to see before.

After Robert had laid out the story of the black box and the dangers to the world if the formula connected with the calculations stored in the ignition chamber of the buried bombs, the doctor held his head in his hands and mumbled incoherently. Robert was afraid that he had pushed his friend over the edge with the urgency of recovering from the drugs the enemy had given him to cloud his brain. He shook his head and looked at Robert with an intensity that made his skin crawl.

"It's not only ze black box......it's ze disc. I had the disc when zhey came for me at ze arsenal. It was in my hearing aid the size of a hearing aide battery. I sink I gave it to......If they have the disc, they could......God! Bobbie! If they discover it and don't know any better, they could destroy us if the bombs are still activated. I wondered why they ordered me to keep the detonating block system intact when they had rendered the bombs inactive. We have got to..." Gregor Olmstead tried to stand and fell back on the bed. He began to tremor and soon was seizing including all parts of his body. The convulsions lasted less than thirty seconds but they were violent leaving him snoring, incontinent of urine and drooling white frothy sputum from the corner of his mouth. Robert wiped away the secretions and turned him on his side to prevent him from aspirating as he snored loudly his cheeks puffing out like a blow fish with each breath.

Robert West stood with his head swimming and panic he had never felt in his life slammed into his gut and grabbed hold of his chest. The disc......it can't be the tracking disc I put in Will's car......it just...oh, my God...if he's got the disc. If they find out......if any of the agents, terrorists or theirs or ours, knows they will have to stop at nothing to retrieve it! Will, oh Will where are you? He knew that he had to find his son, no matter what, he had to find him. He felt that his family was still alive...all of them. He had to believe it, but take action that led the terrorists to believe he thought otherwise. He also had to protect the doctor, locate the black box, and prevent a monumental disaster that would destroy all of them and millions of others. The assignment had become extremely complicated and dangerous. Systematically, he reviewed the knowns and unknowns, put himself in the mindset of the terrorists, eliminated the "rescue" part of the dilemma, and focused on fooling the enemy into believing he held the key to what they were seeking. He needed to be where the bombs were located and he needed to allow the terrorists to locate his whereabouts without raising their suspicions. Bait. To catch a hawk you needed bait. He turned toward the man snoring in post seizure stupor on the cot in the corner of the room. The dim light of morning shone through the murky window as he pulled the cords from the sagging venetian blinds and began to tie his friend's hands behind his back. His watch read 5:14 A.M.

* * *

Charlie recalled flying through the open door of the bus as it tumbled into the weeds alongside the highway. His arm was painful and he had multiple cuts and bruises but he laid on the damp ground looking up at the sky casting its night blanket aside. As he tried to collect his thoughts and orient himself to the last few horrifying minutes with screams and screeching metal echoing in his ears and the bus spinning helplessly then toppling over and over, he felt a shot of adrenalin hit his consciousness. He remembered the thud of Brenda Rivera's body as it flopped over the steering wheel and he was thrown from the bus. He remembered Casey and Will falling against him and then the crunching sound of metal bending into grotesque shapes now strewn around him. In the distance he could see flashing lights of ambulances, police cars, and fire trucks stretched like Christmas lights across the highway. He ran to the more intact portion of the bus that laid against a big tree. The top portion of the bus looked as though a huge club had hit it so hard it had collapsed almost to the floor. The smell of gasoline, wet grass, and metal stung his nostrils and he tried to peer through the jagged, twisted windows. He heard it. The same sound that Adam had heard before he passed out. A growl deep and ominous came from inside what was left of the bus. It sent shivers up Charlie's injured arm that was hanging loosely by his side. He backed away from the wreckage and looked around for a high place away from what he thought might be a mountain lion or bear. His heart beat as he desperately ran toward a tree with some low hanging branches to the right of the wreckage. A dark figure moved out of one of the openings in the bus and bounded toward Charlie's retreating, panting body. It leaped onto his back before Charlie reached the tree and the branch. He felt the claws bury into his skin and the hot breath of the animal on his neck and face. Falling to the ground, he tried instinctively to protect his face from the jaws of the beast. When Charlie turned over to try to throw the beast off of him, he saw the dazed eyes and barred teeth of his best friend. Foam sputtered from the dog's mouth and he whimpered when he saw his human's face. Charlie clung to him and tried to soothe the trembling dog rocking him in his arms and allowing him to cling to him even though his claws were daggers in his skin. In several minutes the scent of his favorite human reached his senses and Casey relaxed his death hold, released his claws from Charlie's bleeding skin and, laid in his master's arms as he buried his head into his wet fur.

"There, there, buddy. It'll be alright. You're a good dog......good dog," Charlie repeated over and over.

A short distance from where the two sat rocking back and forth, a figure laid face down on the ground. It tried to move as it gained consciousness and sensed other persons near him. Will had also been thrown clear of the tumbling Greyhound, had smashed against a nearby fence and fractured his right leg and dislocated his right shoulder. His arms and legs were cut by glass strewn across the field as he rolled helplessly toward the fence. Will could see in the dim light a figure sitting, holding something about thirty feet from where he lay. He tried to call out but little more than a squeak exited his parched aching throat. Charlie thought he heard a voice, but only looked to his left and right. Seeing no movement he continued to clutch his orphaned dog as the canines trembling gradually subsided. Then he heard something again. This time it came from the fractured portion of the bus that Casey had left. It was definitely a human groan and a weak cry for help. Casey ran ahead of Charlie who felt a little woozy when he got up to follow his dog. Casey limped, his bad leg noticeably buckling as he headed toward the bus. Charlie shook his head to try to clear the dizziness as he bent down the look into the mangled window and jagged opening of the wreckage. He saw an arm lying next to a rifle and followed it to Adam's pale bloody form.

"Please help me...p...ple..." Adam's voice was barely audible then fell silent. Charlie could see that the seat pushed against Adam's body was jammed against his ribs and he would have to turn him on his back or stomach to try to extricate him. He looked at the pool of blood surrounding Adam's head and the paleness of his skin and erratic breathing, the distance he would have to run to get help from the slowly diminishing crowd of rescue vehicles and his own inability to focus and decided he would have to get Adam out from under the vice like grip of the seat so he could breathe. Bracing himself against the metal cage that had formed from the buses collision, he slowly turned Adam until he was lying supine. Placing his hands under his shoulders using his injured arm as best he could, he pulled with all his might. Adam screamed in pain as they both fell backwards into the grass. It was daylight now and Charlie could see a couple of other bodies bent and twisted hanging from the parts of the bus and one small figure near the fence who was moving. Charlie grabbed the rifle and pulled back the loading arm to engage the bullets into the chamber and fired it into the air. The kick of the gun knocked him backwards and he crawled toward Will who had only enough strength to whisper "Charlie" before he lost consciousness.

The rescue crews had never seen anything like it when they arrived on the scene. Even with many years of being called to immense tragedies and horrific accidents had they encountered one involving so many vehicles...so many injured and twenty deaths so far. They were exhausted and had sprayed the highway covered with gasoline, oil, and blood with a sawdust-like compound to absorb the debris. They had blocked off a one mile area of highway until the clean up was complete. They heard the first shot coming from the field near the woods where the remains of the greyhound was strewn about. One of the EMTs jumped into a rescue van and headed toward the shots. He saw three figures lying on the ground still alive. One of the survivors was barely breathing and the other two were in shock with broken bones, cuts and possibly a concussion. A matted, bleary eyed dog with his one lip tucked into the side of his mouth lay next to one of the victims. He no longer looked like he was smiling.

Chapter Nineteen

Escape

It was time. Time to use their collective experience to extricate themselves from their prison. There seemed to be only one guard at night who delighted in waiting until the two women and baby captive were asleep then screaming obscenities in a foreign language which would awaken Toby and the ladies. Toby was so weak and his little bottom was scalded from the concentrated urine and dehydration. Though Emily and Kate had sacrificed most of their liquids for him, it was barely enough to keep him alive. Emily's breast milk had dried up shortly after they were captured. Though Toby's cry became weaker and weaker, Emily and even the hardened Kate awakened immediately to his sorrowful cry. Though they were weak themselves, filthy and bedraggled, they were still women and he was a man. Because he was closer to an animal than a human, it would be easier to tempt him. The women washed away what dirt they could from their faces and undressed to their underwear using the water that lay in puddles on the floor. There was just enough light from a full moon that night that one could see through the small opening in the door that the women were nearly naked. The terrorist delighted in watching them startled awake by his yelling and even a sicker delight in watching one of the women try to console the limp child back to sleep only to be awakened by his cursing and hideous laughter. This night, though, he had to take longer look as he saw the hint of breasts and long sinewy legs as he peered through the small door. He drooled a little and his loins began to feel an urgency as his testosterone began to boil at the sight of his near naked captors.

"I could handle both of the infidels in a few moments." He thought to himself as his desire pushed reason to the side. "It would be fun to watch them fight me and I will beat them until they beg me to have them." He boasted. His orders were to keep them alive, not to kill them, but if needed, could injure them. They were the bait. They needed the combination to allow the black box to release its hold on the bombs. They needed all the parts in order to have leverage to get what they wanted. Millions of dollars, all the terrorist captives released, ruling of the Middle Eastern countries, withdrawal of all foreign troupes from their part of the world, and supreme ownership of all the oil fields. The threat would constantly be their finger on the trigger of the invention of the infidels' own scientist that could end the world in a heartbeat.

The door opened and a man with a black beard and blacker eyes entered. He was about five feet ten inches tall and had a belt with a pistol and a knife hanging around his hips. Emily cowered near the bin that held her whimpering child. Kate was several feet from her feigning sleep as she laid on the cold damp floor. The man could see her breasts moving as she breathed and began to grin showing crooked yellowed teeth. He saw the smoothness of her muscular leg and began to move toward her anticipating his attack. Emily moved like a lioness on the prowl lifting the bin above her head and smashing it into the back of the salivating captor. The man reeled and lunged toward Emily. His hairy arms grabbed at her shoulder digging his fingers into her flesh. She twisted her body from his grasp and lifted her leg giving him a hard karate kick to his jaw. His head flew back as she connected and Kate wrapped the blindfold around his neck and twirled to tighten the noose. She used all her strength to fracture his windpipe. His eyes bulged from their sockets and his body seized as it gradually fell to the floor. Emily finished the attack by grabbing the piece of concrete slab that they had loosened from the wall to mark a sundial on the floor. They had gradually sharpened it into a deadly arrowhead. With the pent up anger and loathing she felt for the suffering he and his kind had put them through, she buried the arrowhead deep into his neck precisely where the carotid artery lies. They dressed quickly and grabbed the weapons from his belt and some keys, bundled the baby in a piece of his shirt they ripped from his chest and ran cautiously up the stone stairs to the outer door.

Grabbing a brown leather satchel that was lying on a table next to the door, they sprinted towards a van parked alongside the building. They scanned their surroundings with expert eyes. Once in the van they ripped out any extra wires that they knew were not needed to keep the vehicle running. The two agents scoured the van for any apparatus they thought could be used to track them, stepped on the gas, and took off through a nearby alley. They had both mapped out with a piece of coal they found in the corner of their cell the route they memorized when they were being transported. Emily wanted to stop to get formula and some supplies for her baby, but she knew they had to get as far from the warehouse as possible and had to follow an altogether different route than the one that had brought them to their prison.

"Pretty good for a semi-retired 'agee,'" Kate murmured as Emily tried to get Toby to suckle her baron breast. Emily flashed a look at her prison mate/fellow agent and returned to her motherly duties that had been so sparse in the last weeks. She felt responsible for her chosen profession with all of its dangers, and responsibility for her children and her husband. She would have never had children if she knew they might suffer because of her unbreakable ties to the agency. Her heart ached when she looked at her listless baby, pale and dehydrated, smelling of urine and feces, too weak to grab hold of her nipple even if there was little there to nourish him. "Where was Will? He was a strong, resourceful boy...but that was it, he was just a boy." She prayed he had gone to his best friend's house when she hollered for him to run. He was probably terrified that she and Toby and even his father were dead or injured. "Robert...oh, Robert...what have we done? You have to be alive. You have to find our son and bring us all together again. We will move far up into the mountains and change our names, even our identities," she promised herself as she pressed her baby closer to her aching chest.

"When we get to New Brunswick, do you think Robert will be there? The plan has changed now that there seems to be a reason they wanted to get at Olmstead, despite having the black box." Kate roused Emily from her musings as she weaved through back roads and alleys changing her route while continually heading east.

"That's probably what these guys want us to do. They want us to be pulled together so that they have one target instead of many spread out over miles. I'm sure Robert knows that they will use us for bait and it won't be long before they discover we have escaped. They are counting on one of us to weaken and try to rescue one another. As much as I want to find Robert and Will, I know we have to disappear and put together a better plan, so turn this thing south and I know a place we can hide until we get our heads together." Emily reasoned.

Kate knew that Emily was right and heading south sounded even more palatable since she still wanted to find her sister and her family. They had to be okay because she had so much time to make up for the years she had ignored them. She never was good at apologizing or even realizing she might be wrong once in a while. Her resentments toward her father expanded to the entire family and blocked any forgiveness and healing that could have occurred. Her training and years of stuffing her emotions and feelings did her well in the field, but left an empty hole in her personal life that she was thinking she needed to fill if it wasn't too late. The sun was just peaking over the horizon as the three of them in a stolen van headed southeast toward Atlanta.

Kate switched on the radio. The morning news reporter was just finishing the local news and in his deep voice began reporting a horrific accident involving multiple automobiles, a greyhound bus, and a black van on Route 95 North. There were many casualties and injuries. The injured has been life-flighted to New York General Hospital. Kate listened absentmindedly as she was busy trying to catalog some type of sense out to the events of the past few days. Emily was fighting sleep as she yawned and tried to stretch as much as she could without waking Toby.

"The police are investigating not only the accident but the weapons found in and around what was left of the black van as well as tapes and a video camera that had survived the crash," the newsman said. "It appears there was foul play as well as carelessness surrounding this tragedy. NNOS News will keep you posted."

Kate glanced over at Emily who was suddenly acutely awake. She shivered and her pulse raced as the newsman's last sentence rang in her ears.

"Among the victims were two young boys who were found thrown from the bus into a field nearby. The boys and a dog, who would not leave their side, were taken to New York General Hospital along with the other victims. When tracing the Greyhound's trip from their point of departure, it seems the two boys were unaccompanied by adults. One of the injured is reported to be William West for whom the authorities have been searching in conjunction with the explosion of his home two weeks ago and the disappearance of his parents. The other boy is Charles Peterson whose parents were tragically killed while trying to escape hurricane Helen's fury."

The van careened to the berm of the road as Kate slammed on the brakes and bent her head against the steering wheel. Toby began to whimper as Emily reached for the headlights and for Kate's arm. The radio was playing a country song about beer, bright lights, and lost love as Emily quickly switched it off. Cars and trucks zoomed by heading for work or wherever. They went unnoticed as they had landed a short distance past the berm in a field lined with low hanging weeping willow trees which hid the van from the road. No one spoke and Toby buried his head into his mother's soft breast. Kate had begun to cry; tears hot as pokers ran down her face and onto the steering wheel; tears she had held back for years discounting their usefulness—their existence. Emily knew she had to see her son, to make sure he was alive, to make sure he knew she was beside him. She was willing to leave caution to the wind to be with him. "I've sacrificed enough. I need to be with my son. He must be so frightened. What has he been through? My God, please help me do what you know is best!" She turned to Kate who had lifted her head and was wiping her nose and eyes with her sleeve. She realized they had said nothing about Jake. "Where is Jake? I've got to go to Charlie. He must be terrified and so lost if he knows Carolyn and Jes...Oh, Carolyn I am so sorry."

"So sorry..." Kate said out loud. She took a deep breath and looked at her new partner and they both knew what each other was thinking.

"Want me to drive, Kate? I'm so sorry." Emily said softly as she started to exit the van to take over.

"It's okay. I need to drive. I'm really bad at holding babies...at holding anything. I think I have a plan that might satisfy our maternal side...er. Eh...your maternal side and our 'agee' side."

Chapter Twenty

New York General Hospital

Police guards sat outside Room 576. One of the guards chewed his gum noisily while he glanced the swimsuit edition of *Sports Illustrated*. The other guard yawned and drew his pistol from his holster polishing it with a handkerchief.

"Hey, Jeff gimme that magazine. I'm getting so bored I feel like shooting something," the guard said as he holstered his weapon and blew his nose into the handkerchief.

"You'll have to fight me for it, buddy...this one is super hot!" Jeff teased. They both stood up quickly as they heard footsteps echoing into the empty hallway of the hospital. It was the chief, Chief Andrew Mortelli, one of the "old timers," the ruler of New York Precinct No. 727.

Andrew Mortelli had grown up in a tough neighborhood just on the outskirts of Brooklyn. His father was a steel worker in a factory in northern Pennsylvania. Because they were barely able to make ends meet, Drew's (his dad called him Drew) father worked double shifts at the mill and only came home on weekends. Drew's mother took in laundry for some wealthy families that lived in the new condos beginning to dot Manhattan and the suburbs. She did her best to raise her three boys without a constant male presence, but the gangs in the area became surrogate father figures for many boys who were fatherless because of the war, prison sentences, or shootings. Even though the motives and actions of the gang members were illegal, there was a sense of belonging and a structure that many kids migrated toward, despite the dangers they posed and the deathly consequences when orders were disobeyed. Drew and his brothers were drawn to the excitement, the independence, and the money the gangs seemed to provide. They didn't mind the fights, even the ones they lost, because they felt they were invincible and there would always be someone at their backs. There were no killings or big robberies among the early gangs in their area of the city. They were able to intimidate those outside there group by their numbers and the "tough guy" attitude the flaunted. Drew's father protested vehemently when he was home on the weekends so the boys made up stories as to their whereabouts, vowing to their father that they were no longer involved with the gang. Things changed radically when the "Mob" began to infiltrate the gangs and take over, using them to terrorize business owners in the area into paying for protection from the mob itself. Gang members were taught to use guns and to flex their muscles against innocent citizens. They were paid for their work which increased the incentive and buried morality under greed. Some of the gang members felt uncomfortable reigning havoc on their own family members and friends and attempted to leave the gang. That was a dangerous step and one that eventually meant moving to other parts of the city or even to another town to avoid violent beatings or even murder. Drew's middle brother, Angelo, tried to escape by hiding in his house, not even going to school or seeing any of his friends. His mother was frightened for her sons' lives and spent much of her time outside of the house looking back over her shoulder to see if she was being followed. Marcus, the youngest, thrived on the power of the gang and the fear he saw in people's eyes when he or his fellow gang members were around. His mother begged him to leave the gang and move upstate with her sister and their kids but he gradually had changed into a ruthless, unforgiving menace. Drew and he had it out one day in an alley after Marcus had robbed Mr. Pappas's delicatessen and left him bleeding on the floor of his shop from a bullet to the chest.

"What the hell are you turning into! This is not what we were taught. For God's sake, Marc,

call for help...that's Mr. Pappas, our friend in there...you...you. Marcus...we've got to get out of this gang!" Marcus punched Drew in the face and started to run but Drew recovered spitting out some blood and a tooth. Drew grabbed his brother by the collar and threw him on the damp ground. The glazed apathetic look in his little brother's eyes made him look very different from the kid who used to beg to go along with his big brother everywhere. Drew wanted to pummel some sense into him but that would have made him equally as guilty. He stood over him.

"I'm calling 911 and the cops and we're going to get out of this mess." Drew turned to run into the shop and a sudden sharp stabbing pain filled his thigh and ran down his leg. He crumpled to the ground suddenly realizing he'd been shot.

"Don't try to come after me, bro! I couldn't let you call the cops on me. Stay out of my life if you know what's good for you!" Drew tried to get up but his leg wouldn't support him. He watched his brother back out of the alley the gun dangling from his fingers like an anvil. Drew dragged himself across the ground and into the doorway of the deli. He called out.

"Pappy...it's Andrew Mortelli. I'm here to help you but I've been shot. Pappy! Can you hear me...my brother is gone...I promise I won't hurt you." He wanted to cry. He wished he had never gotten involved with the gang. He heard a groan and dragged himself around the corner of the counter. Pappy was ghastly pale and lying in a pool of blood on the floor. He groaned and a trickle of blood ran down the side of his mouth onto his cheek. Drew grabbed the cord of the telephone and pulled it down onto the floor. He was dizzy and the room was getting dark as he tried to focus on the numbers. His shaking hand dialed 9...1...1 and a lady's voice answered.

"911 emergency center. How can I help you?"

"Shot...two of us...shot...come quick Pappas's Deli on Mart..." The room started to close in and Drew lost consciousness before he could finish.

"Sir...could you repeat the address? Did you say you were shot? I have to call you back to confirm this is a true emergency call. I will call you right back. Do not leave the phone."

Nothing but the incessant drone of a busy signal reached Martha McCauley's ears, but she had this feeling the voice on the other end sounded so frightened that she rang her supervisor and he traced the call to 1480 Martin Ave. where the police and rescue teams found two men. The older man was barely alive and the other man injured badly. Andrew Mortelli was only fifteen years old. Pappy and he survived.

The shooting and robbery had taken place at 10:15 P.M. At 12:04 A.M., two figures dressed in black hooded sweatshirts and black pants doused the house at 101 Parker Street with gasoline, lit a match and watched it explode into an inferno from a car parked a half block away. Maria Mortelli and Angelo Mortelli were asphyxiated while they slept and burned to death along with some rich peoples' laundry and their humble belongings. Drew was in the operating room having the bullet from his own brother's gun removed from his thigh. He left the hospital with a limp that became a trademark for the man who vowed to make criminals pay for their crimes with every breath he took. He signed up for the police academy and double fisted his way to Captain. He became a feared cause to be reckoned with by the mob, gangs, and gangsters. Barely sleeping more than three hours a night, he was relentless and brutal. You didn't want to meet Andrew Mortelli in an alley. His brother Marcus spat on his picture whenever it appeared in the newspaper for some heroic deed or another. Somewhere deep inside the layers of apathy and menacing greed, Marcus knew his brother and he would meet again for a final round.

Captain Mortelli approached his two men guarding the hospital room. The bathing suit edition of *Sports Illustrated* was pushed under one of the chairs as Jeff and his co-guard stood at attention.

"Anyone visit or attempt to get in to see these two while you were on guard?" The Captain glared at the two guards who tried not to show they really were not completely focused on their tasks.

"Well I take it no answer is about what I expected. This isn't a vacation. These boys are in some kind of danger and it seems have been traveling alone with broken hearts and scared to death. If you can't take this assignment seriously then you can be replaced. Get me?"

Both men straightened their backs even more rigidly than when first approached by their commander. "Yes, Sir!" They spouted in unison. Captain Mortelli pushed past them and looked behind the door as he entered Charlie and Will's room. Will was still unconscious and had dislocated his left shoulder. He also had a cast on his right leg after his two lower limb bones had shattered requiring a cage of wire placed in surgery to stabilize the fractures. He was bruised and his face was swollen and a large gash in his lower lip was sewn together making him appear like an oversized raggedy Andy doll. Charlie appeared to be asleep or unconscious. He had his left arm in a cast and his right leg was in a traction set up and his left hip had been shattered and replaced with prosthesis.

"Charlie. Can you hear me, lad?" Captain Mortelli whispered in the kindest voice he could muster. "I'm Captain Mortelli from NYPD and I have to ask you a few questions if you're up to it."

Charlie opened his eyes half way. His lids were heavy and there were halos around the lights making it appear like he was in some surreal place. "Did I die? I can't move. Where am I......the bus..."

"Casey! Casey! Mom...Dad!" Who are you?" His lips and mouth were dry and his voice came out in staccato, gravely tones. He tried to hide under the covers but any movement sent knife like pains through his arms and hips.

"It's okay, son. I won't hurt you. You're in a hospital. We won't let anyone hurt you. I'm a policeman and I want to help you and your friend."

"Max...Will...Is...is he okay? I can't remember. Are the others all right? The teacher...she was trying to get away from them. I hope she isn't hurt or d..." Charlie closed his eyes and could see the panic in her eyes just as the bus began to swerve out of control. She had still tried to get it back on the road and then he remembered everything smashing around him and the screams of the other passengers just before he was ejected from the bus. "Tell me this is all a bad dream...my mom and dad, Jake...God has to help me." He pleaded.

Andrew Mortelli had put God aside when he lost his mother and brother. He still conceded there was a God, but had lost his trust in Him the anger and pain replacing all he had learned of the vastness of His plan for us that included painful human events testing our faith and our trust.

"I'm sure He is listening, son. I know how painful this has been for you. If I am to help you I need to know where you both were going and why, who was following you, and where you have been in the past two weeks. If you get too tired, I can come back tomorrow."

Charlie shook his head as his eyes filled with tears when he talked about the hurricane and the loss of his parents. He told the Captain he just had met Will who for some reason used the alias, Max, when they first encountered each other. Will had told him about the explosion and being followed by two or three men as he tried to get to New Jersey to look for his father. What Will had not shared was the mysterious disc planted in his race car and that just before the crash he had pulled the car from its hiding place in the suitcase and had put it inside the belt of his jeans. He also had not told Charlie about his suspicions that his parents were involved in some type of business that left many unanswered questions and his fear that they were in danger or even more paralyzing—captured or dead. Will had told Charlie that his little brother Toby was also missing and that no bodies had been found in the rubble of his home.

"I have a brother who didn't get into the van when we were trying to evacuate. He…he was nuts about surfing and I told mom and dad that I would try to find him. They didn't want me to go but…I…I…don't remember much after that. Jake…I need to f……" Charlie's eyes slowly closed and he drifted off into a dream world swirling with faces he had met along his journey and his mother calling him into a crooked old house for dinner, rows of bodies covered with sheets and winds howling with painful memories.

Jake…Peterson. That name sounds familiar somehow. Andrew Mortelli stared at Charlie then at Will, shook his head and moved toward the door leading to the hallway. The two guards saluted and stood erect at their posts as they watched the big Italian move toward a briefcase he had left near their chairs. Without a word to them he settled on a couch located in a waiting area a short distance from the boys' room. He typed several names into a laptop he pulled from the briefcase:

Jacob "Jake" Peterson
William Edward West
Robert West
Emily West
Tobias West
Charles Peterson
Jesse Peterson, M.D.
Carolyn Peterson, R.N.

Searching through a police program used to identify missing persons, criminals, suspects, etc., he confirmed the location of Charlie's parents, their backgrounds and close relatives, bank accounts, even their driving history and credentials. His brow crinkled as his search regarding the West family revealed only birth dates and auto license numbers. The newspaper article identifying William West as the son of Robert and Emily West and the search for him flashed across the screen. After attempting a number of search functions and entering a series of dates Jacob Peterson - MedSurg Stepdown Trauma Unit New York General Hospital - Admission date: September 8, 2002; 22:50 P.M.; air ambulance transport; major trauma; condition critical appeared along with similar information about Charlie and Will. The guards tiring of their rigid pose had assumed the "at ease" position and watched as their Captain almost dropped the computer on the floor trying to hurriedly stuff it into the briefcase as he rushed toward the nurses' station several feet from the waiting area.

"Nurse!" He spoke louder than he meant to as Marilyn Porter, R.N. was engrossed in preparing the 8:00 P.M. medications for her patients almost spilled the contents of a liquid she was measuring. She turned to look into piercing brown eyes, a black mustache and a strong somewhat scowling face.

"You scared me, sir. How can I help you?" Marilyn politely and professionally offered as she thought, *"Hmm…not a bad looking guy. I'll bet he's one of those policemen that are guarding those poor kids…no wedding ring."*

"I'm sorry, ma'am. I didn't mean to scare you. I'm Captain Mortelli from the NYPD and wonder if you could locate a patient in the Med/Surg Stepdown Trauma unit? His name is Jacob…or Jake Peterson."

I knew he was a cop. I hate when they call me ma'am. "I really need to have some identification, Sir" *I owed him one.* before I give out any information. It's the rules."

"Of course." Drew reached for his I.D. and laid it on the desk for Marilyn to see.

"Captain Mortelli. Nice picture. Are you here for those two boys in 576?" She lowered her voice and leaned over the desk. *He smells like cherry tobacco. Got nice eyes. No ring.* "They are amazingly lucky to have made it without more serious injuries or worse," She made sure the "v-neck" of her scrub top allowed a peak of her generous cleavage.

"Yes, ma'am, there it was again! They were fortunate. Ah…could you possibly locate Mr. Peterson?" He backed a short way from the desk to avoid starring at the nurse's display of wares. He had business to attend to and no time to flirt or to waste on any normal feelings. He had trained himself to focus on his career ninety percent of the time so life wouldn't break through the wall he had built around his emotions.

Marilyn sighed and picked up the desk phone. "He's probably older than he looks," she mused as she dialed the information desk. "He's in Room 1140, Captain. Just take the elevator to the first floor and the concourse to the new part of the hospital. There are double doors there with a marquis that says 'Trauma Unit'." She reported in her most sultry tone.

"Thank you, ma'am." There it was again! Before she could respond in any tone whatsoever, Captain Mortelli hurried to the elevators.

Jake Peterson had regained consciousness one week ago. He had not only survived the hurricane but also four surgeries, a concussion, hypothermia, and pneumonia. His right arm had been crushed so severely that the surgeons had been unable to save it. His muscular upper arm and youth prompted the surgical team to place an experimental electromagnetic device attached to the end points of severed muscles, tendons and nerves under the skin of the amputation site just above the elbow. The sensors in the device would eventually communicate with a prosthetic arm that was predicted to be indestructible. Multiple tests proved it to have three times the dexterity, strength, and range of motion than its human counterpart. When it was discovered, the boy had lost his parents and many attempts had been made to locate relatives to no avail, the surgeons had obtained permission from the state to perform surgery to save Jake's life. His new arm was appropriately named "Jake" in honor of its first recipient. Jake had not been given the news that his parents had been killed in the storm, nor that his brother was several floors below him recovering from his own nightmare. The press had been blocked from interviewing any of the three young men. Several salivating over a hot front page splash camped outside the hospital waiting for a break in the blockade. What a story! They could see the headlines shouting the unusual circumstances having a one in a million chance of two kids from different parts of the country pulled together by tragedy. A third boy who hadn't been identified as yet but police were pursuing his identity. His relationship with Charlie seemed to be much more than chance and their being found together more than just coincidence.

Captain Mortelli checked with the nurse guarding the entrance to the cubicles in the Trauma Unit. When he had shown all the cards in his billfold and swore on an imaginary bible that he was a cop, the nurse finally allowed him to visit for fifteen minutes. The electronic doors opened with a solemn groan into a large nurses' station surrounded by banks of computers displaying heart and arterial graphics, racks of charts and medical personnel in scrub outfits, suits, lab coats, and isolation gowns. The murmurs of their voices raised and lowered like the echoes in a conch shell mixing with the bleeps of the monitors and the pulsations of respirators added eeriness to the ambiance. Andrew Mortelli walked toward Room 12 with mixed feelings of anticipation and hesitancy. He dreaded being the one to inform Jake that his parents were gone just as he once was the recipient of similar horrifying news. He also had the feeling, perhaps because of his years in the force; that these boys were in danger. There was no concrete evidence to his suspicions, just a haunting sixth sense premonition that there was a connection between the three that posed a threat to their safety. There was a metal cabinet in front of Jake's cubicle filled with yellow gowns, masks, and gloves. A sign in bold red letters read "ISOLATION: ALL PERSONS ENTERING THIS ROOM MUST WEAR GOWN, MASK, AND GLOVES." After obeying the sign, Captain Mortelli, NYPD, stepped into a room filled with poles and monitors, a bed cradling a young man whose face was swollen and bruised. It was partially covered by a venti-mask that clouded somewhat with every exhalation. The right arm was partially missing and bandaged from just below the elbow up to the shoulder. The boy's left leg had a large pin running through the distal end of the femur and a traction device was attached to the pins in a geometric cascade of metal and wire. The bed was fashioned like a large waffle iron which allowed rotation of the entire body 360 degrees. Jake's eyes were closed and his respirations were shallow and rapid. Andrew approached the bed cautiously and laid his hand on Jake's. There was no response to the touch so Andrew leaned toward Jake's face.

"Jake...Jacob," he said softly then repeated a little louder than the first. Jake opened his eyes halfway and stared ahead as though there was nothing to see. "Jake. I am Captain Mortelli of the New York police department. I need you to listen very carefully. Can you hear me and understand me?"

"Yeh...yes," his voice was hoarse and weak, but audible. "Where am I?" Jake asked for the twentieth time that day. "The police? What did I do?" He opened his eyes and looked into Captain Mortelli's face.

"You're in New York General Hospital, Jake. You were injured in a hurricane. Do you remember the hurricane? You were trying to see the waves, maybe to surf them. It was about three weeks ago."

"I kind of remember. How are mom and dad......my brother tried to stop me...and...it is a blur from then on!"

"I need to tell you something that will upset you, I know. I want the nurse to be in here when I talk with you about this." the captain leaned out of the room and motioned to a nurse who was standing near the cubicle"

"What is it? Did something happen to my family? I've been asking but no one seems to know. I'm scared. What's happened?" Jake tried to sit up but he collapsed back onto the pillow. His left arm was restrained but the right arm was free and he raised it to try to remove the oxygen mask. When he did this he could see part of his arm was missing and he shrieked yelling "My arm...my hand...where is my hand! God, what did I do?! Where is my hand!" Tears formed in his eyes and rolled down his bruised cheeks. "What did you do with my hand?!" he sobbed and screamed at the same time. Jake had forgotten that he had lost a portion of his arm. Sedation and pain medication made it difficult for him to recall what he had already been told.

Nurses came running to the cubicle and sedatives were drawn up hastily and injected rapidly. One of the doctors came in and loudly said, "Settle down, Jake. We will tell you everything. You have to lie quietly so we can help you." Jake felt the curtain of pain lift from him in a soft flood of analgesia as the Ativan began to have its effect. He settled back on the pillow murmuring his parents' names and tossing his head from side to side.

"Jake, can you understand me?" the Captain asked. "Your parents were lost in the storm, but your brother Charlie and your dog are a few floors below us. Charlie is doing better and Casey is on constant watch at his bedside. He won't eat or drink hardly anything. He is quite a dog!" Mortelli tried to lighten the blow with a couple of positives.

"Mom and Dad are...dead? They're dead! Oh, God. It's all my fault. They would have..." Jake retreated into a sedative stupor mid sentence but the pain of losing his parents and his arm showed in tears that ran down the sides of his cheeks and the rapid heart rate bleeps on the monitor.

"We hope to get him started using his new bionic arm in physical therapy, get the pins and traction out of his leg, and get him into therapy this week." The somber physician reported. The nurses had returned to their other duties as soon the sedative took effect.

"How old is he?" Andrew asked staring at the tears and feeling helpless. The sun filtered through the tiny venetian blinds giving a staccato-like image to the three figures in the room.

"He is sixteen from the records we received from Florida General. We've not been able to locate any relatives. Both sets of grandparents are deceased. There is one sister, his mother's, we think that lives somewhere in Jersey but we haven't been able to locate her either. The address we have is false...a vacant lot in East Orange. We are kind of at a standstill unless the brother has something for us." the doctor stated.

"Charlie, Jake's brother just regained consciousness and we haven't told him about Jake. He found out about his parents shortly after the storm and it looks like he was headed to Jersey to find his Aunt when he was in the crash." Andrew shared with the doctor. "There is another boy that seemed to have been traveling with Charlie and he was headed to Jersey as well. I need to let him know his brother is here. These poor kids are orphans and also injured physically. It will be a difficult recovery for them emotionally and otherwise." "Plus, there is something really odd about the accident. The bus driver was found at the back of the bus with a head injury that seemed to have occurred before the crash and a woman was found in the driver's seat crushed by the impact of the engine moving into the cab of the bus. A black van was pinned between the bus and a truck carrying metal pipes and two guns were found inside the smashed vehicle along with two men pronounced dead at the scene. A gun was also found inside the remains of the Greyhound. It was all very suspicious. The two other survivors that were on the bus were Frank Goldman, an attorney, and Adam Kresge. Wonder if they know anything about these boys?" Captain Mortelli thanked the nurses and the doctor, hit the metal pad that opened the Trauma Unit doors and walked down the hall toward the elevators.

Chapter Twenty-One

Calling all Troops

The Ulysses Air Force Base was just responding to Taps as Emily drove the van up to the gates. A young Private with starched uniform and sober countenance exited the guard booth and stood at attention on the driver's side of the car. Emily recited a series of numbers and codes to the guard who saluted and clicked a remote hanging from his utility belt opening the gates. The van passed barracks and a large building with several flags in front billowing in the early morning breeze. A bronze replica of the world with an eagle proudly holding an olive branch glistened in the sun as it proudly marked the head-quarters of the U.S. Naval Base. The guardsman had radioed ahead that the persons in the van were here to see the Commander and that the driver had clearly identified herself as one of the highly regarded secret agents for the U.S. government. Kate awakened as the van turned into the circular drive in front of Headquarters. Toby had fallen asleep with his head snuggled into the warm soft corner of her breast. She tried to reposition him into a less "mothering" position, but he kept turning back toward her side. She couldn't dare admit to herself he felt good nestled in her arms and she was surprised that she could feel anything of the kind when a dangerous mission was presenting itself. That was her first love, she told herself. Another soldier walked up to the van and saluted as he opened the door for Emily. She had glanced at her reflection in the mirror and had attempted to straighten her disheveled hair. Vanity being the last thing on her mind at this point, she shook off the image of the dark circles under her eyes, her long matted main and unwashed skin and stepped onto the pavement. Kate had exited from the other side of the van somewhat clumsily having to relocate Toby to her shoulder. Emily came to her rescue looking into Kate's face and silently acknowledging she had found a soft spot in the tough shield Kate wore. The soldier led the trio up the glistening white stairway to two huge glass doors with the emblem of the eagle impregnated in gold. The early morning sun was a welcome change from the damp prison in the warehouse. The two women hesitated for a moment at the door to catch a few more seconds of the rays. A large half moon shaped reception desk greeted the group. The entrance rose from a glistening marble floor to a cathedral ceiling bordered by flags from every country and busts of all the United States Presidents. The domed ceiling of stained glass portrayed battle scenes from early contests as the U.S. fought for its independence and situation in the world. A female soldier was summoned to care for Toby who drowsily accommodated the hesitant release from his mother's grasp. She knew he would be bathed, fed, and checked by the medical staff, but still felt anxious and guilty. The soldier who had greeted them outside the headquarters led them to a group of elevators to the fourth floor. Oak doors with a carving of the state and federal seals opened to an office similar to the President's. Behind a massive desk, Commander Elton Howard removed a cigar from his mouth, stood and greeted Emily and Kate.

"Have a seat, ladies," he said in a gravely voice as he motioned to two leather chairs in front of the desk. Commander Howard was an impressive man, about sixty years old, over six feet tall, trim, and handsome. His graying hair gave him more prestige and his uniform with many bars of recognition for his forty years in the service was perfectly fitted to his still muscular frame. Ice blue eyes that had seen death and destruction, victory and celebration, loss and pain fixed themselves on the two disheveled women in front of him. "Would you like to shower and get something to eat before we begin this debriefing? From what I am told you both have had a harrowing week." He had moved out from behind the desk and stood in front of Emily and Kate, so close they could smell the hickory scent rising from the cigar still in his hand.

"Sir, we need to report to you what we know as we feel many lives are in danger and time is of the essence." Emily spoke for both of them. "My husband is Robert West, agent E-29, and the terrorist cell "Hatham" is trying to lure him into a trap using myself and my son as bait. My son, Will, has been missing since the detonation of our home and I believe the enemy is tracking him as well. There are some missing pieces that neither agent Caputo and I have privy to. I'm sure you are aware of Project RRX42. We have a foreboding feeling that the enemy is trying to manipulate all of us to arrive at an old arsenal in New Jersey, Sir." Showers and food seemed to pale in the urgency in her voice.

"Yes, I am aware of the magnitude of this project. I have been kept abreast of the movements of Hatham and of Mr. West and his charge. The plan to lure the enemy by leaking information on the whereabouts of Mr. West and Mr. Olmstead has been thwarted as the attention of the terrorists seems to be focused on following a signal emitted by some device now located at a hospital in New York. We have notified the local authorities that any patients having been admitted in the past three days be heavily guarded."

Emily gasped. "Will…it has to be Will. Oh, Sir. I have got to get there to see him. There was an accident on Route 95 in which two young boys were found and rushed to New York General Hospital. It might be him. What would the terrorists want with him? He's just a boy." She couldn't help herself. Lack of sleep, dehydration, the anxiety of not knowing where her loved ones were broke the courage and control she wanted to show the Commander. She sobbed. Elton Howard, the man, pushed aside the Commander part of him and leaned over Emily holding her shoulders and allowing her to break down. He straightened after a moment and handed her a handkerchief from his pocket. Kate sat at attention in her seat waiting for the flood to subside. She felt oddly touched by Emily's pain but needed to keep her wits about her.

"Ahem," Kate interjected. "When I was captured the first time there was a black box that seemed to be very important to them so I took it and was on my way to Washington to as directed when I was abducted again and taken to the warehouse where Emily here was being held. Do you think, Sir, that the box is a decoy to confuse the Hatham and what they are really looking for is with Emily's son?"

"Emily, what was your son doing just before the detonation?"

Emily had regained her composure. She straightened in her chair and apologized to the Commander who waved her breakdown away as though he had not seen it. "He was painting his new model race car when I heard the two men asking him questions and I set the detonation device. I knew I would have only a few minutes to get him, myself, and Toby away from the house. I yelled to him to run and then I ran for the woods. The two men caught up with me, but I wanted them to run after me instead of Will. He was just…painting……the model. The race car! Do you think it could be something about the race car? Bob would never have put his son in danger by planting something in his race car! He knew he was going to rescue George. He must have thought we would be out of harm's way if he was away from home. I talked to him the night before he left and he warned me that I might have to destroy our home if for some reason the terrorists would come for us. George had given Robert and me tracking discs that could be activated should we be separated for any reason. Those were specific to one another and could not be tracked by anyone outside of the three of us, and even one that could be placed in Toby. We were the only ones who knew about them…only us…and George."

Emily looked wide-eyed at Kate and then at Commander Howard.

Chapter Twenty-Two

The Eagle Turned Hawk?

George Olmstead could not move his arms or legs. They were bound and he was desperately trying to see where he was. As his consciousness cleared he realized he was in the back seat of a car. He could only see the top of the head of the person driving the car. It was daytime and he could see the sun shining in the driver side car window. He calculated that it would be about two o'clock and they would be heading east. If they were heading west the sun would be shining in the right front window, the side facing his back. Where was Bobbie? Why was he bound? Had they discovered...no...that was impossible. Bobbie is too smart for that. If he suspected anything he wouldn't have taken the chance of moving his precious charge. He would have called in the troops and George would be in a stronghold somewhere. He tried to sit up but he kept falling backwards with each attempt.

"George. Stop trying to get up. I need you to be still. I am protecting you. I have to locate the terrorists and find out where Emily and the boys are. I'm using you for bait to see if I can get them to negotiate a trade, but there will be no trade as I have agents ready to surround them. You know the drill. We've been through lots of these times together. It just never involved a wife and kids before and I look at things a little differently now."

Good old Bobbie. He sure knows how to play his cards. I should have predicted something like zis. I wonder if zey have picked up my signal. Zey promised me Emily and the boys would not be involved. I should have known ze agency couldn't be trusted to keep their word. George said to himself. A large gray cloud covered the sun as the car seemed to turn off of concrete onto a dirt road. The car rumbled over gravel and stones enveloping it in a cloud of dust. After several minutes the car went up an incline and stopped in an area surrounded by trees. Robert got out of the car, patted the revolver on his belt, and opened the back door. He untied the ropes around George's ankles and pulled him out of the back seat. George leaned against car staring at his friend.

"George, here's the plan. When the terrorists see that I have you, they might start shooting. I know they don't want to lose you and what you know so I'm going to have to put you in front of me. I want you to know I won't let anything happen to you. There are guys in the woods all around here and they are waiting for my signal as soon as I find out about Emily and the kids." George didn't respond, he just stared at his friend. Just then a black car could be seen coming down the same road they had just traveled. They could see the dust envelope the car as it sped along.

"Just tell me one sing, Bobbie. Does ze Eagle fly or is it caught in ze hawks talons?"

Robert West just smiled and answered

"What do you think, George?"

The black car was covered in road dust as three men stepped out of the car. One of the men with dark glasses a scar across his cheek and a deep penetrating voice spoke loud enough for Robert and George to hear from a distance of approximately thirty feet away, "What is your business with us?"

"I have the package you were searching for, but I must know where my wife and children are before I can deliver it." Robert's voice was firm and steady.

"I do not know what you speak. I have no knowledge of your wife and children."

"Do you think I am a fool? You visited my house before it was demolished. I know you have knowledge of my wife and boys. I demand to know now or you will never have the answers you so desperately need!" Robert moved closer to the group of men and the car keeping George in front of him. The sun broke through the clouds and was filtered in tiny petals of light on the ground between them.

"Your wife and son are dead. You have nothing to bargain with as we have the black box. We have no need of your friend's knowledge nor of you!" The two men on either side of him raised their guns taking aim at Robert and George.

"Wait! Wait! The black box is not good wisout the disc." George shouted, beads of sweat forming under his thinning gray hair. "You will not be able to do anysing!" the German accent becoming more evident as he shouted at them.

The man with the sunglasses motioned to his two gunman to lower their guns and walked slowly up to George and Robert. He removed his sunglasses and glared at the German scientist with contempt, his eyes burning into George's that were glaring back. "Where is the disc?"

"What disc. George?" Robert spun him around ignoring the man who was also asking the same question. George just looked at his friend with a blank stare as though he could see through him. He whispered in his friend's ear. "What disc are you talking about? The one that you gave me for Will?

You put my son in jeopardy for these maniacs?" Robert whispered with desperation in his voice and dug his fingers into George's arm. He shouted to the terrorists, "You better be wrong about my wife and child or I will hunt you down to the ends of the earth." The two gunman were unable to get a good aim at Robert as the man they wanted was standing directly in front of him. Robert put his arm in the air signaling the agents to come out of the woods. He turned and grabbed George and shoved him in his car as the three men yelled obscenities in another language. He drove down the small hill and onto the dirt road at high speed, the dust billowing behind him.

* * *

"Will...Will! You've got to wake up and talk to me. It's Charlie. We're at a hospital and there are guards outside our room. C'mon, wake up, buddy." Casey heard Charlie's forced whisper and limped over to his master's bed. He pushed on Will's hand that was dangling over the bed and began to lick the healing scratches on the back of it. Will felt the dog's prodding and together with Charlie's insistent call he opened his eyes.

"Charlie. The bus. My suitcase! Where is it?" Will tried to sit up but dizziness and a pounding headache forced his head right back on the pillow.

"Geesh! You almost died and all you care about is that stupid suitcase? What is with that thing?" Charlie looked disgusted.

"Sorry, Charlie. I don't think I know myself, but there is something in there that someone wants real bad. I think it has something to do with my mom and dad. I think they were spies at one time...or are now...I don't know. My head hurts and I can't even think anymore."

"Okay. I'll ring for the nurse. You look kind of pale. I didn't mean to get you all riled up." Charlie ruffled Casey's ears and Casey gave a small "woof" of approval.

"I see Casey made it. What happened? I remember going in my suitcase to get my...something and the next thing I knew I was airborne. Must have hit something big and hard. Everything went black then." He felt around the bed for his race car not expecting to ever see it again. What were the chances that it had stayed under the belt of his jeans? He looked under the covers and could see the blue pajama bottoms only—no jeans. He looked on the bedside table and on Charlie's bed and table next to his, but no race car. Maybe it was a good thing, he thought. It seemed like it was the only way he could be followed. Maybe it was what those men were looking for. He was pretty sure he had experienced more adventure than most boys his age. All he wanted was to find his parents and brother and get a home. He never would complain about trimming hedges or mowing the grass. Never.

A young nurse dressed in a blue scrub outfit and a much too large lab coat came in to the room to answer Charlie's call light. "Your call light is on. How can I help you?" she offered cheerily.

"He," pointing to Will. "His head..."

Will took over "Can I have a pain pill, my head hurts right here," pointing to the right side of his head where there was a large sutured wound with tiny dark hairs sprouting along the shaved areas.

"I'm sure it's painful. You were so lucky being thrown that long distance from the bus. We think you hit a tree because you were lying near one that had blood…sorry, a little too descriptive," the nurse caught the rolling of eyes from the two boys. "On a scale of one to ten, ten being the worst, would you say your pain is feeling?" Her smile was like a warm blanket that made Charlie and Will feel a little more at ease.

"Ah…maybe seven. Yah, seven. Um, was there stuff found at the crash. Like a suitcase or a pillow case with…Um, clothes and stuff?" Will braced himself for a "no." He couldn't imagine much of anything survived from what he could recall; the awful sound of metal tearing apart and the screams of the passengers.

"I think there were a few things. Most of them were pretty damaged. I think the police have some things. Is there something particular you were looking for?" She smiled again. They weren't too sick to appreciate a pretty girl's smile.

"I had two pillow cases and a duffel bag. One of them had a container with my p…p…parents' ashes." Charlie choked on those last words, still feeling the ache in his chest and blinking back tears stinging his eyes.

"I'm so sorry about your folks, Charlie. I will ask Captain Mortelli if he knows what was rescued." She touched his shoulder the same way his mother used to when she wanted to console him.

Will didn't feel right asking about his meager stuff when there was something much more important that Charlie needed. "Nothing now, ma'am. Thanks," he said looking at his hands and bending down to get a petting fix from Casey. Casey had limped over to his area where the nurses had purchased the most amazing dog pillow. It was thick and covered with this fuzzy stuff that cuddled him when he would plop in to sleep. There were rubber bones and pull toys, a dish of yummy canned dog food, and a water bowl that was freshened many times a day. He got oodles of cuddling and petting from the humans that sounded a lot like a human he remembered holding him when he was a pup. He snorted and scratched that place behind his ears he could barely reach, licked his poor injured leg and picked up one of the toys to take back to his post between his master's bed and that other human who he was getting to feel really responsible to protect.

The nurse had exited and came back with a pill tray which Will downed gratefully. He looked down at Casey who whimpered obviously expecting something for himself when he saw Will appeared to be eating. Casey was drooling expectantly and had dropped his toy on the floor next to the bed.

Charlie was about to tell the nurse that Will had some belongings he lost in the accident when Will interrupted, "Holy geepers! Charlie! Casey had the race car…good boy! Wow—what a dog! You're the best!" Will almost fell off the bed as he grabbed hold of the part of Casey he could reach. The room started to spin as he rolled back into bed and the color drained from his cheeks. His head was pounding. Casey sniffed and snorted as he surveyed the floor for one of those treats he was getting regularly when he heard "good dog."

"A race car?" Charlie puzzled. "That's what was so important in your suitcase? Looks pretty beat up. Doesn't look like anything anyone would shoot at you and follow you for." The nurse glanced at the car uninterestedly and checked Will's wristband at the same time handing him two white pills from a small pill holder.

"William West?" she asked. Will was clutching the car which was no longer red and had multiple teeth marks imbedded in what was left of the chassis. The frame was bent and it had only one wheel left dangling from loose connection to the wheel bar.

"Yes, ma'am," Will answered. He took the pills and told Charlie and Casey he wanted to sleep. He would talk more in the morning. He covered part of his head with the sheet as Charlie went to his bed and Casey found a place between the beds to sleep sentinel style. Will peered inside the bent chassis of his mysterious car and saw that the disc was still there. It did not glow or make its buzzing vibrations, but it was still was there hidden in the base of the car as though it had always belonged there. Will had this feeling that it was the one connection to his father and mother that he needed to guard and keep with him. He didn't know why. The pills were starting to take effect as he drifted off to sleep. Casey groaned and kept his eyes half open always ready to protect his two humans.

Captain Mortelli walked from the elevator towards Room 576. One of the guards jumped up from his catnap as he heard the chief's footsteps. He noticed that Stan wasn't at his post and he moved his eyes back and forth while keeping his head rigidly at attention to see if he could find him.

"Where is the other guard, mister?" Mortelli stood facing his subordinate within a few inches of his face. Jeff felt the flush rise above his collar and small beads of sweat prickle his forehead.

"Sir. I do not know where he is, sir."

"That's not good enough, son. Your job was to guard this room and these kids until you were relieved by the next crew. I don't see a next crew and I don't see two guards." Mortelli's face was getting red and so was the lone guard's for different reasons. Jeff knew he messed up by dozing off. Mortelli was trying to piece together the few pieces of a puzzle he suspected had many missing. His gut feeling was that the West kid was trying to find his missing parents and was being followed by someone who wanted to find them too. When he had entered the list of names into the computer, the news story of several weeks before of the explosion and missing West family flashed across the screen. Mortelli had been involved in a big drug bust during the days when the story had aired on national TV for a short time and then was downsized to local coverage in the Ohio area. After two weeks it had lost its sensational charisma appearing in the second section, last page of the city newspapers. Andrew had volunteered to head the bust on a tip that his brother, Marcus might be involved. He had never forgiven his brother for the fire and the murder of their mother and Angelo. He ordered the trembling guard to remain at his post. Mortelli phoned the precinct and reported the missing guard, made arrangements for the next crew to come to the hospital. He also requested a squad car and two officers to track down the missing guard. After hanging up the phone he scowled at Jeff as he passed him and told him to stay put until the next crew arrived. He ordered him to join the two officers in the search for Stan.

The wheels in his brain continued to spin as he approached Charlie's bed and proceeded to tell him about his brother. Andrew Mortelli glanced at Will sleeping after his headache responded to the pain pills and he made sure the mysterious car was tucked away into his bedside stand wrapped in a plastic hospital bag.

"Jake! Oh, God. Jake is here in the same hospital! Will, wake up...he's alive. Officer Mortelli just came and told me Jake was here and was in physical therapy. They just moved him out of the trauma unit to a rehab floor. He made it through the hurricane! My brother...he...he lost part of his arm, but they think they can give him an artificial one. I gotta go and see him! I can't believe that crazy brother of mine survived that monster. Wow!" Charlie was shaking Will and Casey was barking when the morning nurse came swishing in her nylons playing music as her knees rubbed against one another. She was the perfect example of the starched nurse of long ago. Starched white uniform buttoned up to her chin, polished white nurses' shoes, not tennis shoes like those young nurses disrespectfully wore, and a cap pinned to her hair identifying the school from which she graduated. Ms. Cratchet (the boys had renamed her) stood for no nonsense in her ward. These boys were getting a little too rowdy and that dog! It was very irregular to have any sort of an animal in the patient ward, especially one that barks and sheds.

"That will be enough noise, boys." She demanded. "This is a hospital, not a playground. If you are feeling that good, you can take your own baths."

"Nurse Crat...er Nurse Manion, I just found out my brother is a patient here. He's up in the rehab unit. I need to see him. We lost our mom and dad in the hurricane and he almost was lost too. Please, can we go see him or see if he can come see us? Please?" Charlie knew that reminding Nurse Manion he and his brother were orphans would do the trick.

"If you settle down, take your baths, and eat all your lunch, I will see what I can do to get him down here. You are under police guard so he will have to come here." Her voice had softened and she looked less like a Sergeant then she did when she came into the room.

"Will! What are the chances that I would find Jake......Here in the same place? I think I know what mom and dad taught us that God has ways of taking care of us, no matter what happens, as long as we trust Him. I know he will help you find your parents and brother. I know it. I feel it."

Will believed. He really did. He tried to push away the foreboding feeling that something awful was about to happen. The pain medicine clouded the feeling somewhat. Still, the ache in his stomach continued to haunt him.

"I have to get out of here, Charlie," he whispered. "Something tells me that I have to get to Jersey and find them. That is the last place I heard my dad was going on a business trip. I think it was dangerous business and there is a reason why those guys were following me." Will looked so anxious and weary. Charlie watched him look around the room as though he expected a demon to jump out and attack him. "After Jake comes to see you......I...I have a plan to get past the guards and..."

Miss Manion swished into the room with a petulant Nurses' Aide trailing behind. Both had trays of food. It was 12:30 P.M. As she unveiled the over-cooked Salisbury steak, peas, and mashed potatoes with a watery gravy, gestured to the aide to leave the room, she winked at the boys. This was so out of character, the two boys glanced at each other wondering if somehow Nurse "Cratchet" had overheard them.

Chapter Twenty-Three

The Puzzle Takes Shape

Robert West entered the ramp leading to Highway 95. George Olmstead sat staring out the tinted windows lost in a vision of Emily being attacked by a hawk. The dream haunted him especially now that Bobbie suspected him of treason. *If I only knew. I can't tell him that I think there is someone whom we both trust entrenched with the terrorists. He wouldn't believe me anyway.* George closed his eyes trying to block out his thoughts. Robert glanced in the rearview mirror at his longtime friend whose head was bent toward his chest in the pretense of sleep. Robert had phoned in a code to headquarters so they could pick up the signal from the tracking device embedded in the tissue under his skin; the tracking device invented by the man who sat bound in the back seat of the car. He was so confused. Had George been brainwashed by the terrorists to become one of them at the expense of his family? Robert just could not believe his friend would be capable of such a demonic act. Had the terrorists drugged him to the point that he could be deluded into believing he was acting rationally? They were capable of all kinds of intricate schemes. Lives lost, even their own, meant little to them as long as the cause or mission was accomplished. He had to believe that his sons and Emily were still alive. His life would be unimaginable without them. He had come to know a very different side of Emily in the years since the boys were born. The steel armor was still part of the agent part of her, but it had been covered by a lace gown; a gentle, caring Emily. You could still see the armor through the weave of the new fabric, but it had become less visible as her nurturing knitted a more feminine design. If she was able to he knew she would be headed toward a predetermined rendezvous in Jersey. They had their orders. They had been told that there was a plot by the Hatham terrorist group to gain access to a fail-safe system locking the detonation portals of buried nuclear bombs at an old army base. At first, the intelligence sector chuckled as a report on file stated the bombs had been rendered inert almost a year ago. Two agents were sent to verify the system had truly been deactivated. They met with an ambush by the terrorists who seemed to have access to movements within the agency. Before one of the agents succumbed to his wounds, he managed to get a message to headquarters that read "Bombs alive." Security was tightened at headquarters and a leak was found via a computer tech that had been planted within the agency. All the security screenings and background checks had not raised any suspicion that this tech was the enemy. The President alone was made aware of the dangerous situation and a team of top agents was called in to devise a plan. The scientist who had devised the intricate system of geometric and numeric sequencing to hold the detonation chamber in check had been placed in a private sanitarium in up-state New York under tight round the clock security. His co-workers had noticed his memory lapses and questionable decisions increase over the past year. He was relieved of his duties and the details of the monitoring system locked in a vault in Washington, D.C. Though the top officials in the agency felt the security system was no longer needed under the false assumption the bombs had been rendered inert, a Commander at one of the active naval bases urged the agency to keep the detonation hold process activated. He was praised by the agency and the President for his foresight and his security status upgraded. When it was discovered that George was being drugged by the terrorist aide at the sanitarium, Robert and Emily were ordered to come back into active service. Searching through piles of notes and tapes found at George's home revealed the importance of a black box. It held calculations coinciding with computerized sequences if matched by a formula effecting their randomization. The randomization could be halted in two ways. The alignment of the formulas between the black box and a computer could be typed in manually or a disc could be placed in a designated place within the black box that would align the two devices Activation of the denotation chamber would take one hour. If the detonation prongs were married to the bomb's housing it would detonate two bombs. The power had been enhanced four times their original destructive power. The United States, parts of Canada, and Mexico would be engulfed in atomic destruction and the fallout could travel for thousands of miles destroying and effecting wildlife, plant life and human life for years to come. The missing pieces of the puzzle were that there appeared to be more than one black box; exact duplicates randomly displaying sequences of numbers and geometric icons. How did the terrorists know the whereabouts of agents when their tracking devices could only be accessed by top officials of the agency in Washington? Who was aware that there was more than one to cause the two sequencing systems to line up causing the lockup of the detonation chamber to abort? It was decided that only Dr. Olmstead held that key. He had to be personally monitored by someone he trusted and kept in hiding until his mind cleared. Physicians and scientists had examined the composition of the medication the aide had been giving George. They concluded with time and a few drops of antidote each day in a beverage the effects could be reversed. The President himself had requested the Wests be put back into active duty. Because everyone in the agency could be suspect, the President and one of his trusted advisers met with the Wests to devise a plan. Robert was to abduct George from the sanitarium and secure him until Emily could get her boys to a safe location where they would be guarded twenty four hours a day. A second agent, Kate Caputo, would be assigned to retrieve the black box from the terrorists who were hiding out in a motel. Kate would act as a double agent. She would go to Philadelphia and arrange a meeting of the terrorist leader, General Talyasi, Robert West, Dr. Olmstead, and Commander of Navy Intelligence to discuss the terrorist demands. She would lead them to believe she would assist in determining if the black box they possessed was the actual one or a decoy. Kate was informed that she was being placed in extreme danger and her ruse might be discovered by the terrorists. She thrived on danger though she still would go to any lengths to stay alive. "Not quite ready to cash it in" was her favorite saying. Kate knew of Emily but was not told of her part in the plan. All she knew was she was to rescue the black box and take to headquarters in Washington, D.C. Emily was key in the triple decoy plan. She knew when the enemy found out Robert was guarding the key person to solve the black box puzzle they would attempt to abduct her and use her to draw Robert into their clutches. She and Robert, with George's help, had installed a detonation device behind the fuse box in their home. Never thinking they would have to use it to make it appear they had been annihilated, they almost forgot it existed. Robert would take assignments with little intrigue and minimal danger out of town and secretly attend camps for weaponry, computer, and device utilization training, while Emily tended the children. She worked out every day and practiced her weaponry skills under the guise of a Karate class at a private club set up by the agency. There was no way to project that Robert would be called to abduct George before Emily had a chance to secure her children. That was what had caused the animated discussion and tearful send off the night before Robert left the Will had overheard. Robert had hidden what he believed to be a tracking disc George had given him in the frame of the race car he and his son had worked on the night he received the call to invoke project RRX42 at once. Robert knew that Will would take the race car with him as he was so thrilled when they shared that time together. He urged Emily to take the boys to the secure site the next day. If he could have changed things, he certainly would have but both of them knew that time was of the essence and his protection of their friend was essential not only for his safety but for that of the entire country. Robert and Emily were under the assumption the disc they were given was a tracking disc not the one that could halt a disaster.

George had not taken the pills that the errant aide had given him in the sanitarium. He was a genius not only technically but also had developed expertise in undercover maneuvers. He was an exceptional actor and commanded seven languages. After overhearing the aide having a conversation in another language, he knew he needed to contact Robert. During World War II, George had been a dual agent posing as an SS Commandant while spying for the American intelligence in Germany. He had realized that someone was attempting to take over his mind while he was in the process refining the fail-safe interactions of the detonation arresting system. Originally, the plan was to use it on warships and unmanned jets during peacetime to be placed on the ships and planes. The weapons on these vehicles could only be detonated by the U.S. military. Should they fall into enemy hands, the weapons would be useless. George had tested it on the bombs located near his lab at Raritan under the assumption the bombs were no longer able to be activated. When he received orders to keep the detonating block apparatus running, he was puzzled.

Headaches and blurred vision led him to believe that somehow he was being drugged. He embellished the symptoms with his acting prowess, knowing the government would do anything to protect him and he would be removed from duty. He gave the two tracking discs to Robert before he was taken to the sanitarium. George told his friend that they were for his two boys should he ever need them. George felt the discs would be safe with Robert and Emily as they were committed to remain inactive with the agency. He had seen over the last twelve years how both of his friends had become domesticated and totally enamored with their boys and their new life. Though they never could fully retire from the agency and they still kept fit and honed their skills, they had settled into a life much different from when they had met. George knew the discs were critical to the detonating system. Placed in a well hidden portal deep inside the intricate wiring of the black box, the disc allowed the randomization to connect and five sequences would fall into place to unlock the detonating device. Under the assumption that the bombs were inert, he also felt the discs would not pose danger for Emily and Robert. The discs also had the capacity to act as a tracking device when in the "on" position. When held by a human hand the disc would activate and would send out its tracking waves at ninety two degrees. The only way the disc could communicate with the detonation chamber sequencing is if it was placed into the appropriate area of the black box.

The pieces of the puzzle were beginning to fall into place. Missing were the whereabouts of Robert's son, Emily, Toby and the most frightening—someone with power was assisting the enemy in their quest to hold the United States hostage to accommodate their demands. Will had the disc. George was becoming increasingly suspicious that the bombs were alive. He could not trust anyone, even Robert. Robert was suspicious of George's intentions. Kate was focused on retrieving the black box though the other part of her that had surfaced through Emily and her time together was driven to locate her nephews. Emily and Kate were at the Air Force Base being debriefed by Commander Howard.

Jamie, the social worker who had helped Will when he was at the shelter, had been released from the hospital. After hearing the news of the crash and that two boys, one of them, William West, had survived, Jamie caught the first train out of Circleville to New Jersey. He not only was fearful for Will's safety but also wanted revenge for his having been shot and for the plate in his skull that gave him violent headaches. An odd phenomenon occurred when the headaches escalated. During the siege he could perform intricate calculations and advanced deductive reasoning that amazed himself and all the physicians at the hospital. Advanced calculus and intricate formulas were like first grade arithmetic to him. When Jamie left the hospital he kissed Maria good-bye. She had been at his side since the shooting almost every day. The tragedy had opened the door to the love they had put aside for so long. Maria begged Jamie not to go as she felt it was too soon after leaving the hospital rehabilitation program but Jamie convinced her that it was something he had to do.

It was 12:30 P.M. on Saturday, September 27 when Robert and George drove onto Interstate 95 headed toward New Brunswick. There were two black boxes. One was in a vault in Washington, D.C. The other was in the hands of the terrorists. Both boxes continued to list alphanumeric and geometric groups sequentially. Only one of the boxes would respond to the disc to deactivate the detonation chamber inhibitor. Only one person knew the difference between the boxes and that person also knew where the disc needed to be inserted. The terrorists were getting desperate as they were ordered to obtain the release of prisoners at four locations throughout the world at any cost and to demand a bounty for all the time their comrades were imprisoned. They knew their lives were of no consequence but their families would also be massacred should they fail. Under the assumption they had the only black box and surmising that Dr. Olmstead had the disc needed to complete their objective, they would find all of them, obtain the disc, and inform those in power that they held the reigns of the most devastating disaster in history of mankind.

"Bobbie. You haz to believe me that I would never hurt you or your family. You know me. I have been loyal to ziz country all these years, even during ze war. Let me help you find Emily and your boys. If Will has the tracking device und you received a zignal two veeks ago after ze explosion you know it vas vorking. There are two discs zat I gave you. Who has the other von? The lives of all of us and ze rest of ze vorld depends on locating zos discs." George had decided that if there was anyone he needed to trust at this moment it was Robert West. He leaned forward looking into the rear view mirror as he spoke. Robert saw the look of pain and passion in his eyes. He wanted more than anything to trust his old friend.

"What I can't understand is why you would give these discs to me for my boys when you knew they were a potential dangerous commodity? I'm not sure what they are so damned important except they have something to do with those old buried bombs at Raritan. I was to eventually take you back there hoping your mind would clear and this mystery could be solved." Robert glanced at the speedometer which read ninety miles per hour. He eased off the pedal and glanced once again in the mirror at his friend.

"It is complicated." George decided to trust Robert with what he knew or surmised. "There are zeez black boxes, two of zem. Years ago, while ze bombs were still active, I vas ordered by upper level command to create a fail-safe ziztem that would arrest ze detonation chamber until ze agency could render ze bombs inactive. One year after ze order vas given I had developed a mathematical system zat vould do just zat. Two veeks after ze system vas in place I found zat zer vas a million to von chance dat de seqvences would line up and ze detonation zyztem vould activate. I knew it vould be only von more veek until ze agency vould deactivate ze bombs but I vas still apprehensive, zo I programmed one of ze tracking discs to eliminate ze defect and anozer if placed next to ze original disc would magnitize ze system and line up ze calculations to detonate ze bombs. I made copies of ze detonating discs as I was becoming paranoid and finding it difficult to zinc. Zat is ven I suspected I vas being drugged. To be safe I gave von of ze discs to ze President and ze ozer to you. I vas sure ze whole system vould no longer be needed by ze next veek. I feigned being more addled then I really vas zo zat I vould be taken avay from ze arsenal where I felt somevon vas drugging me. Ven I vas at ze sanitarium und overheard ze aide talking in Arabic I realized I vas not safe there either. Zo I contacted ze agency und you ver sent to rescue me. I had to keep acting as zo I vas still demented even wis you. I do not know vat is going on except I suspect zat ze terrorists believe ze system is still active und zat is why day vant ze disc und me so desperately. Bobbie, I think ze bombs are still active und zat someone wis power is moving ze enemy into place to facilitate their leverage. Bobbie...I...I enhanced ze bombs potential inadvertently ven I vas vorking on de zystem...it is four times more powerful zen it vas. I sent a confidential urgent message to ze President. I vas taken to ze sanitarium und I...I didn't receive confirmation he received it. I am zo frightened it might have been intercepted und ze disc ze President has is a fake." The usually calm, unemotional scientist was perspiring and the color had drained from his face.

Robert pulled off the expressway into a gas station. He got out of the car and moved to the back seat with a knife he had taken from a concealed holder attached to his calf. George looked at Bobbie's face contorted into a half smile. In that moment George shivered regretting everything he had just said. Robert West held the blade as it reflected the early afternoon sun into his eyes.

* * *

Emily and Kate were given clean clothes, new weapons, showers, and new orders. They were to personally accompany the Commander and two airmen to the arsenal in New Jersey. There had been a change in Project RRX42 as Robert West had been tracked heading north on Route 95 with "precious cargo." Will had been located at a hospital in New York and Emily was told she would be reunited with her son as soon as the terrorists were captured. Kate had an odd feeling, a gut feeling, about the change in plans as the importance of locating the black box had dropped off the radar. Perhaps the agency were sure the enemy would be following Robert and whomever it was so important to them. That wouldn't explain why she would be headed toward the arsenal as she would be utilized more efficiently in the field attempting to locate the terrorists and the box before they caught up with Robert. Kate's gut feeling had saved her from disaster in the past. It had occasionally gotten her into situations that were difficult to escape, but all in all it was her best detection device. She left Emily who was playfully bouncing a refreshed Toby on her knee. Obviously she was not questioning the changes. The "mom" has taken over. Kate looked at the two laughing together and decided she was on her own.

"Hey, Kate. Don't you think it's odd Commander Howard would risk going to Raritan himself? Maybe the President told him he should, but I have a weird feeling about this whole thing, don't you?"

"At a girl! Guess I was wrong about you again, agee." Kate thought to herself. "You bet something smells about this whole project. I think there is much more to it than they are telling us. I'm going to get out of here while the getting is good and go after those guys. You need to stick with this Howard dude to see what he is up to."

"Kate that would be going against orders. I can't let you do that. Let me go. This is my very last mission ever. They never completely retire or fire anyone, but I would be off duty permanently, which suits me just fine."

"Emily, listen. The bad guys are following your husband. They would so love to have both of you in the same grasp if you get captured. The only guys that know me are blown up in a motel. Let me take this one. You might have the more dangerous job...I don't know. You've got a chance to unite with Will. Take it." Kate said as she began to put her hair into an ensign's cap, took off her bra and wrapped her ample bosom tightly with a towel. She put men's fatigues over her own slacks and shirt and adjusted a belt so that her hips seemed to disappear into her waist. When they were showering and changing in the locker room, she borrowed men's garb and boots from the adjoining male locker room. When Commander Howard was debriefing them he was interrupted by two phone calls. That would not ordinarily happen as all calls would be held unless the secretary would find it urgent and she would have come into the room to ask the Commander to take a call in her office. No calls would have been going in or out of the office due to the sensitivity of any upper echelon issues, especially during a debriefing. That, together with a radical change in the plan for no obvious reason began to seep into the agent's gut and made her suspicious. Kate ruffled the blond curls on Toby's head as she winked at Emily and climbed into a towel bin sitting near the door of the locker room. She made herself as small as she could and covered herself with the towels that smelled like a mix of body odor and perfumed soap. Kind of a nauseating combination plus they were damp. She had been in worse spaces so she waited until the evening crew arrived to clean the locker rooms. The cart moved slowly along the cement floor. Kate could feel when her vehicle made a turn to the right and the sounds of the laundry area came closer. The laundry was a large room at the far east corner of the base. The ceiling was high as large conveyors picked up the laundry carts and moved them to large vats containing boiling water and bleach where the automated system would empty the carts, replace the liners with fresh ones and return the carts to a holding area. The only attendants were stationed at the front of the line to make sure the carts were positioned appropriately for the metal claws that lifted them on to the conveyor. Kate knew the only way to get out without being noticed would be when the cart was tipping its contents into the steaming washer vats. If she could hang on to the cart until it righted itself she could exit before it traveled down the ramp to the holding area. There had to be two fire exit doors at the back of the building. With any luck they would be unguarded and she could get out to one of the jeeps belonging to the laundry staff. They always left the jeeps unlocked and keys in the ignitions in case of a drill or an actual disaster it wouldn't matter who's jeep you were in you could get going immediately. That was a rule she hoped was still enforced. "JR" stood for "jeep ready," not the oil villain on the TV. She felt the hamper jerk as it was lifted up to the conveyor suspended from the ceiling. The whirring sound of the greasy metal pulleys covered up her pounding heart.

"Timing, Kate old girl...don't need to be cooked like a lobster!" She grabbed the material on either side of her and pressed her feet against the thin bar holding the material in place. The ride grew hotter and hotter as the hamper came closer to the vats. Steam surrounding her hiding place made it difficult to breathe through her nose, but she knew she had to as breathing through her mouth would make remaining conscious more difficult. She could hear the bubbling of the ominous vats below her as the hamper tilted forward and the towels began to fall into the inferno. The towels had acted as a slight barrier from the burning steam. Kate's face and eyes watered profusely as the cloud of hot air attacked her face and lungs. She took short breaths pursing her lips. The tops of her hands burned and ached as she clutched desperately to the bottom of the hamper. The pressure of her body pushed against the metal bar as she curled her toes digging into the bottom of her man boots in a vain attempt to hang on until the emptying process allowed the hamper to go back along the conveyor. She stared into the boiling water about fifteen feet below her. She did something in that few seconds hanging there that she had not done since she was a child...she prayed. She prayed to die before she hit the water; she promised that she would be a better person if He would get her out of this. Just before the lack of oxygen and build-up of carbon dioxide from her shallow breathing caused her to faint; just as she was losing her grip on the damp cloth at the bottom of the hamper it flipped her back with a bang. She lay limply in her empty cave, looked up at the windows surrounding the ceiling and said, "Thanks, God...Jesus...angels...all of you!" One errant towel was stuck underneath her and she used it to wipe her crimson sweat drenched face. It smelled musty with a hint of perfumed soap. At that moment it was the greatest smell in the world. The hamper slid down onto a platform. Before another hamper dropped off the conveyor to bump hers onto the ramp, she peeked through a small opening where the hamper was attached to the rail and could see no guards or workers. There was a fire door several feet from the platform and she jumped from the hamper onto the floor. Her legs were rubbery and her vision was blurred as she ran to the exit door. The cool air felt amazing at first as she moved against the cool cement wall toward the parking area and her means of escape. Her damp clothes soon responded to the change in temperature and she shivered as they clung to her flesh. It was 5:15 P.M. when she climbed into one of the jeeps and saw with relief that the keys were still in the ignition. Slowly driving past the hospital, the barracks, the commissary, and Headquarters she glanced over as the golden monument of the world with the staunch eagle holding the olive branch glistened in the late afternoon sun. She passed the drowsy guard who saluted halfheartedly as she headed north toward New Jersey.

Chapter Twenty-Four

The Rendezvous

Jake almost tripped over the foot pedals of the wheelchair Nurse Manion pushed passed the guards in front of Room 576 and into Charlie, Will, and Casey's room. Charlie leaped out of bed to meet his brother who almost ran despite the brace on his left leg to grab his brother in a bear hug like the ones guys give after a touchdown or winning the championship. They had both beaten the most fearsome opponents of all. They had beaten death and loss and fear. Casey danced around the two boys wagging his tail, smiling his goofy grin, and barking to the dismay of Nurse Manion. They both parted and looked at each other as the unspoken knowledge hit home that they were the only ones left of their family. Jake bent down to rub Casey's ears with his remaining hand.

"Hey, boy. I hear you're a hero. What a dog!" He straightened up and looked at Charlie. "I shouldn't have left. It's my fault Mom and Dad are...I was stupid and crazy. What was I thinking? Had to prove I was the big *kahuna*. I'm so sorry, Charlie." Charlie looked at Jake's bandaged arm and missing forearm and hand. He could have agreed with Jake's blaming himself but it wouldn't bring his parents back and they needed to stick together. They both had lost but Charlie had both his hands. They both had been spared a brush with death more than once.

"It's done, Jake. You and me...that's it...you and me. Yeah, and you too, boy." Casey panted and drooled sitting on his haunches between them seeming to understand his humans needed him.

Jake noticed Will sitting in a chair next to his bed trying very hard to be as invisible as possible. "Is this the guy whose being chased by some goons, Charlie?" Jake hobbled over and shook Will's hand. "Thanks for sticking by my bro, man. I guess you've got some problems from what Captain Mortelli tells me. What's going on? I think Charlie has a right to know since he got caught up in this with you."

"Hi, Jake. I guess you had quite a ride. I'm not sure what's going on myself. These guys came to my...our house. One of them shot off the door handle and I heard my mom yell for me to run. Then the house exploded and...and...they couldn't find my mom or my brother. My dad had left for business in New Jersey. I heard them arguing the night before he left. I have to find them! These guys are following me and they shot at the bus. Maybe they think I know where mom and dad are, but I don't. All I know is I gotta get to New Jersey and see if my dad is there." Will lowered his voice to a whisper. "It sounds weird but I think my parents are agents or spies or something."

Charlie, Jake, and Casey were all huddled close to Will. Jake whispered, "Wow! That is awesome. We'll help you. Their getting me a new arm this week. I have to practice with it. I guess it is super strong and can do lots of things a human one can't." Charlie saw that wild look in Jake's eyes. It was the one he always had as he was headed toward the surf. *Here we go again.* Charlie knew his brother never would back down from danger despite what had happened to him. Charlie was the sensible one.

"We've got to know everything if we're going with you and then we've got to have a plan. We can't walk out of here past two guards and Ms. Manion's eagle eye, mosey down to Jersey, and start asking people if they've seen your dad. Will is there more?"

Will got out of his chair slowly, looked around the room and at the closed door to make sure Ms. Manion was gone. He pulled out the drawer of the bedside table and took out a hospital bag with a towel wrapped around it. Will motioned to Charlie and Jake to come over by the bathroom door. They watched as Will turned on the bathroom light and motioned the other two boys to huddle around him. It was dark except for a small night light on the wall by the bathroom. Will unwrapped the race car and held it next to his chest. His heart beat faster anticipating the vibration and the disc messaging system to activate. He hoped it had not been damaged in the accident. He jumped a little as the vibrations buzzed against his chest. It felt much like the shock he got when he was about four years old and had decided to put his mom's keys into one of the light sockets.

"A model car? That's all..." Charlie whispered loudly.

"Shhh. You'll see in a minute." Will held out the vibrating, dilapidated, car as Jake and Charlie watched the green signal flash from its place imbedded in the frame. Two...four...two...pause...five. It flashed the sequence three times then stopped. "I think it is some kind of code. Maybe my dad is trying to find me. I don't know. I think those guys want this or want me to find my dad and maybe my mom is with him. Maybe their captured and trying to tell me something. I don't care what...I have to find them. If they were okay they would have been trying to find me." The door opened and the light from the hallway shone into the darkened room. Nurse Manion flipped on the lights from a switch near the door. Will scurried to the bathroom with his race car clutched to his chest. The vibrations had stopped. His heart was pounding as he looked frantically for a hiding place. The room had a shower stall and a toilet. A hamper with soiled bedding and gowns was the only place he could see to hide the car. He stuffed it down under the linens and pretended to be exiting innocently.

"Mr. Peterson." Nurse Cratchet commanded. "You were to stay in your wheelchair for the visit. You are not to be bearing weight on that leg. Please sit down." Jake put on his most petulant face as he allowed the nurse to lower him into the wheelchair.

"Sorry. I was so glad to see my brother I forgot." He even had a crack in his pitiful voice.

"Very well. I have to take you back upstairs. Therapy is waiting to try out your prosthesis. You boys need anything?" She looked at Will and he felt like she could see right through him into the bathroom where his treasure was hidden. She winked at him again. It was the second time she had done that and it made him feel uneasy and suspicious.

Captain Mortelli knew how it felt to be an orphan. He picked up the phone and dialed a number he found buried behind identification cards in his wallet. When he was a new trainee in the police department he developed friends that had been lost in battles and dangerous assignments, some that had left before the rigorous training was complete, and others that found positions elsewhere in the protection business. Elton Howard was one of the latter. He thrived on battle. Joining the navy two years after graduation fed that appetite and he moved quickly up the ranks to eventually take command of his own ship during the Viet Nam War. In an attack on key enemy arsenals, his ship was destroyed; he lost most of his men, his right leg was shattered and he spiraled into a depression that took almost a year to heal. His wife had been killed in an attack on a plane on which she was a passenger. He was never the same. His focus became revenge and he became known as the "Pit Bull". Anything standing in the way of Elton Howard's goal to regain power and annihilate his enemies, real or imagined, was expendable. He was given a purple heart and elevated to Commander of Intelligence for the United States Naval Forces. Located at Ulysses S. Grant Naval Base in Atlanta, his loyalty and expertise went unquestioned. Mortelli had lost touch with his friend shortly after he had taken command of the Precinct 727. Even though Mortelli saw the change in Elton he respected his courage and his ability to pursue justice no matter the cost. Mortelli needed to find Jake and Will's parents. He had this gut feeling that the parents were involved in some clandestine affair that not only put themselves in danger but also exposed Will to danger as well. He had lost his only living relative to the gangs. Not knowing if Marcus was alive or dead gave him incentive to help the young boys in 576.

"Hello. May I speak to Commander Howard, please? I am Captain Andrew Mortelli from NYPD and I have some important information for him." Mortelli waited as the Ensign at headquarters repeated Mortelli's name.

"Sir. I have to obtain clearance for you to speak directly to the Commander. Can you hold?"

"Yes, I can hold" The line went silent. *America the Beautiful* played by the Naval band filled the silence.

"Mortelli? Andrew Mortelli? You crusty old cop. To what do I owe this honor?" Commander Howard boomed into the phone just as "So Proudly We Hail" played. "You still street fighting up there in the pits?"

"Yeah. They'll miss me when I'm gone. I suppose I should call you Sir but it kind of gives me the willies. I hear they've given you a name that fits you...Hmm...Pit Bull. Got any bites lately?" Mortelli chided his old teammate as he had heard from some men that had served under the "bull" that the nickname more than fit him, it was him.

"Stuff I can't let you in on. What's up? You haven't called me in years. I don't think it's just to chat."

"Did you hear about a family that was missing after their house exploded several weeks ago in Ohio? It's old news now and probably didn't even make the papers in the east, but they never found any bodies and one of the kids is here in New York General Hospital. I think he is being followed by some pretty desperate characters for some reason or other. He thinks his parents are involved with undercover activities. I wondered if you could have someone check and see if that might be the case. His father is Robert West and his mother is Emily."

There was more than a pregnant pause as a slow grin exposed Commander Howard's one gold tooth among several other crooked ones. "Hmm. I don't recognize the name but I can have my staff check for you. If they are involved in undercover work I wouldn't be able to give you any information, but I could try to locate them to let them know where their son is. What's the boy's name?"

"It's Will, William Edward West, Jr. He's in Room 576. Coincidently, two brothers that lost their folks in that hurricane are patients here and one of them has been traveling with Will. I sure would appreciate anything you can do. I know you are an important and busy man but maybe we can get together sometime...talk about old times on the force."

"Sounds good to me. Give me your number and I will get back with you as soon as I get some information. Good talking to you, Drew."

"Likewise, thanks." The line clicked and Mortelli hung up the phone. Nurse Porter watched the cop walk past her nurses' station. She waved and smiled her most fetching smile batting her long lashes flirtatiously.

"Good morning, ma'am...er...Miss Porter." Evidently he had seen her bristle when he called her "ma'am".

"Good morning, Captain. How is it going? I hear the two brothers got together yesterday. Unbelievable coincidence, aye? Would you like a coffee? I have some brewing in the lounge. You look like you've not had much sleep lately. Why in the heck did I say that? I...I mean it must be hard to work the hours you do. I see you in the morning and you are back here when I leave. *Now he probably thinks I'm stalking him…Mari, you are a dork.*

"That would be great, ma…what's your first name, may I ask?"

"Marilyn, but my friends call me Mari," she blushed and shuffled some papers on the desk. "The lounge is just behind the station. Come with me Captain…Andrew. Can I call you Andrew?"

"My friends call me Drew."

"Okay Drew. Come with me" The two other nurses in the station grinned and winked at their comrade as she scored her first victory.

* * *

Commander Howard stared at the phone and walked behind his half circle mahogany desk. He caught a glimpse of the golden eagle perched proudly on the crest representing the United States Navy. The lines in his face from years of smoking and exposure to the sun, wind and sea framed his deep set blue eyes making him look much older than his sixty years. Perhaps it was the fireball of latent resentment and anger that burned inside him. He was known for his volatile temper but few were exposed to the furry that would often ooze to the surface causing him to exit meetings and confrontations without an explanation before it totally erupted.

They were stationed in the bay off the coast of Viet Nam in the South China Sea. This was Elton Howard's second tour. He had requested this assignment despite the negative aura surrounding this war as it was a way for him to climb the ladder to a position of power. The need to be in charge was his prescription for the damaged self esteem he buried deep inside. His parents were successful lawyers and had little room in their high society life for a child, let alone a child with a seizure disorder. His "fits" embarrassed them at functions and whenever they occurred while they were in public places. Thus, Elton was closeted at home under the watchful eye of a nanny and eventually sent away to a private military school. The grand mal-seizures were arrested as he grew older. On occasion he would experience headaches and visual images from a tiny irritable focus in the temporal part of his brain. During these episodes, he had the strange ability to solve difficult mathematical problems with amazing speed and accuracy. Devoid of the bonding and nurturing so essential for a healthy self-image, he saw the recognition and power senior officers and commanders possessed. That feeling of unquestioned authority and ability to order those people under him to do his bidding partially filled that hole left from his lonely childhood. Sarah Conrad was his first and only love. They had met during his first tour in Viet Nam while she was a night nurse supervisor at the field hospital in Saigon. He was drawn to her feisty personality and her innate beauty; no makeup, no frills and no games. She stood up to the doctors and stood up for her nursing staff and patients, didn't back down from her principles, and still remained feminine and tender when the time was right. They married and continued to serve their country each in their own way. Eight months after they married Sarah announced that she was with child and wanted to return to the states by the end of her second trimester. The war and its associated casualties exploded as the fighting drew closer to Saigon. Lack of sleep and the stress of trying to heal critically wounded young men and women, deal with those addicted to drugs and marijuana, and the constant threat that she and her husband could be among the victims took its toll. She withdrew into a deep depression, lost touch with reality, refused to eat, and lost the baby. The navy loaded her on a cargo plane bound for Germany where she was to be admitted to a psychiatric unit at a large Naval base in Strasbourg. Elton kissed the women he loved as she was ushered to the plane. Sarah did not recognize him or anyone. She was buried in a pit of post traumatic stress filled emotions. As the plane flew north toward its destination, an enemy fighter pilot entered the safe flying zone unknowingly and fired repeatedly at the cargo plane. Without weapons there was no way to counter the attack. The pilot of the cargo plane screamed into the intercom attempting to contact the enemy pilot to alert him he was firing at an unarmed ship. The explosion erupted into an inferno of metal, supplies, and humans disintegrating to nothing but a few pieces of charred twisted debris hitting the hills along the border. Elton Howard received the call at 12:15 A.M. That is when the door slammed shut on his emotions. He had finally learned what it meant to be loved and had been cheated once again. That morning he vowed to make someone pay.

He opened the top drawer of his massive mahogany desk and reached for the file hidden in the back of the drawer. The piercing eye of the hawk stared at him from the cover as he reached for the phone with a trembling hand.

* * *

Emily followed the Ensign from the dormitory after she was sure Toby received a generous mom hug and wet kisses. She was prepared to put on her most believable poker face when questioned about the disappearance of her co-agent, Kate. As far as she knew, Kate must have left when Emily was asleep. She had not heard anything as she was exhausted from the arduous captivity and trip to the base. She was surprised to find Kate and her possessions gone when she awoke that morning. Emily explained this to Commander Howard when he questioned her though she doubted he believed her. Her mind wanted to focus on any plan that would allow her to connect with her husband and Will. She had cried herself to sleep praying for their safety promising she would devote the rest of her life to them and stay away from this crazy undercover business.

"We leave at 1600 hours. I will need you to promise you will follow my instructions exactly. No questions. Can you handle that?" Commander Howard stood up behind his desk and leaned toward Emily who was standing on the opposite side of the desk. She glanced at the golden eagle and then into the eyes of her superior. This was the first time she had met the man whose tenacity, bravery, and zero tolerance for incompetence was a legend.

"Yes Sir." Emily looked directly into his deep set black blue eyes and felt a little chill run up her spine. She wondered why he never reacted to Kate's disappearance. *Stop it, Em. He's the head honcho, the chief, decorations all over his uniform. I know I've been in this business too long when I don't trust anyone.*

The Commander was issuing some orders over his intercom and hadn't seemed to have read Emily's thoughts. She stood at attention until he motioned to her to sit in one of the large leather chairs facing his desk. The eagle's piercing stare reminded her of the terrorists' Hatham insignia and of the cold masochistic vengeance of their members she must face once again. There had to be more to this assignment then she or Robert knew. The Commander would not be involved in the rescue of Dr. Olmstead. That black box Kate had told her about must be very important. From what Robert had shared with her the night before he left the good doctor had devised an apparatus that could affect the detonation device attached to some inert bombs buried underground at the old Raritan Arsenal in New Jersey. Perhaps the terrorists thought the bombs were still active and they could...

"Mrs. West, please come with me," a young female officer in a perfectly fitted naval uniform stood in the doorway. The Commander was gone. Emily stood and followed the officer down a long corridor and into a room marked "DISPENSARY". On a table there were fatigues, a beret, dark glasses, a revolver, ammunition and a hunting knife. "The Commander would like you to look as much like a man as you can. If there is anything you need besides these items, please let me know, ma'am."

"I see...do you have any six inch ace bandages?" The officer walked crisply over to the shelves and produced four six inch ace bandages. She stood at attention blocking the path to the door.

"You're excused while I change into a guy. Wouldn't want you to know my secret." The officer stood erect without a glimmer of a smile. She didn't make any move to exit.

"If you don't mind." Her companion did not move and Emily got the message that she wasn't trusted either. She turned her back an undressed removing her bra and wrapping the ace bandage around her chest to hide her breasts. She did the same around her hips to flatten her buttocks. As she fashioned her costume she looked at the shelves to see if there was something she needed to take with her just in case things went sour. She saw Epi-pen and Benadryl injections in boxes on a shelf just to the right of the door.

Emily turned toward her guard, " I really could use some man smell. Could you go to the laundry room and get me some soiled men's socks, tee shirt, and shorts? I promise I will stay right here. You can lock me in if that will make you feel better."

The officer looked at Emily's seemingly innocent face. "Very well, ma'am. I will have to lock the door," as she turned and stepped into the hallway. Emily listened for the click of the lock and grabbed several of the injections from both boxes. She pushed them down under the ace wrap and proceeded to add another layer of elastic bandage around her chest. Just as she was putting on the fatigue shirt, the door lock clicked and the officer stood holding the soiled, smelly underwear out for Emily.

"Thanks."

Commander Howard placed a small package into his briefcase between the two file folders and a revolver. The clock chimed a deep sorrowful nine times as the office door opened and Emily, now looking much more like an "Emile," was ushered into the office by the sober faced officer.

"Emily West, Sir," she announced, saluting crisply.

"At ease, Lieutenant." Howard barked as he zipped the briefcase shut and placed it on the floor next to his desk. "You are excused Lieutenant" he directed as he examined the masqueraded agent and gruffly uttered "Humpffff" supposedly approving the transformation. He motioned to Emily to sit in one of the chairs and began to outline his plan and her part in the play. Her eyes widened as she was informed of the script, the actors, and the possible cost of this intricate and dangerous performance. Her heart pounded against the constricting bands around her chest.

* * *

Stan was waiting in his apartment for further orders. He had removed the makeup from his face that made him look more American and the wig that covered his coal black hair. His real name was Abdul Sharati and he prided himself in his ability to become the person who wore the disguise. He had fooled the police force throughout his training and on several assignments. The phone rang as he was complimenting himself on his allusive prowess. The person on the other end gave him orders that would require another disguise. This time it was to be that of a woman. "Of course, I am a man of many talents. This will not be a problem." He walked over to a suitcase and began to make the transformation. It would be easy to eliminate the real person as she was very rigid about her routine.

Ms. Manion was completing her charting. It was 3:15 P.M. and she had checked on the boys in 576 just a few minutes ago as well as her other patients. This profession was her life. She had no husband or kids, not even a significant other. Though she detested the "spinster" label the other nurses placed on her, she tried to act as though it did not hurt her. One of the two guards had gone on break so she glanced up from her charting occasionally to make sure the other guard was still awake. Her code of ethics rarely allowed her to get attached to her patients but the two orphans and even that silly dog had gotten to her. She had maternal feelings that had never been used stored in her heart that seemed to rise to the surface when she took care of them. She remained stern and practical most of the time. A couple of times she had inadvertently winked at the boys without thinking just to let them know she cared. That was a big step for her.

She turned as she heard someone behind her. A man in police uniform whispered to her that he needed her assistance. She could see his uniform but his face was hidden in the shadows of the medication room behind the nurses' station. Before she could think or call out she was pulled behind the station into a utility room. Ms. Manion felt his hands around her throat tightening, fracturing her trachea. She fought with every fiber of her being digging her nails into the skin of his arms and lurching her body forward. Her heart pounded as it fought for oxygen and her lungs collapsed with the lack of air. The small light that filtered through a window in the door ceased to exist and she fell from his grasp onto the cold floor. He dragged her to the back of the utility room and took her clothes, her cap and her stethoscope. Lifting her into a laundry bag he dragged her to the trash bin at the far side of the hospital. After he dumped her and covered her with garbage he drove his car back to his apartment and washed the uniform. He smiled while he planned the next phase of his assignment. He was ordered to abduct the two boys in 576 and take them to a warehouse several miles from the hospital. There he was to use any method he needed to use to find out where the disc for the black box was hidden. It was somewhere in the hospital. Abdul, alias Stan, was to dispose of the boys and to disappear forever. Ms. Manion's next shift was the next day. Abdul needed some sleep if he was to become the nurse by 6:00 A.M. the next day.

* * *

Jamie, the social worker from Circleville arrived in New Brunswick at 10:30 A.M. He was determined to find Will, alias Max, not only because he felt responsible in some way to help the lad but also because the attack he had suffered proved to him Will was being followed by extremely dangerous people. When he regained consciousness from his head injury, the police questioned him about the events leading up to the shooting. They were still working on finding the missing family members but the investigation had been placed at the back of a pile of local needs. They had made little progress in locating Will's parents and brother. They were told that the Feds would take over and were ordered to report any information pertaining to the case to the FBI. Jamie had given them descriptions of the two men who had come to the Center looking for Will and told the police that he had followed Will to the library where it appeared he was getting directions to a town in New Jersey. It seemed to Jamie that the police had a ho-hum attitude about the entire case and he decided to try to find Will himself. The Mayflower Hotel wasn't the classiest in town but Jamie only needed a bed and a bathroom. He deposited his duffel bag on the bed and stopped at the desk to see if the clerk had checked in any customer with the last name of West though he was ninety nine percent sure that would not be the name any of the family would be using. The lobby was decorated in the early thirties. Dusty crystal chandeliers with candle like bulbs created the feeling one had been thrown back in time. The carpet was worn in paths created by many travelers. In the center of the lobby a large area rug of faded greens, maroon and blue flowers lay under glass tables with gold legs whose scratches and dents were like varicose veins and age spots. Even the overstuffed green couches surrounding the tables sagged with the imprints of the bodies that had rested there throughout the years. Jamie chose pamphlets from a display listing the local hotels and the sites that travelers might want to visit. Among the pamphlets was one about the old army depot that had once been a large arsenal storing weapons and large artillery. The park was located in the nearby town of Edison. Children played in the old dilapidated barracks and had pictures taken standing on a rusty World War II tank in the center of the park.

The headache began at his eyebrows and moved across the front of his skull. Icy fingers clutched his forehead had begun to squeeze. The vice tightened and caused Jamie to lean against the wall adjacent to the revolving doors at the entrance to the lobby. Every sound was magnified and the dull lights from the chandeliers seemed to brighten. Everything that contained a number prompted formulas to flash across his brain; the numbers on the wall phone nearby jumped from the dial into a cascade of calculations and ratios. All the possible combinations of phone numbers rolled across Jamie's visual field. A lady with a red coat and hat passed Jamie as he leaned against the wall. She couldn't help but notice the dazed look in his eyes.

"Are you all right young man?" she asked. "Should I call someone? Are you a diabetic?"

Jamie tried to focus on the person under the red hat that was looking up at him.

"I'm fine, ma'am. Just a little headache. Thank you for asking." The pain was lessening and the numbers began to fade as he blinked to try to clear his vision.

"You should make sure you tell a doctor if you are having headaches. You looked like you were having a seizure…a convulsion or something. My name is Catherine. I'm an old, retired nurse. Are you sure you don't want to sit down? I'll get you a glass of juice from the café. Have you eaten today?"

"I'm feeling much better. I have a doctor who knows about these. It's very nice of you, Catherine, to be so concerned."

"Very well. What's your name might I ask? Is this your first time in New Brunswick? I live here and was arranging for a nursing conference at the hotel. Isn't this old place just beautiful? Are you visiting friends of family? There I go again…asking too many questions. I'm sorry"

Jamie smiled at her. "I'm a social worker and am used to asking lots of questions myself. Please don't apologize."

"Social worker. That is a wonderful profession. A lot like nursing. We're both caretakers. I have to go pick up one of the grand kids at soccer practice. Take care of yourself. I hope you enjoy your visit. Bye now!" Catherine disappeared through the revolving door.

There are sure a lot of nice people in this world. Then there are those few who have no regard for anyone. "I wonder why it has to be that way?" No time to ponder on philosophy. Jamie was on a mission to find a kid who had touched his heart and also inadvertently involved the docile social worker in one of the most puzzling cases of his career.

* * *

George looked at the knife his friend held over him. "Turn around, George." Sweat began to trickle down the sides of the weary doctor's face. He blamed himself for this nightmare. His compulsive need to invent and create had gotten out of hand when he discovered a formula accidentally that increased the power of a rocket launcher he was working on to be installed on naval warships. He had run out of magnesium oxide, one of the components of the rocket launcher's ignition system. Dr. Olmstead had grown to love this country but was thoroughly disgusted with the red tape it took to get things done if it had anything to do with politics. The deadline was approaching for him to complete the project and he could not wait for the paperwork to siphon through security for his supply to be replenished. With a few scientific calculations he found that ammonium phosphate possessed almost identical properties to the magnesium oxide. The fuel injection chamber of the old bombs buried under the barracks in Raritan Park had at one time been filled with ammonium phosphate. He poured over his notes written meticulously outlining his assignment years ago to invent a device to control the ignition chamber of the bomb. The notes came to an abrupt ending when it was decided to render the bombs inert. Having been notified that a team of agents had been sent to Raritan for the deactivation, he was to fly to Washington to meet with the Commander of the naval ships for which he was preparing the rocket launchers. Upon his return he entered the secret passage behind the barracks to extract some ammonium phosphate from the fuel injection chamber. He was unaware that the agents had been killed before the bomb actually was deactivated. The terrorists had been devising a plan to use the backfired project to their advantage and they needed Dr. Olmstead's expertise to have all the cards in their hands to get what they wanted. The "hawk" was circling. The terrorists knew everything about the doctor; even the smallest detail such as his ritual of taking vitamins every morning along with a cup of rich German coffee. They paid a young boy who worked as a delivery clerk for the pharmacy that prepared Dr. Olmstead's prescriptions. All he had to do for forty dollars was to exchange bags with a man who would meet him one block from the doctor's home. It meant nothing to the delivery boy except that it was great pay for doing almost nothing. The vitamins the terrorists provided were injected with a medication that temporarily and gradually produced symptoms similar to a type of dementia seen often in older folks. Before the doctor realized he was being drugged, he had replaced the ammonium phosphate with his new supply of magnesium oxide. He somehow felt in his confused state that he needed to replace the ammonium phosphate he had extracted from the ignition chamber of the bomb. One night, he walked from the lab to the back of the barracks with a case of magnesium oxide instead of the ammonium. He vaguely remembered the codes that would allow four ports to open that led to the ignition tanks. The musty smell of the damp lead vault that housed the bombs reminded him of the tiny cells where he spent months barely existing in a prison camp in Germany. He opened each vial of chemical without performing his usual check and recheck to confirm the appropriate substance. When the magnesium oxide and ammonium phosphate combined it increased the destructive potential of the bombs fourfold. When he realized he was being drugged he poured over his notes to see what combination of chemicals he had used. The rocket launchers were so powerful they could be used from twice the distance they had been used in the past. Commander Howard was ecstatic. The more power that man had the easier he was to get along with Dr. Olmstead was told. When Gregor saw in his notes that on September 8, 1971 he had replaced the magnesium sulfate in the ignition chamber by mistake, he notified the agency Director at once. Thinking that the bombs had been deactivated the Director had not reported it to the President until he was made aware that the agents had been eliminated before they could complete the deactivation and that it was part of the terrorists plan to use the threat of massive destruction to gain their control.

"You know I would never harm you. I know it's hard to trust anyone in this business. I had to make it look like I thought you were still under those creeps' control. Sorry I pushed you around a little. I'm so worried about Emily and the boys. I don't think they were supposed to be part of this mess." Robert helped the relieved doctor sit up as he cut the ropes that bound him.

"It's my fault. Bobbie we have to get to ze old base before the terrorists find Will…if he's still…"

"Alive…he has to be, George. They all have to be. I think I have a plan."

* * *

Robert had a plan. Jamie had a plan. The boys were working on a plan. Emily and the Commander had a plan. Kate had her orders and she needed a plan. Like the individual ends of a boondoggle, if woven correctly, a strong symmetrical finished product would be produced. If any one of the strands were placed in the wrong position or missing it would end up tossed in the trash. The problem was that there was no single director to mesh the plans and to pull the pieces together and there was this dark evil hawk that was ready to pounce on any and all of them and tear them to shreds. The agency had possession of one black box. The terrorists had possession of another black box. One of the black boxes had the capacity to abort the deactivation sequencing if a disc was placed in a well hidden place inside the device. The President, his top adviser, and the Hatham leader, were the three participants who were fully aware of the ominous magnitude of the situation. Millions of people could die and the rest of the world would be devastated if the deactivation chamber was opened setting in motion the eventual detonation of the bombs...The agency tracking devices had lost Emily, Robert and the doctor, and Kate. All the signals from their implanted tracking devices had been blocked. A report had come in that two agents had escaped from a warehouse basement in near Philadelphia and a terrorist was found dead at the scene. The agency were sure it was Kate and Emily but had no way of tracking them down. Left on their own experienced agents would find a way to carry out their orders. Emily had her orders to act as a decoy for Robert. She had not been figured in the equation especially being coupled with Kate Caputo. That was like putting a match to dynamite. Remember the cardinal rule; no two agents or crooks to be in close proximity to one another. Most missions or projects placed agents at various locations so that the targets were small and it was easier to confuse the enemy.

Kate drove as cautiously as she could observing traffic signs and speed limits even though she wanted to push that gas pedal to the floor and fly up the coast to Philadelphia where she was to arrange the meeting with the terrorists. She knew that if Robert West had been called into action, there must be a lot more to this black box thing than she was told. If the Commander of the Naval Secret Service was involved and headed north to some Podunk town in Jersey, it had to be big! It got her adrenalin pumping just thinking about it. Then that other person seeped into her thoughts messing up her reverie. She remembered a rare call from her sister about six months ago asking her to take care of her boys if anything happened to her and Jesse. She hemmed and hawed, making all kinds of excuses. She wasn't good with kids. She had a job (she couldn't tell Carolyn what kind of job) that had her traveling all over the place; she was never home; she couldn't cook; she was a crab most of the time (which Carolyn was fully aware of); she didn't have any room in her apartment; on and on and on. Carolyn listened to the endless excuses and said. "So, I take it you're saying 'yes'. Oh, sis, you don't know how happy you've made me. I'll send you some papers that you will need just in case. I love you. Be careful." CLICK. She ignored the "buts" and the "uh-uhs" and that was the last Kate had heard from her sister. Kate received the envelope with the stamps full of flowers and the return sticker with a dove flying in the blue sky surrounding Carolyn Peterson and her address. She had tucked it in her lingerie drawer so she didn't have to be reminded of the albatross she could possibly inherit. Kate had to find the black box and hopefully could eliminate a few of the bad guys along with the recovery but she also had been given an assignment to take care of her sister's kids. She decided she could kill two birds (hawks preferably) with one stone. The stolen...er, borrowed Jeep continued toward Philadelphia. She needed to find a phone as soon as she arrived to check in with her supervisor. She was sure the agency was tracking her through the device implanted under the skin of her right arm. It was odd that both she and Emily had been captured and held for several days without someone from the agency locating them. She never questioned the actions of her agency. She did her work. They gave an assignment and she carried it out with whatever tools and ingenuity she could utilize. Lots of things were odd about this project. As she turned off the highway onto Scarab Avenue just outside Philadelphia, she had decided how she could fulfill both of her missions. It was risky. She was Kate Caputo and let 'em try and stop her! Kate located the warehouse which was quarantined by the Feds. She talked to one of the agents she knew that was in charge of that part of the investigation and found out that the terrorists had been traced to New Brunswick. That seemed odd. The Commander was headed there with Emily.

Commander Howard had advised the President not to surround the park where the bombs were buried as it might cause a confrontation with the terrorists that would put residents of the town in danger. He had Kate arrange a meeting at the site with a liaison from the Hatham to find out what they were demanding. Emily sat in the passenger seat of Commander Howard's Jeep. He smoked a cigar that reminded her of Robert's father, the General. She wondered if Robert was heading for the same destination. When Commander Howard revealed some portions of project RRX42, she realized that Dr. Olmstead was key to the terrorists' ability to negotiate. Robert was to become just visible enough that the terrorists would see he was harboring the doctor. The doctor needed to send a message to the terrorists by his actions that he was leaning their way. They had to believe he was putty in their hands should they be able to abduct him. The terrorists knew of Robert West's reputation and they had to be cautious as many of their cells had been eliminated in the past by this man.

* * *

Breakfast trays had been collected and it was time for the patients on 5 west who had orders for physical therapy to go to the second floor gym. Will and Charlie had met with Jake several times during that week and planned their escape. The guards never went to the gym as they figured there were too many therapists, doctors, and other patients in that area that anyone trying to get to Will or the other boys would have a difficult time doing it clandestinely. Casey was allowed to sit by the double doors leading into the large therapy room. Every type of exercising equipment lined the walls. There were cubicles for special treatments and a large metal door that led to the hyperbaric chamber. Four oversized doors led into male and female dressing rooms and bathrooms. The doors could accommodate large wheelchairs, stretchers, Hoyer lifts, and other equipment that might be needed in an emergency. Patients from other smaller hospitals, ambulatory outpatients, and the New York General Hospital patients moved in and out of the various stations as they were directed by the therapists. Moans and groans mixed with laughter and clanking of metal bars, walkers, and other transportation equipment would appear to an observer to be disorganized but everything was planned, supervised, timed, and evaluated. Jake usually had his therapy at two in the afternoon but had requested a post breakfast time for this day. Charlie was on one of the mats while Cheryl exercised his injured left leg raising it off the mat and having Charlie pull the leg toward him with a band wrapped around his upper thigh. This stretched the muscles in order to prevent scaring and limitation of movement at the surgical site to repair his shattered pelvis and femur. Will was sitting in one of the cubicles nervously waiting for Kim, his therapist, to perform an ultrasound treatment to his shoulder and upper arm. Jake arrived and checked out the positions of the other boys. He was chosen to be the star of this episode. When he had finally regained consciousness in the trauma unit, he watched patients come and go, some so mangled that they didn't survive, others like him who cheated death and improved enough to be moved to a step down unit. One of the cubicles directly across from his held a young girl who had taken an overdose of her mother's antidepressant, thirty antihistamine capsules and a chaser of cleaning fluid because her boyfriend broke up with her. Her mouth was burned and she was on a ventilator. The nurses and doctors couldn't seem to control her seizures, despite medications used to paralyze and sedate her she would convulse violently. Her mother would sit for hours whenever the staff would allow it and stroke her long black hair singing lullabies, tears falling onto her child's pale skin. When the seizures would begin she would arch her back and her arms would contort into rigid sticks at her sides. The bed would shake as her body would writhe with tremors that caused tubes to disconnect and alarms to sound, lights flashing and nurses running to inject drugs into the intravenous lines. Jake felt a connection in some odd way to the young girl. He dreamed that she had gotten up one night and walked over to his cubicle. She was dressed in a white nightgown, barefooted and her mouth was no longer scarred from the caustic burns of the cleaning fluid. She walked toward him trying to tell him something. She was smiling and her lips were soft and pink. Her hair framed her beautiful face and she smiled as she came toward him. As she came closer, he could see right through her. He heard her whisper "good-bye" as she walked through him and disappeared. Later that day, her heart stopped beating and they called a "code" trying to resuscitate the poor child. She died and Jake knew that her spirit had left her injured body that night before. Her seizures were etched in Jake's brain along with the memory of her visit to him. He knew that was much more than just a dream...it was a gift.

Abdul dressed and disguised as Ms. Manion knew that the boys would be in the therapy room without a guard. Ms. Manion was to accompany the boys back to their room after the therapy and stay with them until the guards returned. Abdul had planned a little diversion from the plan that would not make them suspicious. He planned to tell them that he (Ms Manion) had arranged a little tour of the morgue and some of the other departments in the basement of the hospital because they seemed so bored with being in that hospital room. He (she) had obtained permission from her supervisor and the police to take the short tour. His friend, another terrorist, disguised as an orderly would help wheel the boys into the basement and tranquilizer injections given to them. They would be loaded onto stretchers and wheeled to an ambulance at the back entrance to the hospital where cadavers were loaded and transported to funeral homes. Sometimes the devil is foiled. The boys had their own tour planned and it was about to begin.

The timing had to be perfect. Jake started to wheel himself toward one of the cubicles opposite the area where Will and Charlie were receiving their treatments. The night before, Jake had visited the other boys and stuffed clothes, Will's race car, and the few other items he could stash in the pockets of his wheelchair. Suddenly Jake moaned and arched his back, stiffened his arms and legs and fell from his wheelchair onto the floor. His entire body writhed and he urinated, clenched his teeth into a frightening contorted grimace. Therapists rushed to his side as well as some of the patients who could move on their own. A rapid response code was called and a crash cart along with residents and a special team of respiratory therapists and nurses rushed into the therapy room. In those few minutes of chaos, Will and Charlie grabbed the wheelchair stuffed their paraphernalia into a pillow case, grabbed a drowsy Casey and ran through the exit doors, down the stairs and out into the cool September air. The hospital was located in Allensville, a mid-sized town about twenty miles northeast of New York City. Several large medical buildings, a pharmacy, and a hotel for patients' families flanked the large 845 bed hospital. Shuttles came and went carrying visitors, staff, and even patients to other facilities related to the larger Upper New York Medical Collaborative. Will, Charlie, and Casey ran to the nearest shuttle headed for the local airport. The boys had argued with Jake when he came up with the diversion tactic of having a fake seizure. They needed him to come with them to track down Will's parents and to try and find their aunt Kathy. He assured them that he would find a way to get out of the hospital and meet up with them in two days. The boys were to get as close as they could to Newark New Jersey in those two days and meet Jake at the train station there at 7:00 P.M. If they got there first and he did not meet them by 8:00 P.M., they were to move on to try to find Will's parents. Some of the nurses at New York General had grown very fond of the three orphans and had gotten together a collection for them. It added up to four hundred and fifty dollars. They each took a portion and stuffed it in some jeans the staff had also purchased for them. Will and Charlie left notes in their bedside stand drawers thanking everyone for their kindness and care. They just had to leave to take care of some unfinished business. Jake was taken back to the Intensive Care Unit and a CAT scan was ordered to see if the seizure was related to his injuries from the hurricane or a new problem. When the therapists and guards realized Will and Charlie were missing, they notified Captain Mortelli. An APB-all points bulletin was placed to alert transportation services, radio, and TV stations and other precincts of the missing kids. Mortelli paced back and forth in front of Room 576. The guards were ordered to search the entire room, every inch of it. They found the notes in their bedside stand.

"Those darn kids don't know the danger they're in. I called a friend of mine who has connections with Will's parents and he called me to tell me he knew they were alive and he would make sure they were reunited. He couldn't tell me why but he said the boys had to be protected at all costs and Will's parents would not be able to get to Will for a few days. I think there is something really big going on and Will is somehow an innocent participant. I'm sure Charlie's brother knows something. As soon as the doc's will let us question him we need to find out. He needs to know that Charlie might be in danger as long as he's with Will."

Abdul disguised as Nurse Manion ducked into the linen room to change into scrubs and an OR cap. He shoved his frizzy brown wig into the cap and stuffed the uniform and cap behind a linen cart. Abdul was disappointed when he heard the boys had escaped. He should have gone into therapy with them but was worried that someone might question him and his disguise would be discovered. He knew the boys would try to take off to find Will's parents. He had tried to find the source of the sporadic signal his comrades had detected coming from the hospital, searching the boys room when they were in therapy or for testing, even examining Casey's toys but could find nothing. Jake. He hadn't thought about Jake. Maybe Will had given whatever was emitting that signal to Jake. He was older and less apt to be suspected. He found out that Jake was to have a CAT scan that day. The scanner was located on the first floor radiology wing. He could disguise himself enough to play the part of a transporter and get Jake somewhere he could question him. This hospital was so big no one knew Ms. Manion in the Intensive Care units. Jake might recognize her as she had wheeled him in to see his brother that first time. She could tell him she was working under cover for the police and he couldn't blow her cover. Jake was planning his escape at the same time "Nurse Manion" was preparing his disguise. He remembered the layout of the radiology unit as he had been a frequent visitor there after he was life-flighted to the hospital. No matter what test you were sent to radiology for there was always a period of time you were parked in the hallway waiting your turn. Night and day the unit was full of techs, doctors, patients, and clerks. It was one of the busiest places in the hospital. New devices to search bones, cavities, every part of your body were being invented and purchased by the large hospitals. Smaller hospitals that could not afford the trained personnel to run the equipment, let alone the equipment itself, sent their patients to the larger meccas for testing. It wouldn't be unusual for a patient to disappear either because he was tired of waiting or someone had whisked him off to another area for testing. Transporters were so busy moving patients that those that could be left unattended were parked and left to fend for themselves. Jake recognized Nurse Cratchet despite her disguise. He didn't think too much of it except it was a little odd that a nurse would be transporting a patient who did not require a heart monitor during the trip.

"Getting some extra hours?" Jake asked as Abdul helped him into the wheelchair. Jake insisted on wearing his sweats instead of those useless gown things. His new arm was working out really well and he was feeling pretty cocky that his plan to create a ruckus allowing the boys to escape had worked.

"Yeh, I need some extra cash for Christmas so I take any assignment I can get, within reason." Abdul pushed the wheelchair through the doors of the ICU and down the hall to the elevator. His pistol was pressing against his bare skin. He had strapped it to his thigh and the metal handle had turned under the strap. He felt as cold as that metal. It was never about what was right or wrong. It was always about who wins. Pretending to care about people when his heart had turned to stone through the years of training, multiple wounds and beatings, constant messages that your life here was only important if you followed orders and sacrificed everything for the cause. It didn't matter if the cause was just or ethical, you did what you were told. The elevator stopped on the third floor. Abdul acted like he had pushed number three by mistake along with the button for the first floor. The door opened and he began to push the wheelchair and Jake onto the new obstetric unit that was still under remodeling. The halls were filled with insulation and half completed walls. The lights were dimmed as there were no workers on the weekends.

"Hey you got off on the wrong floor. Radiology is on one." Jake turned slightly in his chair to try to see if the nurse was having a stroke or something when Abdul spun the wheelchair around and pointed the gun at his head.

"What the hell are you doing lady? Why…"

"Shut up! I ask the questions. Where is it? If you don't tell me where the signal device is I will shoot you and stuff you into that shredder." His face had changed from the nurse's caring mask to that of hate and contempt. Jake didn't know what he was talking about at first. Ms. Manion's voice changed to a man's. Then he remembered Will's race car and the glowing disc signaling a code they couldn't understand.

"I don't know what you're talking about. Who are you, anyway?"

Abdul hit Jake on the side of his head with his free hand. "I said I would ask the questions. I know the signal came from that kid, Will. You know where they went and you are going to tell me!" Abdul slapped him again. Jake remembered his new arm had many times the strength of his original one. *No better time to test new weapons than when you're in a battle.* he thought. It happened so fast Manion or whoever she was didn't have time to pull the trigger. When he knocked the gun from Abdul's hand he heard a crack and he fell to the floor. The hand that had held the gun was bent backwards and a bone protruded from the lower part of his arm. Abdul tried to reach for the gun and Jake kicked it across the room. He lifted a plastic bag from the pocket of his wheelchair, picked up the gun, and stuffed it into the elastic of his sweats. He pulled a hooded sweatshirt over his head and walked down the dark corridor to the red exit sign, down the stairs to the first floor. He went to a house phone and dialed the operator.

Jake spoke softly into the phone. "There's been an accident on 3 North. Injured nurse. Need to call a code blue." He hung up the phone and heard the overhead page for the code, walked through the doors and into the parking lot. It was 7:30 P.M. and the night shift had already exited their buses and cars. Most of the day shift staff that took the shuttles had left. A few stragglers climbed on with the hooded visitor. He sat in the back of the bus and patted his new arm. "This sure is more exciting than surfing. Wow! I think I've got a new friend. Wonder what is up with that green disc? Got to make sure I get to that train station. I didn't mean to hurt that nu...person but he was going to shoot me."

The shuttle pulled away from the hospital and headed to the airport.

Chapter Twenty-Five

The Arsenal

Raritan Arsenal Park was filled with kids and their families that Sunday afternoon. The late September weather was cool with brief periods of sunshine wafting through the trees. The leaves had the slightest hint of gold and crimson that soon would replace the lush green foliage and loosen their grip on the branches. The parents sat at the picnic tables discussing politics, school clothes, recipes, and the latest gossip about Mary and her new beau, the closing of Frank's hardware store, and the influx of "those foreigners" into their neighborhoods. Some of the dads pitched balls to their boys secretly dreaming they might make the big leagues someday. When the sun blessed them with a few warm rays everyone would stop, close their eyes and raise their heads toward the sun. For those few seconds, it looked like a herd of turtles straining their heads out of their shells to bask in nature's heater. The older kids took turns climbing the old war tank, posing for pictures and making noises mimicking bombs dropping and the rat-a-tat of machine guns. A black van drove past the park. The windows were tinted so no one could see the passengers or driver. It drove slowly and parked one block away in front of the vacant hardware store. Matt Porter noticed the van drive by and park. He wondered why no one got out and why they parked next to a vacant building but shook off the thought. He was a lawyer for many hours during the week and some weekends. He had vowed that when there were weekends he could spend with his wife and two boys he would shed his lawyer's suit, stash his lawyer's briefcase, and be a dad and a husband only. It was hard to throw off the naturally suspicious nature and analytic thinking that made him a success but he worked hard to do it with his family. Three of the kids, two boys about twelve or thirteen years old and one of the boy's sisters decided to investigate the old barracks at the south end of the park. They had been warned not to go into the dilapidated building as the timbers were rotting and the floor was caving in. The Historical Society fought hard to keep the building intact and had tried to raise enough money to restore it. Many people who had worked at the arsenal when it covered fifteen acres of the town and was dotted with buildings and warehouses wanted to see it preserved. The other buildings and seven other barracks had been demolished including a laboratory and the weapons museum. The General's headquarters had been located just behind the tank. An impressive building designed to look like the White House in Washington used to be filled with uniformed personnel, many of them highly decorated officers. There was a story about the ghosts of the Generals and soldiers marching through the park at midnight that became the key to manhood in Edison. If you wanted to be a "man," you were dared by your buddies to sit on the top of the old tank at midnight on Halloween and wait for the ghosts to march.

Billy and Tammy Newcomer with their friend Kurt Porter were curious about the barracks and what kind of treasures they might find there. Their parents were busy gabbing like adults like to do so they took that chance to sneak away.

"Just a few minutes and we have to get back," Kurt warned as they ran from tree to tree toward the barracks. "If they catch us we're in a heap of trouble." He was trying hard to use the country jargon. Heap of trouble seemed to fit in this case.

"Aw, don't be a wimp. Why did you bring her with you?" Billy pointed at Tammy who was being more cautious then the two boys.

"She's your sister. She follows me everywhere. I can't get rid of her. She tries to walk to school with me. Even if I ignore her, she doesn't get it."

"Kurt's got a girlfriend. Kurt's got a girlfriend!" Billy chided his new buddy melodically.

Kurt punched Billy in the arm playfully as Tammy caught up with them. "You aren't really going into that ugly place are you?" Tammy looked at the building whose boards had lost all of their paint. The door hung loosely on rusted hinges and creaked as the breeze teased it back and forth. The glass in all the windows had been broken. Jagged pieces lay on the ground glistening in the occasional burst of sunlight. It gave her chills just to think that she was standing this close to it and that she was willing to get into to trouble just to be with Kurt. She vowed to marry him someday and have a whole slew of children just like her parents. She had four brothers and two sisters. Her sisters were much older than her twelve years and spent most of the time away from home off to college somewhere. Being the only female around those boys, she learned to climb trees, spit watermelon seeds, skip stones in the creek, dig for worms for fishin', and burp and fart with the best of them. The little bit of femininity left after all that training was encouraged by her mother's dressing her like a lady for Sunday church and curling her long auburn hair into ringlets whenever she could get her to sit still. Both parts of Tammy had fallen in love with Kurt when he walked into classroom 212 at Edison Junior

High a month ago. He was the handsomest, neatest, smartest boy she had ever met. He was nothing like her scraggy brothers and their scraggy friends. His parents were lawyers and they had moved to Edison from New York City. Tammy decided that she would make herself noticed by this guy no matter what.

Billy was the first to pull open the door just enough to step inside. Kurt and Tammy followed hesitantly. It was dark and smelled like firewood ashes that had been left in the rain. The floor boards creaked and there were a few old bunks rusted and twisted resting against the wall. There was a rustling sound coming from a torn mattress at the back of the room several feet away from where the kids stood riveted to the creaky floor and huddled together next to the door. Something ran from the mattress out through an opening in the wall boards and the three kids jumped, Tammy squealing like a castrated pig.

"Enough for me. We saw it. Let's get out of here. This is spooky!" Kurt proposed, his pre-teen voice cracking as it went from boy voice to man voice in mid-sentence.

Billy had regained his composure and was moving farther into the barracks. "Hey, Kurt, c'mere. There's an old chain laying over there on the floor. Maybe it belonged to some of the soldiers."

Kurt wanted to leave but he also wanted buddies. He missed his friends in New York and had to act differently here in this small town so he didn't seem uppity. He talked a lot faster than these kids. Everyone talked fast in the city. Everything moved slower here and the people were friendlier. Tammy followed Kurt as he tiptoed across the sagging floor to where Billy had found the treasure. In trying to pick up the chain, he found it was attached to the floor. As he pulled on it, a trap door opened into a dark pit that seemed to have no bottom. The three of them leaned forward their mouths open and their eyes wide as saucers trying to peer into the emptiness.

"Kurt! Kurt Porter! Where are you?"

"Tammy, Billy! You better not be near those barracks!" They heard their parents calling in the distance and let the trap door slam closed. A few birds dozing in the rafters screeched their discontent and dove at the kids who were desperately looking for an escape route other than the door they had entered. Billy saw an opening between two planks in the east wall. Tammy tore her good sweatshirt on some rusty nails protruding from the board when the boys pushed her through. They ran to one of the outhouses several yards away and hid behind it as their parents approached the barracks. There were rows of hedges lining the perimeter of the park and they scooted behind those until they could circle around to the front of the picnic area. There they waited for their parents to return acting as though they were the ones who were searching for the parents. Whether anyone believed them was questionable but no one could prove they had disobeyed. Tammy said she tore her sweatshirt on a tree branch during one of her historic climbs. That part was believable. When the three musketeers got home they couldn't wait to devise a plan to go back with flashlights and weapons to investigate the trap door mystery.

The men in the black van saw the kids enter the barracks. The van pulled away and drove slowly down the main street toward New Brunswick.

Jamie had exhausted his search for any member of the West family. He had printed copies of pictures of the family that had appeared in the newspapers several weeks ago. Evidently, Ohio news was of very little importance in New Jersey. No one had even heard about the explosion and the missing family here nor had anyone seen Robert West or Will. By Monday morning, he knew he should get back to the Center. He missed Maria and he had spent some of his savings for this failed mission. The pamphlets laid on the hotel bed as he was stuffing his clothes into the duffel bag. There was a 7:00 P.M. train arriving and heading on to Philadelphia where he had could pick up another train going west to Ohio. He figured he could be home by Tuesday. He sat on the bed thinking about Will and the two men who had come to the Center looking for him. He was sure they were responsible for shooting him or hired someone to do it. It was 10:10 A.M. and he had several hours to do nothing but think. Thinking was getting him nowhere. The pamphlet advertising the arsenal caught his eye. Edison wasn't very far away from New Brunswick and he had been interested in old forts and military history for a period of time before he became busy running the Center. He grabbed the pamphlet and his jacket stopping at the desk to see if there was a bus leaving town heading for Edison. The clerk said there should be one about 11:00 and that he would enjoy the park on such a beautiful day.

"Lots of history about that old place. Still have a part of the barracks standing but no one goes in there. Town keeps wanting to restore it but no one wants to put up the money. The tank is from World War II and used to be in front of the Headquarters. Generals, lots of important people, some say even the President used to come there. Too bad they tore it down. Would have made a great museum."

Jamie excused himself as the bus with Edison on the marquis drove in front of the hotel. He boarded the bus and watched the rolling hills of north Jersey pass by his window. He had a twinge of a headache that passed without progressing, to his relief. It was a beautiful day. Jamie wished the anxious feeling in his gut would go away so he could enjoy it.

* * *

The meeting with Hatham was to take place at 9:00 P.M. on Monday, September 29, 2002. There were to be only one attendant for each of the negotiators. Commander Howard and his attendant were to drive to Philadelphia where the attendant for the Hatham representative would meet them to take them to a meeting place. The agency had contacted Robert directing him to take Dr. Olmstead to a site determined by both of the negotiators. The black box would be returned as soon as the terrorists were satisfied there was a reasonable agreement. The disc that could cause the calculations to align opening the detonation chamber was glued to Will's race car. Robert and Dr. Olmstead were the only ones who knew about the disc. They had no idea if the race car was destroyed in the explosion of the West home or if Will was alive and had the disc with him. Commander Howard had been given the black box and a disc from Washington. Both were sitting in his briefcase. The one thing no one knew was which of the boxes was the one that could set a nightmare in motion when the disc was planted. Hatham and the President were counting on Dr. Olmstead to bring sanity to negotiations. He alone would know the difference and could fool the terrorists into thinking they had the upper hand. The U.S. did not wish to genuflect to any demands by terrorists but they had no choice. They were up against a wall. The Hatham had made sure the bombs were alive. The terrorists had thwarted several attempts to render them inactive. The only chip the U.S. had was the black box sequencing preventing the detonation chamber from communicating with the ignition device. If the block was negated it would take thirty minutes for the ignition to occur. If that happened there would be no way to stop the bombs from erupting and no one would win; not the terrorists, not the U.S, not anyone. Robert West wasn't sure if his friend had recovered enough from the chemicals the terrorists had given him. George had said he was faking the past week but the seizure did not look fake, and there was something strange about his friend he couldn't put his finger on.

* * *

Will, Charlie, and Casey had taken another shuttle from the airport to the train station. The cops were looking for them so they got some ladies clothes and dressed in the bathroom stalls at the airport. Casey would have given them away so they hid him under some old clothes in a small grocery cart they purchased at a Good Will. Will made the best looking girl so he purchased the train tickets. Everyone looked suspicious to Will who knew the cops weren't the only ones looking for him. Two policemen were in the train station just as the boys and the cloistered canine started to get on the train. They eyed the pair of young "girls" and the cart but moved past them as the two boys practically threw the cart up the train steps and plopped in the first seats they could find. Will pulled the shade down over the window and prayed for the sound of the engine to start. Casey poked his nose between the clothes and tried to pull himself out of the cart.

"Down, Casey!" Charlie whispered loudly. "Good boy." Charlie covered up the confused pooch. *My humans look weird and I don't like this stupid basket.* Charlie got a look from his buddy that appeared to say just that. He thought about all they had been through together and wondered what made pets more loyal than people.

It was about 11:00 A.M. on Sunday when Jake stepped on the train heading for New Brunswick. By now the cops had to be looking for him too after beating up one of their "nurses" and leaving AMA (against medical advice). He wondered why there weren't any cops following him, but this was a small town and they surely wouldn't bring in the big guns from the NYPD just to track down a teenager. He was really curious about the trouble Will was in and that his little brother was in danger by association. Jake was a tough guy. Charlie was soft and too trusting. He had to take care of both of them no matter what they were into. He patted his bionic arm and closed his eyes as the train moved away from the station. He dreamed of surfing a giant wave with trusty Elmo under his bare feet. The wave suddenly turned into a huge shark and he awoke trembling and sweaty. He pulled the hood of his sweatshirt over his head and stared out the window listening to the sound of the train moving along the track.

Kate arrived in New Brunswick in her stolen Jeep about 11:00 A.M. Monday morning, September 28. She parked at the drugstore and went to a phone booth to call the agency. Her chief was both angry and relieved that she had finally contacted him as she had been missing and they had been unable to track her. They had assumed it was she and Emily West who had eradicated their captor in the warehouse basement. She told him that she was concerned because no one had attempted to follow her or try to abort her escape and that she had a funny feeling the Commander was hiding something. Why would he want to take Emily and Kate with him on this mission? The terrorists knew them both and it opened him up to attack. Her chief told her it wasn't up to her to decide what the top echelon should do and to stay in town until he contacted her. Her tracking device had been blocked so he expected she would be obeying his orders. She assured him she would stay put and that she had a weapon if it was needed. She wanted to ask if they had located the black box but she figured he would have told her if it was something she needed to know. Kate checked in to the Mayflower Hotel and tried to call New York General Hospital to see if she could find out how the boys were doing. They wouldn't tell her if the boys were patients there even when she told them she was their only living relative. She left the phone number of her hotel room and went downstairs to the restaurant. A glass of wine sounded really good. She hadn't eaten for two days. After scarfing down two glasses of wine and a steak dinner she went back upstairs to her room. The room was dark and she could see the message light flashing on the phone. Before she could turn on the light to see who had called her, there was an explosion in her head as the metal butt of the gun connected with the back of her skull. He dragged her across the room and tied her hands and feet, gagged her mouth with thick tape and dumped her limp body into the metal food cart. He picked up the phone with his blood stained glove and hit the message button.

"Ms. Caputo. This is Andrew Mortelli of the NYPD. I understand you are related to Charlie and Jacob Peterson. We need to talk with you as soon as possible. Please call me at 714-462-8117. Ask for me. Do not talk to anyone else. Thank you."

The waiter placed the gloves in the steel cart. He pushed the cart to the elevator and nodded to a couple coming off the elevator. He pushed "B" and wheeled the cart into the alley at the back of the hotel. A van was waiting and the driver assisted the waiter to lift Kate's lifeless body out of the cart. The cart was left just inside the exit door and the waiter got into the passenger side of the van as it drove southeast toward Edison.

Jamie walked around the park not really looking at anything in particular. There were a couple of people on a bench not far from the tank that looked out of place with marigolds and other fall flowers surrounding it. He glanced at the barracks but was lost in his thoughts. A van drove past him and circled the park a couple of times backing up to the barracks with the back of the van up against the back of the decrepit building. That part of the street faced the woods so hardly any traffic turned that way. Jamie decided to walk around the east side of the park where hedges formed a fence that eventually ended near the barracks. Lost in thought about Maria, the weird headaches and how they made his brain work, Will, and the Center, he found himself close to the barracks and decided to peak in just to say he had touched an artifact of history. As he approached the door, he heard mutterings and grunts from someone inside. He hadn't noticed anyone around the building. He peaked through the partially opened door and saw figures dragging something out of the back of a van. They disappeared into an opening in the floor of the barracks and the van drove away at the same time a metal door closed over the opening. His heart was beating so loudly that he was afraid they would discover he was there. He ran to the outhouse just as the van came around the corner and headed down the street past the front of the park.

"What in the heck was that? Maybe some kids found a storm cellar or something. The backs of the two that dragged the thing out of the van were men, not kids. Kids wouldn't be driving." He peaked out of the outhouse and saw the clock on the bank across the street. It was 5:45 P.M. and he had about an hour to catch the bus back to New Brunswick, check out of the hotel and get to the train station. He looked around to see if the van was anywhere in site and he walked to the bus stop. "I'll call the cops when I get back to the hotel. I've got to get home. I hope that wasn't a person they were taking into that place. I can't do this." The headache started as he boarded the bus. He held his head in his hands and the numbers rolled through his brain at lightning speed. His eyes watered as the pain increased. A man in the seat across from him leaned over and asked if he was okay. Jamie grunted a "yes" and the pain started to subside. By the time the bus pulled up in front of the Mayflower, he was back to normal. His insides were far from normal and he felt like he had become a part of a terrible nightmare.

Chapter Twenty-Six

Bargaining with a Hawk

Commander Howard deposited Emily in the Mayflower Hotel in New Brunswick ordering her to stay in her room. He would send a driver for her after a message was sent on the pager he gave her. Emily was trained to follow orders. Even though Robert's M.O. deviated from them at times, she found it difficult to question the expertise and decision making of her superiors. Most of her husband's alteration in plans resulted in successfully thwarting the enemy. He and Kate were similar in that respect. Her exodus from Atlanta caused barely a raised eyebrow from the Commander when he found she had stolen a Jeep and left the base. That disturbed Emily and made her even more suspicious of him. When he had revealed his plan to disguise Emily as one of his male aides, he also had the lab change the codes in her tracking device through an ultrasound technique. The ultrasound placed over her forearm where the device had been implanted was connected to a computer. A technician was given a new code and this was sent through the computer to the ultrasound probe re-coding the tracking disc. Howard explained that this was necessary as the terrorists had found a way to block the devices of all those they knew might be involved in the project. Hopefully, the new code would not be one the Hawks would be looking for.

"I know Will is alive. I just feel it. I've got to find Robert somehow. I can't just sit here and wait. This is one time I can't follow orders. Why did Howard want to bring me with him? I think he is using me for bait to draw out Robert." She knew that Robert was in the same town or headed that way. She had to warn him that he was being tricked. She was sure of it. Emily West stepped into the hallway and locked the door. She walked down the exit stairs and into the lobby. It was almost 6:30 P.M. and she watched as several people exited a bus outside the hotel. Among those was a young man who rushed to the elevators up to his room, grabbed his duffel bag, checked out hurriedly, and headed for the train station. Emily watched him and her sixth sense urged her to follow him. Besides that, he looked vaguely familiar. Jamie paid little attention to the guy in fatigues walking to the station behind him. He was busy looking at his watch and wondering if he should stay or leave.

The teller at the window inside the NB railroad station drowsily took Jamie's money and handed him a ticket. The lights from the engine outlined his troubled face. Emily stood in the shadows trying hard to recall where she had seen him before. The train slowly came to a halt and belched a few times before settling into a gentle hum. Two young girls in slacks and sweatshirts lifted a grocery basket on wheels from the train as they exited along with several other commuters. Will bumped into a guy who was standing there looking perplexed. When they looked at each other, Will couldn't believe his eyes. Charlie was trying hard to keep his restless pooch in the basket. He gestured to Will to get going but Will and the guy were hugging! He thought the masquerade had gone a little bit too far if Will was trying to pretend to be someone's long lost lover. Casey had managed to tip over the cart and was stretching his aching bones. He saw Will with a stranger holding on to him and went into protection mode. Casey leaped from a crouched attack position and jumped on Jamie knocking him to the ground. The train started to pull away as Will and Charlie were restraining their guard dog and trying to help Jamie up. In the process, Will's blond (very becoming) wig fell off and Emily gasped as she recognized her son. She ran from the shadows grabbing hold of him and attempting to embrace him. He didn't recognize her and he pushed her back onto the platform.

"Will! Will...it's me...it's Mom!" She yelled. It was the same voice he heard yelling "Run, Will...Run!" when this nightmare started weeks ago. Emily ripped off the cap and her hair fell onto her shoulders while the tears streamed down her face. Jamie and Charlie stood with their mouths open as the scene began to make sense. Jamie had seen Emily briefly when she had come to the Center to meet Maria. That had been quite a while ago and he had never been formally introduced. Casey stood waiting for a treat for his heroic efforts. Emily pulled the four of them close to the building and they all began to fill each other in on the events of the past few weeks. Emily had forgotten about all the rules. She had become the mother and wife, ignoring the agent programmed inside her.

The two men who had followed her from the hotel waited in their van. One of the men with a scar across his face dialed a cell phone and spoke to the man on the other end of the line. "I've got something that will confirm that our demands will be answered." The sinister grin spread over his face as the van pulled into the dimly lit parking lot behind the station. The man on the other end of the cell phone grinned as well. His gold tooth glistened amongst his crooked teeth and the scent of old hickory filled the room as he puffed contentedly on his cigar.

Emily had pushed her hair back up into the cap. She had messed up. She knew if she left the hotel against orders she would have been followed. At least it would be someone from her own camp. The group went into the station to continue to catch up and to wait for Jake. It was 7:42 P.M. and they were only to wait until 8 P.M. Will and Emily looked like sister and brother reunited. Will had placed his wig back and Charlie was getting acquainted with Jamie. They realized they were a lot alike. Both were caretakers and saw the best in most everyone which was a good and bad thing at the same time. Casey was licking the last crumbs of a cookie Charlie had purchased at the commissary in the station as his reward for attacking Jamie. Emily's only goal now was to re-unite with her husband and to protect her son. His courage and maturity amazed her. All he had been through had made him look much older than his twelve years. She was bursting with pride. He had shared with her the strange disc that was imbedded in the race car and she sensed this was how the terrorists were tracking him. She did not know that the same disc could destroy her, her family, millions of people, the world if it fell into the Hatham's hands. She did not know that her close proximity to her son increased the danger to him and that if her plans to destroy the race car with its tell-tale disc were attempted, her life and all those attached to her would mean nothing.

7:45 P.M. The lonely whistle of the incoming train from New York was pulling into the station. Charlie and Casey left the group to stand on the platform to meet Jake. Charlie's heart pounded as people began to step from the train and he didn't see his brother among them. Just as the train was pulling away and Charlie's heart had sunk to his shoes Jake jumped off of the moving train onto the platform.

"I saw a girl with a dog that looked like Casey but I wasn't sure. You make a pretty good lookin' girl, bro! Wasn't sure if some broad stool the pooch or if he had a twin." He poked at Charlie whose cheeks were turning red as tomatoes.

"You won't believe what happened at the hospital. That Nurse Cratchet...she was a he and some sort of a spy or something. Almost shot me. My new arm...man is it awesome! I broke her arm with one swat!" Jake boasted. Charlie ushered him into the station to meet the others and catch him up. Jake hadn't changed much but Charlie was happy he was alive no matter how cocky he could be. Emily decided they all should go back to the hotel and work out a plan. It would be better if they were being tracked by the Commander's watchdogs so they walked down the main streets from the station. The van pulled from the parking lot and followed some distance behind them. It pulled into the parking garage located beneath Mayflower Hotel when they saw the group enter the lobby and head toward the elevator. All Emily could think of was to get rid of that race car. She was sure that it held the device that allowed Will to be followed.

They were waiting in the bathroom when Emily unlocked the door to the hotel room. Four men grabbed each of them and sprayed Casey with pepper spray. The dog yelped and one of the attackers attempted to hit him with the butt of a rifle. The pepper spray brought out the primitive part of that dog and he leaped at the fuzzy figure he could barely see sinking his teeth into the surprised guy's shoulder. Jake used his arm as a bludgeon pulling two of the men away and tossing them like rags against the wall. Jamie remembered a little karate and pinned the arm of his attacker behind him and was about to flip him when Jake shot him with the silencer gun he had taken from Abdul (alias Stan/Ms. Manion). The guy went down and Jake lifted the fourth attacker off the floor just as he was about to attack Emily. The air went out of the attacker as Jakes grip tightened the collar around his neck causing him to pass out. The five of them locked the door and ran down the nearest exit just as the hotel security people ran off the elevator. Guests who heard the noises and yelps from the room poked their heads out of their doors to see what was happening. Emily felt responsible for the other four and was not sure what they should do next as she had no orders, no plan, and a group of kids, a dog and a social worker who knew a little karate. They huddled in a corner of the underground parking lot. Jamie was shaking and had sprained his wrist during his karate move. Casey was having sneezing fits from the effects of the pepper spray and Charlie, Will, and Jake were ready to take on the world. A little adrenalin in teenagers can be dangerous. Jamie remembered what he had seen that afternoon at the Arsenal Park and asked Emily if it might have something to do with the project her husband had been assigned. Emily knew that Dr. Olmstead had worked at the arsenal when it was active and he had performed most of his experiments there. There was a rumor that some bombs were still housed underground but were obsolete and too large and dangerous to dig up. Some of the chambers were filled with stale chemicals and the city was hesitant to expose anyone to them. She wondered what had happened to Kate as she had said she was going to try to locate the men with the black box. Jake had taken it upon himself to cruise the garage and found a purple van that he was able to pry open the hood to hot wire the starter. When he pulled up in the stolen van to pick up the rest of the gang Charlie shook his head wondering if they were related at all. Emily decided that they would investigate the old barracks to see where the trap door led. She had the feeling the project and that old arsenal were somehow related.

Commander Howard was to meet Robert and Dr. Olmsted in Philadelphia at the site designated by both parties. The Minuteman Hotel was just off Route 95 as it turned into 295 circling the city. Two armored cars were sent to the Agency headquarters downtown where the Commander had deposited his jeep. Robert and the doctor arrived at headquarters and were ushered into the second car by agency guards. The car carrying the Commander led the way. Robert and Dr. Olmstead did not talk. They had agreed that no matter what happened the terrorists would be stopped at all costs if they tried to initiate the mass destruction they were threatening. The moon hid behind a dark cloak of clouds and there was a fine mist that made the city streets slick. The reflection of the lights on the wet pavement made it appear transparent. They passed the entertainment section of the city with its marquis filled with rotating and flashing colored lights inviting visitors to enjoy shows, exquisite dining, and exotic dancers. The lights faded behind the two cars as they turned off of 295 onto the main highway and headed north. The Minuteman Hotel was just two exits from where they had pulled onto the highway but Commander Howard's car did not pull onto the exit ramp. It kept going northeast toward Newark and Edison. Dr. Olmstead fidgeted in the hard leather seat of the car.

"Should I follow the Commander, Sir?" The driver asked as he watched the sign for the hotel disappear behind him.

"Follow him, of course." Robert ordered through clenched teeth. "What in the hell is he doing? If we don't meet with the Hatham, all bets are off!"

George said nothing. He just stared at the tail lights of Howard's car and knew that all chances of surviving this mess lay on his shoulders. He knew where Elton Howard was headed. He didn't exactly know why but he could guess that it was a show down rather than a negotiation.

Billy, Tammy, and Kurt were supposed to be in bed. It was a school night and 9:00 P.M. was curfew at both their houses. All three of them had agreed to sneak out and meet at the Park. They had worn their clothes to bed and stashed flashlights in their dark hooded sweatshirts. Billy and Kurt wanted Tammy to bow out trying to scare her with the possibility of snakes and rats being down in the pit under the trap door. She had no problem with any of those varmints so that didn't work. They met a couple of blocks from home and decided to just shine their flashlights into the pit to see if there was anything down there. They were in no way going to go into the pit or look any further than that. At least that was their vow before they reached the park. They reached the park at 9:45 P.M. just as a purple van parked a block away and several people exited. The two groups stealthily inched their way toward the darkened barracks. The crickets screeched and an owl hooted as the kids came toward the front of the eerie looking building. The three almost turned around as a rabbit ran in front of them stopping their hearts. Emily decided to have her group wait behind the hedges that ran from the outhouse along the east side of the park. She wasn't sure what they were waiting for but they were waiting. She heard the door creak at the front of the barracks and slithered over to the side of the building. Three hooded figures were entering the door at the front. She could barely make out anything distinguishable as they ducked inside quickly. She pulled out her trusty pistol and was preparing to go inside when two cars pulled up to the back of the barracks. When the headlights were turned off she hurried back to the cover of the hedges and her cohorts. Whoever was driving the cars did not get out. Charlie was glad he had left Casey in the car as he would be announcing his presence for sure with all these people lurking around. The local trio was just about to lift the trap door when the lights of the two cars filtered through the loosened boards of the barracks. They scurried over to the rusty cots leaning against the wall and hid behind them. The sounds of their panicky breathing seemed to echo off the walls of the room like ghosts from the past. Two more cars arrived and two people came out of each car. They carried rifles or machine guns Emily deducted from the silhouette she could make out. They walked over to the two cars that had arrived first and barked some orders in another language to the passengers in those cars. The passengers seemed to understand them as two persons, who appeared to be men, stepped cautiously out of both cars with their hands on their heads. The four men pushed aside two of the loose panels of wood that was attached to the building just at the top and ushered their captives (they appeared to be captives) into the old building. One of the men had brought a portable camping lamp. He lit it and the three kids hiding behind the beds made themselves as small as they could. They were all wishing they had stayed in their safe cozy beds instead of giving in to their curiosity. Billy could see the two men with guns were young with dark hair and beards. They looked like the pictures of the people who had flown planes into the towers in New York last year. One of the other two men was in uniform and looked terrified. He was young and apparently was a driver for the fourth man. This man was tall, muscular, with graying hair and did not look at all afraid of the two guards who kept barking orders at the driver who was visibly shaking. The guards made the driver open the hatch to the pit and climb down first. There must have been stairs as the driver disappeared below ground gradually. The second confident looking man went down the steps as well and the two with guns followed. They left the hatch open and the lamp lit beside it. Just as Billy, Tammy, and Kurt were about to make a quick exit, the lights from a fifth car shone into the spaces between the buildings' boards as it pulled up next to the other cars. One of the guards who had entered the pit must have heard the car drive in and came up with his machine gun pointing at the opening. Robert West and Dr. Olmstead walked into the barracks and when the guard saw who it was, he lowered his weapon and helped the older man down the ladder into the pit. Robert talked for a while to the guard and the both of them disappeared below ground.

Emily was completely confused. Who were all these people going into an old broken down barracks and not coming out; some hooded ones through the front and several cars full in the back? Maybe it was a séance or a bunch of kids having a party where they could drink and smoke without being caught. She wasn't sure…then she saw the three people with hoods run out of the broken front door. They looked like they were running for their lives and disappeared beyond the park and into town. Emily quietly moved up to the front door with her revolver cocked and ready. She could see a light coming from one corner of the building. The light cast eerie shadows as it outlined pieces of ceiling dangling from the rafters and old rusted cots leaning against the walls. As she peered around the open doorway cautiously, she saw an opening near the lamp and did not see anyone in the building proper. She could hear voices coming from the opening though they seemed to be quite a distance away.

Will and Charlie had gotten pretty tired of being dressed like girls. They had ditched the wigs and put on sweatshirts and their tennis shoes. They wiped the make-up off on some rags they found in their "borrowed" car. Emily had told Will they had to destroy the race car because the disc was probably how the terrorists were keeping track of him. The attack in the hotel had diverted her from destroying it. Will felt it was the only thing that connected him to his father and that his father had put it there for a reason. Emily was still wary but hadn't pressed the issue. It seemed odd that a simple tracking disc would send a coded message and light up anyway. Most devices she knew about did none of that. They were small, ultra-sensitive capacitors that emitted radio waves that could be tracked by a computer. Will felt the vibrations in the pocket of his sweatshirt. A faint hint of green light shone through the thick cloth as the familiar sequencing began. It lasted all of 45 seconds but it was enough to be picked up by someone in the pit of the barracks. One of the guards poked his head out of the hole with his machine gun ready to fire. Emily saw him just in time to plaster herself against the outside wall. She ran quickly back behind the bushes and saw the last bleeps of Will's disc emitting from his pocket.

"Will. There are guards here and other people. I don't know what is going on but I need to have you, Jamie, drive the boys back to town and call this number. Let the agency know E-7 is missing and R-22 is in need of help out here. You boys need to stay in the car. I don't want you to get hurt." Emily whispered.

"I'm staying, Mom." Will looked at his mother and at the car in his pocket. "If they want this so bad they will have to fight me for it"

"So are we." Jake and Charlie both stated firmly

"I'm coming back as soon as I call," Jamie added.

The man with the gun stepped out of the front door and stood listening. The crickets and frogs had stopped chirping as it was getting close to midnight. Emily had her revolver ready as they all froze behind the hedges. They began breathing again when the man stepped back into the barracks.

Kate was getting really tired of being drugged, tied up, blindfolded and deposited in strange places. It wasn't that she hadn't been abducted, beaten, tortured, and imprisoned on other missions but she had always been successful completing them. She had neither recovered the black box nor interrogated anyone. All she had been able to do was to set up the meeting at the Minutemen Hotel. She had contacted her agency so they could be ready to surround the hotel. If Kate was good at escaping she was even better at interrogating. The only terrorists she had met up with so far were the ones she killed and the ones that tried to kill her. When she regained consciousness from the most recent blow to her skull she felt she was in a huge room or cave. When she grunted and screeched her prison echoed. Most times when blindfolded she could see a little light if she was in a place where there were windows or some type of lighting. Here the darkness enveloped her…totally black……so black it made her dizzy, almost claustrophobic. Her bladder was full and her back and head throbbed. Both wrists were bleeding from her attempts to wriggle out of the ropes that bound them. It seemed like hours before there was any sound other than her grunts and a drip…drip…drip coming from quite a distance. Suddenly there was the sound of metal scraping on metal and a tiny halo of light filtered through her blindfold. Her body tensed and she listened as a man yelled, "Go down the steps and then follow the corridor" in Arabic. All agents were fluent in at least four languages.

"When do you think the Leader will arrive, Matsua?" another voice said.

"I don't know but we better make sure everything is ready." There were footsteps on a stone or marble floor coming closer. "Ha! You think you can escape from Matsua's bindings? I could cut off your hands for you if you wish and make it easier for you. Or would you like me to rip your arms from their sockets?" He laughed in a way that sent icy shivers up Kate's spine. She steeled herself for whatever torture he was about to inflict.

"They are coming. You had better leave the hor alone." The other man seemed to move away as he spoke. Matsua spit into Kay's face and she tried in vain to bend her face to her shoulder to wipe the putrid smelling slime dripping down the side of her face into her tousled red hair. As soon as she was freed, she would make sure she returned the favor to Mr. Matsua.

His eyes were dark and covered with thick black eyebrows set in dark olive, tan face. His black oily mustache perched above lips that were thick and curled in a half smile as he watched the guard move aside for him as he entered the dimly lit corridor. Matsua's countenance changed from an arrogant, taunting assailant to a meek, obedient servant as the man walked close to him and looked through him as though he were nothing.

"You were told to capture and hold the agent. Who gave you the orders to ridicule and revile her? Do you want me to cut off your hands, Matsua?

"N...no, Sir. I am..."

"You are going to untie her and give her a drink of water. Then you are going to wipe the spit off her face and tell her you are sorry."

"But she is......yes, Sir I am you servant," Matsua walked over to Kate and removed the ropes from her wrists and ankles. The light was intense as the blindfold and the gag were removed. Kate could see the outline of a person standing over her and behind him a group of metal structures half sunken in some sort of a pit. The room was very large with cement walls marked with the tears of underground moisture. There was a low hum that throbbed intermittently for several seconds then quiet followed by a drip...drip...dripping sound.

"I apologize for the inconvenience, Ms. Caputo and for the poor manners of my compatriots. We had to make sure you would not be attempting an intervention. That would have been unwise and disastrous."

Kate recognized him from his pictures at the agency. What would Omir Talyasi be doing here? There must be something very important for him to take a risk to come to this country.

"We both have jobs to do," Kate looked into those dark eyes and could see that whatever mercy she was being given might only be temporary. One of his men yelled down from the entrance that the rest of the men had driven in. General Omir Talyasi turned away from Kate and walked over to a table with six chairs several feet from the bench where she was sitting. He was carrying a briefcase which he placed on one of the chairs gingerly. There were muffled voices, shadows moving across the wall of the entryway and then Robert West and Dr. Gregor Olmstead squinted as they entered the room. This is getting better every minute. Don't they know this is exactly what they wanted. The old geezer has the answers they need to get whatever they want.

"General Talyasi. This is Dr. Gregor Olmstead." Omir offered his hand to the doctor who hesitantly shook it unenthusiastically.

"I have heard many things about you, Dr. Olmstead. They tell me you are quite an inventor. Perhaps you can show me some of your work while I am here." Kate had moved to the edge of the bench and was preparing to stand.

"Please sit down, Ms. Caputo." He ordered in a deep menacing voice. Kate returned to her seat and looked at Robert who acted as though he did not know her. She could not tell if he actually didn't recognize her or was acting as though he didn't. She turned her attention to the two large cylindrical tanks housed in thick walled metal coffins sunken into the ground. Two towers rose at the far end of the cement fortress. These were joined together by a half wall covered with dials, computer screens, and levers. Suspended from the towers were a series of cables that appeared to be attached to the second set of tanks. Just as Kate was leaning forward to see if there was another entrance, she heard a group of voices coming from the entrance of the cave.

"I thought we were to meet at the Minuteman Hotel. You disappeared after I parked. Can you let me in on what's going on, sir?" Robert questioned respectfully.

"It is best you just do as you're told, Robert. I can only tell you to be on your guard and watch those two men who ushered us down here." Commander Howard entered the room and stood staring piercingly at the General as a cloak of silence fell between them. Their eyes met and Commander dropped his cigar on the ground. He overtly crushed the smoldering stogie with the heel of his boot. General Talyasi appeared to get the subliminal message and cast his eyes at the boot then back up to meet the Commander's eyes once again. General Talyasi motioned the group over to the table.

"Would you like some coffee gentlemen? It was made by my guards so I am not sure you will like it as strong as they are accustomed to drinking in our country." The General's smile was chilling as the double message he sent was evident. What he wanted to get across to the three of them was the men with rifles were his and that they were used to dealing with others that may not have the same motives. They all passed on the coffee offer and took a seat at the table. One overhead light shone on the scratched surface as General Talyasi placed the briefcase on the table. There was one empty chair.

* * *

Billy, Tammy, and Kurt ran as fast as their legs would carry them to the Porter's house. Billy and Tammy's parents had found their beds empty and had called Matt Porter. The Newcomers decided to join the Porters in a search for the kids. They were both angry and worried as the clock chimed twelve midnight and no sign of their errant teenagers.

"I can't imagine where they would go on a school night. They are in for some strong punishment when they show up." The Newcomer's middle son was still at home for a few more days before college re-opened. His parents had rousted him out of bed and told him to report to them if the kids returned. Matt and Catherine were not surprised that Kurt had joined his new buddies. It had been difficult for him to make the change from his big city school and friends he had known all his life to a small rural school and town where he felt like he didn't fit in at all. If he had been included in an adventure it surely would have taken precedence over his parents' curfew and rules.

"I thought they were hanging around the old army barracks yesterday when we were at the park. They had said they were going to the john, but I'm wondering if they went back there?" Matt questioned as he looked out their front picture window for the fiftieth time. "If I were a kid that place sure would make a good clubhouse or spook house."

"I always wished they would take that place down. It's an eyesore and probably unsafe, it's so old. There are lots of stories of seeing lights coming from the inside at night and cars that come and go in the back of the building. It might be a drug drop off site for all we know. Ben, you guys should probably call the police." Ben's wife, Phyllis, paced back and forth wringing her hands.

"Maybe you and I should go over to the park and see if the kids might have sneaked over there." Matt said to Ben. Ben shook his head and grabbed his jacket. "You ladies stay here and if we can't find them at the park or on the way we will call the cops." Matt and Ben walked down Ivy Street and turned onto Providence, the main street that ran in front of the park. The three adventurers arrived at 2265 Emmet Street out of breath and their eyes wide as saucers. They almost knocked over a sleepy-eyed Peter Newcomer as they barreled through the door into the living room.

"Boy are you guys in trouble. Where in the heck have you been? You look like you saw a ghost!" Peter listened as the threesome tried to tell what they had seen at the barracks all at one time. "Hold it. I can't understand you talking all at once. Billy, tell me what happened?" Billy began to tell his brother about the trap door and the men they saw with guns. There were other men who drove up in Jeeps and went down into a tunnel or cave or something. He hardly took a breath as he spoke his voice shaking. Tammy and Kurt sat together on the couch and it would have been one of the best moments of her life as Tammy's arm touched Kurt's side if she wasn't so frightened and also mad at herself for going along with the boys.

Jamie crept along the hedges as silently as he could until he reached the sidewalk on the main street. Most of the stores were closed except for the all night Subway shop and the hotel a block away. Jamie was hesitant to go to the hotel as he could see two police cars parked in front and two policemen standing at the entrance. He didn't think anyone had all the pieces to this crazy puzzle. It sure was a far cry from running a shelter for indigent families though he really was invigorated by the intrigue and mystery. Will's glowing race car; Will's mother probably a spy or an agent; the explosion at their home; the attack in the hotel; the mysterious goings on in the old barracks—it was like being an actor in a movie but much more dangerous. He thought of Maria who must be frantic wondering where he was, especially after the shooting. He would call her in the morning. He entered the Subway restaurant and asked if there were any phones. The kid behind the counter motioned to a booth in the back corner of the store. Jamie dialed the number Emily had given him.

"The Federal Bureau of Investigation. You must have a clearance number in order to speak with anyone at this agency," a computerized voice message played repetitiously. "Please enter your clearance number and push pound," it repeated as Jamie faltered on the first try. Jamie's hands were shaking as he dialed the code and there was ringing on the line. "This is the Special Forces Division of the FBI. Please identify your project number and clearance code distinctly. This is a voice recognition line and will only verify with the owner of the project and the clearance code." Jamie looked at the scrap of paper on which Emily had scribbled her code. She must have known I couldn't get information…she must have wanted me away from the barracks. The boys!

There were only a few more loose ends in this crazy assignment. Emily hadn't planned to involve any of her children…When Robert told her he had placed the disc George had given him in the race car he was building with Will, she had no idea that the disc had more abilities than just being able to track someone. The two men who had come to the house were not the ones the agency hired to stage the explosion and her capture. They were not supposed to place Will in danger, they were supposed to protect him. Her plan to stage a capture and then to locate her husband and get to Commander Howard had not gone well. Her agents had been replaced by terrorists and she wound up in a cell with Kate. When the Commander filled in the holes of the project—the disc and the potential disastrous consequences if it were placed in the correct black box; George's addled condition; Robert's orders to protect him at all costs; the location of bombs that could be activated and ignited destroying much of the continent—she knew what she had to do to make sure the perpetrator of the plan would be exposed. The bugs in the plan were four innocent young men, Will, Charlie, Jake, and Jamie. She had to find a way to get them away from the barracks and the park. Time was running out. She had sent Jamie on a wild goose chase to call her agency. Now she ordered Will, Jake, and Charlie to go back to the van, lock the doors, and remain there until she returned. The van was a couple of blocks away and that would give her the time she needed to do what she had to do. Placing Will's race car into the belt alongside her knife and the holster of her gun, she inched her way around the back of the barracks and knelt between the cars as she contemplated how to draw the General's guards out of the barracks.

The chair was not for Emily. The chair was for Kate. Kate feigned confidence as she took the chair next to General Talyasi. Commander Howard lit a cigar as he surveyed the confused faces of Robert and Dr. Olmstead. Elton Howard had waited for this moment to make them pay for the loss of his only love. He had manipulated documents, requested favors so he could gain the confidence of the President and the General. Only he and the President knew which black box was the original and which was the decoy. Only Dr. Olmstead knew where to place the disc to abort the block on the detonation chamber. The sequence of numbers and alpha characters was unstoppable. There was no human that could realign the sequences to halt the detonation which would take 30 minutes once initiated. It seemed like one of those scenes in the game of *Clue*. Who'd done it? Who had it? Who was the bad guy? Who was the good guy?

Matt and Ben reached the edge of the park and looked toward the barracks outlined by the moon. It looked eerie and desolate. Matt grabbed Ben's arm as he thought he saw a flicker of light coming from the inside of the building which was about fifty feet from where they were hidden behind the rusty tank.

"I think it's just the moon, don't you?" Ben said as he stared as hard has he could at the barracks. There it was again. The light seemed to be at the ground level and a tiny flicker came and went. "Maybe it's the boys with a flashlight or something. Wait 'til I get my hands on them!"

"Let's move closer. I think there are some hedges that run alongside the building. We should circle around. If it is the boys we might scare the heck out of them and it will serve them right for sneaking out." Matt led Ben around the tank to the east side of the park where the hedges formed a fence up to the outhouse near the barracks.

Will, Jake, and Charlie went back to the van as they were told to do but they didn't lock the doors nor did they stay in the van. They got Casey who was panting with enthusiasm and had to relieve himself as soon as he was released from his prison. If Charlie told Casey not to bark, he didn't. If Charlie told Casey to sit and stay he did unless he felt his human was in danger. That was Casey. He had been through a lot with his human and had an instinctive need to protect him. They had survived a hurricane, starvation, loss, an attack by a crazed veteran, being thrown from a bus, shot at, chased and ambushed but they had made it. Casey also needed to protect that human who loved the wet monster that picked him up and tossed him around at the beach near his humans' home. If it is possible for animals to miss their owners Casey missed the soft spoken lady that used to pet him and cuddle him from birth.

Emily threw a rock at the trap door and waited as Matsua leaned cautiously out of the trap door peering into the darkness. He could barely see the outline of the cars as he moved towards the opening between the barracks wall boards. Emily crept around the cars and came up behind Matsua who only grunted as she shot him in the back of his head with her silencer gun and dragged him into the bushes. The other guard noticed that Matsua was gone and called up to him from the bottom of the stairs leading to the chamber.

"What is going on?" General Talyasi growled as he was waiting for Commander Howard to respond to the demands of Hatham. They wanted forty million dollars and all the prisoners released from Guantanamo Bay prison and three other prisons throughout Europe. The money was restitution for the families of those who had been incarcerated for over a year. They had the black box and knew the sequences to obliterate the block on the detonation chamber. They had recovered the real disc and would force Dr. Olmstead to place it in the box, connect it to a computer unless their demands were agreed to in one hour from now. It was 12:38 A.M. "See where Matsua went." The General returned to the table and pointed at the doctor. "You think that everyone at this table is here to protect you except me? You never know what people will do for money and power."

The second guard saluted and cautiously pulled himself up the ten steps leading to the opening in the trap door. He did not relish this assignment. Jaboul Tamarisa was not a violent man. He had taken the position of computer specialist in the office of the General because he could not provide for his family on the meager profit he made repairing and programming old computers for his village. The only reason he was able to complete his basic education was through hard work and the encouragement and support of his parents. Even as a young boy he was mesmerized by any object that had parts, especially electrical parts. He would search through trash and storage units for anything that resembled a motor or a device. When he wasn't in school or studying he would work, sometimes without pay, in fix-it shops and computer stores as well as neighbors' farms to earn enough money to attend the trade school in the city. When he was hired by one of the Aides at Military Headquarters to trouble shoot the office computers, his talent was recognized and he was chosen to travel with the upper echelon to keep the communication system intact and running efficiently. Anyone working with the top brass was automatically trained to fight, to shoot, to kill, and to obey orders without question. For two years he was sent to military camps to learn to do all those things. The trainees were put through rigorous and dangerous exercises, fed only when they completed each segment of training perfectly, and allowed to see their families twice during the two years. If you failed, you paid, often with your life or by being tortured or starved. Jaboul was wise enough to play his part well, proving his loyalty and Pavlovian prowess. Because of his technical expertise he was sheltered from combat thus not having to kill and maim as his fellow soldiers were forced to.

I don't know if I can kill someone. I have never had to do such a thing. I must protect my General, but I am not sure these people are the demons I have been told they are. Jaboul thought to himself as he lifted the trap door just enough to peer into the darkness. The musty smell of the barracks reminded him of the few times he was thrown into a solitary, damp cell when he dared to question the incessant harangue of slander shouted to him in his two years of training by the camp leader. The infidels; cheaters; killers of babies; and many other more flammable terms were used to describe the Americans and their allies. A tiny ray of light from below filtered through the cool morning haze and crept across the weathered floor of the barracks. Emily thought she saw the hint of light as she crouched between the vans. Jaboul called out softly for his fellow guard who now lay dead in the bushes. "Matsua......Matsua......where are you?" He opened the door a few more inches and stepped up one more rung of the ladder. He held his rifle against his chest and his heart pounded against its cold metal housing. It rushed toward him before he could see what or whom it was. His rifle fired into the air as he jumped back down into the cave. He slammed the two bolts across the seam of the door and rushed down the corridor to the great room.

"My General......My General! There is someone up there! I cannot see Matsua anywhere!" Jaboul reported breathlessly to his scowling Commander.

"No one was to know where we were to meet! If you have broken your promise you will have brought destruction on your country and the world!" General Talyasi's face was dark and contorted. He looked directly at Commander Howard who had stood up as well when he heard Jaboul's report.

"I promise you, General, this meeting was arranged according to your in-structions. No troops, no publicity, no politicians." Commander Howard glanced around the table. Only Dr. Olmstead looked at this decorated, revered soldier and realized he had plans far beyond the negotiation table in that room. A veil of hatred fell over his face as he countered the General's accusations.

"Jaboul. Go back into the barracks and bring the intruder here to me," he shouted at the trembling computer specialist. "Take the other entrance."

"As you wish, my General." Jaboul had no idea how many intruders there were and was getting concerned that Matsua had been put out of commis-sion. He never would have deserted. Matsua lived to kill and maim. If he had any ethics or feelings for his fellow man, it had been crushed like a cigarette on the pavement. Jaboul checked the knife dangling in its holder on his belt, confirmed his rifle was loaded and moved swiftly toward the far end of the chamber. The cylinders housed in the floor of the cave only caught his eye for a moment. He entered a large steel door and climbed steps to a tube that ran perpendicular to a small landing. The tube was only large enough to accom-modate a mid-sized person and there was a row of metal rungs that led upward to a round door bolted shut at the top of the tube. He climbed to the top and unbolted the door pushing himself through the narrow opening. He stepped out onto the damp grass, closed the grass covered hatch, and pulled some branches over the area. He was now on the opposite side of a dead end street hidden by thick foliage and trees that ran down a hill to a small river that ran through the edge of town. He looked around him and suddenly crouched down into the brush as he saw the outline of a group of people come toward the park and the back of the barracks. It looked like three persons and perhaps a dog crouching behind the vans parked at the back of the barracks.

Emily had reached the trap door just as it slammed shut. She tried to pull it open with the rusty chain but it would not budge. Her body was slammed to the ground and her arms pinned to her sides. She kicked at the heavy weight lying on top of her and rolled quickly out of the grasp of another attempting to restrain her. She used all the tactics she had learned to throw one of the attackers against the fragile barrack wall. The ancient boards groaned with the weight of the former football player. Her legs lashed out at the head of the second assailant as he tried to recover his footing on the uneven floor. Matt took the blow to his head and fell against the old bed frame. His nose and mouth began to bleed as his head throbbed. He tried to see who the Karate Kid was on the other end of the shoe and realized it was a woman. She held a gun steadily pointed toward him and then at Ben who was slowly attempting to get up off the floor.

"Who are you?" the three questioned almost in unison.

"Lady, we are looking for our kids who we think came to this park tonight. We aren't here to harm anyone. What in the heck is going on here?" Matt could make out in the dim light from a single lamp post at the edge of the park that the person had to beautiful a face to be a guy. She wore fatigues and looked like a soldier ready for combat.

"I'm not sure what is going on here but I do know you both will not want to be here when I find out. I haven't seen any kids around here tonight. You need to leave and not tell anyone what you saw here. I will take care of this. This is government business and very dangerous. You really need to do as I say." Emily heard a noise in the back of the barracks where she had entered. She shouted, "Stay put!" as she grabbed Matsua's rifle and pointed it in the direction of the noise still pointing her revolver at the two frightened and confused fathers.

"Who goes there? I will shoot if you don't identify yourself"" Emily moved back a few steps so she was hidden in the shadows.

"Mom, it...it's us. We couldn't sit in the van. We want to help you." Will announced as he, Jake, Charlie, moved from behind the space in the wall boards.

Just what I need...a bunch of amateurs. They have no idea how dangerous this is. "You boys need to go back to the car now. There is nothing you can do here except get yourself killed."

"Is this a movie scene or something? Where are the cameras? This is friggin' awesome! Matt, we're in a movie!" Ben practically jumped up and down.

"Uh, I don't think this is a movie, Ben. Those are real guns and she looks like she means business." Matt rolled his eyes and looked at the boys, the dog, and then Emily, "I don't know what's going on here but suppose our kids stumbled on something going on just like we did and they are in danger. I'm not leaving until I'm sure the kids are safe. Evidently this is your son, so you know what I'm talking about."

"I'm sure not leaving either. I've got two kids who might be in trouble." Ben said as bravely as he could.

Jamie had worked his way back along the hedges and was circling around the outhouse heading toward the back of the building. He could see what appeared to be persons moving inside the barracks. He didn't see Emily anywhere. The he saw someone bent low to the ground crossing the road at the edge of the park behind the building. He plastered himself against the outhouse and tried to see if it might be Emily. The figure moved stealthily behind the vans and the rifle he was carrying caught the light just enough for Jamie to see it was a gun. Emily, as far as he knew, did not have a rifle, just a revolver and a knife. He hadn't been much help in the last confrontation, but he had to do something.

Jaboul was so confused. In fact so was everyone else in this scene. He was sure there were no additional guests invited to this meeting with his General. He could make out several people standing near the trap door. One of the people looked like a soldier as he appeared to be in fatigues. He was holding two guns pointed at the others. It was difficult to see any faces and how many were there as he was looking from behind the van through the small opening in the boards. If he attacked as he was trained to do his aversion to killing would make it impossible to gun down a group of people that he couldn't identify as enemy or comrade.

The group sitting around the negotiation table heard the commotion above them. The walls of the cave were nine feet thick and built with cement and wire mesh so the sounds were muffled. There were no shots fired so General Talyasi assumed whomever had invited themselves to the party was being captured by his two men. Kate and Commander Howard were hoping the message had gotten to the agency that they suspected the meeting place might be changed. If Kate or the Commander sent a signal by pressing on their tracking devices it would be time to send reinforcements. Until then there would be no backup as they had promised the Hatham. Robert West didn't trust anyone at the table at this point. He had been informed that Kate was involved in the project. He was ordered to act as though he did not know her though she could reveal that she knew of him. Dr. Olmstead did not believe that the General had one of the original discs to the black box in his possession as he had boasted. He knew that it was because of him this nightmare had gotten to this point. If it meant he would have to die to make sure the detonation block was intact until the government could confirm the bombs were no longer able to be ignited then he would die protecting it. Kate and the Commander had been dealing with Hatham for over a year to convince them they were willing to work as double agents for a large sum of money. When it was revealed to them that the terrorists had aborted the deactivation of the bombs and were gradually drugging Dr. Olmstead, they informed the President and began to devise a plan to regain possession of the box, the disc, and defuse the bombs forever.

Jaboul did what he thought he had to do. He screeched the call of a Hatham soldier his tongue vibrating against his upper palate. He fired first into the air and then randomly at the group of people in the barracks. Everyone except Emily scattered to hide behind overturned benches and cots toward the opposite end of the building. Emily ducked behind a cot leaning against the wall as Jaboul made his entrance into the building, his gun firing randomly around the room. She raised her pistol, aimed toward the leg of the intruder and fired. Jaboul felt the bullet pierce his thigh like a hot poker being thrust through muscle and bone. The soldier/computer specialist fell to the ground his rifle falling several feet from where he landed. He grabbed his leg as the blood oozed onto his pants. Emily stood over him with the rifle pointed at his head.

"Tell me quickly what is going on here before I kill you. Can you understand me?" Emily could easily translate her request for him but Jaboul had learned English and several other languages. He knew what the soldier was saying to him.

"I am here as a computer specialist and guard. That is all I have been told. Allah be praised." Jaboul looked into the eyes of his captor and saw very little empathy there but there was something; a hint of kindness or a few seconds of belief in what he was telling the man. This is a woman. This is not a man, he thought.

"What is under that door? Are there any more guards?" Emily persisted with her interrogation pushing the barrel of the gun closer the Jaboul's face.

"It is a cave and there are many guards in there." Jaboul wondered where Matsua was...perhaps he was...he didn't want to think he was the only protection for his General as he already botched up the job. He was losing blood from his leg wound and he felt woozy. "Who are you? How did you find this place?"

"I will ask the questions. I need to know how many guards are..." Emily looked up as she heard a noise from the back of the barracks. She leveled the rifle she had taken from Jaboul at the separated boards. Jamie rushed at Matt and Ben knocking them to the ground. Emily chuckled as the three of them laid on top of one another. "Jamie, what are you doing here? I told you to make a call. These guys are looking for their kids. What am I going to do with all of you amateurs!" Matt, Ben, and Jamie had managed to right themselves and were staring at Emily in her "man" disguise and Jaboul lying in a pool of blood on the floor. His eyelids were drooping and you could almost see pallor to his olive skin. "Listen to me. I can't tell you everything but this is a very dangerous place to be for anyone who is not trained. You two men (she motioned to Matt and Ben) can see your kids aren't here. I need you to help me. You have to follow my instructions to the letter." She whispered to Matt and Ben whose eyes were as big as saucers and Ben was almost salivating. They turned immediately and ran toward town. Whatever Emily had told them certainly hit home. Jamie was both embarrassed and puzzled—not that he hadn't been confused from the beginning of this crazy adventure. He starred at the trap door, at Emily, and at the man lying on the ground. Suddenly it began. The pain started at the back of his head and crept toward his forehead. Like a vise slowly tightening itself it seemed to be squeezing his brain intractably. His eyes changed from their usual softness to a piercing dark purple. His pupils dilated as they focused on Emily. Numbers began to roll through space like a transparent screen on a computer. Each column rolled past Jamie's visual field. Numbers, symbols, and letters comprised the sequences. Emily started to walk over to him as the look on his face gave her chills. When she had gotten within a few feet of him she was thrown back by an electrical field surrounding the once docile social worker. The myriad of characters began to slow until three columns matched. Emily noticed a buzzing in her pocket and reached for the race car she had placed there. She tried to hold on to it as it zapped her hand and she dropped it. Will grabbed the car with the sleeve of his sweatshirt protecting his hand. The buzzing stopped as the glow of the disc imbedded in the chassis subsided. Everyone looked toward Jamie who was crouched against the wall holding his head in his hands. Jake noticed that his bionic arm felt warm to the touch while the rest of his body was cool in the early morning air. Charlie and Casey stood frozen to the ground. Charlie didn't know what to think and Casey was eying the injured man on the ground wanting desperately to lick his wound. Emily ran over to Jamie as she ordered the three boys to tear up one of their shirts and fashion a bandage for the limp Jaboul. Will pulled down one of the cots leaning against the wall while Jake took off his hospital tee shirt and wrapped it around the wound in Jaboul's leg. Jake and Charlie took off their sweatshirts and laid them on the rusty cot. The three boys lifted Jaboul and placed him gently on the bed. Emily reached under the Ace bandages binding her breasts and pulled out the injection marked Benadryl. She injected Jaboul to lessen the pain and to keep him from loosening the pieces of bandage she used to tie him to the bed.

Jamie shook his head as the pain subsided and the numbers disappeared. He told Emily about the strange phenomenon that occurred when these spells would happen. He had told Emily how he met Will and the strange men that visited the Shelter before he was shot. Emily wondered if there was a connection between the signal from the disc and Jamie's visions. There wasn't any time to waste. The Commander had told Emily that he and Kate had been posing as double agents for some time in order to gain information about terrorist activity in the U.S. They were recruited for this mission to uncover the identity of a spy for the terrorists who had foiled many attempts to capture him or her. This person was responsible for aborting several attempts to defuse the bombs located at the old arsenal, the drugging and attempted capture of Dr. Olmstead, and the plan to use the bombs as a negotiating tool to free enemy prisoners. The identity of the spy had led to dead-ends so far. This person had established a perfect cover for his real identity. He seemed to be able to direct activities from a remote site that was almost impossible to detect. He had to be a genius; a person driven by greed and contempt for the U.S.

The group in the cave barely heard any of the commotion above them due to the thickness of the walls and the trap door. The Commander thought he heard a shot fired and then nothing. Both guards had not returned. He wasn't sure if that was a good sign or a bad one, but he had just twelve minutes left in the hour he was given by General Talyasi to decide to give in to his demands. General Talyasi was not a fool. He was not convinced that this Howard person was working for the Hatham and still pretending to be loyal to the U.S. The 911 had been a victory for his organization. Patience was the one virtue the terrorists possessed.

The plan to wreak havoc in the U.S. and to depose it as a leader was devised over many years. There had to be contacts placed in the United States that had untraceable relationships with the Hatham. They had to be enmeshed with the American culture and seemingly aligned with the beliefs and lifestyle of the American Dream. The actual disaster would not be nearly as effective as the fallout over time. Disruption of the belief the United States was immune to and defensible against an attack from an enemy would cripple the economy and damage the trust the people had in their leaders. Now the Hatham needed allies in their own camp. Because of skirmishes in the Middle East, many of the Hatham leaders and soldiers had been killed or imprisoned. The clock was ticking and each minute that passed chiseled away a portion of the confidence he was to have this man would be sure their demands would be met without a confrontation.

Kate watched the Commander pick up his briefcase from the floor of the cave. She had also been able to arrange the meeting and assure the General there would be only the persons there that would be key to negotiations. Over the past year she had been beaten, detained, interrogated, tortured, pursued, and humiliated by both sides. America was convinced her allegiance was to this country. Hatham was convinced she had been drawn to their philosophy of supremacy. Quite an actress. Tough and ruthless with little regard for the pleas of her captors. Until now. Something had opened up a place buried deep in her heart that cared. It may have been the fact that her only relatives where orphans and she was all they had left to guide and protect them or that darned baby she held in the car cuddled against her breast, warm and needy. The Commander looked at her as he pulled out the black box and laid it gingerly on the table. General Talyasi pulled a similar black box out of his briefcase and placed it next to the other one.

"Eight minutes, Commander." Tiny beads of perspiration were forming on the General's forehead and below his eyes. "Dr. Olmstead. You have been chosen to examine these two boxes and to tell us which is the decoy and which is the actual device halting the detonation process." The General leaned across the table glaring at George as though every bit of contempt he held for this country was focused on the doctor. Robert West reached for one of the boxes and the General hacked down on his wrist with all his might. Robert stood and grabbed the General by his shirt collar and sat him in his chair. He reached into his coat pocket and drew out what looked like a pen.

"Enough of this fooling around. Elton you have to come clean. This crazy man is not fooling. If he has the disc and places it in that box, the only one who can stop the end of the world is George." Robert's face was noticeably red and his eyes were blazing.

George looked at Robert and the Commander, and then at Kate. He thought about his awful dream of Emily being carried off by a hawk and knew that his life was over no matter what the outcome. He had never forgiven the world for the loss of his family, his friends, and his career during the war. He had worked both sides of the coin and had never developed an allegiance to any country or any person. His wife had died and his children were estranged from him as he had buried himself in his work and his inventions. He had fooled them all. Worst of all, he had grown to like some of his victims yet his inability to forgive enveloped him and washed away any empathy or sentiment that could have change his course. He had programmed the original box to activate the detonation chamber at exactly four in the morning on September 29, 2002. That was his birthday. It also would be the end, the end of the tortured soul that caused him to never be free of the vengeance that consumed him. He felt powerful. None of them knew that the process had already begun. The only thing that could halt it would be a miracle or the disc placed deep within the device in a very precise location to inhibit the magnetic field of the activator disc preventing the detonation process.

He had given it to Robert to protect his sons. No one would discover it nor had any idea that it could save the country and much of the world from destruction. He was a genius. He had made the mistake of trusting a terrorist to disguise himself and abduct the boys. It was difficult to even think of the boys at this moment.

"I cannot tell you which of zese is the actual box. It matters little now as one of zem has been programmed to open ze detonation chamber in thirty minutes from now." Dr. Olmstead stood and smiled at the amazed faces of the rest of the group.

"What the...George...you...you are the one! I can't believe you would hurt us! Emily...the boys......what have you done?" Robert reached for his friend. "You have the ability to stop this......George you have to stop this!" Gregor Olmstead looked into the eyes of his friend and slowly peeled away Robert's hands holding his jacket.

"You need to say zoz prayers you ver saying before, dear Bobbie. I am sorry I has to do zis but it is time to develop a new race. Dis old von is damaged. It needs to go."

"You are crazy!" Robert exclaimed.

Kate and the Commander were counting on Emily to save the day by capturing the mystery terrorist once they found him. They were not prepared for that person to be one of their own trusted allies or for him to be insane. General Talyasi had lost his bargaining chip if this madman was telling the truth. He had little fear for his life as he had been programmed to believe this life on earth was worth very little. He wasn't too sure he was ready to leave just yet so he drew a pistol from under his cloak and pointed it at the doctor.

"Go ahead. Shoot. It makes no difference to me."

The Commander reached for one of the boxes and stared at the display of characters moving across the screen. Kate moved beside him to gaze at a weapon she could not defend herself against. He felt the hate for the man who represented those who had killed the only person he had ever loved. It made little difference now. Emily and Robert should be together in these last moments. He rubbed his right arm and triggered the notification device.

"You two are not allies of the Hatham are you?" the General slumped in his chair muttered. "It makes no difference in the face of death with whom we choose to align ourselves, does it. We all become allies then."

Emily and the boys had tied Jaboul's limp body to the bed. They had no idea who was in the cave, whether there were more guards with weapons, or what actually was taking place. Emily was to take into custody the mystery terrorist as soon as the Commander pressed the alarm hidden in the tracking device under his skin. He had told her that Kate had arranged the place for this meeting and was trusted by both the terrorists and her agency. She looked at her watch and wondered why he had not signaled her. It was 3:35 A.M. when the signal vibrated under her skin. She had given the revolver to Jake who had some lessons before the hurricane. She didn't want Will, Jamie, or the other two boys to come with her. They were glued to her. She insisted the boys stay hidden behind the vans until she could scout out the situation.

At 3:40 A.M. Jamie helped her lift the trap door. A ray of light shone from the cave as she stealthily lowered herself down the ladder leading to the cave. She crept along the cold walls of the small tunnel leading to the cave proper. No guards halted her progress. She could only hear an occasional muffled voice. Other than that and an intermittent pulsation followed by a dripping sound in the distance, it was quiet. Her heart pounded against her chest and for a moment she longed to be holding her baby against her breast feeling that bond between them only a mother can feel. As the light grew brighter and the pulsations grew louder, she reached the end of the tunnel that opened into a massive room. In the distance she saw the huge metal housings in the floor of the cave and what looked like two immense tanks or bombs resting in them. To her right was an arch and beyond that she could see a table and some chairs occupied by several people. It was difficult to make out who the people were but the one facing the entrance surely was Commander Howard. She breathed a little deeper relieved to see he was still alive and that none of the people looked like they had weapons. A man with a turban was sitting on the left of the Commander. She could not see his face. She surmised this might be the mystery terrorist and the one she was to detain. There were three other people with their backs to her. One person appeared to be a soldier dressed in fatigues as she was. One of the remaining two was standing and holding something in his hands. Both appeared to be men. The man sitting next to the one standing was dressed in a sweatshirt and jeans. She could not tell who the three of these were. She wondered about Robert and George and prayed they were safe. Now that she had found Will she could wonder what had happened to those two. Robert knew how to take care of himself and of those for whom he was responsible. She did not worry about him. She missed him.

3:46 A.M. When you know you are about to die, there are strange things that come to mind. You remember scenes from happy times and you want to dive into them and feel nothing. You wonder if it will be painful and if you believe the things you have been taught about the hereafter or if that it...blackness......nothingness. For a moment, you regret some things you have done or not done, people you will miss and who will miss you, what it looks like in heaven...if you believe in heaven.

Emily entered the anteroom with her rifle pointed at the head of the person she believed to be the terrorist she was to detain and capture. When she saw Robert and George looking at her with utter amazement, her heart almost leaped into her throat. She couldn't show her feelings as she was sure the Commander had summoned her to do what he had ordered. General Talyasi clasped his hands over his head in submission and smiled. It seemed ludicrous at this point, less than three minutes away from the detonation device being released, that he was being captured...

"Emily," Robert came to her and tried to wrap his arms around the stalwart agent. "Em, put down the gun. It's George. He is the one. He has programmed the detonating device to be released at 4:00 A.M. We don't have any time. Just hold me. Just hold me." Emily looked at her husband and then at George who could not look at her.

"George......you...you are going to kill us all! Why George...Will...the boys. My God. The boys!" She dropped her rifle and clung to the man she loved.

"Will is here? Toby?"

"Will and his friends are in the barracks" The pulsations stopped and a loud rumble could be heard from the far end of the cave. Huge prongs exited from a large metal tank and began to inch their way down a channel heading toward the two atomic bombs.

Will and his companions, including Casey couldn't wait any longer. They went down the ladder, through the tunnel and out into the cave proper. Will saw his parents holding each other and ran toward them.

"Dad......oh, Dad." Robert wrapped his arms around Emily and Will. Tears streamed down their faces as the roar grew louder. Robert saw Will still had his mangled race car and grabbed it from him peering into the chassis to see if the disc was still there. He grabbed George.

"George. You said this was the disc to halt the ignition process. You love Emily and the boys. Please do it for them. Do it for God. Please!" Robert begged his old friend.

Gregor Olmstead looked at Emily, Robert, and the boys. He picked up the rifle that Emily had dropped and held it against his chest as he pulled the trigger and slumped to the floor. Emily pulled the boys away as the shot splayed the doctor's chest open. Robert had tried to wrestle the rifle away when he saw what George was about to do. George had a death grip on the weapon.

Robert felt the vibrations of the race car as it began to flash its eerie green light. The shock stung and he dropped it on the table next to the black box. The roar from the detonation chamber grew louder and the dripping sound echoed in the background Will grabbed the vibrating car and peeled back the bent metal frame. He reached into the chassis and tried to remove the flashing disc. The detonation prongs were less than fifteen feet away from connecting with the ignition chamber of the bombs. The world as all of them had known it would end in less than fifteen minutes from the time the prongs were set into the female end of the ignition chamber. The chain reaction would begin and there could be no stopping it from that point forward. Robert pulled off the back cover of the black box searching inside its complicated mass of wires and ports for the other disc allowing the sequence to align. Jamie stood mesmerized by the scene he barely understood. Casey noticed the man with the turban inching his way around the table and picking up the rifle. He growled sensing the human looked like he was going to attack his humans. Jake saw the General aim the rifle at Will and he raised his bionic arm in front of Will's head blocking the bullet from killing his friend. Casey heard the shot and went into attack mode leaping with ferocity, teeth bared and guttural sounds emitting from his throat. The General went down and Jake pushed his bionic hand against the terrorist leader's throat.

"You may not want to move. This arm is new to me and I'm not sure what it can do." The General did not fight Jake and Charlie as they sat him back in one of the chairs and tied his hands with Kate's belt. Kate hadn't had time to be properly introduced but she saw these kids were tough and brave and felt pretty proud to be related to them. They had a little bit of Kate in them, she thought. The roar stopped suddenly as the prongs married with the ignition chamber. Then the warning lights and alarms began to flash announcing the ignition process had begun.

4:06 A.M. As Robert and Will frantically searched both black boxes for the port that held the disc chamber, the sequences flashed in concert across from each other on the screens. They had only one disc, fourteen minutes, and did not know which box was the decoy. George knew, but he was dead. Jamie felt it again. This time the pain engulfed his entire head and face. His eyes blazed purple, pupils dilated, and his face became contorted. The numbers began to cascade across his eyes and the people staring at him from around the table blurred as the characters and numbers became more vivid in the foreground of his vision. The disc inside the chassis of the race car began to flash two......four......two......pause...five. Jamie stood rigid as it traveled from his head to his arms, down his chest.

4:11 A.M. The disc had turned a bright red. Robert burned his fingers as the heat from the disc increased. Two...four...two...pause...five. The flashes occurred closer together and Jamie saw the pulsations hit highlighting numbers in each of the sequences as they raced by. He moved toward the black box on the right and grabbed the race car crushing it and extracting the glowing, vibrating disc. A sequence of numbers flashed in Jamie's brain and he pulled a compartment from the port that matched the numbers and seated the disc into the holder within the port.

At 4:16 A.M., four minutes short of disaster, the warning lights stopped flashing, the alarms were silenced and the reactor groaned to a halt. Jamie collapsed on the table and Casey ran up to give him a hug. The dripping sound stopped. The silence was interrupted by the cheering of all except the General.

Meanwhile, Jaboul had regained consciousness enough to extricate himself from the cot. He winced with pain as he stepped into the tunnel leading to the cave. He limped on his injured leg but knew he had to show the General he was there to do his job. He heard the cheering and saw his leader bound to a chair some distance away for the jubilant group. He thought they were cheering the capture of his leader so he attacked with the only weapon he could find...the chain from the trap door. He ran toward Charlie twirling the chain in the air and yelling his warbling warrior call. Jake twirled around and knocked his brother away from the whirling weapon. The chain wrapped itself around Jake's bionic arm. Before Jaboul realized what happened, Jake had jerked him, chain and all, into the air and slammed him to the ground. He lifted him from the floor into the air with his amazing prosthesis and threw him against the wall. Jaboul slid down the wall and crumpled into a lump on the floor. At least he had shown his General that he was more than just a computer geek and that he was willing to die for him.

Matt and Ben were out of breath when they finally got to Ben's house. Matt's wife had come over and both were wringing their hands wondering what had happened to their husbands. The kids had come home breathless a couple of hours before telling this unbelievable story about cloaked men carrying a body into a trap door in the old barracks. Both moms were less than impressed even though the kids kept begging them to believe it was true and that they should call the police or something. It was 3:55 A.M. when they burst through the Newcomers' door. Ben and Matt hugged their wives so hard that they were both breathless as well. The kids got big hugs too and starred at their fathers in amazement. Ben looked at Matt.

"It's 4:00 A.M. You call Matt." The group of moms and kids watched with their mouths opened as Matt slowly dialed the number Emily had whispered to him.

"This is the Federal Bureau of Investigation. No calls will be connected without the proper identification." the militant attendant announced. "Please enter the code followed by the pound sign within fifteen seconds or the call will be traced." Matt entered Emily's code he and Ben had recited over and over as they ran from the barracks.

"You have given the code for Emily West. Please remain on the line." Ben's wife tried to ask him what was going on but he shushed her. "This is Lieutenant Martindale. Please state your code." Matt repeated Emily's code as though it were his own. "Who is this answering for Emily West?" the deep rough voice asked.

"Ms. West asked me to give you this project number and is requesting backup sir. Location coordinates are being sent through Ms. West's tracking device. Project RRX42 completed, Sir."

Matt felt like he was the star in a spy movie and Ben puffed out his chest like a quail during mating season. Both of their wives looked at each other and their kids and husbands. Somehow, those guys looked different. They oozed manhood and were kind of sexy that way.

The agents and Reserves came in jeeps and helicopters. The town was full of spectators as the barracks were leveled and two huge bombs were dismantled and the reactor hauled away in a huge armored truck. The cave was converted into a museum for old weapons and memorabilia from wars and times gone by. Matt and Ben were heroes and received a medal for bravery from Commander Howard. Billy, Tammy, and Kurt were stars at their school, telling the story over and over, each time embellishing it a little. Raritan Park became a tourist site and brought hundreds of tourists to the two hotels and to the other businesses in town. The Mayflower Hotel in nearby New Brunswick had a waiting list for people who wanted to stay in the room where terrorists had attacked the U.S. agents and her crew. They adopted a name for Charlie, Casey, Jake, Will, Emily, Kate, and Robert. "West's Orphans" were a group to be feared and revered. Kate, Robert, and Emily had new homes built by the government with every protective device available installed. Kate, Jake, Charlie, and Casey lived a few blocks from the Wests. They even went to church together and shared many great memories together with the Newcomers and the Porters. Robert and Will built a clubhouse in a big oak tree on their property. It looked very much like the one Ted Swanson's grandfather had built. Ted and his mom came to visit and heard the amazing adventures they all had experienced. Jamie married Maria and was given a large cash grant from the government for his bravery and for saving the lives of millions. He invested it in several beautiful shelters for the homeless around the State of Ohio. He continued to have occasional headaches and strange visions, but none as extreme as that morning in the cave. They visited Kate and the Wests whenever they could.

It was rumored that the Wests and Kate had officially retired from the agency with a large pension and many accolades from the President. Hmmm. Some who knew them wondered if it was really true.

The End

ORPHANS
by Nancy Jasin Ensley